Text Classics

KENNETH IVO BROWNLEY LANGWELL 'SEAFORTH' MACKENZIE was born in 1913 in South Perth. His parents divorced in 1919, and he grew up with his mother and maternal grandfather on a property at Pinjarra, south of Perth. He was a sensitive child who developed an intense love of nature.

At age thirteen Mackenzie was sent to board at Guildford Grammar School in Perth. His experiences there informed his first novel, *The Young Desire It*, published under the name Seaforth Mackenzie by Jonathan Cape in 1937. The author was just twenty-three.

The novel drew praise from *The Times*, *Spectator* and *Sydney Morning Herald*; the *Liverpool Daily Post* called it 'amazingly brilliant'. It was awarded the Australian Literary Society Gold Medal.

By this time Mackenzie had studied law, worked as a journalist and moved to Sydney. There he met the leading lights of the literary scene—among them Kenneth Slessor and Norman Lindsay—and married. He and his wife had a daughter and a son.

Mackenzie's subsequent novels were *Chosen People* (1938), *Dead Men Rising* (1951), based partly on his experience of the Cowra prisoner breakout, and *The Refuge* (1954). He also produced two volumes of poetry.

Kenneth Mackenzie's last years were spent mainly alone, in declining health and battling alcoholism, at Kurrajong in New South Wales. On 19 January 1955 he drowned in mysterious circumstances while swimming in Tallong Creek, near Goulburn.

NICOLAS ROTHWELL is a senior writer for the *Australian*, and the award-winning author of *Heaven and Earth*, *Wings of the Kite-Hawk*, *Another Country*, *The Red Highway* and *Journeys to the Interior*. His most recent book, *Belomor*, was shortlisted for a Prime Minister's Literary Award.

ALSO BY KENNETH MACKENZIE

The Young Desire It
Chosen People
Dead Men Rising

The Refuge
A Confession
Kenneth Mackenzie

Text Publishing Melbourne Australia

textclassics.com.au
textpublishing.com.au

The Text Publishing Company
Swann House
22 William Street
Melbourne Victoria 3000
Australia

First published by Jonathan Cape 1954
This edition published by The Text Publishing Company 2015

Cover design by WH Chong
Page design by Text
Typeset by Midland Typesetters

Printed in Australia by Griffin Press, an Accredited ISO AS/NZS 14001:2004
Environmental Management System printer

Primary print ISBN: 9781922182654
Ebook ISBN: 9781925095593
Author: Mackenzie, Kenneth, 1913–1955.
Title: The refuge : a confession / by Kenneth Mackenzie ; introduced by
Nicolas Rothwell.
Series: Text classics.
Dewey Number: A823.3

This book is printed on paper certified against the Forest Stewardship
Council® Standards. Griffin Press holds FSC chain-of-custody
certification SGS-COC-005088. FSC promotes environmentally
responsible, socially beneficial and economically viable management
of the world's forests.

CONTENTS

Hunting Different Game
by Nicolas Rothwell

CAN a work of genius, a masterwork—a classic—be imperfect, flawed in its essence? Can a great book be made from unbalanced or ill-fitting parts, and can those flaws and quirks actually be the crux of its strength, in much the same way the crystal imperfections of an Argyle diamond cause its prized pale-pink sheen? On first encounter, Kenneth Mackenzie's *The Refuge* certainly seems a strange beast of a novel: it is not a tale told, but an act remembered. It doesn't really have subsidiary characters, so much as walk-on cardboard cut-out figures. The first-person narrative strains credulity until you surrender yourself to its flow. It is by turns wordy and rapid to a fault; its focus jumps here and there; it is distinctly dreamlike, if not nightmarish—yet life, at least the life we expect to see reflected in a mid-twentieth-century realist Australian novel set in a busy media landscape, does not generally have the texture of a dream. We are caught up in a most unconventional kind of classic, then.

Securely designated classics are often venerable treasures, famous for being famous, so well known we cannot really read them: grand human tapestries in prose, depicting with assured simplicity all the breadth of a particular society's jostling, intermingling life. In the Australian context, the term has been eagerly affixed to well-loved novels, to period pieces with a certain enduring verve, to essay-tracts that traffic in grand ideas and national themes. Sunshine, more than shadows and the night. Critics want the books they call classics to have a consistent confidence and energy about them, and to radiate enlightened social attitudes. Works of Australian literature judged worthy of canonical status are thus often those that portray man's nature as fundamentally benign, or within the province of possible redemption. A sense of progress in the narrative, a journey towards resolution and greater understanding—such features are desirable as well.

None of these are obvious attributes of the best-known work of Kenneth Mackenzie, and they are wholly lacking in *The Refuge*, the last book he published in his lifetime. How to frame and approach this novel, without doubt one of the most peculiar and least known of the texts included in the eclectic Text Classics series to date? *The Young Desire It*, Mackenzie's early masterwork, was revived by Text in 2013, a full three-quarter century after its first appearance, and was well received by respectable authorities. The case for it was clear enough: it is a vivid tale of youth, and coming of age, written in lyrical prose, its themes in fine balance, its exploration of the tensions between master and pupil in a sylvan West Australian setting exquisitely done.

The Refuge, first published seventeen years after that novel, in 1954, is something else: a murder mystery that is no mystery at all, a seeming thriller set against the backdrop of wartime Sydney with an introspective crime reporter as its controlling, narrating central presence. As is clear from the outset, he is himself the killer in the case—the author and the reporter of the crime. After this initial set-up, the story is inevitably a retracing: the plot is preordained, it has a fated quality about it; we see the characters move in uncomprehending lock-step towards the narrative's final point. But this crime business is not the key to the work, or even its matter, so much as its pretext. The Mackenzie of *The Refuge* is hunting different game.

The novel's opening scene is set in a magnificently tangy Sydney newspaper general reporting room—'in the corner annexe the overseas teletype machine kept up a continuous solid rattle and ring, working away on its own inside its heavy metal case.' Foreign influences are flooding in—we will not stay long in familiar, parochial territory. Our reporter, the van Dyck-bearded, grandly named Lloyd Fitzherbert, sets down his tale in poised, self-conscious fashion: he is mazy, he is artful; he meanders into questions of psychology and family dynamics, pedagogy and inheritance, ideology and world politics, the nature and reproducibility of female beauty, the light and look of Sydney Harbour, and the landscape of the Blue Mountains and the surrounding Australian bush.

Indeed, Sydney is a principal presence in his narrative: one could almost say, as with the works of Elizabeth Harrower, that the city has a speaking part. 'There would be dawn,' Fitzherbert muses early on,

> turning the harbour slowly from light-pricked nothingness to an unfolding mystery of black and silver; aslant the twin bluffs of the Heads, day would break in melancholy tones of yellow and grey and the scraping cries of seagulls above the leaden water would herald the winter sunrise.

So what genre are we dealing with: a philosophical novel? A self-examination? No: another kind of classic. *The Refuge* is in fact a tragedy, a very precise one, conforming in its own fashion to the tragic unities of time and place. The tell-tale signs are there in the early pages: the initial unfurling image sequences; the central character's propensity for clear-eyed, paradox-courting psychological explorations; the long soliloquies, the sudden shafts of rather Shakespearean prose—the harbour in the early morning is like music, 'there is a cool, voluptuous quality in the light of air and water.'

It is impossible that the hyper-literary Mackenzie was unaware, as he wrote, of the genre that lay concealed inside his narrative, or of the specific precursor from which, somehow, he derived his initial premise—a play first performed in 428 BC, the gruesome, distinctly perverse *Hippolytus* of Euripides. In it a kingly, potent father with a handsome young son on the brink of manhood decides to remarry; this father who loves youth takes as his new bride a much younger woman than himself, a creature from the depths of Europe, beautiful, exotic. Trouble ensues.

Those who seek the humdrum in a novel may well struggle with *The Refuge*, for all the beauty of its language, the force of intellect present in its architecture and the terrifying logic of its progression from first page to end. But the open reader will be caught at once by Mackenzie's overwhelming ability to convey the texture of subjective experience: his hero, or anti-hero, is not relating or describing the events of his life; he is living them afresh in the manner he first grasped them, through the medium of words. We are in his head, we see into his poor heart: we have his perspective only. And so we cannot help but be with him, as we are with a great tragic hero whose thought and fate dominates and shapes all the dramatic landscape.

Mackenzie achieves this by a simple procedure. The narrator controls all: the novel is not just his confession, his manifesto. It is his vision. This is a filmic book, and the cinematic genre it borrows from on almost every page is film noir. Odd angles, sharp cuts, extreme close-ups, schlock movie-script coincidences—Hitchcock and Fritz Lang stand like plot consultants at Mackenzie's shoulder. The twists begin with the early pages, and build to the bleak disclosures of the last.

Police reporter Fitzherbert of the *Gazette* places his regular late-night call to the CIB in the full knowledge that he will be told of a mysterious drowning in the harbour. What he does not know is that his close friend the duty sergeant will kindly invite him to take a ride to view the corpse—the body of the woman he loved too much to forgive. And so, with this Grand Guignol gauntlet thrown down, the narrator at once in supreme control and off balance, his tragedy in flashback begins.

The cast of characters we meet is limited: Fitzherbert himself; his love object, the impossibly glamorous mid-European refugee Irma, trailing a concealed Communist Party back story in her wake; his teenage son, Alan; and his female confidante, Barbara, who plays the dialogue-sustaining role assigned in Greek tragedy to the nurse or family retainer, conversing, disclosing, moving the drama's action relentlessly on.

None of this would be sufficient to lift *The Refuge* beyond the realm of quirky thrillerdom: Agatha Christie's *The Murder of Roger Ackroyd*, done with a garnishing of literary style. But Mackenzie has a further aim, intriguingly realised in the sweep and atmospherics of his book. Wartime Sydney and the Australia of the setting constitute the 'refuge' of the title. Irma is fleeing persecution in Nazi Europe, but she is also bringing the sophistication and the complexity and the paranoia of Europe in her wake. She is a character from the fictive world of Victor Serge or the real world of the exiled Trotsky. Murky agents are on her trail; she must seek shelter, she must hide her unforgettable face away.

Lloyd Fitzherbert, a distinctly provincial, establishment Australian with pedigree and fine principles, finds himself swept up in this net. His investigations and questionings quickly bring him into contact with sinister-seeming party apparatchiks. One foreign pursuer pays a call on Fitzherbert in his newsroom:

> He was one of those Europeans who seem to have been born to shrug, roll their guilelessly watchful eyes, and to do things with their mouths and hands in a fashion so hypnotic that, without remembering a word they ever say, one has a lasting recollection of them always doing those things, like images on a motion-picture screen not wired for sound.

With great indignation, Fitzherbert winds himself up to resist this sinuous intruder and all the machinations and conspiracies he represents:

> 'Look here...you have come to the wrong man. In fact, I suggest you have come to the wrong country. Wherever your sort go, they expect to inspire fear, or to arouse a fear already dormant. In Australia we have never had to live in that sort of individual fear as yet. I doubt if we ever shall.'

And Fitzherbert sends him packing. But the worm is already deep in the virginal Australian rose. Foreign spirits, sultry and intoxicating, have drifted in upon the tide, and they are spreading through the old, staid country, hinting at elusive, hidden knowledge, sowing temptation and confusion as they go. Lovely Irma has seized on Fitzherbert as her refuge, just as he believes he has found refuge from the drab succession of his life in her. In the Indian summer of their romance it is clear to him: refuge is what people give each other. She is the bird in flight, and she has come to 'her final refuge within the cave of my mind, the walls of my arms'.

But those walls do not remain a solid place of safety, given Fitzherbert's slow realisation, in his repeated dealings with his new love and her milieu, that all emotions are ambiguous, that there is no rational or appointed order in the flux and flow of the wide world: 'It is not hard,' he concludes, 'to love that which will destroy the lover, and earthly love and fear are in essence equally strong, equally self-destructive.' A few pages later, Irma is dead by his hand, her body is adrift in the harbour, and the seagulls are once more on the wing against cloud cover the colour of themselves. The refuge has failed. Australia has lost its simplicity; the equations have come out to their inevitable solution: the tale is at its term.

Much has been at stake; much has been resolved. This is a novel of lingering looks and breaths on the skin, of imagined closeness and wide distances between characters. From its opening pages on, it is also a duel: between eye and object. Our reporter first meets the woman he will love and kill on a passenger ship in the harbour. She is in his mind from that day on. Time drags: eventually, she comes to him, in appeal. He rescues her: he abstracts her to his retreat in the Blue Mountains, another space of shrouds and life-threatening edges. There, she is safe, away from the world. They talk through the night, and the book's central scene unfolds—a scene that really must be read through without pause, both attentively and with tenderness. It has few parallels in modern writing: it is mature and sophisticated, and naïve and adolescent. It is a description of intimacy and intimacy's limits; of longing, gazing, and the way the self can lose its boundaries and become unmoored. Such conversations are only possible by night, and are probably best confined to fiction. Another such is the endless-seeming talk between the heroine and the doctor in Djuna Barnes's *Nightwood*, a strange jewel of the 1930s that *The Refuge* resembles in its baroque linguistic glow.

Irma confesses herself to Fitzherbert, she tells him all her secrets, she offers her body up to him. 'I knew that such a moment could never again in my life come upon me with this fierce, unpardonable surprise.' His choice is abstention, and honour: it is also possession in words, and obsession. Better to write than to live; better to know one's thoughts and feelings with analytic precision than to be caught up wildly in the flow of love. This is the choice that is no choice. The memory of it tempts him until he betrays it. His depth of feeling compels his surrender. Like all tragedies, *The Refuge* is the tale of a hero who is trapped. His gifts and the strengths in his character are what destroy him.

Books can reach out beyond their frame, and dictate, in some sense, the lives their authors lead. By the time he had reached his fortieth birthday, Kenneth Mackenzie was living at Kurrajong, beside the flank of the Blue Mountains. He was drinking; his world was in disarray. He was the author of majestic books that were received with puzzlement; he was a Bohemian in an austere new post-war realm. The *Australian Dictionary of Biography* entry devoted to him signs off in sombre tones: 'His financial situation and personal life were fast deteriorating.'

In January 1955, Mackenzie made a visit to a friend in

nearby Goulburn, and was arrested for drunkenness. That same night he was, though a strong swimmer, 'accidentally drowned' while bathing in Tallong Creek, a fast-flowing watercourse that few would choose for an early evening dip. Death by water—refuge, release, a literary end.

The Refuge

Author's note from the first edition:

The Refuge is a work of fiction. All the characters, except those mentioned by their given or assumed names—Neville Chamberlain, Adolf Hitler, Winston Churchill, General D. MacArthur, H. E. L. Townsend, Jesus, *et alia*—are fictional characters. Thus there need be none of the misunderstanding which prevented the publication in Australia of *Dead Men Rising*. I trust that even the oldest-established legal firms in my own country are in no doubt about this matter.

K. S. M.
Sydney, 1953

To
G. A. Ferguson, Esquire
in friendship

'All treaties are by their natures false, since they pretend on either hand . . . a willingness to gratify the other's desire that they may the sooner gratify the one's: save only that which a man enters upon with his own soul, to be true unto her.'

Michael Paul, *The Anatomy of Failure*

ONE
THE END

It was, I found, the most difficult night telephone call I had ever made.

No one would describe me as a nervous man. Years of police reporting give a necessary control of all emotion, not merely a command of the show of it. I have seen men hanged, and the raped and mutilated bodies of young women, and children's bodies that fire has burned, and drowned people on whom fish have been feeding; and for such sights great calmness of spirit is essential. One does not even allow an inward weeping for pity, or for shame at being oneself a man. One looks, and makes notes, and forgets. Nervousness does not come into it.

Yet this telephone call . . . To all the world it was but a routine night call to the headquarters of the criminal investigation branch of the State Police, and all I had to do was to lift the receiver and say 'C.I.B., please,' and the girl would say 'Yes, Mr. Fitzherbert,' and put me through. Or—though it was less desirable—I could use my own direct line, which I prefer to keep clear for incoming calls, for it is the one the police themselves use, ringing me personally instead of the office switchboard. The digits of my home number are the same—1939—and thus, if I am not on duty, they have merely to use the other call-symbol; the number is, of course, unforgettable.

The general reporters' room was fairly busy still, though the country edition must have been just going to bed, for it was eleven o'clock. The tide in the harbour would be flooding westwards towards the bridge under a lowering sky. I had waited for that hour, with, as I thought, no feelings whatever. The management had not yet given me a private room and an assistant for full-time duty, and my table was in the big room with eighteen others; I walked about, sometimes, between nine and eleven, talking to one man or another, and sometimes sat at my table thinking, hoping that perhaps my own telephone would ring first. But they never bothered me about suicides unless there were peculiar circumstances, or unless it were very late, when they would ring me at home and I would get into touch with the office from there if there were a chance of catching the final or the city edition. If it was not late, they knew I would ring them as usual, at eleven o'clock.

I am certainly not a nervous man. What I had done I had done without fear or fumbling, cleanly, knowing the way—though it was not easy—and the most probable picture it would all make to the police mind, which is as a rule impatient of suicide. Now, however, I found that my hands were sweating profusely, my throat was dry, and in the lower part of my abdomen there was a trembling, jumping sensation; and I felt again the terrible emotion of triumph mixed with and outweighed by black and utter despair, guiltless yet horrified. I forced myself to think of Alan, to remember that what I had done was done for his salvation, not my own, and that I had him to live for; that now he was safe, that dear and beautiful boy.

It was after eleven. If you knew the office sounds in that vast building, you could hear from deep underground, far below street level, the presses running off the country edition, well away by now. At the airfield, the *Gazette* aeroplanes, two of them now, would be warming up out on the runway in the silvery blaze of light. One suicide more or less must mean nothing at all to the men and women of the Australian countryside, who are familiar with death in many forms by the violence of fire and water and the blind malice of accident . . .

By water. The perspiration tickled the roots of my hair and beard. I took up the house telephone receiver, and said to the girl on the switchboard in my usual voice, 'C.I.B., please, Molly.'

'Yes, Mr. Fitzherbert.'

At this, I felt the excitement and sickness leave me. It was a strong physical sensation, like that of an urgent bodily function timely performed. I sat on the edge of my table swinging one foot and watching the reflection of the ceiling light overhead come and go on the polished toe of that shoe. Often enough I had waited like this for Hubble

7

or one of his men to answer my routine night call, and had been content to wait, assured and at ease. Tonight, it seemed that a long time passed before the harsh click at the other end of the line was followed by the sound of a typewriter working at speed under heavy hands, then by a familiar voice.

'C.I.B.'

'Fitzherbert here, Sergeant. Anything doing?'

That question was the climax of the whole business, and—as happens with so many climaxes—I had not realized it was upon me until I spoke. The sweat ran a little way down my wrist even before the sergeant answered; on my shoe the light was still, and the voices and typewriters in the general room where I sat sounded suddenly loud and many.

'Hullo, Fitz. Nothing much in your line. A gent drove his car over an embankment half an hour ago in Chatswood. Minor injuries. I'll give you details in a minute. A bit of a do at Kings Cross—the patrol car's there now, if you can wait half an hour. No details yet. No sign of the chap who got out of the Bay—yes, Manser. Still loose. I'll let you have some reassuring words about that, too . . . And that's about the lot. Dull life, isn't it?'

Sergeant Hubble I liked. He had put more than one good thing in my way, and given me valuable leads without betraying the trust placed in him by his organization. Tonight, however, his cheery and casual voice was that of a stranger, that of a man I was trying without words to persuade to tell me something he did not know, though I knew it. A sudden compelling desire to prompt him had to be suppressed so strongly that I found my teeth were clenched painfully, my body rigid with a species of helpless anguish.

'Just a minute, Harry,' I said. 'I'll have that Chatswood smash. Is it worth a picture?'

'Not unless you're light on. A ten-foot drop, not much damage, no one of importance—not even a pinched car. Are you right?'

Moving into the chair, I changed the receiver to my left hand so that I could write. In his most official voice, deep and clear above the bang and rush and ring of the typewriter in the room with him, Sergeant Hubble gave me the story, and then some pointers about the escapee, Manser, who was also a nobody—not even a dangerous criminal. Because the public (which has a perverse and nervous sympathy for those who evade that justice the public itself has decreed) enjoys reading about such evasions, as well as for the reputation of the force, the police are extremely touchy in the matter of these escapes; and this was the fourth in the State in less than three months. My paper's policy has always been to play up the police efforts in such cases—in all cases, in fact, from murder down—and in return we have had a most satisfactory co-operation from those strange, suspicious, arrogant and often frightened men whom I have known to be as brave as at times they have been brutal. I listened and made notes; or perhaps I should say Lloyd Fitzherbert listened and made notes, in a neat shorthand on a tidy block of paper, while I, the secret self of that efficient, experienced and even esteemed police roundsman of the *Sydney Gazette*, stood aside watching with renewed anguish of mind the swift performance of a routine night task. For I had not heard from Hubble what I must hear if I hoped to sleep that night (or, said the subdued, unreasoning voice of despair, to sleep ever again); and, thinking of the tide in the harbour, how it must now be approaching its fullness, I knew it was time; it was time . . .

'And that's that,' Hubble said at last. 'Make what you like of Manser. He's been sighted, which means we ought to have him by tomorrow night at the latest. They're coming in now from the Cross after putting two men and a woman in Darlinghurst for the night. I think it was only a bun-fight. Ring you back. So long.'

He hung up before I could speak again; but that did not matter, for I had nothing to say that could be said to a police sergeant, however friendly. The nauseated sensation came over me again, and the dark and as it were drunken despair of mind. I put the receiver back on its trestle and sat looking at it. This period was one I had only half-foreseen, knowing it must be lived through but not realizing that a nervous exhaustion such as I had known only once before in my life—when Alan was born and my wife of less than two years' marriage died—would make the endurance of it so hard.

Behind me, the last man on late duty was packing up to go. In the big room, with its barren spread of now vacant tables under the insufficient ceiling lights of white glass, the air was as stale and vitiated as that of an empty theatre after a show. It felt warm, in spite of the bleak May night outside in the streets; I knew that once again the air-conditioning system was out of order on our floor, and the general room, windowless, set in the middle of the building and surrounded by corridors, became at such times almost uninhabitable, and smelt of lavatories. My mind in a sort of frenzy underlined the physical discomfort; I felt I must go out and breathe the cold air of the emptying streets which by comparison would seem sweet. Only when I had typed out my notes taken from Hubble, and was about to carry the copy to the sub-editors and go on down the imposing lower staircase to the street door, did I realize that I was still waiting—I could not yet leave that telephone lying silent as if in exhausted sleep on its rest, not for more than a minute or two. When I did leave—probably at about midnight, perhaps later, if the call I must hear had not yet come—Hubble could briefly be let know I was to be found at home within half an hour; within fifteen minutes . . . A taxi would do it.

The subs had their heads down above the broad table which ran like a great brown polished horseshoe from one door to the other in the inner wall of their room. Unlike the general reporting staff, they could seldom leave their seats at that table during the eight long hours of duty. It was safe to put them into a room with windows overlooking the street—safe and healthy, I suppose. Now for the most part they were absorbed, for it was a busy time, with the cables still coming in from daytime Europe. In the corner annexe which also overlooked the street, the overseas tele-type machine kept up a continuous solid rattle and ring, working away on its own as though moved by a human conscience inside its heavy metal case. I left the door open into the passage so that I could hear my telephone if it rang, and took my copy to the basket in front of Blake, the chief sub-editor, who was reading a page-proof. I did not wish now to talk to anyone, but Blake did; he had got the main body of the so-called final edition away, and as usual at this time of night he was bored, and boredom made his thin, sharp, white face with the ginger-red Chaplin moustache and penetrating green eyes look to be consumed with anger. However, as I knew by now, he merely wished for a cup of coffee upstairs in the staff dining-room, and a break away from that table where he must spend more than half the night, five nights out of seven.

Until I put my copy into it, the wire basket was empty. The chief cable-sub was getting paper direct from the tele-type machine at the hands of a gum-chewing boy whose face in the harsh light was almost as white, though by no means as thin, as Blake's. Blake snatched the few sheets out of the basket, glanced at them, called out '*Bill!*' in a sharp tenor voice that perfectly matched his own red-and-white colour, and sank back in his wooden armchair to look at me at last.

'Nothing big, Lloyd?' he said. 'We're short of crime. No, seriously. How about going out and committing a nice juicy murder? A man with your experience, you ought to be able to get away with it.'

Such is the untrustworthy state of a mind battling with strong emotion that for the flashing part of a second I was impelled to answer by saying, 'I have done that once since sunset, and once is enough for a lifetime.' Instead, I laughed, though I had not meant to, nor to laugh so loudly. The room seemed to echo with it, but no head was raised, no face turned. Only Blake looked slightly surprised, and his thin mouth relaxed into a smile of sudden, complete charm.

'Oh come,' he said, 'it's not as funny as that. In fact, it's not funny at all, I know. I did once see a film—or maybe it was in a book I read—where the ace crime reporter goes out and commits the perfect crime, just to make news. Hollywood and the Johnson office being what they are—to say nothing of the deep-seated moral rectitude of the film-going public, or so they say—the poor blighter wasn't allowed to get away with it. I forget what happened, but I know he was duly and fittingly punished.'

All this was spoken at nervous high speed, and ended with a snap-to of his thin lips, unsmiling again. Blake was said to have been one of the really crack officers of the Australian army during the recent war. Looking at him sitting there bored and impatient in the urgent stillness of that room, I could easily believe this to have been so: with his profound and unconscious personal charm which only his friends were allowed to see went all the secret signs of an impersonal ruthlessness, perhaps cruelty, so perceptible to me that sometimes when I was with him I felt that for him the state of war never had been and never would be ended. He had about him always the air of immediate command, even—as now—in his times of greatest boredom.

My eyes saw him, part of my mind was yet again summing him up, but all the time I listened for the bell of my telephone; and I found I was feeling cold in every part of my body. That laugh had done me no good; it was as though it had come near to shaking loose my grasp on something on which I must retain my strongest hold, or perish. I had turned to go, to cross the room to the door, cross the passage to the big room opposite, with its faintly foul atmosphere, and once more sit at my own table, waiting, when Blake with a muttered exclamation in a tone of impatience and disgust rose from his chair and like a boy vaulted the shining curve at the very centre of the subs' table, and stood beside me, as still as though he had been there all the time.

'Come up for some coffee,' he said. 'You don't look your usual self tonight, Fitz. Too much petty crime, no doubt. Come and have a cup of coffee—my shout.'

'I can't,' I said. 'I'm waiting for the C.I.B. to call me about some trouble at the Cross.'

'How much?' he asked instantly, seeming to forget about his cup of coffee. 'We're full.' However much he might pretend, and jump about like a schoolboy, he was never off duty in that office; he had translated his war into an alert battle against space and time—literally—and this he pursued with a vigour of mind equal to that of his lean, trim body. It was thanks to him more than to any other individual that, in spite of the whims and vagaries and occasional rather petulant modifications of policy higher up, the old *Gazette* had become more concise, cleaner in outline, more readable and so more influential than it had ever been.

'Three or four inches, I imagine—no more,' I told him. 'Keep it for the city if you like.'

'We'll whittle a bit more off that Chief Secretary on the sanctity of the kangaroo, if necessary,' he said. 'With a little less publicity he might show a little more sense. I don't know why Scotty insists on using him—except, of course, that he's always good for sending the correspondence columns mad. Can't your 'phone call wait ten minutes?'

'No,' I said. 'They've all gone home in there. I must stay about for a while.'

He marched away briskly, but with one hand trailing limply along the curved rail enclosing the well of the main staircase, so that it was as though two men, one soldierly, one idle and bored, walked with a single step round and out of sight. I went back to the general room, and just as I reached my table the telephone bell rang. The sound of it gave me a very strange feeling, mixed I think of relief and fear—a fear not for myself but lest even now I should not hear from the police what I could have told them myself hours earlier: for the waiting was becoming almost more than I could bear, I found. Nevertheless, I let the bell ring three times.

The receiver seemed to leap from the trestle to my ear and my mouth. It surprised me to hear my own voice saying with what might have been the weary calm proper to the hour and place, 'Police rounds. Fitzherbert speaking.'

'Yes, Fitz—about that Kings Cross rumpus.' It was Hubble again sounding amused. 'Have you a boy named Alan, A-L-A-N? If so, he's in the cells at Darlinghurst. Have you?'

'Good gracious,' I said; and I did not know what to think, or indeed how to think at all. The message I had been challenging fate to let me hear was gone from my mind in an instant.

'Keep calm—if you're ever anything else,' Hubble said, laughing. 'It's all rather funny. No real damage to anyone except a dog. Here's how.'

15

He then told me that a dog-fight had started in one of the better-lighted back streets of Kings Cross, that square mile of passions and violence and bright colours which never quite sleeps. Alan, on his way home from a show I had persuaded him to go to, as a break from hard study (I said), came on the scene just as the man who owned one dog started kicking in the ribs of its opponent; whereat the woman who owned the second dog set upon the man, who took to her with his fists. Alan, it appeared, tackled the tough in his turn, only to find himself up against not merely the man, but the infuriated woman as well. The two dogs apparently pursued their own fight uninterrupted in the half-darkness between lamps, and as for Alan, only the fortunate arrival of the district police night patrol on a routine cruise saved him from probable serious injury; for the man, they found, was wearing a knife.

'All right,' I said. 'Thank you, Harry. I don't think we need to do much about that, do you? How is the boy? Can I get him out?'

'You can,' he said. 'We'll let him off with a caution to keep the peace. Listen—I thought you Fitzherberts were gentlemen?'

'We are,' I said; and like a tide the immediate past flowed and fled over me again, and again I was in imagination prompting him to tell me what no one but myself seemed yet to know. It was with real physical discomfort that I withheld myself from shouting at him, *There is a dead woman in the harbour tonight, waiting for you to find her. A dead woman, do you hear? A dead woman, a dead woman . . .* It would not really have amused him to think I had gone mad, since we were good friends.

He was speaking again. His voice steadied me, the uproar in my mind quietened, and I remembered Alan with a sudden tender yearning to have him beside me.

'If you're free, I'll pick you up in a minute,' Hubble said. 'I'm off at zero—five minutes from now. We can collect the younger Fitzherbert too, and I'll run you both home. How's that?'

'Who takes over?'

'Smithy.'

'Leave a message for him to ring me at my home about anything at all, other than drunk and disorderly, and I'll accept your offer very gratefully. I was going soon, in any case.'

While I listened, he wrote the message for the man next on duty, reading each word aloud as some people do: 'Ring Fitz *Gazette* at home for anything above d. and d. . . . Right?'

'I shall be at the front door in five minutes,' I said.

When we had hung up, I suddenly saw the night stretching ahead of me, vast, sleepless and terrible. To rid my mind of that vision, I deliberately thought of Alan, whose affair pleased rather than fretted me. It was pleasing to think of what he had done for a mongrel dog (I supposed) in a back street. He would be let out of the cells, and come home with me unaware of what had happened since he left in the morning; I would keep him close, so that even if it were for the last time he might sleep soundly in the room next to mine, the laughter of the whole escapade still lingering about his sleeping mouth, as I had seen it many a time since childhood. He was good, and he was handsome and strong in his body, upon which neither I nor anyone else now had any claim. I felt again that inward melting sensation rather like the heart itself weeping, when I thought of him. His strength was youth, and youth had been his only weakness; and not long ago I had taken care of that, at the same time losing him altogether . . . This thought brought my mind back to the vision of night stretching ahead, as certain and as mysterious as a wet and unknown road stretching beyond the delimiting headlights of a car driven by a stranger. It led somewhere, that was sure. There would be dawn, turning the harbour slowly from light-pricked nothingness to an unfolding mystery of black and silver; aslant the twin bluffs of the Heads, which I could see almost entire from my high bedroom windows, day would break in melancholy tones of yellow and grey and the scraping cries of seagulls above the leaden water would herald the winter sunrise—grey and cold, no doubt, but day indeed, with its feeling of renewed security and purpose; and at some hour between now and I knew not when the telephone would ring, the final message would come.

Only an infinite patience was needed, a patience of the soul itself to withstand yet a little longer the terrible onslaughts of memory and imagination; and I had always been a patient man, never a nervous subject, never . . . until tonight, when something seemed to have been weakened in me, as though by the final spasm of a supreme effort.

In the street it was raining, very softly, little more than a breath of bliss on the night air. Already the city was quiet. Between the clanking rumble of late trams, near at hand and far away in distant streets, I could just perceive—it was both more and less than hearing—the pulse of the presses, deep underground in their brilliantly-lighted chambers of ferro-concrete, a pulse so slight that only one who sought for it would have detected it. Nevertheless it was the pulse of a most violent life, roaring in a muffled scream down there in the earth, where one of the greatest morning papers south of the Line was being printed by hundreds of thousands between now and dawn. Night after night, for more than twenty years, I had been aware of that sound, that terrific activity, and from the first I had never been sure of the rightness and sanity of its purpose, nor ever felt myself to be truly related to it.

The *Gazette* had long had what seemed to me an influence out of all proportion to its own, or any other's, value as a daily newspaper. Its history proved beyond argument that the very real power of the Press is based chiefly upon the ignorance of its readers; yet the *Gazette* had brought about changes in State and Federal Parliaments; it had forced the setting-up of Royal Commissions and caused the downfall of Ministers; the divorce laws, the gaming and betting acts, the licensing act, the administration of public transport and the care of public health and education—with all these it had ever busied itself, as well as sponsoring many charitable causes, to the tune of millions of words and allegedly in the interests of the people and the nation; with an air of having said the last word that could be said, it considered music, letters and the kindred arts, talking pictures, wireless programmes, sport, and the whole political and economic scene; periodically it announced an increase or a decrease in the incidence of crime and other popular diseases; and its comments on international affairs were occasionally quoted round the globe.

And I—I had never felt myself to belong to it wholly, as most other men did, with a sort of contemptuous pride. It is likely that I was never of the stuff of which true newspaper men are made. I was not, above all, sufficiently a nervous man. By upbringing and by tradition I had never learned to yell loudly or to get drunk, to relieve any nervous tension induced by the often freakish exigencies of the life; and so, as the years passed, the need for such relief had diminished and gone, and I had achieved a certain stillness of the spirit which had long stood me in good stead, in the sort of work I was required by the *Gazette* to do. As Sergeant Hubble had implied not long since, the Fitzherberts were considered to be gentlemen, among the motley throng who had somehow come to be known—to all but themselves—as gentlemen of the Press.

Even as I thought of Hubble, he drew his car up softly alongside me where I was standing near the glistening edge of the sidewalk, looking at but not seeing my own shadow thrown by the light of the main entrance behind me into the more weakly lighted street.

'Hop in, Fitz,' he said. 'Sorry we're late. Last-minute job that won't take a moment. Doc Maybee's in the back there, going to examine a body. You may as well come along.'

I crossed the glare of his headlights to get in beside him on the front seat. For a moment the light blacked-out everything. At the same time my mind seemed to stand still abruptly in its forward movement. I felt it all again—the sweat, the nausea, the overpowering sensation of pervading coldness. So this was it! I had no doubt, no doubt at all; and I found I could not speak, not even to ask a casually curious question that would have needed no thought. Hubble turned from Martin Place into George Street, going north towards the bridge, and towards the city morgue behind the coroner's court. After a silence he spoke to me again.

'Fish bait. The vulgar boatmen' (his term for the water police) 'netted this one in the harbour off Woolloomooloo. Coming in with the tide, I suppose. They tell me it's a real beauty—a woman, and not a mark on her. Luck, eh? Only the colour's wrong for a drowning, it seems, though there was enough water in the lungs. The doc's going to have a look-see, then we can go. You can do me a service by asking in your rag for help in identification. It appears she's wearing only night attire—not even a handbag. Inconsiderate, these suicides. By the description I had over the 'phone, she'll be missed by more than one male tomorrow, if not before. I wonder why they do it?'

Missed, I thought. Missed by Linda Werther, by Kalmikoff, by Alec the caretaker, by the girls at *Chez Madame*, by a whole crowd of exclamatory foreigners, people who, like her, had come to the country as to a refuge, and had turned much of it into a moral and aesthetic and material bargain-basement. Missed by Alan, by me . . .

Yes, she would be missed soon enough, but—if I knew them—not for long by many among us.

'Old or young?' I said at last, to show I had been listening. In the back seat the police surgeon yawned. The car slowed down, turned in the empty street, and came to a

21

halt facing the way we had come, in front of a lighted open doorway. Through the mist of rain under the sickly green pallor of the overhead street lights, this front entry to the house of the dead looked almost warm, almost comforting against the crowding shape of midnight.

'Young and beautiful, from what I hear,' Hubble said, easing his big body away from the steering-wheel and backwards through the open driver's door. 'We'll see in a minute. Let's go.'

'You don't want me,' I said. 'I'll wait, if you are not to be long.'

'Come on, come on,' Hubble said, with a sort of cheerful impatience. Maybee now stood beside him. 'It may be murder, for all you know, my boy. Then how would you feel tomorrow, if some of the other lads got it and not you?'

He was amusing himself. He would never have allowed me to be scooped if he could have helped it, and we both knew this. Hubble never let me miss anything. But at that moment, outside the lighted doorway beyond which lay the unwanted dead of the city, dead by accident or by design, I felt my body weighted as though its flesh were lead, as though I must be lifted from the car if I were ever to leave it. The feeling of nervelessness affected even my hands and feet. Hubble and the doctor stood together on the sidewalk.

'I am rather tired,' I said, 'and one cadaver is much like another, after all.'

Hubble, with the light, quick movements of many fat men who have lived active lives, was round the front of the car, at the door on my side, opening it, pulling me out with great firmness.

22

'Listen to him,' he said to the empty street, with laughter in his strong voice. 'This is a corpse, boy. Cadaver, indeed! This is something to put in your paper.'

I imagined I heard again the tenor voice of Blake: 'We're short of crime . . . The ace crime reporter goes out and commits the perfect crime . . . How about going out and committing a nice juicy murder? A man with your experience . . .'

We walked along the lighted passage. Under the brim of his hat Hubble's face was benevolent and without other expression; in his heavy overcoat he looked enormous. No doubt from habit, he held me by the arm. Quite suddenly his touch made me feel uneasy, and I disengaged myself from his light, friendly grasp. He looked sideways at me, smiling with lips and eyes round his plump red cheek, as we stepped among the echoes of the dark and empty courtroom, from lighted doorway to lighted doorway; and we were there.

I had been thinking very rapidly over what would now ensue. If I had made any plans, done any but the most elementary things in advance, to cover myself, they would not have included arrangements for a visit to the morgue. If I had foreseen this moment, no degree of imagination could possibly have warned me of the feelings which, I found, must accompany it. Clearly, I would have to identify the body; a thing which, did they but know it, I could have done in utter darkness with the fingertips of one hand, or—to be melodramatic—with my very lips. Identity having been established, I must tell all that was necessary to be known of my relationship to the dead woman; and we should need to go to the flat next to my own, where Hubble would

23

find an almost-empty coffee cup and a note—a genuine suicide note, too—addressed to me. The time had come, with the sudden shock of a thunderclap, to act my part; and I perceived very clearly the difference between passive and active participation in such a scene.

Certainly, I had foreseen much of this, but not, as I say, the emotions that went with it, which must be not only hidden but inwardly suppressed, lest they confuse my mind in its present task of making some show of emotions I did not quite feel. As the grey-haired attendant opened a door in the refrigeration unit and began to slide out the tray, I silently made a great call upon that stillness of spirit which is beyond all physical and nervous and mental strength.

I must have closed my eyes for a moment, for suddenly, as Hubble said 'Ah!' with deep appreciation in his resonant voice, I looked—and she was there, there before me again.

Her head was turned away, with closed eyes and parted lips as though in sleep. I knew the pose; it wanted only the light of dawn gleaming like pearl upon her shoulder and cheek and arm, and I should have forgotten where I was. However, there was now only the hard overhead glare of an unshaded electric bulb, merciless and brilliant upon her eternal serenity. The dark hair clinging to the skull and swept by some not-unkind hand in a loose coil beneath her right cheek and that shoulder and arm would have lost its subtle human smell mixed with the perfume of geranium—the hair she had cared for with such absorption each night, each morning; now it must smell of salt water and the undying bitterness of the ocean in which she had drifted back to us. Shining but lustreless, clinging close with moisture, it gave

24

her averted head a sexless, formalized appearance belied by all else about her; for the cover had been folded down to her waist, and her hands, closed listlessly as in sleep, were exposed in all their final helplessness, and the 'night attire' mentioned by Hubble over the telephone was a loose suit of white nylon pyjamas in which, even when it was not made completely transparent by sea water, she (as I had told her with an irritation I could not control) might just as well have gone entirely unclothed. This very evening I had told her that . . . poor soul, poor doomed and destructive creature with whose fate I had tampered too much.

Her bosom through the fantastic material was actually emphasized, and there, too, was the faint, childish thumb-print that was her navel, the sign of mortality more pathetic and pitiful than any other in the whole estate of the flesh. But what was to me most suddenly disconcerting was the utter absence of movement, of the subtle stirring of breath.

I had not realized how she would look. I suppose I had expected horror, the terrible nibbling depredations of leather-jackets and other small harbour fish, such as I had seen too often before, with the bleached bone and bloodless tissue exposed. Instead, here was beauty, more than she had ever seemed to have in life, even in her most harmless moments when she slept. Now that face, quite free of all expression, robbed me for a moment of breath and caution. I went away and sat on a wooden chair. Hubble and the doctor looked at me: even while I rested my face in my hands I could feel their regard of surprise and wonder.

'Can't you take it?' Hubble said, watching me closely.

'I know her,' I said.

25

There was a short pause. Then 'Hell!' Hubble said softly, with great emphasis. He came to where I sat hiding my face in both hands, and rested his own plump hand, gentle now and giving no inkling of its tremendous strength of a former professional wrestler's hand, on my shoulder.

'Take it easy then, Fitz,' he murmured. 'Take it easy.'

'It is the surprise,' I said. 'I was not ready. I feel rather tired, that is all.'

'Take it easy,' he said again. Maybee had turned away and was looking down with an expression of deep thoughtfulness at that averted face. Through my spread fingers I saw him extend his hand and delicately raise one peaceful eyelid; then he went round to the other side of the tray, took from his pocket a pencil torch, raised the eyelid again, and shone the minute beam of light full and steady on the dead, unseeing eye. I felt a passing relief that her face was turned away from where I sat. My view was of her cheek and ear and wet dark hair, and the police surgeon's swarthy and morose face peering, peering with a look of angry concentration into the terrible emptiness of the exposed eyeball. With what seemed an enormous effort, I restrained myself from jumping up and rushing at him to dash the little torch from his hand, to cover again that bared torso with its look of indescribable virgin innocence, and to hide beneath the sheet that lovely sleeping face of clay.

Hubble removed his hand, and I let mine fall on my knees, and looked up at him.

'My identification will be all you will need,' I said; and the time had come to speak with an exquisite care I feared might be beyond me. 'She is known as Irma Francis or

26

Irma Martin. She has lived in the flat next to ours for three years. Martin is an Anglicized form of Maartens—Dutch. Francis was a professional name—she modelled women's clothes at a shop in town here. Actually I believe she was Lithuanian, part-Jewish, with a name no one but her Lithuanian friends—if she had any—could have pronounced, even had they known it, which I understand they did not. She claimed to be Dutch, anyhow. Irma Martin. Or Francis. A mannequin.'

The room was very cold, but again I felt the perspiration prick my hair and beard, and the palms of my hands were damp again. Yet this was not because of any fear. I must suppose it was caused by the not inconsiderable effort of telling Hubble all he needed to know, yet telling nothing he would not have found out for himself.

'Her legal name,' I said slowly, looking up steadily at him as I spoke, 'is Irma Fitzherbert. As you said, the Fitzherberts call themselves gentlemen. We were married three years ago, with two old men, strangers picked up outside the registrar's office, for witnesses. Besides them and the registrar, you are the only person who knows of this. My son does not know. Her friends did not know. We each had reasons for not appearing to be more than old and close friends. I can tell you about that some other time.'

'So long as it has nothing to do with—this.' He gestured with his elbow, keeping his hands in his pockets.

'Nothing more I could possibly tell you has anything at all to do with it.'

It was my first lie, but for the moment I did not realize that. In spite of that inward stillness beyond life and death, beyond fear and desire, I felt my voice tremble on the brink of uncontrol; and at once I saw there was no danger to myself in allowing it to become uncertain. Hubble was staring into my face with a mild look of mixed incredulity and compassion. It was one of the few times when I had known him to look anything but cheerful or officially expressionless.

'As for this, itself,' I said, satisfied that my voice was still noticeably shaken, 'I cannot tell you anything about it. I do know she had been subject to fits of inconsolable depression and would talk rather wildly about killing herself' (this I had heard from Miss Werther, long ago) 'probably because she had been through such hell before she escaped from Europe.'

'A Communist,' Hubble said quietly, as though to himself; but I was not sure of the ground there; I felt I should answer his comment.

'She had been a Party member, in Europe, and had left the Party. She told me only a little of it, but quite enough to explain her occasional states of mind that were like a sort of insanity. Yet when I saw her last, late yesterday afternoon, she was perfectly happy and cheerful.'

It was true. As I handed her the cup of black coffee, which she took very strong with much sugar and a tablespoon of brandy in it, she had been laughing . . .

'She talked so easily of suicide, now and then, that I firmly believed she could never do it. I was sure she was incapable.'

Above all, I must not let him know she had once tried to take her own life.

28

'It is a hard thing for me to consider,' I said. 'As you know, my Church considers it one of the basest sins—something inconceivable to the ordinary mind.'

'How long have you known her?' Hubble said suddenly.

'A long time, I suppose. I saw her first on the ship when she arrived with other refugees in nineteen thirty-eight. Quite a while afterwards, I met her again by chance, at a friend's flat. Little by little we became friends, at first because I was sorry for her, and later for other reasons. I was able to be helpful to her once or twice. Three years ago she agreed to marry me. That is all.'

'That'll do for now, Fitz. I'm dam' sorry you had to find it out like this. If I hadn't insisted on dragging you along . . .'

He touched my arm and turned away.

'Anything unusual, Doc?'

'One of the opiates, and a hell of a lot of it,' Maybee said. I could clearly hear their murmured talk, subdued for my sake in that place where lowered voices mattered no more. With a quick, casual movement the surgeon unfolded the cover and flicked it upwards, so that she was gone from sight completely, and there remained only the hinted outlines of a lifeless anonymity stretched out under the harsh glare of the light overhead. I knew I should never see her again.

'They got water out of her lungs, Doc.'

'They might have. One breath, perhaps. This stuff had about done its work when she went in, I'd say at a guess. Better fix it for tomorrow, Hubble.'

Hubble murmured something hurriedly, and then raised his voice a little to speak to me.

29

'Would you like us to go on ahead and wait, Fitz?'

'No,' I said, 'I had better come with you. We ought to go up to the flat straight away, if you don't mind. There may be something.'

'Right,' he said. 'The doc will want a p.m., you know. Mind?'

'Nothing,' I said, 'can hurt her now. Why should I mind? It is all part of the job.'

I saw the look of slightly puzzled embarrassment about his steady eyes and full, firm lips.

'Queer devil,' he said, as if to himself. 'Perhaps you're right, Fitz. Part of the job. Perhaps you're right. But look—what about that boy of yours?'

'Later,' I said. Now Alan would have to know—tonight; by far the worst was yet to come, I thought. 'He's in good hands where he is. Let us go to the flat first. He need not know about this yet. They were tremendously fond of one another, in spite of the age difference. It will be a shock to him.'

More than anything else in this affair, I had plagued myself with thoughts of how Alan would take it. At the moment, it seemed to me best that he should stay where he was, safely locked up where I could find him when it was time. A growing anxiety to return to the flat next to mine, in the company of this friendly and intelligent police sergeant, this professional detective, now quite obsessed me. As we went out the attendant came back wiping his lips; when he gave us good night as he passed, I could smell he had been drinking tea, and that made me hungry, for I had had no proper meal that night. In the passage, I heard behind us the tray slide home into the cold blackness, and the soft and final closing of the airtight door. They were sounds I heard with something of relief, something of reawakened old despair. Then we stepped out into the greenish-black air of night in the empty street. The small rain was still falling.

In the car, driving back along George Street towards the centre of the city, Hubble and Maybee were silent, until the sergeant, as though reaching the end of a train of thought, said suddenly, 'Now then—your story, Fitz. "The body of a young woman clad only in pyjamas was found by Sydney Water Police late last night floating in the harbour off Woolloomooloo Bay. The dead woman was later identified as Miss Martin or Maartens, also known as Irma Francis, age so-and-so, a Dutch migrant who had worked in Australia as a professional mannequin. Medical examination indicated that the dead woman had taken a large quantity of a—a sleeping-draught, and police believe she may have entered the water while not fully aware of what she was doing. This theory is borne out by the fact that death was caused by drowning. Detective-Sergeant Hubble of the C.I.B. is in charge of investigations."'

After a pause, he said with a coldness I guessed was affected, 'Is that in the best *Gazettese*? I think it tells the truth without bringing in personalities.'

'Thank you,' I said. 'That will do very well. To tell you the truth, I was wondering how to put it.'

'And some day,' he went on, as if he had not heard me, 'you can tell me the whole story.'

His voice now was as cold and heavy as a stone. I took a deeper breath, but he was too quick for me.

31

'Don't interrupt, Fitz, until I've said what I'm going to say. Whether you like it or not. Firstly, I don't mind telling you it looks a dam' funny way for any woman, especially a young and beautiful one, to put her own light out. Apparently she had enough of whatever drug it was to do her business, so why the water? Did she think of the water first, and take the dope to make it easier and to make certain? That's possible, I know. We've had these double-header jobs before and they're always puzzling. But usually they use a rope for their second string, so to speak. You know that yourself. Was she worried about what she'd look like afterwards? Suicides nine times out of ten are what you writers call consumed with vanity. They are. If she had that in mind, she forgot the fishes and sharks *et cetera* in our lovely harbour. It's only luck that they got her so soon, that she's not unrecognizable at first glance. How long would you say she'd been in, Doc?' he said in a louder voice, without looking away from the upward incline of William Street, now almost empty of traffic, which we were ascending at some speed towards the sleepless brilliance of Kings Cross.

Maybee said glumly, 'Hard to tell. Anything from two to six hours, at a guess. My guess is no better than yours. All I can tell you is that she must have been alive when she went in, if they got water from the lungs. Whether she was conscious or not is another matter. The p.m. may give us some idea. You can make that for eleven o'clock if that suits Weatherall.'

'Right . . . How would she get in if she wasn't conscious? The answer is either A or B. A says she might fall in. B says she might have been pushed or dropped in.'

I felt compelled to interrupt at last.

'B would be murder.'

'Right.'

'Impossible.'

He laughed through his nose briefly.

'Fitz, Fitz, nothing's impossible when you're dealing with human frailty. You of all people should know that. Had she any enemies—people, foreigners, who might want her out of the picture? You know what these refugees are. Had she?'

'Ten years ago I would have said "perhaps" to that,' I told him. 'Anyone who leaves the Party always has enemies, depending on how important the apostate may have been as a member. She was . . . just a member, I imagine, and on the other side of the world. No, I know of no enemies in the last few years, none at all.'

Except herself, I might have added, and it might or might not have sounded right to Hubble in his present state of mind. I said no more.

'Well,' he said, with a sort of reluctance, 'I suppose you'd be the one to know. All the same, I agree with what you said. When they talk a lot about suicide they seldom do it . . . Look here, Fitz, don't misunderstand me. I'm sincerely and deeply sorry about it for your sake. But for me it's a job—just another job. I have to get these things out clean with no tangles or implications or loose ends. The fact that you and I've been friends for donkeys' years mustn't be allowed to make any difference. When I say I hope for your sake it was suicide, don't get me wrong. If it had happened to be murder, your own part in the story would have had to come out, and I quite realize you don't want that. Jesus—how the Sunday papers would go to town about you. What was it they called you that time—"the neatly-bearded and aloof Mister Lloyd ('Sherlock Holmes') Fitzherbert, bright boy of the *Gazette*'s secret sleuthing department", wasn't it?'

'It's more for the boy's sake,' I said, 'than for my own. He knows nothing of the marriage, and I think it would upset him a good deal if he found out about it now, in that particular way. Some day I shall have to tell him, of course . . . Not that you could call it much of a marriage, in any case, I suppose.'

In the back seat the morose police surgeon laughed suddenly and harshly.

'You people will never face the facts about women,' he said, 'all you bloody gentlemen and policemen. No man on night duty and on call at all hours should ever think of marriage. Who's ever known a happy doctor's wife? Unless she had a second string to her bow, as most of 'em have. It's so obvious. It's only at night that women have any use for a man. Bloody nuisances in daylight. Ask any house-frau.'

We reached the Cross. Light seemed to swallow us; the coloured glare of the neon signs made the face of humanity into a livid mask. By contrast with the empty city streets we had just left, the place was still restless with life, sleepless and hectic, a gleaming nightmare of faces and eyes seen as it were through greenish-red water, drowning. We had turned cautiously left into Darlinghurst Road, the street of greatest activity at any hour. At this time of night people were walking in the roadway without care, and the clearest

34

sound, rising above the throb of engines and the scraps of music like torn flags in a wind, was the intermittent blare of taxi-cab horns. When we were forced to halt for some seconds at the Springfield Avenue corner, the voices reached us; and I thought again, as always, how there must be less English spoken in this quarter than in any other equivalent area in the whole country. As the world's most thickly-populated district of comparable size, it had long ago become a refuge within a refuge. Every foreigner who landed from Sydney harbour or stepped to earth at Mascot aerodrome knew of the Cross already, and went there as though drawn by an irresistible passion, there to fade—if he chose—into a consoling anonymity until, like the beetle or the butterfly from its chrysalis, he was ready to emerge, full of plans for conquest.

Irma had come here from her ship, she told me; and I knew she had never lived anywhere else in Sydney, never sought or thought of another refuge until she was driven to it; for here she felt at first she had reached her Ultima Thule, the end and the beginning of the world. Like thousands of others in the years just before the second world-war and during it, she felt the safety of the place, its air of plenty, the security of many tongues, most of which she herself knew, and the more animal security of the herd actuated by one itching idea, which was, as I had learned with dismay and a sort of shame, to outwit the Australian hosts in every way, at every turn in every affair, however small. It was when I myself had become a dupe, a voluntary victim of this almost unconscious intention striking at my most real life, my integrity and my very self—it was then that I had been driven, by a force beyond analysis and so beyond proper control, to act.

'Thank God for the Cross,' Hubble was murmuring; and he seemed to have forgotten the matter to which he had been giving such cold, intense thought two minutes earlier. 'Where would we poor policemen be without it? Crime—I dote on it. Don't you?'

'Like you,' I said, 'I live by it. If it interests me, it is for reasons you would not understand.'

'Ho-ho-ho.'

At the end of Darlinghurst Road we turned right, and the car's headlights swept through sudden comparative gloom and silence. Through the cleared half-moon of glass before me, on which the windscreen-wiper was working with awkward urgency, I could see the wet street above which the night brooded, heavy with rain. We were going downhill now, to the maze of dead-end streets at water-level on the city side of Rushcutters Bay; we were nearly home. Again the despair, the fruitless sense of completion, the loneliness, came upon me, as for days past they had done hereabouts when in the small hours I made my way back, usually on foot from the Cross, to my own flat night after night, knowing that only a wall divided from each other the only two people I had ever fully loved, disinterestedly with my mind as well as with my heart and, indeed, all my flesh, all my spirit, my whole self. Now the two flats would be empty.

'Right at the end still, isn't it?' Hubble said doubtfully.

'Right at the end, on the right.'

'On the very edge of the water.'

'Almost in the water. The harbour-side foundation is carried straight ahead to make a tidal breakwater for the swimming pool belonging to the building.'

We ran gently down the last incline, almost as steep as a ramp, and stopped before the dimly-lighted front entrance. When he cut off the engine, a profound silence enveloped us, emphasized by the faint contracting clicks of hot metal cooling under the bonnet. This was one of the quietest parts of the whole city, for the streets were all *culs-de-sac,* and there was no passage for through traffic within half a mile. Cars could not even approach at speed without risk, and the noise of accelerated departures up the steep street was always a diminishing noise; nor did we whose flats faced north-east, looking out across the vast beauty and peace of the outer harbour, hear any sounds of street traffic at all—nothing but the hush and splash of the ocean, landlocked and serene, against the breakwater and the boat-house piles, the grating screams of the grey gulls shearing for ever across the sky's huge disclosure, and the mild and distant sounds of the ceaseless traffic of the sea as the ships came and went, by night and by day . . . Yes, it was a place of peace, where the spirit could, if it would, be still.

This time I led the way, and Maybee stayed in the darkness of the rear seat, smoking in silence. The caretaker's small flat was on the floor below street level, and while Hubble waited I went down the single unlit flight of stairs, and rang the bell. It was a bad hour in which to wake a man out of his first sleep. For some time there was no answer. I tossed up my keys to Hubble and told him to go up to the third landing and let himself into the flat next

37

to mine. A deep silence filled the building, for it was almost one o'clock, and though we who were tenants lived near the Cross we had, for the most part, suburban habits. Irma was the only one, besides myself, who had kept late hours; and now, of course, time would never again mean any more to her than she meant to time, or to me. She was gone, and sometimes during this long night my own desire to live had wavered, as though willing to be gone with her; and only the thought of Alan, so young and proud and bright with happiness and intelligence, had steadied and fed the flame of that desire when it seemed to weaken within me.

I realized now, as I listened to Hubble's ascending steps soften into silence on the carpeted stair, that never again would I return home in the hours after midnight to find her lying on the blue rug, open-eyed and quite motionless before her low-tuned wireless receiver, listening to foreign broadcasts; never again would she pull me down on to the floor beside her, roughly and without a word, and invariably begin to rub my hair with almost ruthless fingers until, although refreshed by this and by her bodily nearness, I could bear neither without moving for a moment longer.

Standing down there in the dark, I felt very tired. No sound of movement could be heard from Alec's little flat, and I pressed the bell-button a second time, holding it down a little longer. The abrupt opening of the door inwards, away from my face, startled me, but in spite of the sensation of profound weariness, I had command of myself; and in any case, I am not a nervous man. Alec's daughter, prepared I think to be indignant, stood against the light of the small entrance hall, wearing like a cloak a woollen dressing-gown that partly concealed her winter pyjamas. She was still half-asleep.

'It's Lloyd Fitzherbert, Emmy,' I said quietly. 'I'd like to see your father for a minute.'

''S asleep, Mr. Fitz,' she struggled to say. 'Won't I do?'

Alec had no wife alive, but had got his job of caretaker on the understanding that his daughter shared the work and the living quarters with him. He once told me she was better than any wife, as she would not bother to quarrel with him and took his mild orders obediently; and it is certain that this was one of the best-cared-for buildings in the whole rabbit-warren of a residential district in which it unobtrusively stood. It is no less certain that I never knew a young woman, as generally presentable as Emmy, who gave such an immediate impression of having no private life of her own whatever.

'I think you had better get him up for me,' I said; and though we spoke only in casual murmurs, our voices seemed to echo up the stair-well with a ghastly hollowness, like the voices of conspirators in a cellar.

She went away from the door, and I heard her call her father in a hushed and regretful tone, and heard his sudden answer in the brisk voice of a man who wishes to be thought wide awake and expectant. A minute later he came himself, owl-eyed in the light, hitching his dressing-gown about his shoulders.

'What's trouble, Mr. Fitz?' he said in a surprised voice.

I told him, and explained that I wanted his master-key. I did not tell him Hubble had used my own duplicate and was already in the flat next to mine.

'Don't go to bed for a few minutes,' I said. 'There is a police detective with me who may want to ask you a few purely formal questions, as you are in charge here. It is for him I want the key.'

Speechless, he took a ring of keys from somewhere behind the door, looked at them and pushed them about until he could isolate a particular one. I saw he was well awake by now; when he spoke at last, it was with his own peculiar intonation and emphasis which always put me in mind of some radio comedian I had once heard on a B.B.C. programme.

'*That* one is *her* key,' he said in his queer falsetto voice. 'There *is* no *master* key, Mr. Fitz, but *that* one is *hers*. Or . . . should I *say*—er—*was*? Dear me. This is *indeed* a dreadful *thing,* and *you* and your *boy* and *her* such *friends*. Dear me, what a dreadful *thing*. I do *hope*, Mr. Fitz, it doesn't get in the *papers*, I mean to *say*, the *flats*, you know—it's the *letting* what I'm *thinking* of, Mr. Fitz. People don't *like* it, goodness knows *why*, but they *don't*.'

'We'll keep the address out of it, Alec,' I said. 'Just wait for a minute or two, and I'll call down to you if Sergeant Hubble wants you.'

'As you *say*, Mr. Fitz,' he said rather doubtfully; and I left him there in the doorway with his pinched, precise face turned up as he watched me go with some anxiety, and began the climb up that so-familiar stairway to the third landing and—as I hoped—the beginning of the last act in this drama of my own devising, which would be almost at an end when I brought Alan home. It was a heavy and an interminable ascent, for while my will led me up and on with desperate determination, my whole body was in open rebellion now, and I had actually to resist a strong urge to sit down on the top step of the first flight and lean my forehead against the coldness of the pale-green wall. Only the knowledge that Hubble was in her flat, alone, drove me on without a pause. When I reached the landing I saw the lighted doorway, and saw his bulky shadow move slowly across the slab of light on the corridor carpet outside it. Without hesitation I went in to join him. One look about, as I entered the big room from the entrance lobby, assured me that all was as it should be. Hubble, very solid and serious in his heavy overcoat, stood still now in the middle of the deep-blue carpet. His regard met mine without suspicion, with— I thought—an expression of simple compassion at last.

'There's a note for you on the radio,' he said. 'I want you to tell me, for the sake of formality, if it's her hand-writing. If you have any letters of hers you've saved, you'd better show me one. Just formality, you know. The note about settles it, I think.'

I took up the note with both hands. In these matters you cannot be too careful, particularly under the very eye of the police; and that folded sheet of paper, did he but know it, already had my finger-prints on it, as well as Irma's. I did not enjoy this active deceiving of a man who had long been my good friend, but I had determined that it should be he, and no one else from his branch if possible, who would be with me at this moment, for now much depended upon his casual goodwill towards me. It must be understood that I was thinking throughout not of myself and my own safety, but of Alan. Once determined upon, once begun, the business must not be botched through any over-confidence of mine, for the boy's whole well-being depended upon me now.

Our friends, as well as those who love us much, are of course our easiest dupes. I had recently tasted this duplicity myself, and was as yet no judge upon it; but it was then that, by the action of that terrible and subtle poison, part of my inner self had withered and died, in a space of minutes, like green leaves in a quick fire. Not for the world would I have had Hubble experience, through my own action, anything like this.

I read the note. Though I knew it by heart, I read it again with an irresistible fascination now, for now, after so many months, it had true and fatal meaning. That meaning I myself had infused into the half-hysterical words so clearly and neatly written:

'Lloyd darling, I have no world of my own and can't can't live in yours any more. I look at the water of the beautiful harbour and it calls me all night and day even when I sleep. So I am going. This time it is true. I thank you for loving me so kindly and I kiss you

Goodbye Fitzi darling—IRMA'

After handling the paper a little more, turning it over as though seeking some added word, some more definite explanation of that least natural of all human actions, suicide, I held it out to Hubble.

'You'll want this, I suppose,' I said. 'It's certainly her handwriting.'

42

Without speaking he took it, folded it, and put it neatly into his large wallet. Then he walked to the window, and from the light folding table that always stood there, at which we had taken so many good and happy meals, he lifted up the empty glass tube by sliding a pencil into it. Turning back to the room, he waved it briefly at me.

'Morphine hydrochloride,' he said conversationally. 'Quarter grains. I wonder how much there was in this? Did you know she had the stuff?'

'I knew she used to have it. She used it with a needle, she told me, years ago when she had some painful trouble—I think she brought it into the country with her. A great many of them—the refugees—did that. They carted the stuff about with them wherever they went in Europe, after nineteen thirty-three, I believe—only it was usually one of the cyanides. In small glass capsules that could be hidden, or even swallowed unbroken and recovered. You will know all about it, I expect. She had one of those too, but I threw it into the harbour. About the morphine, she told me she had lost that years ago. She must have come across it again since. I could not disbelieve her, anyhow. Possibly she got more. They used to get those things easily enough from Jewish chemists in Europe. You know what the casual traffic in it was like here after nineteen thirty-nine. They were the people responsible, the refugees. And it all began because they were frightened even of Australia. They made sure they had a way out. Apparently she did too. If I had known she had that . . .'

I left it to him to finish the sentence, for although not a nervous man, I am a bad hand at telling lies.

'If you'd known, she might be still alive, you mean?' Hubble said softly. 'Well, Fitz—maybe. But in view of that note I doubt it. She meant business, Fitz. But why in God's name do they do it?'

I sighed. He was not, in his manly kindness of heart, to know that it was a sigh of relief, as well as of utter weariness and that sick despair which I could neither understand nor fight down. All was now ended—all but the task of getting Alan home and telling him, somehow without lying, of Irma's fate; and such was my unforeseen relief at Hubble's last remarks that this task did not now seem so hard in prospect. Often before tonight I had consoled the boy's grief and hidden my own caused by the sight of his; I could do it again, I could do it as long as I lived, for this love knows no exhaustion, asks no return; it is like the spring of water near Hill Farm, in the mountains: no man has ever known it to falter or dry and cease from flowing.

'I've looked round,' Hubble said. 'There's that coffee cup on the radio—can you find me a bottle of some sort, I'll take the dregs for Maybee. It's likely she took the stuff in that.'

In the kitchen, off the small passage that opened upon the service-staircase outside, I looked about for a small container. The complete tidiness of the place, scrubbed and immaculate as though never used, gave me again that subtle feeling of pleasure I had always had when looking at the indications of her manner of living; for she was tidy and clean to a truly exquisite degree, yet in so casual a manner that one never seemed to catch her at it. This was especially true of her person, though her natural physical perfection was nothing at all like the aseptic and repellent American magazine-advertisement sort, but arose and emanated rather from an abundance of good health and her use of leisure for being idle than from the pursuit either of health or of leisure so miserably characteristic of the age. I never knew a woman with her capacity for immobility and ease. Like her strange, animal ability to sleep at will, from which I think it sprang, it was at first disconcerting, though in time I learned its virtue and lost my earlier desire to make her move and speak; to ask—like any love-sick boy—'What are you thinking about?' Her reply, which in another woman might have sounded foolishly affected, was the simple truth: 'I think of nothing at all. My mind is a blank, so do not talk to me, darling.'

I could hear that voice with its light, strong, un-English inflections and accent as I opened the doors of the cupboard under the shining sink. It was so clear in my hearing, memory was so faithful and vivid, that an inadvertent thrill of intense, unreasonable happiness passed through my nerves and seemed to lodge like an obstruction in my throat, bringing a sting of tears, while I bent down to search for one of the small brandy flasks she kept for replenishments, to lace her morning and evening coffee with the spirits. I had forgotten she was dead.

'Fine,' Hubble said, when I took the little flat bottle in to him. 'Did she drink much of this, by the way?'

'Two tablespoons a day,' I said. 'One in the morning, one in the evening, always in coffee. She considered it a sort of tonic medicine. Otherwise, she drank wine sometimes with meals. Not always. She was as abstemious as—as I am myself.'

Hubble laughed softly as he drained the porcelain coffee cup with delicate precision into the flask.

'What a nice sober couple you must have been, then,' he said. 'Personally, I could do with a drink right now.'

'When you are ready,' I said, 'we can go next door and you can have some whisky, if that will do. I have the caretaker waiting, if you want to see him.'

'Fine,' he said again without much interest. 'Better see him, I suppose. He may be able to give us some idea of the time.'

While he took the empty cup and its saucer to the kitchen to rinse them—for, like some fat men and not all police officers, he was a neat and tidy fellow in all things—I looked in at the bedroom. It was, of course, just as I had seen it last, like the rest of the flat, not many hours before. On the white dressing-table lay her hairbrush which I had picked up from where it fell out of her hands; and I thought I could see still on the bedcover the faint imprint of her half-conscious form, though I had smoothed the ruffled material after I got her off the bed and into a chair in the big room. Neither of us would ever wake again in that firm and comfortable bed, as until recently we had so often done when the light of dawn warned me that it was time to go softly back to my own flat. I supposed that to the rest of the world it would have seemed a fantastic marriage, had the facts of it been known; but as it was it suited us both very well, for there was something innocently clandestine about it besides the freedom of movement made possible by those two separate and adjacent establishments, each of which one of us commanded without question.

Standing there just inside the doorway, breathing her most intimate atmosphere for the last time, while she lay cold and lifeless in an airtight refrigeration chamber, a body among other unwanted bodies each in its narrow deathly little cell, I decided that Alec should arrange with the owners, if possible, to purchase the entire furnishings of the flat for what they cared to pay, so that like certain others in the building it could be rented furnished. I would probably never enter or see into it again, and I was not inclined to have anything more to do with what had belonged to her, even though many of the material things I myself had given her cried out softly to be remembered and taken away. Miss Werther could look after it—that would be better still, better than Alec. For the rest, all was ended tonight, all, and there must be no loose threads. On this I was absolutely determined, just as I was determined that Alan too should never come in here again. There must be no loose threads for him either, for youth can become entangled in such things more easily even than maturity, to its own confusion.

I became aware that Hubble had returned to the room behind me and was waiting, so I switched off the bedside lamp at the door switch and closed the door. As I turned to him I saw again that look of simple compassion in his blue friendly eyes.

'Shall we go?' he said. 'There's nothing more, I think.'

The place suddenly felt dead and empty, as though no one had ever lived there. I looked at none of it as we let ourselves out; I would have welcomed the suggestion of a haunting ghost, but there was no ghost, nothing but a still emptiness containing nothing, expecting no one.

There was still much to be done, and I clung to that thought. When Hubble was settled in my flat, I went down and called Alec from the first landing, apologizing for having kept him out of bed for so long. He followed me up in silence. No doubt the thought of meeting a policeman professionally in some way outraged his law-abiding soul. But Hubble was all kindliness and brevity now, when he questioned him.

'I heard *her* wireless,' Alec said in a more confident tone. 'That would *be* at seven p.m., sir, because I had just gone *up* to *look* at one of the off-*peak* hot-water *tanks*, and it was coming *down* I heard *it*, quite a while after Mr. Fitz, I should say Mr. *Fitzherbert*, had gone off to the office, which is why I remember, for as you know Mr. Fitz and Alan was very friendly with Miss Martin, poor thing, and they was always in and out of one another's flats when at home. Oh—I hope I do not divulge unwanted information, Mr. Fitz?'

'Go ahead, Alec,' I said. 'Did you hear the wireless stop?'

'No, sir, but one of her *friends* came, and when he *knocked* he could not *get* an answer, so *he* came downstairs to *me* and says was Miss Martin *out*? and I says not that I am aware of, because mostly I hear the tenants *come* and *go*, and he says "*Well*," he says, "she does not *answer* her door so I presume," he says, "she has gone *out*, though *she* was *expecting* me." So I said to him, "*Well* . . ."'

'What time was this?' Hubble asked gently. Alec, interrupted, looked confused for a moment; his fixed stare over Hubble's head wavered and came back to the present.

'About eight o'clock I think it was,' he said.

'And what was the visitor like?' Hubble asked.

'Like, sir? *He* was one of these *foreigners*, very foreign in his way of *speaking*, with a big dark mo and glasses.'

'Kalmikoff,' I said. 'He's a musician, an irritating fellow she seemed to have known for years. One of those fugitives from Communist Russia who become rabidly communist the moment they reach a country of refuge. Like most of them, he is quite futile and harmless—irritating to talk with, but an excellent musician. You may have heard of him, even if you have not heard him play. He is a violinist.'

'I may have heard of him,' Hubble said. 'As for music, I know nothing about it. Did he stay or go?' he asked Alec.

'Him? Oh—*he* went away, sir, and rather *angry* I should say *he* was, muttering to himself in some foreign lingo. *I* went upstairs again, but Miss *Martin* had turned her wireless *off*, and if she has gone *out*, I thought, why, *she* has been pretty quiet about it. Most likely she didn't want to see *this* chap, I thought, but too kind to say so. She was always very kind in that way, sir. And that is all I know.'

His information could not have satisfied me more if I had dictated it to him myself. Fortunate fellow, he would return to sleep not knowing that when he had heard her wireless tuned to Radio Luxembourg—the only foreign station I knew how to find—Irma was already dead in the early darkness of the placid harbour beyond the break-water; while I, not she, had heard his quick steps softly pass that door and continue the descent towards dinner and a peaceful evening with the papers and the commercial broadcasting programmes. Before Kalmikoff banged at the

49

door, before Alec returned to listen, I had gone by the way I came after my earlier and more ostentatious departure.

'Thank you,' Hubble said. 'This is quite helpful. And now you had better be off to bed—catch up on your beauty-sleep, lucky man.'

Alec made a sudden clucking noise, his queer way of laughing, and went towards the door, saying, '*Beauty*-sleep. That's a good one. Wait till Emmy *hears* that one. Good night, sir, good night Mr. Fitz*herbert* . . . *Beauty*-sleep!'

He let himself out and clucked softly downstairs. Hubble smiled at the closed door while I set out whisky and a soda-water siphon on the book-table beside my reading chair where he sat, and poured us a stiff peg each. As he took the tumbler, he motioned with his head at the telephone on my work-table in the corner near the windows.

'Hadn't you better ring your office?' he said. 'Then we'll go and get that boy of yours out of the clutches of the law. He must have cooled off enough by now.'

'What about Maybee?' I said. 'Would he join us?'

'Don't bother him. He's most probably asleep, if I know the doc. A hard-working, hard-tongued chap, but one of the best. Now.'

I went to the table and unlocked the only drawer in the whole place that had a key to it. It contained my small revolver, which I had bought and had licensed in my early, youthful days on police rounds, and had never used; and weighted down by this were some half-dozen letters from Irma which for reasons of somewhat weakly sentiment I had kept, meaning always to destroy them yet somehow never being quite willing to part with them or anything else that had been hers. I had never looked at them again. The most recent one, more than three years old, I took out and carried to Hubble where he sat holding his glass near his mouth, enjoying the whisky and at the same time smoking his pipe for all the world as though he were seated by his own fireside. I was pleased to observe the finality of his relaxation; it made my own mind easier, and I filled and lighted a pipe for myself. Then I went back to the table and sat down, and took up the telephone receiver to speak to Blake. As I did so, it occurred to me that I had never had and now never would have that telephone call on which my whole future had seemed to hang; and this I took as a warning not to count on the preconceived mechanics of a carefully devised situation when such a situation depends however lightly upon tides and men and other factors not mechanical.

'Thanks,' Hubble said, coming over when I had given Blake the brief story. ('Can't you do better than a bloody suicide, Fitz? Give us blood, man,' Blake said when I had finished.) 'That puts it beyond doubt.'

He was holding out the letter, looking down at me, his fat, strong face serenely quizzical and apologetic. We met each other's gaze for some seconds; then he smiled.

'Don't forget what I said earlier. One day you can tell me the whole story. You can answer all the questions you know I haven't asked you . . . And now let's go and get that precious boy of yours.'

It was then that I decided to write this down, as time allowed, partly to ease my soul of a burden I had not even then foreseen, partly to help memory shrug off the weight of what is now past and irrevocable. Until I die, it can remain in that locked drawer with the useless revolver and the now meaningless letters from the woman I loved, for whose death may God forgive me in the end.

TWO
THE BEGINNING

The harbour in the early morning of a winter day, when the eastern sky is cloudy, is like music. I am reminded—against my will—of the opening of Brahms's great E-minor symphony: there is a cool, voluptuous quality in the light of air and water, and an underlying rhythm much like that of the horns playing their slow and serious melody above the faint *pizzicato* of the strings. Sunrise is the moment when the strings themselves take over the melodic line and shed a clear light upon the triplets in the *tempo*.

It is not encouraged, by true musicians, to associate the sound of music with any visual impressions. Hearing the music, one should see the score; seeing the score, one should be able to hear the music and nothing more. With this I cannot but agree, in theory and argument; yet despite myself music has its visual associations and brings its own visions, so that even now as I imagine the sensuous fourfold first theme of the first movement of the Franck violin sonata I feel that speechless constriction in the throat, that faint tingling in the palms of my hands which a sudden sight of Irma unawares always gave me.

These sensations developed much later when I began to realize and admit what I felt about her. Nothing so personal and intimate touched me on the occasion when I saw her for the first time, although that first meeting remains as vivid in memory as any later one—more vivid, perhaps, since for my part no emotions were involved. I was merely a newspaper man doing a colleague's job, and not liking it much.

That was in August of nineteen thirty-eight, years ago now, when many of us knew that war in Europe was inevitable, this year or next year, though none of us could have foretold its direction or development or who all the participants would be. The shipping editor of the *Gazette* was ill for some weeks, and each day one or other of us who were senior staff men was invited to take some of the weight of the job off the shoulders of his junior assistant. Socially and economically, shipping was still more important than airways; most of the people who made news still arrived in Australia by sea, and the *Gazette*'s cover was thorough.

It meant very early rising as a rule, usually—in my own case—after late night work, and it was not relished; but ships arriving from Europe even then were bringing refugees by the score and the hundred into this country, and were certainly well worth watching, though few of the new arrivals from the dangerous antipodean Old World (which seemed to us to be very old indeed, and increasingly ill-tempered and grotesque) would say much. Many of them had left families still living in the Nazi shadow, and dared not talk, for the remote young continent was fairly well watched by German agents. Most of the newcomers had themselves spent the years since nineteen thirty-three in secret terror or open flight. Australia was their last refuge. They were not going to spoil things here right at the start by indulging that inclination to personal publicity which was, we found, perhaps the most obvious if not the most deep-rooted of all their common characteristics. (Their next most obvious one, it quickly became clear, was an established contempt for Australia and Australians, even before they had descended the ship's gangways; and this was some-times so open and arrogant, with such a display of ignorant self-conceit, that there were occasional regrettable scenes between members of the well-disposed host nation and their seemingly unwilling and curiously resentful guests.) By far the greater percentage of them was Jewish, and not notable for emotional stability or outward control, though I always knew the hard inward core was there.

With other journalists and our photographers, I went out in the Press launch to meet the *Empire Queen* as she came into the harbour. It would have been a Brahms early morning but for the bitterly cold north-east wind coming straight in through the distant Heads and ruffling the steel-grey of the enclosed sea to a troubled darkness streaked with white. It was blowing not hard but steadily, without a pause, as though it had never ceased to blow since the dawn of time. The big passenger vessel, later sunk while acting the futile role of armed merchantman in the Indian

Ocean, had just entered the Heads from the cold unease of the winter Pacific outside. For once, we were early on the job, and had to wait, rocked in a sickening swell, until a police launch pulled away from the gangway on the port side to give us room. I had been informed, the night before, that three rather important Communists were aboard in the guise of refugees; this had come from Melbourne, where it had been discovered, or at least confirmed, only after the ship had left two days ago, and I wanted to be in time for any scenes that might develop after the plain-clothes men had gone aboard. I might have saved myself the trouble of being first up the slippery and unsteady gangway, as it happened, for, having identified their men, the police separated to help the Customs officers who had begun a routine search of the vessel for contraband. Passengers' luggage would wait until it was unloaded into the sheds at Darling Harbour, on the other side of the bridge which, from where we were, looked like a delicate, fantastic silver-point drawing against the pallor of the western sky. Its huge single arch now had a faery quality, and the dim, incessant rumble, like sustained and remote thunder, made by the electric trains and trams roaring across it without a stop from south to north, from north to south, seemed to come from another world. The screaming of the scavenging gulls in our wake, and the occasional whooping sirens of the tugs ahead, were sounds much nearer, more proper to our dead-slow passage through the white-flecked dark water between distant foreshores green with dark trees or pale where the red-and-white of story-book buildings came down to the harbour's very edge.

We were seven men and three women in our party (I could seem to hear the voice of every news-editor in town automatically intoning, 'Get the women's angle. That's what we want these days—the women's angle.'), and as they came up one by one, some carrying cameras, heads were turned and blank or suspicious or dully curious eyes looked us over before the faces were turned abruptly away; for most of the passengers must have been on deck, and there was a subdued noise of excited speech in many languages as these creatures neared the end of their bitter flight, and studied with passionate excitement the shores of final refuge.

Sydney in that year was a hundred and fifty years old, and the ordinary troubles of the Press were being aggravated by what was called—with almost American infelicity—'the sesquicentenary celebrations'. *Post urbe condita ann. CL*—if indeed the city ever had been actually founded; and it is still one of the world's ugliest, beyond the lovely approaches from the sea, as those who work in the heart of it know. It developed without plan from the original huts near the water's edge, spreading southwards in a tangled sprawl of narrow streets, and westwards to the complex shoreline of the inner harbour; and south and west the factories appeared as time passed, right in the path of the strongest prevailing winds, so that the ineradicable grime of smoke and dust from the enclosing semicircle of high chimneys spiking the horizon is never absent from the exterior and interior surfaces of the cramped and hideous Victorian buildings which scowl above the hopelessly overcrowded traffic lanes. Macquarie and his ex-convict architect Greenway had all too short a term together in

57

their intention to make the town as beautiful as its site must once have been. When they were gone, no other inspired mind followed them with authority to pursue their quest for grace and space; the town became a city irresistibly and without plan, and from the south and west the dirt settled upon it. The men of the good Queen's era built their mean buildings behind grotesque and hypocritical façades, and the ownership of street frontages passed securely and unalterably from one generation to the next, so that today it is impossible to walk in comfort on the street sidewalks, or travel in comfort on the roadways—or, indeed, to be comfortable and at ease anywhere at all in the public places. Greed, more potent and less patent than even the sincerest show of civic pride, has kept the main streets to a mediaeval narrowness across which office boys can throw paper darts from window to window, and typists and their employers can observe other typists' clothes and *maquillage* with unstrained critical eyes. And over all, indoors and out, lies the dark and metallic film of unconquerable grime.

Nevertheless, from the mighty bosom of the harbour the skyline to the south and west is mildly fascinating. With unrestricted ground space it has no cause to tower like the incredible aerial skyline of New York. The clouds may lie low over it without obscuring it, and on mornings such as this, when the wind is fresh from the ocean outside the Heads, the blue haze is gone from the narrow ravines of the streets, and the whole scene has the accurate unreality of a detailed stage backdrop. As I looked at it over the heads of the new arrivals crowding the port rail, the weak August sun rose above a seaward bank of heavy cloud and veiled it in an illusory mist of gold, chilly and pale, and in our wake the grey water coldly sparkled under the following wind.

The *Empire Queen*'s purser, busy and harassed, with four interpreters adding to the confusion of his last half-hour before the ship berthed, yet made time to go hurriedly through my passenger list with me. After the brisk air of the open deck, the atmosphere below was thick and stale and still, tepid as used bath-water. While I made notes of half a dozen names of possible interest, a melodious gong sounded through the broadcasting system the call to the second breakfast sitting, and the crowd round the gilded grille of the purser's office thinned somewhat. At such moments, when the journey's end is near, meals are subtly reassuring to the traveller who feels a strange and alien world at hand beyond the ship's rail. It was now I, watching the faces and listening to the excited greetings of those who were making their way to their familiar seats in the saloons, who felt like a stranger among the powerful and evanescent friendships of that long voyage into the unknown. The imminence of final separation, after the closed and intimate and unworldly life on board, and the strong community of their alien origins regardless of nationalities, were for the last time uniting them as though, like an army on the eve of invasion, they were wholly of one mind in a simple and desperate purpose. There was about them, in their eyes and speech, a kind of gay defiance of whatever fate awaited them in the crude, traditionless, uncultured country of their choice. I did not doubt they sat down with good appetite.

Ten minutes after that tuneful gong had sounded through the amplifiers, the lower decks had an air of emptiness and desertion as positive as the whole ship would have when, lying at her berth in the still and torpid water of the inner harbour, she was finally emptied of her human freight. Without any certain objective, I made my way down the stair opposite the purser's office to the second saloon deck, where the atmosphere was even more like used bathwater, slack with steam and the smell of oil, cigarette smoke, linoleum, soap and crowded humanity. Here the cabins, most of which had their doors hooked back as the stewards, in a sudden passion of attentive service, made ready to take up what they could seize of the fantastic assortment of luggage, were of four or six berths, according as they opened inwards, or out upon the second-class promenade deck. Much of the baggage had a cheap smartness about it, the *ersatz* smartness of poverty, or of wealth disguised as poverty, which characterized so many things—and people— arriving at these shores from Europe in those days of fear.

I walked aimlessly aft along the starboard-side corridor, with the bathrooms and toilets and stewards' offices on the right, the open cabin doorways on the left. There was a softly-vibrating silence and a noticeable smell of women passengers, their cosmetics and clothes and bodies, mingled with the steamy, astringent odour of hot sea-water and the smell of the imperfectly aseptic toilets. No doubt I noticed this atmosphere more than the passengers would. I was already beginning to find it intolerable, and hastened my steps towards the after companionway which would take me up to the air of the winter morning, when a glance inside one of the cabins made me pause; and so it was I first saw Irma.

She was sitting on the deck of the cabin, on the bare linoleum, with her feet stretched out straight before her, her knees together and her face hidden in both hands. Her dark hair, cut so that it hung like a mediaeval page's almost to her shoulders, fell forward over her fingers and wrists, and what made me pause, instead of passing on more hastily still, was that as she rocked back and forth she was moaning to herself like someone suffering the pain of a badly aching tooth. It was of toothache, in fact, that I immediately thought; and some impulse entirely foreign to my character, something I can still only describe and think of as a fatal prompting of chance, made me turn towards the doorway and say, 'What is the matter, mademoiselle? Can I help you?'

I was surprised at myself, and she too was surprised, as she showed by taking her hands from her face and springing easily to her feet in an uninterrupted single movement, like a dancer or an acrobat. Erect, she stood quite still.

I saw she was wearing pyjamas. Later I learned that she wore pyjamas at all possible times of the day, hurriedly changing into them the moment she came in from the street, and sometimes even wearing them out of doors when she walked at night about Kings Cross, visiting friends. I have never considered them proper garments for a woman, even to sleep in; certainly not to wear, uncovered, by day, when they give a grotesque emphasis to whatever bodily beauty they affect to conceal; but her they suited unaccountably. It was not until the last evening of her life that I remarked on what seemed to me their impropriety, and that was only because the pyjama suit she had then put on—a new one added to her large collection only that day—went beyond all bounds of decency, being of completely transparent white nylon.

This morning the pyjamas were wholly decent, and over them she wore a knee-length house coat of some thick warm stuff like felt, dark green and cut in the Chinese style with a high collar closely fastened by a gold button the size of a florin. I imagine she had been up on deck with the rest of the passengers, to observe by dawn's light the end of the run up the coast past Botany Bay to the dramatic turn and entry into the huge harbour between the vertical cliffs of the Heads. Below decks in that atmosphere of fug such a coat was unnecessarily warm, even though these people from Europe feel the mild Australian cold more than they ever felt their own white icebound northern winters.

I had looked at her apparel, from the thin black leather slippers to the gold medallion at her throat, in one glance and entirely from habit. Even in those early years of my profession I had had to look at many dead bodies, and clothes had come to have a deep, probably an abnormal, significance in my eyes. In the two peaceful years of my marriage, which had ended with my wife's death eight years before this when I was still a junior on the *Gazette* staff, I doubt whether I could have described any of her outer clothing with comprehensible accuracy, and her other garments remained to the end something of a mystery, though I suppose I could have enumerated them by name after looking at the clothing advertisements and the shop windows. We had both come from Catholic households which were strict in the matter of personal privacy, when we married. Always we had undressed separately, never had we beheld each other's body wholly naked—it would have been unthinkable. All this had much bearing on my subsequent association with the young woman who now stood before me.

When my gaze reached her face a second after she had gained her feet on the deck, I saw that it had been distorted by emotion, the wide full lips stretched in apparent anguish over startlingly white teeth, the eyes of curious opaque grey-blue staring at nothing under contracted brows. But abruptly, even as I looked, all expression vanished, and her youthful countenance became like a mask; even the eyes, those habitual traitors of the mind and spirit, contrived to express nothing. I had a moment to observe the cool adolescent perfection of her face and head as she brushed her dark hair back with the back of one wrist, before she spoke.

'Police?'

The word came, seemingly despite herself, in a sort of gasp.

'No, no,' I said, smiling to reassure her, as well as at the mad thought of an Australian policeman with a van Dyke beard and moustaches; for in spite of her lack of expression her voice had betrayed a stabbing alarm. 'I happened to be passing, and thought perhaps you were in pain—*souffrante, vous comprenez?*'

'Pain?' she said, ignoring my offer of a French translation. 'No pain . . . Oh—pain! Yes, here is pain.'

She put her right hand to her heart so that under the thick stuff of the house coat her breast stood out innocently above the spread thumb and forefinger. Still I could detect

63

nothing of feeling in the mask of her face, which I now saw was not only elusively beautiful but also tragically young for the habit of such immobility. Despite myself, I was moved by this attitude, and by the strange combination of beauty, youthfulness and self-command. When I was a youth myself we did not know such girls.

'I am frightened,' she said with a sort of indifference, as if we knew one another well, and never taking her regard from mine. Her English was precise, like the strange control she always had over her body's attitudes and movements, no matter what was happening to her body: the perfect and natural control of a full-grown animal whose physical dignity you cannot destroy or pervert. She spoke in the light voice of a young girl, sweetly and with a marked but not distorting accent which she never quite lost; even among a crowd of her fellow-refugees her voice, with its buoyant quick precision, could be heard apart, idiomatic yet forever strange. Only in moments of deepest and most tender passion did it become slurred, as though by an extreme exhaustion which her body's vigour frankly denied.

'There is nothing to fear now,' I said, and at once the words sounded foolish. How was I to know what would be fearful to her, what indelible terrors of memory and what vaguer terrors of anticipations she and all those in her position brought with them from Europe's mounting nightmare of the flesh and the spirit?

'You are in Australia now. You are safe. What is your name?'

Self-assurance had come back to me. It was not I, after all, who was the stranger here, but most of the people on

64

this ship, who would disembark and disappear, for the most part, from official ken, and become woven into yet never quite lost in the Australian fabric like the minute individual threads in a tremendous tapestry. I was on my own ground, a newspaperman, a police roundsman, used to asking every sort of question, knowing the most difficult of the ropes, familiar with all sorts of violence, passion and death, securely employed and well paid, with a growing son and an outgrown sorrow for background. As this remembrance passed swiftly through my mind, I stepped through the cabin doorway and looked down into her face. She had not answered my question. I repeated it gently.

'Irma,' she said, turning her head away. 'Irma Maartens—Nederlander. Dutch.'

'Why were you frightened?' I said, making my voice as casual and kindly as possible; for something in her mask-like face, something no mask could have concealed, something like the very essence of feminine beauty which is not of flesh or feature but emanates from the depths of intensely conscious being, had as it were gripped me by the throat and stormed imagination, and in that instant I felt what today I still believe to have been a perfectly sane impulse to take her face between my palms and kiss her closed lips. So strong was this impulse that I instinctively stepped back from her again, placing her out of my reach. Whether she correctly guessed what had been in my mind—she with her already shamefully extensive knowledge of men's passions and compulsions—I did not know; but she smiled, sudden and faint, and her face was no longer so rigidly on guard.

'Yes, frightened,' she said; and having begun, she continued rapidly. 'All the time I am frightened, ever since we are leaving London. Like you, they all tell me Australia is safe, there is plenty money, friendly people, all that. But where is safety for a woman, tell me? Me—I am just another bloody refugee, isn't it? Go to Australia, they say. There you will be orright. Now I am here. What happens next? What do I do, in Australia? What do I *do*?'

I learned, long afterwards, that she had been private secretary to the secretary of a local branch of the Dutch Communist Party in one of the smaller industrial centres in Holland. This followed a fantastic escape from Berlin, where she had lived mostly in hiding, though very active in Party interests, since nineteen thirty-three when, like many older and wiser people—in that year she was a precocious thirteen—she had offered her services to the Communists after the election of Adolf Hitler to the Chancellorship of the Reich. During the vigorous training that had followed her acceptance by the Party, when she had been investigated by agents from Berlin to Kovno, her forgotten birthplace, her name with thousands of others became 'known' to the Nazi police. Just in time, she disappeared from the day-light scene and from all her former haunts. It is likely that her political colleagues would have abandoned her in those days of stealthy terror but for two things: she was already a consummate linguist after a childhood spent wandering about Europe with her father, a musician of sorts; and her integrity, youthfully impassioned though it was, was nevertheless absolute and unwavering. She was thought of favourably as being of great future usefulness, and during her

66

year in hiding she became a sort of pet or mascot—for at that time, I suspect, she was something of a *gamin*—among the fearful and fanatically determined members of the Party in Germany, and had proved her luck moreover by successfully carrying out, before her fifteenth birthday, several missions of some slight importance within and outside the Reich. She usually dressed as a boy, she told me until the attentions of various official and private members of the Nazi party became dangerously personal. I believe her love of wearing pyjamas began during that period of her life.

'Well,' I said, and I was again quite in control of mind and body, 'what can you do? Have you a profession? What did you do in Holland?'

She said, tilting her chin with a sort of haughtiness I afterwards learned to mean she was not telling all, 'I was secretary—to a gentleman.'

It seems she was at last allowed to reappear in Berlin, after some months spent in Switzerland letting her hair grow long again. She was manoeuvred into a job in one of the best fashion-houses, where wives of higher Government officials, with much more money to spend than most of them had ever dreamed of gathered to look at and buy the new gowns and furs from France and Britain and America. For security reasons, and others which they did not mention, her directors thought it best for her to join the Nazi Party with a show of enthusiasm, and with the false papers provided by the experts in her own Party she had been able to do this easily—as easily, in fact, as many Nazis had joined the Communists in the same way and for the same purposes.

67

Meanwhile, she began to enjoy her work in the dress salon when it was discovered that she had a fresh gift for design as well as a natural ability as a model—an ability sprung, I think, from her intense and perfectly controlled femininity. Though she did not much care for the mere wearing and display of clothes, she somehow transformed them; and by this time, Nazi-trained, Communist-schooled, and mercilessly drilled by the mistress of the salon, her control of face and body was perfect and instinctive, without thought, a part of the sum of her conscious being. She began to feel that there was nothing she could not do, no part she could not play.

Today, in the artificial light from the cabin ceiling, she looked forlorn, but not helpless. I never did see her look to be unable to help herself, except once. Now the expression of defensive hauteur faded, and again her face relaxed; again I saw that faint smile move the corners of her mouth, though it did not warm her eyes or soften the cool severity of her brow.

'I am also,' she said, '*couturière*. You have those in Australia, no?'

'Yes,' I said, surprised; and I had to laugh, for the remark was characteristic of the ignorance of this country which nine out of ten of those foreigners brought with them: an ignorance amounting almost to an unwillingness to know, which largely explained the mixed suspicion and contempt which coloured their whole attitude towards the land and the people who gave them refuge. Today the Government-sponsored immigrants, who—though they are infelicitously styled New Australians—are still refugees

68

from conditions, if not from groups of individuals, over which they have no control, at least learn something of the social and political and economic character and the material resources of the world's only island continent, the huge leonine mass of barrenness and fertility pitched between the tropic and polar oceans, before they arrive; at least they are aware, however vaguely, that much of human history and forced nationalistic development was crowded into the century and a half of measured time that had passed before they came; at least they have known they were leaving an old and in some sort moribund civilization for no new barbarity of existence. But the earlier ones, the frightened and arrogant refugees from the terror of Europe, exhibiting that remorseless egomania which is the result of intolerable dread seemingly suffered indefinitely, yet suddenly left behind—those came convinced that a land in which black-skinned tribesmen still roamed at large in the west and the north must be a waste-land of beachcombers and bushrangers and futile remittance-men and ignorant fossickers. Like Irma at first, they supposed the social and cultural arts were their own prerogative to reveal as they saw fit and to dispense as they pleased; and this had always made me laugh a little, because so many of them seemed to us to have, not quite concealed beneath the gesture of habit and the glance of scorn, the half-developed minds of badly spoiled children. Even their suffering could seem, at times, like something they had indulged in and whose memory they vainly cherished.

'You are laughing at me,' she said in a soft voice, with her strange blue gaze now focused and intent upon my face.

'Indeed no,' I said. 'I was laughing at Europe.'

The casual remark, scarcely a hint of what I had been thinking, effected a startling change in her face, which seemed to darken as though under the shadow of a hand. With a sort of animated impatience she shook her head several times emphatically. Looking back, I realize that by now both of us had to some degree forgotten where we were, and the hour, and the future unrevealed beyond the hour; I because without knowing it I was already fallen under the spell of her young enchantment, secret and ineffable, of absolute womanhood, and could not see the violence it concealed; she because with speech her troubled fear was abating steadily, and also because she was at last confronted with a native of the unknown, whom she must certainly have found to be much like other men on the opposite curve of the world.

'At Europe?' she said. 'Then do not. You are not police. Would you laugh at Jesus while the men hit the nails through his wrists? Before the cross is lifted up? No. That is Europe.'

If there is one human manifestation for which I have neither sympathy nor compassion, it is this sort of melodramatic speech which seeks to impress both by emphasis and by far-fetched metaphor. I was not impressed as she had meant by what she had just said; any hack writer could have thought that up, and even got it into print, in those days of mounting sentimental hysteria, when none of us knew where we were heading. What I did feel was a sense of shock and disappointment, that so much youth and vitality and feminine beauty should have been so well-schooled in the mouthing of spiritless clichés; for I could not then and cannot now believe that the passion for their maggot-eaten

70

homelands which these people so readily put into words is a real passion of body and mind and spirit, and not largely a guileful parade of perfected artifice. What I did believe is that they were profoundly glad Australia did exist and was there unguarded for their exploitation.

Furthermore, I have no patience with the easy use of the image of Jesus which is become in these times of loose and vitiated language a commonplace and a habit. I am a Christian and a Catholic, as the men of my family have been since the sixteenth century; I am not actively devout now, but it is there in my consciousness, never to be spoiled, and I can no more listen to the name of my own inspired prophet lightly spoken for the sake of a phrase than I can myself speak it, or for that matter the names of the other prophets before and since Jesus, lightly for the same purpose.

It brought me at once to my senses: I remembered the work I must do before the ship berthed, and realized that the young woman looking at me so intently and even angrily now could very well take care of herself—this *couturière* who had been 'secretary to a gentleman'. An unaccountable disappointment came upon me; I felt that these few minutes in the company of that young stranger, whose mood could change with such apparent sincerity so bewilderingly, were so many minutes apart in my life, to be lived only once but remembered always, with that catch at the throat for something exquisite for ever gone which in the end becomes a conviction that an obscure and priceless opportunity within one's grasp was in that instant irretrievably lost.

I made a sort of bow without saying anything more, and turned to go, and had taken one step into the dead air of the corridor when I heard her move and felt a touch on my arm. In the same soft, humble voice in which she had accused me of laughing at her she now said, 'One moment, please. Please? Do not go for one moment.'

Her touch on my arm was like that of a dog asking for food and words; it was at once urgent and diffident, and when I remembered it later, thinking all this over, I was reminded of my golden cocker bitch, Donna, whom I kept at Hill Farm, in the mountains. She had just that trick of asking, shyly but impressively, with her paw on my hand or arm and her eyes, as brown as oiled cedarwood, fixed on my face. There was certainly nothing doglike about Irma's eyes when I faced her. Their slate-blue gaze shone in the light with perhaps tears, but her voice was steady enough in its softness, her hand was firm and her lips calm.

'Tell me what I shall do,' she said. 'Help me. You are clever, I see it. You will know what is for me to do. I have no friends.'

'Not on this ship?' I said. 'Surely.'

'Surely not.' She removed her hand to make a gesture dismissing her fellow-passengers. 'They are not for me. They talk. They make love. They eat. They sleep—and when they wake up they start the talking again where they stopped, and all the rest—where they stopped. Folly and waste of time.'

Her voice was severe, and its tone expressed perfectly an intellectual disgust which had nothing to do with whatever might have been her physical reactions to such behaviour. She nodded her smooth head weightily, like an old man sitting in judgment.

72

'No friends. Five weeks I have of this, this chattering, this—*five weeks*! And on the ship are three men who would like to kill me. Communists, you understand. Bad men. They come to make trouble here, I tell you, and they hate me because I know them. Once I too was Communist, but not now. I left the Party. It is not permitted, but I do it. And these three men know this. They know I know them. So one of them, he tries to make love to me—it is orders, they wish to find out what I will do, they do not trust me. All three try to make love. It is like the Nazis. I tell them I am no more Communist, and they laugh, but they look—you know—dark.'

She scowled heavily to illustrate.

'"Once a Communist, always Communist," they say, but they are a bit afraid.'

She was speaking rapidly and without passion or gesture, her hands clasped loosely together, her opaque eyes on mine as though to compel belief. I was to learn that she had left the Party in a spirit of bitter revulsion, when she heard what went on in the higher councils and what was to be directed eventually by Moscow, and realized that their aims differed from those of the Nazis in the north and west, the Fascists in the south and east, only in name. She who had believed herself to be risking her life and giving her body and her mind for the cause of man's freedom had finally perceived that she too was fighting, plotting and living only for a rival form of world-domination by a select group of political bigots no less fanatical and one-eyed than the very men against whom, in her small sphere of action, she had fought with all her youth and goodwill, all the zeal of her immortal soul up in arms.

73

Her revulsion and defection had been complete. Someone had betrayed her 'gentleman' and herself to Nazi agents in Holland, whither she had been hastily removed from Berlin when the fact of her Party membership had come fatefully to light. In broad daylight, wearing borrowed furs and jewellery, carrying a mass of hot-house flowers and escorted by inconspicuous fellow-Communists whose laughter hid terror and whose tears were effortlessly real, she had swept on to the main city railway station pretending to be a famous actress leaving for a season in Paris, and with so much glamour and gaiety had tricked the German railway officials into smiles and bows of delight, and their Nazi overseers into a benign tolerance; and so had made good her escape into Holland and a freedom she hoped would last until the inevitable outbreak of the war in Europe. It was the boldest acting of her brief career. She was then sixteen.

Her orders were to make herself known to the Communist secretary of a district whose solidarity was questionable, and to engage herself as his private secretary. As this man's own adherence to the Party line had for some time been suspect, she was to do what she could to strengthen his loyalty—for he was popular with the masses of workers, and so potentially valuable to the higher organization, which had long foreseen the southward movement of Germany the moment war came. At the same time she was to forward secret reports on him to Berlin. For this purpose, it was made clear to her that as quickly as possible she must become in all ways intimate with him.

Because he was a new type of Communist in her

experience—witty, cheerful, usually intelligent and gentle, and fond of all the simpler pleasures of existence—she did not find it hard to obey this order, with the help of her appearance and her vigorous youth; but now for the first time she made a tragic mistake, in spite of the years of indoctrination, in spite of her own judgment and reason. Though he was twenty years older than she was, she found herself after a while to have become deeply in love, for the first time in her life.

The Party did not tolerate bourgeois weaknesses such as sincere and unselfish love among its members, wisely perceiving these individualist emotions to be small defects endangering the whole structure of Party action; and her problem now was to keep her feelings secret, from the world and particularly from her lover. For a young woman of sixteen, however hard the schools through which she had passed, this was no easy task, and she failed, somewhere or other, to round off and seal away her deception. Her directors gave no hint that they knew what they knew. Such was not the way of the European Communists, any more than it was the way of their Nazi opposite numbers. One might have thought that it was only by an unfortunate chance that Gestapo agents in Holland became of a sudden fully cognisant of her lover's secret political connections, but thanks to a last-minute message from one of her former admirers in the Berlin headquarters, Irma was aware that something was about to happen—and aware of it too late. She found his crushed and shapeless body in the gutter at the shadowy street-corner where they were to have met that night. It was evident that the wheels of a heavy car or truck had been run backwards and forwards over it more than once, to make identification difficult. There were no papers in the pockets except an envelope inscribed in a hand she did not know with her own name and the address at which she lived by day. It had obviously been put there after the wheels had done their work.

Within an hour, she was on her way to England, where she lost herself in London for the best part of two years. By now, both the Gestapo and the hunting-dogs of her own former Party, from which by formal notification she had 'resigned', were trailing her, for she was potentially dangerous to both sides—what is called 'hot'. In the end, silent and alone after having for so long been afraid to speak to or make a friend of anyone, she decided to come to Australia, the unknown and remotely isolated continent farthest from the scenes of her youthful joys and griefs and terrors and triumphs, farthest from what seemed at last to have been a life of evil futility in the service of a murderous ideology and a savagely reactionary ideal.

And, now that she was here at last, the very fact of arrival, of the final journeying finally ended, gave her the feeling that the whole world had actually fallen away from beneath her feet, vanishing downwards into timeless space without a shudder or a sound of warning. She found herself facing Baudelaire's *néant vaste et noir*, unable to turn away, without any power or impulse to go forward. It was the realization of this that had as it were struck her to the cabin deck where for one of the few times in her life she gave way to unrestrained, unfathomable despair; and thus I had first seen her.

'You need not worry much about those three men,' I said. 'Their identity is known and the police are already here watching them. They will be watched from now on, and perhaps sent out of the country—it will need only one mistake, perhaps not even that. We too have a law to take care of undesirable aliens.'

'Yes?' she said, with what seemed an insincere eagerness concealing utter disbelief. 'Then me—what will they do to me, these police of yours?'

'You,' I said, to make her smile again, 'will be noted as a very desirable alien indeed, and left alone.' But she did not smile; her eyes did not waver from my face, and so close was their scrutiny that I felt it like a touch on the skin.

'You are very kind,' she said at last. 'You will help me. I must work, I have very little money, no place to go. You are not police. What are you then, please?'

I told her, and when after some explanation she understood that a police roundsman was not a police officer but a newspaper reporter doing special work, she looked relieved but not impressed. Her look seemed to allow that perhaps it was no worse to work for the capitalist Press than for the Communists; for she had by no means rid her mind of the deep imprint of her early teaching.

'You must go to your consulate,' I said. 'If you have Dutch papers they will help you there more than I can.'

I had no intention of entangling myself in any way with an unknown young woman refugee; I had already seen them at work too often to be readily deceived by the superficial charm of foreign lips speaking bad English. I gave her my card, never foreseeing the day and the circumstances in which I would see it again, never expecting to see it again at all. She read the name and address on it, moving her lips slightly as she looked down, and I took the opportunity of studying her averted face for the last time.

At the time of her death she had a matured beauty proper to her twenty-eight years, which was in fact part of her power of complete repose; and it cannot be denied that such reposefulness can cast over the observer a spell stronger than that of any other womanly characteristic, mental or physical. Already, at eighteen, this ability to become quite still was evident, but the mobility of youth had not yet softened in her face, and its changes were abrupt, not subtle as they later came to be, when knowledge and experience had ripened into a deep wisdom which in any other woman would have been disconcerting, since it had about it more of intellect than of instinct.

Evidently the Nazi investigators did not discover that one of her Kovno grandmothers had been Jewish; but there is no doubt that from that old woman, whom to her knowledge she never saw, she inherited a certain skin-pigmentation which gave her whole body, and particularly the exposed surfaces of hands, throat and face, a colour of creamy ivory most pleasing to see in its subtle contrast with the opaque blue of her eyes and the high line of her wide cheekbones. Apart from this, no trace of Jewish ancestry could be discerned (if even this were indeed Jewish, not Slav)—none of the exaggerated elaboration of line you see in women of that race. Beneath the delicate glowing skin the fine bone-structure was strong and Slavic in its width of jaw and brow, and the faint upward slant of her eyebrows and the outer corners of her eyes gave

78

her an expression at once wistful and mischievous. This was emphasized by her mouth, which suggested in its width and controlled fullness much generosity of heart and hand and a pleasant temper, and in the upward line of the corners an optimistic humour at present modified by her attitude of despondent self-absorption. The heavy house coat and the pyjamas of apple-green linen, creased from sleep, concealed the rest of her, except the fact that she was full-bosomed, and that her back was beautifully straight, like her shoulders. I recalled my recent foolish impulse to take her face between my hands and kiss her mouth; and as I looked at her now I could understand it well enough even while I deprecated it, ashamed of myself. It was an impulse every man who had ever been near her, within the strong and reassuring aura of her intense personal being, must have felt as I had. Not all of them resisted it, I know; for long afterwards she told me she had for years thought of men in terms of hands and mouths to be evaded, and had bathed whenever possible because of a feeling of continual uncleanness. Too many people, she said, touched her.

She looked up at last, after a longer time than it could have taken to read the few words on the oblong of paste-board which she was now holding out to me diffidently.

'No,' I said, 'you keep that. Then if things get too bad for you, you will know where to find me. You understand that?'

'Oh yes,' she said. 'I understand. If things get too bad.'

'But they will not,' I said. 'We are in full recovery in this country, after the depression. There is work for all. You will be all right.'

'Oh—I will be all right. But there will be war,' she said gently, as though speaking to a child. 'It is certain. He is not ready this year, not yet. It will be next year.'

Again she nodded her head in that weighty and ancient manner that went so oddly with her youth.

'That is why,' she went on to say, 'those three men come here. They know. They hope to make trouble. We do not know what Moscow will do. We think there will be a— a treaty, yes?—between Stalin and him, sometime. We feel it must be so. Then he will not be afraid of war. Because of Russia, he is still afraid. Of England, no. Of France— ah no! But of Russia, yes . . . But war, it is certain. Inevitable. I have seen it. I tell you.'

Then with another swift change of mood she turned up her face to shake back the smooth dark page-boy hair, looking suddenly gay and mischievous.

'You know what I think?' she said. 'I think that these Nazis have—shall we say?—ripened too quick. You have a proverb, I think it is about money. It says, "Easy come, easy go." It is true of so many things, you see. That is what I think—it is true of the Nazis. They come quick, they go quick. It must be so. They have no history. People without a history, they always want war—to shed the blood, to make the sacrifice, to become blood-brothers with their own national past. They have no political past, so they make one. Do you agree? It is what I think.'

'How old are you, Miss Maarten?'

'I am eighteen years one month. You think that too young? My friend—no! I have lived.'

She looked at me consideringly while neither of us

spoke. I had thought her two or three years older, and while I watched her grave eyes regarding me with unselfconscious thoughtfulness above the high cheekbones I felt again the uneasy sensation of pity I had felt earlier, before that remark about Europe on the eve of crucifixion. At length she broke the brief silence.

'You must call me Irma,' she said decidedly. 'Maartens—that is just a name. When the gentleman in Holland was—when he died, I changed my name to his. He was so kind to me, it was—you know—a memorial.'

She looked steadily at me again in silence. Then, quite unexpectedly she stepped forward and took my hand in her two hands, cool and surprisingly strong within their softness. I felt my card being bent across the back of my knuckles.

'You are very like him,' she said, 'but not so old. It is very funny. When you came here, I was almost for one moment frightened. He was always what he called saving me from myself.'

She laughed, for the first time; a half-hysterical laugh with tears beneath its amusement. At the same moment I was aware of steps and shrill voices far away along the corridor, approaching. I withdrew my hand from between hers. Her laughter ceased abruptly, and she sighed, quick and short with a sort of impatient resignation; but the look of mischief haunted her eyes.

'You must be my friend,' she said in almost a whisper. 'My first Australian. You agree?'

'I do,' I said, not quite sure where we were now in that fantastic conversation between strangers. 'I do agree.'

'Ah yes,' she said. 'Now it is a treaty. Now . . .'

With unexpected swiftness, as the loud voices and the steps drew nearer, bringing with them something of the excitement that seethed through the whole ship and affected both, she raised herself on her toes, took my head between her hands, and kissed me full and lightly on the lips; and was standing away from me, smiling. For a moment I thought I must have imagined the whole thing, which could have taken no more than a couple of seconds; but no—my own lips and her faint smile assured me it had indeed happened. I was so taken aback, in such a confusion of mind whether to be annoyed or glad, that I had nothing to say. It was she who spoke, hurriedly now.

'A treaty. That was what you wished to do before, I know, to kiss me. I could feel that. And you did not even try. You are a funny man.'

'Goodbye,' I said, and went away in haste, to avoid the people coming noisily along the stuffy and dimly-lighted corridor and put myself beyond the reach of that strange young woman's gentle mockery; and the last impression I had of her was of her voice, calling out quite loudly from the littered interior of the cabin, 'Do not forget—a treaty. We are friends.'

I'm damned if we are, I thought, going up on deck in considerable confusion of mind, not knowing, of course, that I should ever see her again.

We had passed under the bridge. The sun was once more behind clouds, the whole world was grey, and the cold wind in my face restored me to my normal senses quickly enough. My interview with the youthful refugee

82

below decks soon began to seem like a fanciful and unlikely dream, impossible to perceive whole in retrospect and so impossible to forget.

The voice of the purser beside me made me think of more immediate matters.

'There's one of your victims, Mr. Fitzherbert. That chap in the fancy ankle-length black coat there by himself on the rail. That is your German baron—or so he says.'

I thanked him, and went towards the stranger, sorting out a series of questions in my mind as I approached.

THREE
ADVANCE AND RETREAT

In the last months of that terrifying year, the European fugitives came in greater numbers, and more hurriedly; and the ugly panic of August flowered and seeded freely in September, and, with the coming of the hot and avid summer months, died and seemed to have vanished. But the seed lay waiting in our hearts and minds—seeds of a blank and mindless fear for most, who had seen from a great distance the first purposeful parade and triumph of the new German military and air strength unmatched, it was plain, in the world or history; the Colossus shadow fell across southern Europe, the Middle East, the Indian Ocean and beyond, across this greatest and youngest of the continents, to which the refugees were coming like locusts, swift, shy and ravenous.

For some, however, there was a thrill of excitement in the brief threat and eventual postponement of war.

To these groups, the profit-makers and the armed forces in particular, the withdrawal of the threat at Munich that September, the apparent shelving-away of a promise that armed force would be used in the end, was not so much a shame upon British integrity and a bloodless defeat of the Imperial arms as a sort of personal betrayal. One man, a clothing manufacturer whom I had long known as a man of intelligence and peace, asked me to luncheon with him expressly, one would have thought, to show me the account-books of his father's firm (of which he was now managing director) for the years between nineteen-fifteen and nineteen-twenty. On those figures, which even I could see were enormous, the whole present wealth and solidarity of his company were based, he explained. The business done then had enabled the firm to survive even the depression years, to gather strength up to this very day, this moment, when another war would have made him a millionaire.

He was unusually excited.

'The chance was there,' he said, his mild eyes snapping strangely. 'The Empire could have fought and won a war, as it did before. Hundreds—thousands of men in my position were waiting for it. Don't imagine I'm a complete scoundrel, old boy. What I know, what the rest of us know, is that a war would have been the making of this country. Not just financially, though that would have come. It would have brought us political maturity. When a young country gets that, it goes ahead in a big way . . . And now that bastard Chamberlain . . .'

'Pardon the interruption,' I said, for I was beginning to feel angry, 'but I think if you take a long, calm look at the situation you will see that that bastard Chamberlain, as you call him, has done more than any other man living to guarantee you your war all in good time. Think it over.'

'These fluctuations in the popular state of mind,' he said, 'are bad for other things than business. A war all in good time is not what I meant. It might be another five years—another ten. We can't afford to wait that long.'

'All my information points to next year, and at about this time,' I said, made reckless by anger. That caused him to put on a blank face, to hide the suddenness of his feelings, no doubt. He wished to appear neither dubious, out of respect towards me as a newspaper man with—as he had always supposed—a huge store of secrets; nor yet hopeful, out of respect for himself. He looked down to stir his coffee.

I had, in fact, told him the truth as far as guesswork could hit upon it. The men and women with whom I worked had shared, perhaps too freely and more fully than most, that appalling wave of panic of which I have spoken. The raw cablegrams and wireless messages, in the very brevity of the jargon in which they are written, at these times always look so much worse than the fluidly formal English into which the sub-editors translate them, according to the *Gazette*'s invariable 'no-panic' ruling on the handling of crisis news of that sort. It was the crude messages: 'Chamberlain Munichwise tomorrow conciliatory more Sanger' and the replies: 'Urgent Sanger Hellbach Munichwise full cover Sydney'—things like that were what we saw or heard about, before the more shocking and reassuring copy began to flood in after the office rumours, let loose somehow by private secretaries and made impetuous by the very lack of facts, had taken hold of all imaginations.

The same thing happened as happened when even the least of domestic office changes was foretold. The men fell into murmuring groups, the women came down more than was customary from their own floor, and the talk went on and on, turning supposition into fact, and from fact brewing a slow-working but potent fearfulness. I recall most particularly the strange new look of life in the women's faces. It was partly fear, partly an unconcealed nervous excitement such as I have seen on the faces of women at the scene of some filthy crime, or in the streets when a brawl is on the point of beginning. It was the few older women on the staff who were the more frankly excited and wet-lipped; the younger ones and the cadets were no less frankly scared; but I recall also, still with the same sense of pain and shame now dulled by time passing, that on the day when the agreement at Munich was made known to the world, when I paid my usual brief afternoon visit to my friend Barbara Conroy, who had recently become women's editor of the *Gazette*, I found her in tears at her big table, in a distraction of grief over something she could not express or even understand, and of relief that the shrill strain of the foregoing days was ended.

Her son Brian, barely seventeen, had been accepted by the Royal Australian Air Force fourteen months earlier and was training at Point Cook; and though there were two other boys she favoured him most, secretly and with much self-criticism as I knew, because he was most like her dead husband, whom she had loved with joy and passion. Her feeling of relief, I could perceive, was intensely personal to herself, and would not last; the other distracting emotion, of mysterious physical shame which many of us felt, as at having touched in the dark some disgusting substance, was beyond description or measurement to her—'a world of shame' was what she said when she had composed herself after I entered. It was the shamed feeling, almost too deep to be borne, which a good man suffers after having done a bad deed unwittingly. The deed is so foreign to what he knows himself to be that he wonders in the end whether his own sanity is in doubt. Seek as he will, he cannot find in himself the fault which, he now perceives, had momentarily endangered the structure of what he was used to think of as a life of integrity; and such moments of remorseful bewilderment can sound as it were the frightening prelude to calamity.

'Why is it,' I said to Barbara, 'that so many of us are simply disappointed, instead of feeling what you and I feel—this sort of shame? Who is right? If we do feel shame, does that mean that we would have preferred to be party to a state of war? Surely, if we had preferred that, we would have even more cause to feel ashamed? No sane person deliberately wishes for the sort of war the next one must be.'

'Must be?' she said. 'Do you think it's inevitable?'

'I know it is,' I said, 'and so do you. Words are irrevocable. "Peace in our time" was a mad thing for that unfortunate man to say. The ancients would have killed him on the spot for defying the gods. The best that can be said about this business is that it gives Britain a little more time, a very little, but some, anyhow.'

Unexpectedly—for I had as I thought forgotten her—there came to my mind the grave face and clear voice of the refugee girl on the *Empire Queen* in that airless cabin just after sunrise, several weeks ago now. 'There will be war. It is certain. He is not ready this year. It will be next year . . .' she had said in her suddenly gentle tone as though speaking to a child.

'It will be next year now,' I said vaguely, not seeing Barbara's fine, tired face and beautifully kept grey hair in the September afternoon sunlight that fell down into the narrow ravine of the street outside. 'Germany is not quite ready yet, it seems. One of these refugees who has been mixed up in politics in Europe gave me to understand that there is still a good deal of consolidation to be done in Europe before Herr Hitler feels he can defy the English-speaking world openly.'

Woman-like, Barbara brought the conversation back to the personal.

'What will our children say of us—what will they think of us, Lloyd?' she said with passionate inquiry.

'Does it matter?' I said. 'All children think unkindly of their parents at some time or another, for this reason or that. I recall a period when I disliked my father because of his Homburg hat and his beard. Beards were going out of fashion. To me he seemed coarsely conspicuous, and I hated being seen in his company by boys of my own age who knew me. Well—look at me now.'

'I love your beard, Lloyd. It's perfect for you. In fact, I love you altogether, probably because I'm nearly old enough to be your mother—your sister, anyhow,' she added, looking at me with a deep, tired look.

'Whatever they think of us,' I said, 'they will know in time that although we were ashamed of Munich we were

89

not among those who were disappointed just because there was no firmer stand—and so no war this year. They will know we were not on the side of the people who are ready to shed other people's blood. Could you kill anyone yourself, or even agree to someone else's death, if it lay in your hands?'

'No more than you could,' she said. 'You know that. Excuse me just a moment.'

She used the house telephone to speak to the printer, referring to a page-proof in front of her from which— a minute sign of the times—a twelve-inch double-column advertisement had been dropped the day before. From time to time she looked up from the proof to me where I sat in the comfortable visitors' chair facing the light. Her eyes were unseeing, but although her face looked weary there was no dullness in it; the strained and hectic manner of most of the older newspaper women I knew was not her manner, but instead she had an air of constant and intelligent watchfulness which, with her perfection of dress and bearing, made her always seem younger than she was. She was, at most, twelve years my senior—in her early forties, perhaps, a splendid age for many women of her physical type, so long as they be not employed on a daily newspaper.

In addition to editing the special Women's Supplement which we published in the middle of each week, and supervising a small staff of variously dependable juniors, she personally covered most of the city's important social occasions. She was related to the paper's chief proprietor in some obscure tie of blood; but in spite of all this, and because she had what I can only call 'style', she never looked completely at home anywhere in the building outside her own rooms. Meeting her walking quickly along one of the corridors, you could well suppose her to be some visiting society woman whose slight eccentricity was to come hatless into the city's fretful afternoon; but the sight of her down on the printing floor, apologetically making last-minute cuts on the stone, or in cool, smiling conclave with a few members of the chapel, was—to me at least—always rather astonishing. I had known her, we had been friends, since we joined the staff of that newspaper almost at the same time, and in all those long and sometimes embittered years I had never heard her say an unjust word or do anything petty or ungraceful. Among newspaper people this would not be a common record. If I say also that she was as easy in her generosity as she was shy in the frank bestowal of her affectionate regard, I flatter not her but myself, who had admired the one and enjoyed the other.

Not in spite but because of these two characteristics, she might well have been out of place even among the fairly conservative members of the *Gazette* staff of those days before the war; but she had social as well as personal grace, and moved as easily in vice-regal company as in that of the overalled, ink-stained members of the chapel downstairs. Nothing quite dismayed her, until today.

At this time—above all at this particular time—I had never so much admired a woman since Jean died when Alan was born. That girl's death, as it were in the very ecstasy of life, so affected me that I very soon came to believe I had had and done with love for any woman. The fact that in time I found absolute celibacy no painful or unnatural

91

state confirmed me in this belief, nor was I any way moved from it by my quite intimate association with Barbara. In marriage, my young wife and I had known, in due course, something near the absolute of bodily and mental and spiritual union and content. Death came like a wind; but, while it extinguished her as a lamp that has burned steadily and bright may be extinguished in an instant, to me it gave— I thought in my despair of those days—only a mortal coldness from which I could not die.

My mother, who lived on disconsolately after my father, reminded me at once that I had the child to think of, and must not give way to grief for too long. In fact, I had not given way to grief at all. Grief had given way to me. If I speak of despair, I mean chiefly the state of mind that would be suffered by a musician who had lost one hand, suddenly and for no apparent earthly or divine reason. Such a man, fatally wounded in mind and spirit, does not die. He lives on, perhaps in immaterial ways a little nobler as in obvious ways he is a little less perfect, physically, than his fellows. He does not die.

Nothing died in me except (as I thought) the power, and it is indeed a power, to love women. I see now that to say merely 'the power to love' would be wrong. Few who have had it lose that and live on. I had been deeply schooled in affection all my life; there remained, as my mother had hurriedly reminded me, the child; and I decided that another life, particularly a life so newly begun, so innocent, and so buoyantly sprung as it were from the dying body of my love, must be well worth cherishing with all my heart. I did honestly think, at that time, that it was indeed a conscious decision, so extremely had I come to rationalize and in a sense excuse even my simplest natural impulses. It is plain enough now that I had been intellectually over-educated but left in a pretty state of social ignorance. As a father and a newspaper reporter I was obliged, without knowing it, to narrow the gap between the two states. What happened, in fact, was that in most ways I put the child in the place of my wife. His life and being came as near to obsessing me as anything human ever did, until I began to know Irma: and even my relationship with her was conditioned, intensified and of course finally concluded by my deep and compassionate awareness of the whole identity of my son.

At the time of the Munich conference, in nineteen thirty-eight, he was in his eighth year. As Barbara pointed out, with simple pleasure on my account, I had nothing to worry about there. She was right, but only in a large and limited sense; for she could not really know how profound had become my mistrust of a world in which wars could still come into evil flower, and in which individuals could play with and brutally alter the myriad personal fates of whole nations of men and women. In such a world I thought I could find plenty of cause to be concerned for Alan; in such an insane, dangerous world, where the very soul, unawares, was vulnerable, I could impersonally imagine a father willingly and painlessly ending the life of a son before that life should fade and fray into the common background pattern of greedy passions and deliberate violence which is also the pattern of inevitable self-destruction.

Barbara was not to know of that grievous secret distrust of the human world and human society which later found

93

its only self-forgetfulness in the Lithuanian refugee, for I could put it from my conscious mind in her calmly observant company. As I looked at her across the wide table's spread of files and clippings, across the still, listening telephones and the first, earliest Queensland roses standing sweetly in a crystal bowl between us, I thought for one unwonted moment how strange it was that the extreme of our physical intimacy had been, in all these years, only an occasional brief handclasp at parting, after one of our rare evenings spent together when it had happened that we were both off duty; for I very well knew that she was a healthy and desirable woman. Possibly we were both impressed more deeply than we ever realized by the fact, scarcely spoken of between us, that we had first met in almost identical circumstances of bereavement; for though I had known Brian Conroy slightly, as a staff man much my senior, I did not even see Barbara until the day after his death, and did not meet her until some time later.

Conroy's death left her with insufficient means to pay for more than food and clothing for herself and her three young sons. She owned the house they lived in, but there was not enough money to educate the boys. No real alternative to finding work could be envisaged, except marriage, which was then, as it continued to be, unthinkable to her. Her slight connection with the *Gazette*'s chief proprietor, and with the paper itself through her dead husband and through occasional work she had done for us as a contributor of special articles on everyday social and domestic problems, made it not unnatural that she should for rather more than charitable reasons be accepted as a new member of the staff which I myself had joined only a few months earlier.

I see now that the secret and intensely personal lone-liness we must each have been enduring, which held us helplessly aloof from anything like intimacy with our new colleagues, did also perhaps inevitably urge us to take special notice of one another; for, of course, we soon knew something of each other's story from hearsay. I do not doubt she learned mine with less impatience and disinterest than I did hers. She was by nature compassionate, and death at a blow had enlarged the springs of her sensibility as surely as it had frozen mine at their innermost source. Years later, she told me she thought she had never seen any man so desperately in need of pity and at the same time so remote from pity's approach. It may well have been so, for I still had a horror, based on ignorance, of easy and casual human associations; I was, I suppose, afraid of the insensitive mutual intimacies to which such associations too often led.

For my own part, I never did tell her that my first impression of her had been of a woman secretly flaunting her widowed motherhood in a circumscribed world marked *Men Only*. I never told her because before long I was hotly ashamed of myself, not only for the cheap and unkind thought but even more for what it revealed of my appalling, unimagined egocentricity. Indeed, the eventual realization of this egotism so confounded me that sometimes, sleep-less in the bitter vacuum after midnight, I caught myself groaning aloud and giving thanks to god that Jean had not lived to learn of it.

Or, I would think, had she? and was that why she had from the first treated me with a passionate and as it were wondering and watching tenderness such as I had never known? Later, when Alan had first learned to walk, and believed that this was the sum of all human learning, the final achievement of man's highest ambition, I felt what I think was a similar tenderness in myself, compassionate, wondering and watching. It differed from hers mostly by the addition of a faint uneasiness lest physical harm come to the infant in his gay extreme of confidence on the brinks of unimaginable abysses; but later I thought: Perhaps to Jean in her womanly native wisdom I was much like that child—in my egotism which was childlike because it was unconscious and absolute; in what might be seen as the supreme conceit of my unthinking assumption of my right to love and adore her. The wise lover must surely have at times a lively doubt of the perfection of his selfhood? Looking at her, I had none—never . . .

Looking at Barbara across the buoyant roses and the telephones that seemed to lie on their trestles for ever ear-to-ground, like black men listening for mysterious tidings, I had doubts and to spare.

'The worst thing about this Munich business,' I felt moved to say at last, 'is not the immediate sense of its ignominy—I for one do not care what France and America will say. It is the feeling that what you and I always thought of as a secure and robust social structure is really very shaky, on its higher levels at any rate.'

'Not shaky, Lloyd,' she said. 'Simply just for the moment at the mercy of someone else's ruthlessly mad conviction. As people, the British—you and I and most of them in this building and this city and this country, say—are very slow and unwilling to be ruthless, and we don't feel too proud of ourselves when at last we've been forced to be. Whereas the Germans seem to me to prize ruthlessness in fact as much as the Americans do in theory, now that they have been taught for so long that it's the only means to all worth-while ends. No end ever justified wrong means. We know that. Your father would have agreed that to justify the means by the end aimed at or even achieved is to throw aside what we call the law . . . Just because we're not equally ruthless, I wouldn't say we're shaky.'

'To me it's shaky,' I said. 'And I do not mean the British empire, or any other empire or commonwealth of nations or what you will. I mean human society as you and I and all mankind have always known it. I mean the world of men—shaky in a way that the world of birds or animals or fish has never been, could not be. But perhaps I am being rather too heavy about it.'

She laughed as though I had suddenly said something pleasant.

'You're never heavy,' she said, 'but sometimes you're rather—what shall I call it?—grave, and far too profound for a simple mind like mine. Con used to say that women arrive at a remarkable number of correct conclusions by thinking with their livers. When I said, why their livers? he said, "Well, any of their organs that happens to be unnaturally affected at the moment." Of course I took the opening to point out to him that the brain is also an organ, but he said that was different—a woman never allowed her brain to interfere with what she called her thinking. He said we think organically, not cerebrally. He was really very nice about it.'

97

I was used to her talk of her dead husband, whom she called 'Con' very naturally still, as though he were away on a journey. It occurred to me now that, in spite of what the world inclines to think of female journalists, and to think with reason enough that they are febrile, nerve-ridden creatures functioning on the energy produced by the friction of fear with vanity, there are—as every newspaper man knows—worthy and admirable exceptions, where the woman fulfils her exacting, distressing, often ridiculous assignments easily and gracefully, and writes good level copy. Such an exception was Barbara. She was a woman of quality.

'I believe women think as well as men do,' I said. 'The purposes of their thinking may differ because living is such a personal business for them, but not the mechanics of it. Still—I have been told,' I said, 'that I have an exaggerated respect for women.'

'I think you don't know a great deal about them,' she said gently; and at that moment one of the telephones—as though the intensity of its recumbent listening had been at last rewarded—rang sharply for attention. She took it up at once without haste.

I watched her face while for some seconds she listened, and I had never seen it change so suddenly from calmness to an unfamiliar look of astonishment and anger. Finally she said, 'No thank you, Mary—it's not only impossible in fact, but it seems to me impossible even to think of it . . . Goodbye.'

I had never heard her speak so before. My astonishment must have been apparent, for when she had returned the receiver to its rest she looked over at me and laughed apologetically.

'Did I sound as bad as that?' she said. 'Well, I'm not sorry, my dear. I'm not sorry. That, believe it or not, was—Yes, Nan, come in.'

The door behind me had opened, and the girl who went past me to the table said rather breathlessly, 'Hullo, Mr. Fitz—excuse me, Mrs. Conroy, Mr. Franklin would like to know whether you can personally cover a party tonight at Lady Solomon's?'

Barbara looked suddenly very tired again, very sick at heart.

'Why didn't Mr. Franklin ring me, child?' she said quietly.

'He was just going out when the call came, and I was near his door, so he asked me to ask you. He said to say he was sorry he hadn't time to run along himself, but would you do it if you haven't anything else important? He'll be out for half an hour.'

'All right, Nan, thank you. I'll see him when he comes in.'

'Thank you, Mrs. Conroy.'

The girl, a brilliantly pretty youngster of eighteen newly employed in the office, smiled at me as she went out. Her lips and eyes were all innocence and cleanness. She was on Barbara's staff as a cadet. On that day of all days, I felt a pang of compassion for such beauty of youth and girlhood caught up in the excitement of the hour; and then I thought of Irma Maartens, irresistibly and for no reason other than that she too was eighteen. The comparison was

99

ridiculous, but it made me realize how far the refugee girl had gone in her eighteen years; she was nothing like this— by contrast, she seemed aloof and ageless, invulnerable in the completeness of her femininity—but only eighteen, I thought. I wondered how she was thinking today, and what her own particular despair was like. That she would indeed despair of the world, if only for a moment, after the triumph and disaster of Munich, I never paused to doubt.

'Now I'm in a proper fix,' Barbara said ruefully, as the door closed upon the shapely figure in its delicate haste. 'There's more than mere coincidence here, Lloyd. I was just going to tell you that the caller I shocked you by being so rude to was Lady Mary Solomon, who considers herself a friend of mine as well as being some sort of a relative. Oh, Lloyd—I shall have to go. But I can't now! What am I to do?'

'Go to Franklin and tell him you're tied up for this evening,' I said recklessly. 'What did she want?'

'That's just it,' she said in exasperation. 'She asked me to go to this party, don't you see? Her exact words were—and this is what made me so mad—"Barbie darling, we're having a whopper of an impromptu party at home tonight to celebrate the Munich victory, and you simply must come. Absolutely everybody will be there. I got in first on the 'phone the moment the news came through." Do you wonder I was rude, Lloyd? I don't care how many millions they're worth—I just can't do that sort of thing, I just can't.'

Her distress turned again to anger, the anger of which I had not known her capable; her eyes, ordinarily so kindly watchful, became dark with pain.

'What do they think we are?' she said bitterly. 'Do they think we're all—all *fools*—like themselves, living from one minute to the next, without two consecutive thoughts to string together to make a third? Ready to dance round the open grave of our own children? Drunk with ignorance? Whatever in the world do they think—or do they?'

'Barbara,' I said, shocked in spite of myself, remembering the last time I had had to listen to wild metaphors springing from the lips of a woman, that morning on the *Empire Queen*, and wondering if perhaps all intelligent and educated women had to relieve their feelings in that unpleasant way instead of simply stamping and swearing and making a noise. Now she had turned her head away not to let the sudden tears be seen, but I had seen them as she turned to face the light of the spring afternoon lingering above the street outside the high windows.

I got up to go and finish a report that wanted some police confirmation. I am no good as a comforter, I thought. It is against every instinct as well as against reasoned habit to show what I feel, and Barbara's distress, coming at such a time, had distressed me in turn. I was of no use there. No doubt she was thinking of her boy Brian, thinking he too and she with him shared in the general reprieve; no doubt Lady Solomon, who 'considered herself a friend', was not unreasonable in supposing that Barbara, the mother, along with the majority of the citizenry, would be very willing to make celebration. The Munich victory. It surprised me, that expression.

'Where are you going?'

Her steady voice made me pause at the door. The tears were gone from her tired-looking face; she was smiling.

'What is the good?' I said. 'We cannot really comfort one another—no one can comfort anyone in real need of comfort at a time like this. We must face it—I mean the fact that each one of us is alone, Barbara. Even Lady Solomon, whether she knows it or not. We cannot alter other people, or their lives, or their destinies, by offering them sweets to take away the bitter taste, any more than they can alter us. You and I happen to have children whose whole lives, as we foresee them, mean more to us, we think, than our own lives do. But do you not see how we do our utmost to shape those lives as we think best, we who say we cannot alter another human destiny? Who are we, anyhow, to know what is best? They are just as much individuals as we are. How can we interfere? The most we can do is to cherish them and love them. Our thoughts and beliefs cannot come into it. They will grow up to have different thoughts from ours, different ideas of how a society should work and enjoy itself and preserve itself. You wondered, a while ago, what our children would think of us for being—however unwillingly—a party to the Munich agreement, in the sense that each one of us is in some degree responsible for the world we live in, and what happens in it. Well, I doubt whether our children will think of Munich at all, outside the textbooks. Do you or I worry ourselves about the Versailles Treaty? No—not even as an episode in world history which has made a Munich victory possible. It does not affect our hearts. Munich will not affect our children's. The best we can do is act in such ways that they will know we never intended evil or craved for power over others. To cry out aloud against the rest of society is as unfruitful of

102

any lasting good as it would be to withdraw personally from that society altogether. It happens that to cry aloud sometimes relieves the heart of what seems—but is not—an intolerable burden of grief and pity. As for the cry itself, it does not get us very far, and I think we may be sure our children will never hear even the echoes of it when they are old enough to listen.'

She was looking at me very intently. 'Go on,' she said.

'There is no more I can say. There is probably nothing I can say which would be new to you. Why do you look like that?'

'When you talk as you were then,' she said, 'you make me think Con is in the room with me. If only you did it more often—No, don't be impatient. I don't want you to think I expect you to be like him, except to clear my mind when it needs it, as it does quite often these days. I think it's good for you yourself to talk like that. My dear, you are altogether too silent.'

'As I said,' I reminded her, 'words and cries don't get us far, in my opinion. Now listen to me, Barbara. What I would do if I were you would be to ring Lady Solomon and say that after all you would like to go to her party. She may not have understood that you were being rude—sometimes those wealthy people don't, though nothing is more vulnerable, to my mind, than the sense of invulnerability large quantities of money give the average person. Make some sort of explanation of your telephone conversation if you must. Thus you will have nothing to explain to Franklin, who is more important to you than Lady Solomon, I imagine. You will also be taking the correct bitter draught for such a time, if you go. Nor will you need to stay very long. Your photographer will be doing most of the work on the spot, won't she?'

'Perhaps you are right,' she said slowly. 'I think you are. Perhaps the flagellants were not as mad as I've always thought. A little self-discipline . . .'

'That is not it,' I said. 'We have a far harder thing to do. We have to live with the belief that this is only the beginning. Let them give their parties. I suspect the future is going to wipe out Munich even for you and me and all those like us.'

At the time, as our minds and feelings then were, it was an easy thing to say. Heard in memory, after the dark years and all the shames of war, it merely sounds like an example of politico-philosophical cant of the worst sort. But that was how our feelings were that late September day when spring was blooming round us like a cold flower, from earth to heaven; that was how we felt, despite the most determined efforts of self-control. It is clear now that to have said 'even for you and me' was a mighty piece of egotism; but that was how we had been driven, by the state of the whole human society in its heart and its head and its corporal body, to feel: that there were not only good and bad people, but people blessed with degrees of goodness.

I had confidently put myself on the side of the angels, like the vainest of all the blessed Saints surrounding my Lord.

It happened that, after all, the winter of nineteen thirty-nine did not seem so frighteningly oppressive as the same months of the year before it. Seeds of panic dropped in our hearts and minds in that year did germinate and flourish, as though the autumn and winter rains from April onwards had softened them like other seeds in their resting-place of summer; but with them grew, as it were, the herb resignation, the mild bane so recommended by some sorts of Christian as an anodyne against the darker passions of misanthropy and despair.

As winter increased through June and July and in August hesitated, we witnessed a sterner repetition of Germany's parade of incredible armed power during the— to us—antipodean summer in Western Europe; and again we were afraid, but this time with the more courageous fear of certainties.

My refugee acquaintance aboard the *Empire Queen*, whom I still sometimes remembered with all the vivid unreality of a brief dream, had not been wrong, that earlier August morning. For the Germans, even more than for Britain, Munich, as it now appeared, had been *reculer pour mieux sauter* in very truth. Lady Solomon had indeed had a victory to celebrate, provided she had been indifferent as to whose victory it was; the Berlin-Moscow pact of the twenty-third of August confirmed her in that, as surely as it showed war to be not only inevitable but imminent. Up to the time of the pathetic Henderson reports from Germany we had looked at one another daily in the turmoil of the *Gazette* office, where by now a kind of gay madness began to be evident, and silently or aloud had wondered, *What week?* but afterwards, through the latter part of August, through the mists and moonlight of the first slow turn of the year towards spring, we were wondering merely, *Tonight—or tomorrow night?* We did not know, from moment to moment of each working day, when the wireless and the clattering teletype machine sweating in its annexe off the sub-editors' room would bring the one word *War*, an end and a beginning.

The days of the Russo-German pact I remember for two things. The second, which can be dismissed as of little importance now, was that on the Wednesday following the signing of the treaty between Hitler's and Stalin's governments, when much of our surprise had been replaced by reorientated speculation, I saw on the corner of Bligh and Hunter Streets, on my way towards Philip Street and the C.I.B., the bright pink street-poster of the *Bulletin*, most admirable of Australian weekly papers, and read with a shock of disbelief the three words in heavy five-inch type: *HITLER PLAYS FALSE.* A shadow not of rain-clouds seemed to fall over the early afternoon, and the corner-newsvendor's monotonous clamour of the latest scare-headlines from the incoming European cables seemed suddenly more monotonous, trivial, meaningless than ever before. At that moment I had an impulse, rare enough with me, and without object or reason, to do immediate violence in some overpowering way to the consciousness of my fellow-men: to shout into the stuffed ears of mankind, *Stop*. Had I done any such thing, in any degree, the echo (as I knew even then) would have come back: *Too late*.

The other episode, which proved to be the most important personal event in my life since Jean's death nearly nine years ago, took place some days before the non-aggression pact between Russia and Germany was made known. At first it seemed no more than an incident, surprising certainly but with no ominous aspect apparent to my ever-increasing self-preoccupation, my striving to discern in myself and my own life what was common to the self and the life of all men, and to come by that ultimate discernment to an ultimate understanding of the passions which must govern human behaviour; for through this understanding of common human passions I hoped to arrive one day at wisdom.

This ambition was not always in the forefront of my mind. It did not interfere with work or ordinary behaviour, nor did I bore and exasperate friends by talking about it; but it was there, like my religion, and it had the effect of making most of the immediate personal contacts and incidents of my days seem of no great importance. Overbearing all our intercourse at that time, in any case, was the talk of war; behind that, the thought of it.

When, therefore, one Friday afternoon in mid-August a boy brought me an envelope containing only my own business-card I supposed some colleague was playing a meaningless jest on me until I turned the pasteboard slip over and saw the words *Irma Martin* and *Empire Queen* inscribed in an impeccably neat hand on the back. The card was quite clean, and smelled now of some perfume I did not then recognize. The boy waited, grinning cheerfully when he caught my glance up from the card; and I thought briefly how reserves and barriers were already being broken down among us by the looming shadow far away beyond the equator to the north and west, and thought too that before all was over this gaily impudent lad would be in a uniform, perhaps in a grave or at the bottom of the sea.

'Where did you get this?' I said.

'Lady out there gave it to me, Mr. Fitz.' he said. 'She said you would know her.' He added gratuitously, 'Some dame.'

'I don't know what you mean by that, but bring her along, will you, Peter?'

When he went away I glanced from habit at the stark face of the office clock on the wall above and to the left of my table. It stood at 3.20, and this was a Friday. Half an hour earlier I had left Barbara's room, even more unwillingly than usual, for we had had some agreeable conversation, about her boy Brian and more particularly about Alan. He spent part of his summer holiday with me at Long Reef, and now thought of my flat as 'our place', rather than my mother's house in Cremorne where he had been reared for eight years by a middle-aged companion-housekeeper whom he called Moley, and by my mother. Thoughts and talk of Alan, and of all the delicate problems of childhood and parenthood, more certainly than anything else moved my mind from preoccupation with the imminence of world calamity. I had found it hard enough to come back to the realities of the day's engagements—a boring coroner's-court session that morning to be written up briefly; talks with various people in the C.I.B.; a cabled special from New York, about drugs and juvenile delinquency, to read and return to the news-editor—and now to be obliged to talk to a young woman who, in memory, had suddenly become disturbing, for reasons I could not explain to myself in my surprise, made me feel thoroughly impatient. I wanted to return to the warm, dreamlike world of my own and Barbara's children.

What did the young scallawag mean by 'Some dame'?

When I was a boy, the expression would have been meaningless. The whole of the language was becoming corrupted by the drug known as the American way of life, by heavens. I looked round the room, which was emptier than usual because it was Friday afternoon. A typewriter pattered and stopped and pattered on at a table hidden from me by a concrete-and-plaster column, and a few men were talking noisily near the door; but many of them had done most of their work for the week and were out for a quiet afternoon drink before putting in the last hour or so of their day in tidying up details. Occasional fragments of conversation, punctuated now and then by a telephone bell ringing, by an arrival or a departure, let me know that as usual the talk was of war; but the atmosphere of the room was one of tired week's-end peace. I heard the footsteps approaching, the boy's and that young woman's, and did not turn in my chair until the lad announced her presence.

'Lady to see you, sir.' Evidently she had given no name.

Even as I was about to turn and rise from my swivel chair, the picture came in a sudden, embarrassing flash, like the unexpected opening of a door upon privacy, and I did not want to look at it: the badly ventilated second-class cabin, the young woman wearing over her apple-green pyjamas a heavy, dark-green house coat cut in the Chinese fashion, the high collar fastened with a large gold button; the quick step forward, the upturned young Slavic face with wide-open eyes, the unexpected, unnecessary kiss, too swift to be astonishing, full upon my lips . . . Like a small dream it had been, and like a dream it remained. I turned and got up, watching the boy go before I allowed myself to look at her squarely.

She was looking round the room, guardedly and quickly, like an animal in strange surroundings. I remembered that look later, when I placed it correctly: it was just so I had seen accused persons look when led into open court. Her face was expressionless and almost rigidly blank, taut and hollow like a mask, and her smile when I greeted her did not show in her eyes as they at last met mine.

'How do you do, Miss Maartens? Please sit down.'

'Martin, please,' she said in a low voice. 'Irma Martin.'

Of course. It had been Martin on the back of my card; I glanced down at it to make sure. She must have found herself a job, or a reason for concealing her previous 'adopted' name that had been a memorial to her dead gentleman.

Instead of taking the wooden chair my various visitors of those days used, she stood where she was, resting one hand on the back of it. All around us the earnest or desultory talk proceeded, the raised voice of someone speaking on the telephone on a bad line, the occasional sound of feet in the corridor outside. Had anyone told me then that years later I would wait in this big, fusty, familiar room for news of her death, I would only have believed it because I seemed always to be waiting for news of death and violence and lawlessness.

'Can we go where it is private, please?'

The words seemed to force themselves through her half-smiling, mirthless lips, as though they had nothing to do with her. Many of my callers asked the same thing; to most of them I gave the answer I now gave her.

110

'We can talk as privately here as if we were in Pitt Street.'

Still she remained standing, her other hand holding a leather handbag swung from a shoulder-strap against her right side. She looked as though she were about to go, as though she regretted already having come; but her eyes held mine with such a direct look rather of command than of appeal, and so entirely without embarrassment, that I resigned myself to an interview in the wireless room, off the library, which was for my private use in emergencies— that is, if it were not occupied by the wireless programme monitor listening to news broadcasts. Wondering what the devil the mystery was all about, I led her between the tables towards the door. Not until later did I realize that she had not asked a second time for privacy, and that it was her look I was complying with. If I had, I might not have been so ready to go. As it was, I took her along without further argument.

All I knew about her at this time was that she had arrived a year before, with a shipload of other refugees, that her name was not Martin nor even Maartens, and that she had been a *couturière* and 'secretary to a gentleman' (her own vague expression) in Europe under the Hitler shadow. I supposed then that she had merely been the 'gentleman's' mistress. I also knew, from her own account, that she had once been a member of the Communist Party, but not that she had also been a Nazi Party member. Because of my ignorance, what followed during that afternoon's interview seemed to me at first both melodramatic and suspicious in the extreme. Only the fact that my year-old memory

111

and my present observation of her disturbed me in some obscure and nervous way, which I did not yet try to understand, withheld me from passing her on to some unoccupied colleague—and the fact, too, that when I had given her my card it had been with an offer to help her if ever I could, if ever she needed it. That was, after all, a year ago, and in those days of August, nineteen thirty-nine, a year could seem an inconceivable nightmare stretch of time.

I led the way along the corridor to the library, feeling fairly sure that the wireless monitor's room would be unoccupied, since we did not receive the next news-broadcast from London until four o'clock. On the way we passed Barbara coming towards us with her quick, confident step of a much younger woman; she and I greeted one another with our eyes—we had been talking intimately together barely half an hour before—but I understood later that she must have observed Irma with womanly shrewdness and accuracy during the few seconds of our approach. (She told me, for one thing, that the girl was noticeably well-dressed, though my eye had merely recorded, from habit, that with a black skirt and jacket she was wearing a white blouse done up to the throat with silver buttons, and that her small lopsided black hat suited her pale face well.) It was not until we were seated in the small, quiet wireless room, with the big cabinet receiver silent against the wall between us, that I had much opportunity to look at her at all. Then I realized that she was afraid.

She lit a cigarette, after I had refused one, and her hands from which she had drawn off the long black gloves were shaking slightly as she held the cigarette and a small gold automatic lighter. This in itself was not unusual, for people who visit newspaper offices for some purpose of their own are usually in the grip of one excitement or another—anger, indignation more often, a natural nervousness of their surroundings, but seldom fear. An interview deliberately sought with a particular member of the staff is quite another matter, especially when, as in this instance, the man sought out is in close daily contact with the police force of a city as cosmopolitan and as large as Sydney was even in those days. In such an instance, the visitor is often nervous of the reporter as an individual.

But Irma was not nervous of me. She seemed indeed hardly aware of me for a time, while she inhaled her cigarette smoke sharply, exhaling it each time with a sort of finality as though about to speak, yet saying nothing, merely looking vaguely at me as though there were someone standing behind me.

There was no need to hurry her; she was a delight to look at, afraid or not, and to be alone with. I filled my pipe and lit it at leisure. We had been in that small, cramped room scarcely two minutes, though I would have supposed it to have been longer; and, in accordance with a habit which I have found to save time even while it seems to waste it, I was not going to break the silence. Let the visitor speak first. Meanwhile, setting aside my feeling of disturbed impatience, I was able to observe her at my ease.

'Some dame', the scamp of a boy had said. If he meant he found her beautiful, why, so did I. The taut, blank mask of her face—the same look, now I thought of it, with which she had faced me on board the *Empire Queen* a year ago,

113

as she uttered the word 'Police?'—in no way hid the fine underlying modelling of the bone; the slant of cheekbone and eyelid and eyebrow was alive with youth and intelligence, Slavic and glowing like the glowing ivory of her throat above the formal neck of the white bodice. Again I was forced—it is not too strong a word to say—forced to notice her disturbing power of imperturbable stillness. Only her bare hand, carrying the cigarette to and from her parted lips with a gesture of ineffable leisure, broke the immobility of her seated pose; and this physical appearance of being undisturbed was all the more remarkable to me because, with the passing of every few seconds, I knew as surely as if she had told me that she was afraid—not as afraid, perhaps, as she may recently have been, but still afraid, and unhappy in it.

Fear is like a smell to men trained to detect it; and in my particular job we so accustom ourselves to its aspects, in so many citizens, that if it is not there when it should be we wonder why. I had quickly known that Irma was afraid, or at least in the ebb of fear. I waited for her to speak, and for another full minute we both smoked in silence, and I listened to yet hardly heard the familiar quiet voices of the women of the library staff, the intermittent patter of typewriter keys on index cards, and the opening and closing of the drawers of cabinets where the incessant work of filing reference went forward in peace. Those peaceful sounds through the open door emphasized the dead hush of that little room whose only window, very dirty on the outside with the rough grime of the city, gave on to a central light well from which no light penetrated.

'You told me, come to you if I wanted help?' she said abruptly, and her questioning tone was as it were underlined by her hand holding the cigarette arrested in mid-air in front of her face, so that now only the upward rippling ribbon of bluish smoke moved where she was sitting.

'Yes, I believe I did.'

'You did . . . Now I think I shall need help.'

My first thought, of course, was that she must need money, yet when I looked at the obvious quality and newness of her handbag, her gloves and shoes—the usual points at which a woman's impoverishment first shows itself—at the perfect condition of fingernails and hair and unobtrusive *maquillage*, and above all at the lack of speculation or embarrassment in the regard of her opaque blue eyes beneath the slanted brows, a request for financial assistance by her seemed wildly improbable. Nevertheless, stranger things had happened to me before this.

'In what way do you think I can help you?' I said; but she did not answer the question. After looking in vain for an ash-tray, she dropped the end of her cigarette on the linoleum covering the floor, and extinguished it with a quick movement of one foot. It was very neatly done, a curiously masculine trick which, in her, quite surprised me. I was still looking at the arched firmness of her black suede shoe, which had a very high heel and sported a silver button as big as a shilling, when she spoke in a low, confident voice, leaning forward suddenly without haste.

'I have remembered you since that day when I arrive. You said we are to be friends—you, my first Australian friend, eh? I have thought of you often, again and again,

115

and wished sometimes to see you. But, you understand, there was no occasion, was there?'

'No,' I said; and I was curiously moved by the calm, low-voiced confession of one of whom I myself had thought so seldom, and then with almost distrust, almost distaste, and no pity.

'No.' She sat back in the chair, her hands lying still in her lap. The fear was leaving her while she spoke.

'I always thought, "Anyhow, that Mr. Fitzherbert is there," and I look at your card, often—then,' she smiled apologetically, 'not so often.' Her eyes were steady on my face. 'One makes other friends. One learns to live in the new country. I have done it before. But I did not forget you. I can speak?'

Her rapid words somehow confused me. I could not follow as one usually can follow in advance the direction of this interview. Without my having suspected it, it had become a personal matter between the two of us—the last thing I desired or ordinarily allowed to happen in that office.

I could only nod my head and murmur rather coldly, 'We are quite alone . . .'

'I must *trust* you,' she said with sudden enormous emphasis. 'I am in danger, and you can maybe help me. Maybe not. If not, what I say you must forget. It is understood?'

Yes, it was personal now, beyond all doubt. Again I nodded, this time saying nothing. She seemed not fully reassured. I witnessed one of the impulsive gestures I was later to come to know so well, to delight in yet almost to shrink from. Leaning forward again, she took my right

116

hand in both hers. Quite automatically—the man's instinctive gesture of calm self-possession—with my other hand I put the mouthpiece of my pipe between my teeth and held it there.

'You see,' she said, 'I must be sure. If we waste time, I go. If not, I tell you. It is all true, but you may say it is—what?—*fishy*. If you think that, you may also think it does not matter that you tell. My friend,' with great weight, pressing my hand hard, 'you must not talk. If you talk, it may harm you too.'

Freeing my hand, I pretended to be feeling for matches as I said, 'Look here, you had better tell me. You have my word that whatever you say will be strictly between ourselves.'

She looked down at her two hands clasped together empty of mine. I could still feel the earnest, excited touch of her fingers, the only indication she had given of how profound her feelings were at that moment.

'So,' she said, with a sigh, whether of relief at the assurance of secrecy or of disappointment that I could not return stress for stress, I do not know. Leaning back in the leather armchair she let her hands lie again still and empty in her smooth lap, and looked at me intently, sidelong across her cheekbones with eyes half-closed—the look of so many foreigners I have known who wished to be impressive. Cautiously, I waited.

'Those three men on the ship,' she said. 'You remember what I tell you?'

'The three Communists. The police have not lost track of them, I can assure you of that.'

'They are dangerous,' she said with bland simplicity. 'But I must tell you everything—everything. You know Russia?'

She spoke of Russia as of a mutual acquaintance. The remark was rhetorical, and again I needed only to incline my head as she went on with suddenly tense and joyless excitement.

'Those three men say there is going to be a treaty with Germany. Soon, very soon. A treaty of non-aggression. For you it is perhaps already a rumour. Now I tell you it is fact. They know.'

I was so immediately astounded, my mind so jolted and incredulous, that it was like being in a street accident, in that moment before feeling and reason again take charge of action.

'Impossible,' I said quite automatically—exactly as one says the word in one's mind at the instant of mechanical impact in the street; but a moment later I was crying inwardly, as the accident victim so often cries aloud, in the small self-deafening voice of horrified belief, 'No . . . no . . . no . . .'

'But no,' she said. 'You do not know Russia. He copies what he admires. What Hitler did at Munich, he too can do—that Stalin, that Molotov, and the others. I know. You see, Mr. Fitzherbert, I have been a member of the Party, in many European countries. I did many missions, I did many things for the Party, learned many things. Not any more—do not suppose.' She made a gesture of cancellation without raising her arm from her black-clad thigh. 'That is why I am in danger. Those three men, they did not come here because of me, but they know me. You see . . .'

118

She paused and looked at the window, which was closed as it had probably been since the building's construction half a century earlier; and at the open door. With a movement of her head towards this, she said authoritatively, 'Please close it.'

I do not mind confessing what I would not for anything have let her know—namely, that I was for the moment in a state of much mental confusion and distress. She did not seem to feel it. Perhaps she had known too long what even a child would have realized in those nightmare days, that a non-aggression pact between Russia and Germany was in fact a clear signal from Moscow to Berlin, to move, and that this time there could be no Munich. With a sensation of physical weakness, I rose and took the two steps necessary to bring me to the innocently open door. The whole brief series of movements between leaving and returning to my chair seemed to take a long time. I was thinking so fast that every act of mine appeared to me to be performed with dragging slowness. When I sat down she was looking at me with a sort of satisfaction.

'You see,' she said at once, as though there had been no interruption, 'I know too much. And I have left the Party. This is not allowed, if you know many things. Now me—I will never tell of what I know—never. But this, of course, they do not believe. Why should they?' She shrugged slightly. 'I am a woman . . . If you do not help me, there will be an accident. An accident—you know. Today or next week. They hate me, because they are uncertain. I have friends here, I call them friends, who are Party members. These do not know how much I know. They think I was

119

just a file-and-rank member, you see. Of my active work they know nothing. They hear these three men talk, and they wonder why they hate me, and so, because they are such friends, they tell me how these men hate me and what they say they would like to do. It is all a joke, my friends say. And Mr. Fitzherbert . . .'

For the first time, with the breaking of her quiet voice on my name, she openly showed emotion. She had talked fear back into herself. I waited while she took out and lighted another of her cigarettes; then, once more unemotionally, she went on.

'Mr. Fitzherbert, what they say they would like to do, they will do that. Have no mistake—they will do it. That is why I am so relieved to know there is this treaty.'

It seemed to me the extreme of irrelevance.

'I do not see what the possible treaty has to do with your safety,' I said rather coolly, for, irrelevance apart, her words had rather shocked me. How could one possibly feel the gladness of relief at the spectacle imagination was pitilessly unfolding?

'Possible, possible,' she said impatiently. 'It is sure. This is from Moscow, do you understand? And as for me, you cannot know your own government. They too are frightened—yes, yes, like me, as you so kindly do not remind me. Your Mr. Menzies will do the only logical thing when war comes. You know what I mean?'

As always, she began to speak with a gentle patience when she talked of matters political. I had noticed it, in retrospect, that morning on the *Empire Queen*; I noticed it again now, and was not offended even though, watching

120

her while she spoke, I could not help remembering that she was much younger than, from her dress and self-command and the secret, as it were impatient, authority of her manner now and again, one might have supposed. She was no more than nineteen, I told myself, and was surprised that I should give her such attention and such credence; for at thirty-one I still supposed that years, rather than experience, demanded one's chiefest respect.

'I don't know that I follow you,' I said, 'but if we were at war with Germany' (I ignored her slight gesture and went on steadily) 'and the pact you speak of had been signed and still existed, then the governments of the British empire would inevitably make the Communist Party illegal. It is the only logical action.'

'Exactly,' she said, pressing her hands one upon the other over her heart; and for a moment her widened eyes seemed to burn not blue but violet. 'And those three men, they go—out of your country. I know the police watch them. *Then*, they are for deportation, yes? Yes. And I am safe again. Even if they try to denounce me to your police, I am safe from—from accident.'

She sighed, and let her hands fall to her lap, and lay back in the deep chair, staring blindly at the white wall opposite her. This attitude of repose, though it appeared exhausted, was merely a resuming of her beautiful mask of indifference. When she spoke again she spoke slowly and clearly, without looking in my direction.

'That treaty. Do not be alarmed. I laughed when I heard. Your own secret agents will be laughing. It is just like Moscow. Hitler, he will now take Poland. There will be

121

war with England this time, and France. Soon, my friend, there will be war with Russia too.'

Her voice, low-pitched and very clear, became dreamy as she looked into a future I myself could only envisage as indescribably terrible. She seemed to see it, like a play already played, a tale told. Had I but realized it, her vision was the measure both of her potential danger to the Party she had so recklessly quitted, and of the danger she herself was in. She had, in fact, that sort of fanaticism which fellow-fanatics do not dare to tolerate, even if they would, in a young woman who is also beautiful. All her life her physical quality must have been her worst enemy. Men put their real treasures into unprepossessing steel safes, dark and soulless, not into the frail and springing delicacy of a porcelain vase. Had I known it, she was in even more danger than she herself could have realized.

'You talk of war,' I said, 'as though it were easy, desirable.'

She shook her head, but not impatiently; again she was talking to a child.

'It is not easy. It is terrible. All that killing and dying for a few men who do not kill or die, all that hatred and fear. But, my friend, it is inevitable. You know it. There will always be these men . . . You are a Christian?'

'Yes,' I said.

'Your Jesus was just such a man,' she said, with the unemotional simplicity of a child who has learned by heart a lesson far beyond its powers of thought or reason. The argument was not new to me, and I had given it much earnest thought. I was not going to waste time on it now, here.

'What do you want me to do?' I said.

'You?'

She had been deep in her dream again, as though caught away from the present by some profoundly absorbing memory of the incredible past. Even as she breathed the one word, her momentary bewilderment vanished. She performed that boyish trick with the smouldering cigarette-end again.

'Yes,' she said, looking up straight into my face with such an unexpected look that to my surprise I felt my heart leap like a lad's when he sees his girl in the distance. That delighted leap of recognition should have warned me, but did not; she was too close for me to see how far I had gone to meet her.

'I thought—if you could tell me how to hide?' she said. 'I must disappear, you see. This is why I come to you, but when we talk so honestly together about the bigger things I forget, see? It will not be for long, I think, but I must get away. Do not worry—I have thought to leave the country, but there is nowhere else I could go, now . . . America is too hard, also too dangerous. And—you know—you got to have money and visas and all that. And a job. No.' She shook her head quickly. 'I must stay here, and I must hide. Other States are no different. They have agents all over, and all your laws are the same. Anyhow, I am too tired of this running.'

She looked at that moment too young to be tired of anything. Later I realized that what really tired her, intellectually, was her own youthfulness. She always tried to look older than she was; that explained the extreme

123

sophistication and excellence of her dress, and in part the deliberate air of authority she often assumed towards people who did not know her real age, and even towards me, who did. As I was to find out for myself, she was driven by passions of a tempestuousness almost beyond belief or reason, or decency. That is why she had done whatever she had undertaken so well, with a sort of precocious genius, one might say 'perfectly' without misusing the word.

'You must let me think,' I said.

'Think,' she said quietly; and she subsided into that old chair in such a way, effacing herself so completely by means of some mysterious withdrawal of her consciousness of me, that I could have believed—save for my eyes' irresistible evidence—that I was alone in that small cold room with the silent wireless receiver and the steady beating of my own heart.

I am not a rapid thinker as a rule. Looking at my watch, I saw that some twenty minutes remained before the wireless monitor would be coming to listen to and transcribe the four o'clock B.B.C. news broadcast. There were several things to be considered.

First, the question whether this young woman really was in danger of being attacked in some way, perhaps killed, as she said. It seemed to me, even without knowing then that she had, by direction, been for a time a Nazi Party member in Berlin, that her danger was quite credible enough to give her cause to be afraid. Already since the first stream of refugees had become so to speak a flood, we had had more than a few extremely mystifying crimes of a sort we could only think of as 'unAustralian'. The character of a crime depends, of course, not upon the method by which it is committed but upon the original motive. At the back of every major crime of violence is someone's conscious or subconscious self-fulfilment, which is why the *cui bono* approach in attempting to solve such crimes is often a heart-breakingly difficult one; for only too often the answer to the question *who benefits?* concerns gratifications not material but emotional, spiritual or even—as in the case of a crime arising out of a conflict of political ideologies—intellectual. So, at any rate, my friends in the C.I.B. had learned, as I in turn had learned from them. Thus it had been found that the 'unAustralian' crimes, from common assault to murder, demanded a deal of new thought based on new knowledge of a sort seldom called for during the previous century and a half of this community's existence.

Looking at Irma absent, as it were, in the dark depths of the leather armchair, I had to admit that more than one crime still unsolved even during my own short experience had had about it many of the obscure but unmistakable characteristics of ideologically-inspired violence; and by no means all had stopped short of murder and the victim's absolute silence thereafter. More difficult in fact were those where the criminals (there were usually at least two) had refrained from actually taking life, leaving the victim capable, sooner or later, of helping the police, but so badly terrified by his experiences and the threat of further persecution that he would literally rather die than speak. I wondered which of these two methods her mysterious 'three men' might have had in mind for Irma. My guess was murder. Women do not react to torture and other methods

125

of terrorism as profoundly as do men, chiefly because their nervous system is not nearly so cerebral and complex.

On the whole, it was safest to assume that she was in serious danger of her life from now on; and my immediate suggestion, which I made to the armchair in which she had effaced herself, was that she seek police protection—what is known as protective custody, which the police are not eager to give unless there has been some actual threat or attempt against the safety of the individual, but which I thought I could arrange through my newly-promoted friend, Detective-Sergeant Harry Hubble of the C.I.B., for whose intelligence in his most difficult profession I had admiration and respect. He would see to it for me, I said. But, emerging from her voluntary self-effacement, she showed such scarcely-controlled alarm at the mere suggestion of involving the police at this time that I was compelled to question her further.

It was thus I found out at last, with mixed feelings, that she had been a passive but genuine member of the Nazi Party during her Berlin operations for the Communists; and for the first time I realized—knowing the dreadful persistence of those people, of both parties—that her danger was indeed real and probably immediate.

For the first time, too, I felt a sudden deep pity for her, in her youth, her unorthodox beauty, and her unconsciously pathetic alienation, wherever she might find herself, anywhere in the world. She had no country now. Australia itself was for her no more than a refuge. As she herself had said, so recently that the tones of her voice seemed still to hang upon the musty air in all their sad dispassionate

126

sincerity, 'there is nowhere else I could go, now . . .' That 'now' summed up, in one evanescent breath like a sigh, her whole life.

'Well then,' I said, 'you must move from where you live now, for a start.'

'That I have done, of course,' she told me calmly, surprised.

'Where are you living, then?' I said, and she laughed, a true laugh at last such as I had not heard in her voice before; and for all my gloomy state of mind at that moment I was charmed by it.

'At Wynyard station.'

'Good lord,' I said, 'how silly. You mean you have nowhere to sleep?'

She gave me a very curious look, almost as though to assure herself I was in earnest; then, seeing I was, she sighed shortly, and once more reverted to that air of patient gentleness that hid god knew what thoughts.

'My friend, look at me . . . Now tell me if you think I shall ever be in want of a place to sleep.'

It was said with such gentle irony that if I was shocked it was only with a new thrill of pity and understanding. She was quite right, of course. With that face, and a form which the fitted black jacket and skirt by their very severity revealed quite frankly to any imagination not utterly moribund, she would, if she chose, never lack a bed.

'You say you have friends,' I said. 'Could they not help?'

'You must understand,' she told me, as though it were an instruction I should already have learned, 'that I am in danger. Yes, I have friends—and I would not go to them to

127

save my life. They are not such friends as that. And it would not be fair. Do you see that?'

'Yet you come to me,' I could not help saying, 'because you think of me as a friend.'

'Ah—see, though, the difference!' she put in quickly with sudden animation, as though I were at last showing some real sense. 'Who are you? A decent respectable gentleman who writes for a sort of proper paper like the *Gazette*, non-political and not very interesting. You must forgive me. It is so it seems to my friends.'

'And to you?'

She waved that aside with a small gesture, smiling.

'I read all your newspapers in Sydney. To me they are all interesting. But do you see? No one knows that I know you, no one who matters. The place where I have been living, at Kings Cross, that has been under surveillance of a sort. I tell you, there are more things going on in this city than you and your policemen will ever know. How could you? For you, there is not time to study all these passions, these ideas, these ambitions and all things in the refugees' world here. But I tell you, I am watched. So I take my luggage, all my luggage, and it is not much, to the Central station and then I go by train to Wynard station and leave it there, and come to see you. At Wynard is a man waiting for me to go back for my luggage. Let him wait, eh?'

She was quite amused at the thought.

'You are earning your living?' It was a silly question, perhaps, but I did not know if a straight inquiry as to how she lived would force her into unnecessary evasions or equally unnecessary and detailed truths.

She answered readily enough.

'I am a model—in a dress salon. Also sometimes I design for Madame.'

'And there is no help there?'

'No—they do not like me very much. I do not talk enough. There is too much I cannot say. Also I do not have boy friends'—she made a wry mouth, giving me a sidelong look out of the corners of her eyes, a look that was not challenging but baffling—'and this they do not understand. I will not tell them lies, so I tell them nothing. I have no past.'

That seemed to amuse her, too.

'All I can see for it is to leave Sydney,' I said. 'You will never lose them here, if they mean trouble. I know the comrades.'

'They will never lose me,' she said, nodding her head. 'And—forgive me—I do not think you do know the comrades. You in Australia do not know them. I have lived in Europe. These three men come from Europe. There are some others here like them already when they come. Already in one year these men have done much trouble. Australia is so hospitable to the poor refugees, and the vision of the Party is very far—I tell you. It remains a few details. I am one—and, my friend, not a very important one. But I want to live. For them, you see, there is no hurry. Here, no one feels the alarm in advance. A kind but foolish country. No one is afraid—only the refugees, yes? Refugees like me. So, you understand, I must disappear.'

She concluded with smiling resignation, watching me. The talking had done her good; the fear was gone from her flesh. I suspected also that for some reason of her own she now had no hope of aid from me—she had talked away her own blinding urgency, she saw me more clearly. I had been too unmoved, it would seem to her, when what she wanted was a spontaneous impulse to meet her half-way, to share her fear. Nothing she could say had made me show excitement, once I had mastered my first concern over what she had told me of Russia and Germany.

Nevertheless, even while we spoke so quietly of such fantastic matters, an idea had been forming on the edge of conscious thought, waiting like a newly-engaged player to walk the stage of consciousness and submit to appraisal. I would have scorned the suggestion that this idea arose from any personal interest I felt in Irma then. To me, she was still a young woman unfamiliar and so to be dealt with cautiously. For all her physical attraction and the young, cool swiftness of her mind, she was a stranger, remote, speaking rather good English with a light, agreeable foreign accent that suggested not any one country but Europe itself, a fair part of which she might be said to represent in her moody self-control, her quick alarms and discontents and eagerness to be moving on, always moving on.

She was a stranger still, and so she remained to the end; and I seek comfort in the possibility that, since I never had a profound and complete understanding of her, so she too may have been aware to the end of some few mysteries, some final reserves in me. It would be obscurely comforting to believe this.

Anyhow, my idea turned out to be not so absurd as it might have seemed to anyone else who knew me as little as she did.

'I have a place in the Blue Mountains,' I told her. 'There is some land and a cottage with no one living in it. An old fellow I have there farms part of the land and keeps an eye on the whole place for me. I suggest you go there for a time. I suggest you take a friend and go there,' I added more firmly, not only because I thought for a moment she was looking doubtful and I had nothing else to offer, but also because the idea, once it had been put into words, seemed to me curiously attractive.

What I had taken for a look of doubt was in fact an expression of slow pleasure, doubtfully entertained, which lit up her whole face. Again she allowed herself that rather theatrical gesture of putting her hands over her heart, and breathed deeply in, sighing out the breath with such an exaggeration (as I thought) of relief that I thought she was laughing at me, and was embarrassed to the point of stroking my beard—a detestable yet irresistible gesture as theatrical, I suppose, as hers, and one which my father used now and then when he wished to hide what he thought might be considered unseemly amusement.

'I knew you were my friend,' she said with delight. 'You see?'

'The only thing is,' I said repressively, 'have you someone to go with you? Quite frankly, I would not like you to stay there alone, for two reasons. The first is that old Jack, my man there, would quite possibly leave if he thought I was making him responsible for you. Freedom from all ties is a passion with him. It has been ever since he escaped from his wife and daughter.'

She looked interested, but I had no more to say about Jack.

131

'The other reason is that it is very lonely and isolated. You could quite easily get lost in the mountains without knowing it, if you went walking alone. That would mean the police, search parties, and publicity—the very things you are trying to avoid,' I could not help adding.

'I understand,' she said gravely. 'I must not go alone. Good. Then if I find a friend I may go? When? Now? Tonight? It is far?'

'First of all,' I said, 'about this friend. Who is he, and is he to be trusted?'

She looked at me in utter amazement; she was so amazed that for a moment her mouth hung open and her eyes went wide like a very caricature of surprise. I cannot say why I should have felt such a lift of the heart again when she began to laugh: for I repeat, she meant nothing to me then more than the symbol of a sort of problem I had not previously met with, and one which for the time I was finding increasingly absorbing.

Her laughter was not loud. Indeed, our entire interview had been so quiet that had the door remained open none of the women working diligently and peacefully in the library would have heard a sound, I think. With it closed, they had probably forgotten we were there; at any rate, I hoped so. Nevertheless, such was the impression of conspiratorial secrecy she had made upon me, with her talk of non-aggression pacts and 'accidents' and hiding from pursuit, that I could not repress a gesture of warning, which silenced her.

'My friend is not a man,' she said abruptly. 'You Australians.'

Following upon her stifled laughter, the remark should perhaps have embarrassed me. Perhaps she intended it should; for, as I was to find, no matter how serious her situation might be she could seldom resist a thrust of words or intonation, an ironic glance or a shrug of her straight shoulders, apparently just to see what the reaction might be. It gave the impression sometimes that she was for ever watching herself and her fortunes from without, and it was very disconcerting. Already there had been moments when I was inclined to think her scatterbrained, or at least prone to irrelevances which she would pursue with an enthusiasm equal to her pursuit of the main theme of talk. This was not true. She could keep the main argument sharply in mind while playing all sorts of trivial small games with word and look as opportunity offered. Such had been her training. It was this, as much as anything, which left me to the end mystified by her, even after I had realized that she was a creature prone to sudden devastating passions which she never allowed to devastate her, whatever their effect upon others might be.

'Who is this friend, then?' I said with assumed indifference, though once more I had felt that ridiculous stir of relief in my breast.

'Her name is Linda Werther,' she said almost repressively, as though that should satisfy me.

'Who is she, and what does she do?' I said, not satisfied at all. Irma I could almost imagine at Hill Farm, but I was not going to have the ragtag and bobtail of the refugee *milieu* clustering over the place like flies.

She began to answer with a shrug of the shoulders, and then thought better of it, I suppose; for she leaned forward in that sudden leisurely way, so near me this time that I could smell the same faint, inscrutable perfume my business card had taken to itself, apparently through being carried about with her.

'Linda is a German Jewess,' she said. 'She is a good woman, but rather fat. She is very kind and not at all sad, though her father and her brother have been killed already by the Nazis. She has no husband, no lover now, only me. She is not a Party member. In Australia in a few years she has made much money in a shop—furs. If you let her come with me, she would look after me. Because of these men, I have not been seeing her for a long time. But we talk on the telephone, often. She is very brave, a brave woman— but too fat to walk far in the mountains and get lost,' she added irresistibly. 'As for me, I do not like walking alone. And Linda—she is a German Jewess, she understands this hiding.'

I put a match to my pipe again. Certainly, by its very attraction for me, the suggestion she had accepted so readily was already taking on in my mind the suspect character of an irresponsible escapade. I thought of my cottage fifty miles to the west, looking down from its unusual mountain plateau across the eastern coastal plain towards the unseen Pacific; and I thought of these two foreign women there, disturbing the peace of the man and the dogs, and the forest behind the cottage, hanging over it like a guardian thought, and the enveloping silence, with clear, lilting talk in some language foreign to everything there that was mine; foreign to the listening trees and the earth itself; to the fearless blue wrens coming for crumbs into the kitchen and to the swift grey thrushes whose large liquid eyes matched the liquid notes of their singing in the apple and apricot and peach trees outside the kitchen door; foreign to the faint voice of the stream from the spring that never died, and to the thin, pure mountain air, itself like spring water, that drifted or rushed down the lonely mountainside, or ran softly up it like an ocean in flood when the wind was in the tender east . . .

Drawing at my burnt-out pipe that would not relight, I thought of all this, my only personal refuge from the smell of that city life that meant to me violence and coarse human passions and ceaseless essays against the immaculate spirit. Suddenly, though only for a moment, what I contemplated appeared as a subtle act of treachery, a piece of selfish vanity, or worse: as though, like Faust in legend, I had suggested trading my mind's and spirit's sanctuary for the gratitude of this young and lovely mortal.

If it were indeed treachery I contemplated, it was a treachery against myself; from another point of view it could have looked like an act of decency, for the girl with me was helplessly in danger from circumstances against which, whatever part she had played in creating them, long ago, she could not now defend herself alone. She was afraid to ask the law's protection in the least degree, for her past record made her presently unfit for official investigation; and I later found on inquiry that she had never been near the Dutch consulate for the good reason that her papers were false. As one of a crowd of foreigners, she might have got away with that as she had done in England. As an individual she must have felt she had little chance. Once in the hands of the police, she would have faced deportation as surely as did the men she feared; and deportation to Holland would now have meant certain death. Treachery or not, to dispatch her for a short while into the oblivion of my mountain hiding-place seemed not merely obligatory but somehow inevitable, I thought; and I avoided looking deeper into my mind for other reasons.

She was still leaning forward, watching me without much expression. I could detect that faint perfume breathed from her body and her hair by which, if by nothing else, she must remain unforgettable.

'That sounds suitable,' I said. 'Can you get into touch with her by telephone?'

Immediately, she said, and this too was satisfying, for having made my decision about Hill Farm I wanted to get the matter moving at once, that very minute—almost as if I feared I might lose her by a moment's delay.

'How soon could she be ready to go with you?'

'In one hour, or less.' She smiled with that light irony I already began to look for in her replies to simple questions of fact. 'We are practised in these matters.'

'She will not be missed?'

'She often goes away. She has money, you understand. At the shop is a woman in charge of all. Linda trusts her. She does not go there always.'

'And you?'

'Yesterday I leave my job.' She laughed impulsively. 'My job, my room—finished. My friends will not be surprised. Also, do not worry—I too have a little money now. It is easy to save money in your country. There is nothing—nothing . . .' She hesitated, then said instead, 'I know how to live poor.'

136

On top of the wireless cabinet there was a direct-line telephone. I indicated it to Irma.

'Ring her. Ask her to come here and ask for me in an hour's time. Tell her where you are going—never mind, tell her you are going into the mountains for a while, to live in a comfortable cottage. You will not need much clothing—strong shoes and warm undergarments. You understand? Food we can arrange about later. There is nothing else. I keep the place always in readiness, and old Jack is there. He has two cows and some hens. You may be lonely but you will not starve. And there are books. You will not die of boredom. Now tell me—can you imagine what it will be like?'

'Yes,' she said gravely, and to my surprise she repeated what I had just said, word for word, with hardly a pause or hesitation. 'It is a trick I was taught. But the sentences must always be short.' She rose to use the telephone, standing in that way I remembered, with her feet together and her back straight like a well-bred child. I supposed it to have been part of her training as a mannequin, and, finding I was staring like a boy at her shape from behind, so straight and flat across the shoulders, straight-backed and trim at the waist above the well-developed pelvis and strong legs, I looked down quickly at my two hands turning about the cold pipe, and found myself listening without comprehension to her conversation in what I guessed was German, rapid, low-toned and emphatic, with her friend Miss Werther.

Meanwhile, I tried to think unemotionally what I must do. One of the garage attendants would bring the car I seldom used except in Alan's holidays and to go to

Hill Farm occasionally; a telephone call would arrange that. What really troubled me, what had been worrying at the edge of consciousness for some time, was the question whether, without involving her, I could pass on at once Irma's warning about the impending pact. Scott, the editor, the news-editors and Blake should all know about this; but I did not see exactly what use it would be to pass it to them as something more than hearsay yet less than fact, and in any case my connection with political rounds was still of the slightest. Their reception of anything I had to say would, I saw, depend necessarily upon their opinions of my integrity, not as police roundsman but as a source of information that had at present nothing to do with my own job. When the pact was signed—if it ever was to be signed; professional caution forced me to remember this condition—the police would at once start moving quietly and secretly to complete their checking not only of German-born immigrants (a task they had begun, I knew, the previous year) but of the Communist members of the community. When that happened I should of course be involved, technically at least. It seemed right that I should strongly hint the probability to Scott and Hubble.

There was, above all, the ethics of my proposed action in helping Irma herself. Her past activities might easily make her, for no reasons other than those suggested by official caution, as 'hot' here as she had become at the time of her 'gentleman's' murder in Holland. No one, on the facts, would blame the authorities if they treated her as a dangerous alien, carrying false papers and with a record which could be traced at the London end easily enough. My own position would be, to say the least, invidious.

I decided to keep secret my whole acquaintance with her and what I was about to do. Judged by the ethics of my profession, as it held me close to the police and in their confidence, my proposed actions would be wrong—in fact, a sort of felony; and of this I had no doubt at all; but another, older ethical code, inherited through a dozen generations of variously law-abiding and devout but invariably gentlemanly Fitzherberts, gave me confidence not to hesitate. My idea, quite in keeping with the melodrama of this whole interview, was about to become actuality, with myself as the chief and only responsible mover.

Irma finished speaking, and hung up the receiver.

'She will come,' she said soberly.

'Listen to what I am going to say, Miss Martin,' I said. 'It is to do with what you tell me about Russia and Germany. I want to ring my editor on this telephone, and warn him. You will not be involved—no names, no mention of any one person, you understand? You can stand here and listen, and if you do not like what I am saying you can press down this hook on the telephone. No questions will be asked that I cannot answer safely.'

She agreed more readily than I expected, as though it were of little importance. 'I trust you. I must, now, isn't it so?'

That seemed in its simplicity quite the most pleasing thing anyone had said to me for many a day. My gratification must have been apparent, for with a smile of sudden intimacy and charm she put her ungloved hand on my arm and added gently, 'You are so kind.'

It is quite likely that at that moment she was hardly aware of me at all, as a person. I did not then know her mannerisms, developed since childhood as a sort of bright, protective armour and also as weapons to win for her whatever contest she undertook. It is probable, too, that in my concentration upon what I was planning to do I had already half-forgotten the original causes of this action—her fear of violence, her direct appeal to me before anyone else, and something more . . . a vanity of my own, a sense of obscure flattery . . . I could not have said, though now I know, that her obsession of my mind, my body, my imagination—I would sometimes even think, of my immortal soul—had begun, at some unplaced moment during our scant half-hour in that dreary little room with its two old-fashioned leather chairs, its brooding quiet, the bulky wireless receiver and the outmoded telephone instrument outlined against the grimy blur of the closed window.

Hill Farm, as it was already called when I bought it just before my marriage, is high on a mountain plateau and faces east. Towering forested spurs wall it in to the north and south. The sun sets early on it behind the main crest which runs north and south like a dark, gigantic wave, but until afternoon subsides into final darkness, it receives from the east a cool reflected light that casts no shadows and seems, indeed, to become brighter than before during the hour or more of sunset and dusk before night falls like a caress over the land.

By driving at a speed uncomfortably fast for my liking, I managed our arrival there while there was still a little of this beneficent luminosity falling shadowless from the high eastern sky. In that direction, the vast coastal plain below was ocean-blue and cold, with lights pricking through the misty air as far as vision reached, to south, east and north. Nearest at hand, twelve miles or more away below, the street and aerodrome lights of the old town of Richmond glittered in rigid stillness; far off, Parramatta was a haze of bright crowded points of illumination, and beyond that, fifteen miles more in the concealing distance, the huge sprawling glow of the metropolis outshone the advancing night that had already hooded the Pacific in a starry darkness.

My last hour in the office had brought upon me a feeling of unreality. Irma, introduced to the monitor as a friend of mine, remained in the wireless room during and after the B.B.C. news broadcast, while I hastened through what I had to do. No one but the monitor, a small, grey-haired woman of modest demeanour, realized that she was still in the building; probably no one else except Peter, the pert and cheerful copy-boy who had brought her to me, knew she had come at all. Throughout the place, the haste and self-consideration of Friday afternoon spread like a fever, almost supervening upon the fretful fever of the times themselves; throughout the building and through the whole city. The irrepressible Australian week-end optimism in the streets made the dirge-like cries of the newsvendors on the corners sound hollow and desperate. This air of adventure and unreality began to pervade my whole mind.

Scott's manner of receiving my rather diffident warning over the telephone—he did not know I was ringing from within the office: it was a chance I felt I must take—was in keeping with the character of the man and the paper he edited in more than name only. His interests were world-wide, and he had a long vision of national and international

141

affairs as they developed. Like most thinking men among us (and every newspaper has a few such), he was at once ready to believe that what had never been ruled out as a possibility—namely, a *rapprochement* between the apparently antithetical Foreign Offices of Berlin and Moscow—might well become an accomplished fact before, as he put it, 'our overloaded stomachs are ready to digest any further morsels of that sort of meat.'

'I felt bound to pass it on to you,' I said, 'because it sounded of particular significance that we here should hear of it so far in advance—if it is far—in Australia itself, and not from overseas sources'.

'You can't give me your source of information, I suppose?' he said in his booming voice, which usually made it necessary to hold the telephone receiver away from one's ear. I looked at Irma standing near, her body inclined forward as she listened with deep concentration frowning slightly but with no other expression; I felt her light, even breathing on the back of my wrist and inhaled half-unconsciously her faint unknown perfume, and shook my head as though Scott himself could see me. (Clearly I could envisage his tanned yachtsman's face with the crest of white hair and the look of benevolent anger he always wore, whatever was going on.)

'No, sir, I'm afraid I can't. Even speaking to you is rather a breach of promise. My informant is quite clear of any political involvement, but you know that with these foreigners there is a deep-rooted fear of the police—particularly the secret police. I find that the very fact of not seeing even a hint of anything like Gestapo or N.K.V.D. activities in Australia only makes them the more sure such things do go on.'

'Yes. Well—we've had rumours of this from London already, of course. It's one of those occasions when one man's guess is as good as another's. It may be as well to let them know at that end what you tell me, especially if what you tell me has come on the red tape.' This was his way of referring to what scanty news we had direct from Russia, from our own men there.

'We can at least get a few things ready here, too,' he shouted thoughtfully. 'Thanks, anyhow, Fitz. Sorry we can't check your sources, but I suppose we'll know the worst soon enough . . . If the whole thing wasn't so calamitous and final I'd like to get in early with it. Still, it's not a time for scoops, I suppose—not even for scooping the *Herald* . . . Goodbye.'

The unreality took hold of my mind as I put down the receiver and looked again at Irma. I wondered for a moment whether it was not all some mad prank being played upon me by someone who knew my temperament; until I remembered the card she had kept for so long. She was standing erect, very close to me, still now with the stillness of overmastering decision. We remained for a few seconds staring steadily at each other, like a couple of conspirators committed to something far more fateful than a plan of escape and disappearance. It almost seemed to me as though, unwittingly, we had somehow pledged ourselves to a deep and timeless association of the mind and the spirit—as though, even if after this moment we were never to see each other again, we should live out our days in the obscure conviction of a frail yet indissoluble union.

143

Such an experience; for all its brevity, was new to me. It was all part of the unreality of that hour, and had not the slightest effect upon my subsequent thoughts and actions up to the moment I left the office finally, soon after five o'clock. We stood so close that when I looked down and saw without surprise that our hands were joined and clinging idly together I did not know whether the childish, unfettered gesture had been hers or my own. Her fingers were cold, and I could feel a faint trembling, too slight to be visible, running down her arms from her whole body. For the first time I realized, in spite of my self-absorption, that since she had come into that office she must have been in a state of the most intense nervous strain, which she had managed to conceal or disguise the whole time. She knew my connection with the police; she was risking everything, she must have felt, on one chance meeting a year old, and on a vague promise made then and perhaps forgotten, or—worse—regretted.

'Courage,' I said to the chilly air above her head, and for a moment she leaned heavily towards me, resting her forehead against my breast and gripping both my hands with hers in a clutching grasp. Then she freed me of herself entirely, stepping back to look up at me.

'It is you, my friend, who will need courage,' she said gently. 'You must pardon me—I am very tired.'

Then she moved quickly back to her chair and sank into it and crossed her knees, taking her cigarette-case and lighter from her shoulder-bag and motioning me sharply to the other chair. No sooner had I sat down than the door behind me opened—she must have been watching it all the while, listening—and the wireless monitor stepped briskly into the little room.

After her unflurried apology, I introduced Irma to her by the first name that came into my mind, and explained that she would wait there for me. Then I went out, forced to admit to myself that my heart and mind were by now considerably disturbed by the interview just concluded. am by no means of a nervous temper, and even in those distracting days I knew I had a fair command not only over my outward expression but also over those inner tides of ebb and flux which most men feel when abrupt changes outside themselves find inward echoes and responses; when new circumstances which the mind alone can fully comprehend and assess prove to have the power also of calling, as it were by surprise, upon the secret life of the emotions.

These unknown quantities in the ratio of behaviour to outward events I believed I could, if not know, at least control, to the end that I might live and work well. But it must be remembered, as I myself was remembering with a sensation of physical pain, that until a few minutes ago I had not been in such familiar proximity to the youth and beauty and compelling bodily power and subtly exhaled essences of womanhood for more than nine years. I had already assured myself that complete celibacy caused me no bodily distress now. Was I to have to reconsider that assurance, and perhaps to start out on that hard and secret road to physical peace all over again?

It was, somehow, unthinkable; and as I opened the door of my locker in the general room to take out my hat and overcoat I swore to myself that it would not be so.

I would avoid the occasion. I had had, I believed, all that one man could hope for from the mysterious hoard of woman—love, and a boy-child, and perfect companionship; in return I had given faithfulness of heart and mind. Oh Jean, Jean, I thought desperately, let me feel again the reassurance of your imagined touch. Blind me with the fair clouds of your hair. Let the memory of what was so good bring quiet in a bad moment.

Evidently I had said some of this audibly, for over the door of the locker on my left, open like my own, a voice I knew said sternly and gaily, 'What's that you're muttering into your beard there, Fitz?'

The speaker was Tim McMahon, at present doing State political rounds, and a more amiably dangerous man I never knew. As it was Friday afternoon, he was as usual already drunk, in his unobtrusive way. His beaming, bespectacled face, the perfect mask of innocence for one who could recite more recondite scandal, of a personal sort, from the Australian political sphere than anyone I ever heard of, regarded me affectionately as we closed our locker doors (his causing a heavy *clink* of bottle against bottle). For some reason which he probably understood as little as I did, he considered me his closest friend. As far as I knew, he had no other, for men were wary of him. It had begun when he was at last recalled quietly from Canberra, where for years he had surveyed the Federal political scene in weekly articles that varied between the brilliant and the useless, and whence he had sent us, time and again, items of news almost too scandalous not to be true, and far too libellous to use—much to Scott's regret, for Scott was a bold man who combined a conservative policy with a love of truth-telling and a bitter contempt for most politicians. McMahon's own usefulness there was deemed to have ended when he began repeating news-items in subsequent dispatches. His weakness for liquor, like the weaknesses of most members of that large staff both at home and overseas, was known well enough. The day came when complaints of him were received from more than one Minister in the Federal capital. Because these were of a personal sort, he was replaced. In common with most publications, the *Gazette* held that a man's private life was his own affair until it affected his work, when it became the concern of his employers. In Sydney he could be watched.

McMahon, however, seemed pleased to be recalled, pleased to be given the comparatively less important assignment of State Parliament; but at first he was naturally lonely in Sydney, where he had never worked since his engagement by the *Gazette* some years earlier. (He was a Melbourne man.) As I was in the office a good deal during the earlier part of the day, I saw him often, and occasionally gave him lunch or a drink—usually both. Like others of his sort, he seemed never to have much money, although he was a high-salary journalist and had been for years. His borrowing habits soon became known, and few men now cared to find themselves alone with him between pay-days. However, I was obliged to enjoy his company—and perversely enough it was worth enjoying, even when he was not sober—more than most; and although he never offered or attempted to project our association outside the varying limits of our working day, he did linger near my table, or sit nonchalant

and laughing in my visitors' chair, for long hours sometimes when we should both have been finishing our work,
entertaining me against my will with his scandalous and
witty reminiscences. Hours meant little to him; like many
a lonely journalist I have known, he was never quite happy
away from the office itself, where he was to be encountered
at any time, on most days, from morning till late at night.

The fact, too, that like him I had had a Catholic upbringing was soon known to him—he had this unashamed
flair for the personal in every human contact he made—and
without trading on it, in that predominantly Protestant
atmosphere of the *Gazette* of those days, he took it, as so
many Catholics since the time of Henry Tudor have taken
this irrelevant matter of religious denomination, to be a
secret additional tie between us.

Today I not only had no time for him: I definitely and
actively wanted him away from me, out of the building and
away from Irma's neighbourhood, for though I liked him I
trusted him no more than one can trust a cat. He followed
me to my table, disappointment in his round thin face where
every feature was of a pinched, classic neatness, almost feminine, from the small square jaw and the little, tender mouth
topped by a restrained moustache to the round brow with its
widow's-peak of dark hair, and the almost wistful directness
of his blue eyes behind shallow lenses in dark frames.

I took up the telephone book without a word, and
quite rudely turned my back upon him while I looked for
the number of the garage where, for most of the year, and
year after year now, my car stood on chocks, polished and
unused—'part of the furniture' the garage men called it,

patting it in a friendly fashion as newer and smarter models came and went.

McMahon for once took my crude hint, and wandered away among the brown wooden tables of the general room. I asked for the car at the side entrance in an hour's time, and then stood fingering in my pocket the receipt slips for Irma's luggage which I had got from her at the last minute, and wondered what to do next. The luggage would wait until the car was at hand. There remained the C.I.B.— particularly Hubble—and a vague feeling that I ought to let Barbara know what I was about. For some reason or other, I felt as though I were about to say goodbye to these two people, like a man making preparations for a long journey.

Above all there was Alan, and at the thought of him the old loneliness and longing for my own kin ached like a healed wound in threatening weather. I seldom left town for long between one annual holiday and the next, except on occasional police assignments, and until this year had never gone away even for a weekend at Hill Farm without first seeing him at my mother's house.

Now, however, things were different, for at the beginning of the year he had been enrolled at S. Johns, the Townsends' unique (as it then was) co-educational school in Vaucluse as a boarder, and had long since learned to be happy there—so happy, indeed, in the company of boys and girls of his own age and social origins that my jealousy at our parting soon gave way to a lonely contentment at the rightness of my own and my mother's decision to send him there. He was in any case an extraordinarily happy child, from the days of his earliest infancy, and though it

149

sometimes made my throat ache to think he must live his life without having ever known the arms and the breasts and the tender lips of an earthly mother, I felt a deep joy in watching develop the innocence and optimism of his nature towards a replica of Jean's own. Being myself inclined sometimes to moods of black gloom and despair, both of myself and of my kind, I could observe with admiration his freedom, so far, from a single moment of self-doubt or self-consciousness, and the sturdy growth of his child mind towards what promised (and indeed proved) to be a healthy and cheerful independence of thought sweetened by much spontaneous and untutored affection for those with whom he lived. He was in fact all Jean in his nature and temperament, and all Fitzherbert in his physical appearance.

Townsend and his wife, who ran the domestic side of the small school between them, discouraged visits by parents. Boarders came home for one week-end each month, and there was only one full-scale holiday each year, covering the Christmas and New Year celebrations during eight flying weeks of summer. May and September holidays were observed by the usual termination of class studies, but the children remained at the school as though it were their own home—as indeed it seemed to them to be—and the course of social training which to the Townsends was designed for the greatest good both of the individual child and of the future community was preserved without serious interruption the year through.

Alan had been there for six months, and I knew he was already benefiting from the well-disciplined informality of that environment. Without doubt, for all her affection and good-will towards her only grandchild, my mother had had some repressive effect upon him. Her love, starved now of almost all other outlets, would have seen to that . . .

I rang S. Johns and spoke to Townsend briefly, asking after the boy and letting him know I would be out of town overnight. He seemed surprised and impatient, as he always did when I made these, to his mind, unnecessary calls to warn him of my absences. His attitude towards parents was one of suspicious tolerance, at best, and of blunt and outspoken criticism when they threatened any interference with his thoughtfully-devised 'system'.

I rang off, supressing a great longing to hear the boy's voice lightly saying my name, and went up to see Barbara.

Still overwhelmed now and then by the recurring thought of what I had learned from Irma, I believe I was fully intending to tell her what I had told Scott. If I was, it was for different reasons—mainly because of the habit of friendship's confession; for we had become over the years such firm friends, so easy in each other's company, that many of the staff, I think, supposed us to be lovers. Our innocent intimacy was of the sort that makes all but the most personal secrecies impossible. Matters that affected our professional and private lives and the lives of our children we discussed with the day-to-day ease of brother and sister, with the same sense of kinship and the same lack of much emotion; and at that time the precarious balance of our civilization on the crumbling cliff-top of incalculable disaster was indeed such a matter.

However, I changed my mind abruptly when she looked up with her invariable smile of welcome and I observed— not without a soft wrench of envy—the expression of calm

151

anticipation in her face, and realized that she must have been thinking with contentment and joy of the two days of freedom before her, and of herself surrounded by her sons—for Brian was at home on a short leave. That look of almost animal well-being, when the flesh itself is informed by the mind's contented purpose, is so peculiar to motherhood that only in the face of a priest who once befriended me in my university days have I seen anything comparable with it in a man, on whom, as it happened, not a child but a fatal cancer was feeding.

Barbara had no bodily ailments that I ever knew of, but she had some of the mental sickness and the sickness of the heart from which our generation suffered in those unbearably threatening days of August in that year. It was like waiting for a blow which we knew must fall, but which would not. Now, in the last hour of her usual working week, she had shrugged off the worry and the fear, setting them aside as firmly as she was setting aside the week's completed tasks. I could not spoil her rare moment of pleasure in seeing herself as once more all woman, all mother.

'You are off, Lloyd?' she said with cheerful surprise. 'Free? Come over and have dinner with us at home. Brian will be there, and the boys haven't seen you for an age. Do us all this favour.'

When I said it was not possible, she seemed unusually disappointed. Then she smiled and remarked teasingly, 'I know—it's that rather startling young woman I saw you with.'

'It is, in fact,' I said. 'I'm taking her up to Hill Farm with me tonight.'

152

'It must be her clothes,' she said. 'I'll bet anything you don't know how particularly well dressed she is. I was almost going to ask you where I could have seen her before. Is she Australian?—no, forgive me. It's no affair of mine, except that her clothes are perfect and she wears them perfectly. Did you know that?'

'I have not your trained eye in such matters,' I said, feeling suddenly depressed. 'The fact is, I really am taking her and a friend of hers to the mountains this evening, and I can't stay long now. I need not tell you the whole story at this time, but briefly, she is in danger and wants a hiding-place, and I could only think of the farm. To tell the truth, I'm not very happy about it. I don't know how Jack will take it. You know how he is about women. I don't want to lose him . . . I could think of nothing else except protective custody, and when I did suggest that, she was pretty badly frightened.'

'Dear me,' Barbara said, 'that sounds bad. I suppose my place wouldn't be any good?'

'No,' I said. 'She has to run for it, you see—right away from Sydney, if what she tells me is true—and I have some reason to believe her. As for your question—no, she is not Australian, she is a refugee I happened to speak to about a year ago, when I was doing a boat for Bob Roberts. She tells me she has been a mannequin here for some time. That is all I know about her life here—a mannequin or model and an occasional designer somewhere in town.'

Barbara nodded.

'I knew I had seen her before,' she said slowly. 'She's first model at a rather posh place called *Chez Madame*—a really

153

lovely creature. I remember her particularly because she has never let herself be photographed. I must say your taste is good, Lloyd.'

'I assure you this is none of my choosing,' I said irritably. 'But that would be the girl.'

'Why no photographs? Usually the particularly lovely ones are particularly vain.'

'She was probably frightened,' I said. 'Off and on for the past five years she has been running for her life—literally. She is doing it again now, she believes.'

'Oh, the poor little thing . . . Tell me, is this part of the general European picture?'

'Yes,' I said. 'It has come near home at last—a rather unusual sample of it, for this country, but common enough over there, I gather. They take their politics rather more seriously than we do. And now I must go and see my police friends. I just came to let you know I shall be at Hill Farm until tomorrow evening or perhaps Sunday—I cannot simply set them down there on old Jack's doorstep and disappear. You see how it is. And thank you for this evening's invitation.'

'Let me know if I can be of any help,' she said earnestly; and, as I was closing the door, she added, 'And take care of yourself as well as of other people, my dear.'

On my way to the main staircase, I called two of the boys from where they sat chattering on their long bench, waiting impatiently to become special correspondents, and gave them Irma's cloakroom receipts and some money.

'Bring whatever it is to the side entrance not a minute later than five to five, will you? I shall be in again about then. One of you please wait with the luggage until I come. Divide the change up between you, and keep sober.'

I got on rather well with our copy-boys. Because of my van Dyke beard and moustaches, they at first thought me rather a comic figure; because of their confident youth and friendly impudence when no one else was near, I thought them comic too. As each of us knew what was in the other's mind, and no harm was meant, we rubbed along very satisfactorily. It is an unfortunate newspaper man who cannot get on happily with his office subordinates. They were still alternately thanking me, hinting at corpses in trunks, and telling each other to shut up when I went down the staircase, past the front business office, and into the street.

A taxi took me to Phillip Street and the C.I.B. The tremulous August afternoon was fading, the air already turning cold. I had a flashing glimpse of the gilded globe high above the entrance to the *Sun* building, where our afternoon colleague was running off final extras: it was catching the last of the city's sunlight, while a dozen floors beneath it the news-editors were sorting out late cables and home news under the shaded glare of desk lights. Over the whole city was spreading the care-freed Friday afternoon mood. Seeing so many week-end suitcases being hoisted into trams and taxis, I was reminded of the need to buy food as soon as I had seen Hubble.

He was sitting, as in imagination I always saw him, with his shirt sleeves rolled up, leaning his elbows on the table and smoking. His pipe was drawing well and his brow was clear and untroubled as a boy's. Like many professional wrestlers'—and in his youth he had won belts—his body

155

looked ill-proportioned while he was seated; as soon as he stood up you saw that, unlike a lot of them, he had the height to carry his weight, almost majestically I sometimes thought; and he had brains and intelligence enough to carry the weight of his present exacting job as a senior member of the criminal investigations branch. He might have been ten years older than I was. The shining fairness of his short-cut hair at the temples might have been silver. No one, in either case, could have said with any certainty.

'Hullo, Fitz—how's crime?'

It was his unvarying greeting. To the clerk busily typing at a small table near him he indicated the door and added, 'See if Mr. Inkpen has finished with that Dodds letter, Bill, and put it back in our file if he has, or we'll lose track of it. I won't be long.'

When the constable had gone out, I told him why I had come.

'As near as that, is it?' he said. 'It's something outside my own sphere just now, this political stuff, but forewarned is forearmed, eh?'

'To coin a phrase, yes,' I said. He gave me a sharp look, then slung one large knee over the arm of his groaning swivel chair and let his head fall back as he laughed. I knew, however, that he was watching me and thinking of what I had told him.

'Where did you pick this up?' he said abruptly, putting his knee down again and leaning forward.

'I'm not free to say—and you need not think you can catch me out with your trick questioning,' I said. 'It comes from a refugee, an ex-Communist who still hears things from Moscow occasionally on the grape-vine. You know what chance there is of keeping a thing as big as this secret in countries like Russia and Germany. It actually came out during a personal conversation. Needless to say, we ourselves cannot do much about it either, until it is official, but, to borrow your phrase, forewarned may be to some extent forearmed. Like you, I don't see myself connected with it—yet. Both of us may be in it if this pact does happen, if we do find ourselves at war with Germany by next month, and if our own government acts quickly. As far as I am any judge, the whole of the immediate future depends on the relationship between those two countries. I imagined your people would like to know it is talked about here. The country's full of aliens.'

'Lousy with 'em,' he agreed, taking up his pipe again when I lit my own, which I had been filling while I spoke, 'And now tell me, my dear Watson, what's really on your mind?'

'Nothing more.' He was always surprising me in this uncanny way, though I knew him well. I believe it was partly habit, partly shooting in the dark; I knew he had more than once found the trick useful when he saw himself stopped in an investigation by his own ignorance of where he was heading, at a certain moment; but invariably his instinct, his choice of the exact instant for asking that direct question, was infallible.

'Nothing?' he said. 'I thought you looked paler than usual—worried.' His own plump red-brown face of a healthy and active man still showed no trace of worldly care.

157

'Not unless you can give me something to worry about.'

'The trouble with you and me, Fitz,' he said amiably, 'is that we don't trust each other like partners in crime should. All right. Have it your own way.'

It had not taken long, but I was anxious now and felt a need for haste, like one approaching the real purpose of a mission. By the time I got back to the side entrance of the office, carrying several food parcels that did not fit together anywhere, it was ten to five.

Fortunately, my boy was already waiting inside the unostentatious steel double doors beside a small collection of travelling luggage.

'Go and stand somewhere near the inquiry desk,' I told him. 'A fat woman will be asking for me at about five o'clock, probably carrying a suitcase. Bring her here, will you?—tell the girl I asked you to meet the woman. Is that clear?'

'Yes, Mr. Fitz,' he said, impressed by these mysterious goings-on so obviously that I forgot my own nervous irritation and had to hide my smile from him.

'All right, all right,' I said, 'there's a couple of shillings waiting here in my pocket for your trouble. Now be off with you—and listen—if anyone wants you, say you're doing an urgent job for me. It won't keep you late.'

When he had gone, skipping up the shadowy concrete stairway rising round the lift-well, I looked at Irma's luggage. There was a small cabin-trunk, as well as two suitcases and a heavy coat; nothing more. It seemed unlikely that she could have lived the life she had lived for a whole year with so little. There was something pathetic in the thought. I stared at the luggage, and at my own parcels—two *batons* of bread, coffee, fish, a dressed fowl, two bottles of white wine—and wondered momentarily if it were not all a dream, the whole afternoon and these last minutes of it, so far was it all from my life as I had taken it up on waking that morning. Then I began to wonder what Irma was doing up in that little cold room alone, and why I should find myself in this fantastic, nerve-wracking and yet fascinating situation. No criminal investigation in which I had ever taken part had seemed so improbable; and it was made all the more unreal, yet somehow all the more convincing, by one sound familiar to the hour above all others—the beginning of the tramp of feet in the street outside.

This sound, to one who is not part of it, is like the sudden rise of a tide that as suddenly ebbs. The feet and the voices surge in ruthless crescendo between the darkening walls of the narrow streets with the lighted windows of shops at their base. At first the onlooker, absorbed in thought perhaps, waiting in a backwater of time, does not know that he hears, but abruptly becomes conscious of the sound and its significance: the leeching from the city itself of all that which, living, keeps the city alive. As the exodus increases, when men and women in their hundred thousands spill from the entrances of the drab buildings into the drab thoroughfares, so the sound increases; and with it the sense of release, in that vitiated air that smells of petrol fumes, metal, tar, humanity, tobacco smoke, food, heat and grime, becomes almost irresistible, and the moored onlooker feels impelled, as if by a mob's panic, to turn, leave his place, and join the hurrying, intent throng. With every

159

second that passes, he sees himself left behind, left behind like a strayed sheep at a crossing; he feels homeless, lonely, unwanted, of no significance to the stream of human life and affairs, and a sense of gloom and defeat emphasizes the creeping melancholy of his situation.

I stood in shadow, and listened to the beginning. Already on the doors of the lifts in the lobby behind me the drivers, physically disabled men, were hanging out their *Automatic* signs. One leaf of the double doors of the dark office building opposite was closed; and at my back, as I stood staring into the street watching lights go off and others come on in unforeseen places, there sounded on the shadowy stairway the footsteps of the first people to leave the business offices upstairs.

It was my car I looked for in the street outside, with a futile and increasing anxiety as the minute-hand of every timepiece in the city moved upwards to twelve. When there were still three minutes to go, I saw it slide in to the kerb opposite the door-way, and the driver, whom I had known for years, edged himself across the seat and got out by the near door, leaning in again to remove the ignition key.

When he turned and, seeing me, raised one hand in casual salute, I beckoned him over and together we quickly stowed the luggage, and the coat and the clumsy parcels in the back seat. We had just finished this to our satisfaction when the boy Peter appeared on the darkening stair looking down over the smart hat of a small round woman who was descending the last steps in front of him carrying a big travelling bag. When he caught my eye, he made a short indicative gesture, and grinned with some

160

embarrassment. I approached the round woman, who was glancing about her with eyes as black and polished as ripe berries, and whose face even in its present watchful expectancy was full of signs of laughter. Indeed, when she saw me she laughed outright, her dark red lips curling back like thick rubber bands from teeth as white as Irma's own, and perceptibly larger; and as she came sailing forward with the light step of a fat woman whose insteps bulge above the cut of her shoes without apparent discomfort, she was holding out one plump hand on which the fingers were being eternally strangled by rich rings that sparkled in the pallid ceiling lights of the lobby, and saying with an air of merry joy, 'Mr. Fitzherbert? Ah—Irma told me. I am Linda Werther.'

'Go up to the wireless room off the library,' I said to the amused boy, who was hovering, 'and show the young lady there the way down here, will you, Peter? Tell her her friend is waiting.'

Miss Werther, dark-eyed and happily smiling, turned to me in the impulsive, enveloping way those people have, and said with subdued intensity, 'Mr. Fitzherbert, Irma told me all, over the telephone. How terrible it is for her— terrible—here where she thought she was safe at last. You know her well, Mr. Fitzherbert?'

'I don't know her at all,' I said, looking down at the Jewess's distressed, smiling face and wondering what I had let myself in for. 'She came to me for help, and I suggested this cottage of mine in the mountains. That is all.'

'But it is perfect,' she said. 'It is the *only* thing, Mr. Fitzherbert—she must get away from cities for a while.

Too many accidents happen in cities. Every day, if you read the papers . . .'

'I help write them,' I said gloomily.

'Yes—ah, of *course*!' she said, laughing heartily. 'So you know . . . Irma is a real refugee, you see—not like me. I came here when I could have stayed, but there was nothing left to stay for. The accidents had not started in Germany then. But Irma, she came because she must. To her, Australia is the refuge. Forgive me if I say I think it was also a refuge from herself. She was taking life the hard way. You know her story?'

'Only in broad outline,' I said, 'from what she was obliged to tell me this afternoon. You must understand, Miss Werther, that this sort of thing is all very unusual to me. I have no experience of playing St. George, you know.'

She exuded optimism and confidence in a dark world, just as the diamonds on her fingers and ears and bosom gave out a mad light where there seemed to be none to awaken them. In spite of my distaste for many of her sort I have seen and met, I could not help but begin to feel a wary liking for her rich, simple cheerfulness, and a sort of respect for the shrewdness with which, as I knew, she was watching me out of her black, shining eyes while she talked with such subdued feeling about Irma.

'St. George?' she said. 'Ah yes—of course. The man that rescued the lady from the dragon.' Her voice was like a nudge in the ribs; she assumed an air of great slyness, deliberately. I turned to look at the last visible flight of the stairway where it emerged downwards from behind the lift-well.

'I only remember him,' I said, 'as a symbol of a sort of chivalry I seldom have time or cause—or inclination—to practise.'

She was unabashed. She put her jewelled, throttled fingers on my sleeve where I let them rest, thinking that I should, after all, be grateful at this moment for her mere existence.

'You are too modest,' she said. 'Though you say you don't know her, Irma has mentioned you to me sometimes since she met you on the boat. She always said how kind you were to her that day, obviously a gentleman. Forgive me laughing. It is at what she said: "Not at all like what one supposed Australians to be, and not at all like what one finds they are".'

'Perhaps,' I said, 'she has not met many Australians in the world she seems to have lived in here.'

'No, how right you are. We are so ready to judge, we Europeans, without knowledge. We expect to find all the world is Europe. When we find it is not, we make a little exclusive Europe of our own, speak our own languages, and have the cheek—it is nothing less—to think of the people of our adopted country as the foreigners, the interlopers.'

She said all this in a very lively way, as one who had said it before—as one whose appeal perhaps lay partly in her willingness to admit, on behalf of the foreign community, what most of us had already seen for ourselves, with varying degrees of anger, amusement or indifference. I could only guess: whatever her mannerisms might be, however well-developed her inevitable façade, they did not really conceal a shyly confident good-hearted quality

163

which made me begin to find her not preposterous but like-able. I was pleased that Irma, so much younger, volatile, more unpredictable, would be in her care and her cheerful company. How would old Jack receive her? I frankly could not say. Judging by her whole appearance, one would have supposed that to pack a travelling bag, however capacious, and at a few minutes' notice leave everything for a wild and unknown destination, must have called for a generous sacrifice of the creature comforts to which, clearly, she was used. The shining black fur of her long coat, whose name I did not know, absolutely smelt of ten-pound notes in large, soft quantities; yet there had been no moment when she showed either surprise or uneasiness, any impatience what-ever, since she had arrived. From her manner of unforced gaiety and friendliness, she might at that moment have been judged ignorant of Irma's very existence.

'With her it is not so,' she was saying in her lilting and accented colloquial English. 'She is truly cosmopolitan, but she has known so much unhappiness and fear, you see, that she really feels she has no world of her own anywhere. A world of one's own is a place of safety. She has been so lonely, and so brave . . . You see, Mr. Fitzherbert, it came to this, that no one would what you might say *claim* her— she seemed too dangerous for everyone, in Europe, even in England. That is why she comes here, and then—*pfft!*—on the same boat are three bad types, who know all about her. It is too much. Certainly, they come on other business, to make trouble with the leaders of your workers, that is well known, but also they do her all the harm they can, on the side, and so—all through this country too her record is known here and there, people are afraid. She is called a traitor. For myself, it does not matter, and I have friends, too, who do not know or care. For us, she is a woman. But even so, there are too many people, Party members, who know about her, and so she is never at peace, in her own mind. She has nothing—no religion, no lover, no family— no future, you might say—yet because she is brave this does not break her heart. The worst you can say of her is that she must always act first for herself, and most of us do that. If it were me, I should go mad.'

She drew the distressing picture with cheerful, dispassionate precision, making Irma for the first time a third person in my mind, and so real that I was increasingly impressed by the clear accuracy of her mind behind the flowery, bejewelled and ornate exterior. Over her tilted head I had been looking at the stair so unseeingly, my mind so filled with the growing portrait of that unfortunate young woman which my companion's lilting, murmured words built up, by stroke after stroke, that when Irma herself did appear at the turn of the stairway, coming quickly down with my boy following, it seemed as though she had been there in the very flesh all the time Miss Werther was speaking.

The two women embraced one another in their different fashions, but briefly, before Irma stepped back and turned to me. Her face was like a wooden mask now—not expressionless, but stiff with the strain of waiting there alone in a strange office, held there by her desperate determination to risk, as she thought, at least her freedom if not her personal safety by trusting me and taking my word.

165

Later I learned that she did not know, until the boy came, whether I would not return with the police, or whether, instead, I might simply have washed my hands of her affairs after all, and have left her there to wait until she was asked to leave the building. It was the sort of thing that could happen to her. She had had similar experiences, but this—if it had happened—was to have been the last of them; and it was then that she showed me the innocent-looking little ampoule of potassium cyanide which they called 'the death capsule'. She had had it all the time, that day, in her glove, fitted into the tip of the thumb. She showed me how, as the glove is casually removed, the glass ampoule falls unnoticed into the palm of the hand and can be slipped into the mouth in the middle of a yawn. I had seen the result of the swift working of that particular poison. In a sweat of retrospective horror I took and threw the shining little thing into the waters of the harbour . . . That was long afterwards, however.

Now, the tramping of feet outside on the pavements was rising with the roar of traffic and the yelling interjections of the newsvendors in their final frenzy of the day to an obliterating tide of sound. All over the city, young women of Irma's age were leaving the doorways of buildings and stepping into friends' cars. It was the natural moment for our departure. I dismissed the boy with a few shillings and thanks—indeed, I could not have hoped to manage the business so unobtrusively without him—wondering at the same time whether the watcher at Wynyard were still loitering there; and then, just as we were about to walk quickly to the car, the women following me, McMahon came in, bumping lightly against the door-frame as he turned out of the crowded street, lightly but with sufficient speed to send him straight into my arms. His hat fell off, and in the dim light from above, his face, blandly drunk and smiling already in senseless apology, was revealed. I heard Irma step behind me with the ghost of an exclamation, and then McMahon drew himself free and upright, and said in his soft voice, with that damnably accurate perception of the practised drunkard, 'Ah—the little Communist lady. Pardon me, Fitz, old boy old boy—sheer clumsiness if you know what I mean, I mean.'

I picked up and returned to him his hat, murmuring in a voice I could barely keep from sounding thoroughly cross, 'For heaven's sake, Tim, keep out of the office and go home. Don't be a fool. Take my tip and go, or you'll find yourself going for good.'

'Hey—easy, Fitz, easy,' he mumbled, trying to get another look at Irma, as, acting mechanically and from instinct, she walked quickly out to the car with her face averted, and opened the door of the rear seat, Miss Werther at her elbow all the time. Without difficulty—for he had taken hold of my wrist in a strong, drunken grasp—I kept myself between McMahon and the very ordinary street scene of two women dressed in businesslike black getting into the back seat of a car, and, when the door was closed, settling themselves in the interior darkness to wait for the driver. When I heard that door slam shut, I stood away from McMahon, whose breath and clothes smelled strongly of a mixture of beer and rum. He stared past me into the shadowless light of the street, a mixture of daylight and lamplight, and frowned in hazy puzzlement.

167

'Funny thing,' he said conversationally, 'I could have sworn I saw a young dame here I know quite a bit about . . . A very choice piece, Fitz, old man, honestly, no, honestly. You see her? or am I a bit—you know—seeing things?'

'Why don't you head for home?' I said, my annoyance going as his bewilderment persisted. 'You know quite well you will only make trouble for yourself with the subs if you go up now. Blake has his eye on you, you know.'

He would not listen to me, but muttered something unrepeatable about Blake and made for the lifts. While his back was turned, and his attention focused uncertainly on the choice of buttons to be pressed, I almost ran from the building and round the back of the car into the crowded roadway beyond. A passing driver, important with the moment's crazy haste, called out irritably, 'Look out, whiskers,' as I got into the driver's seat, slid home and turned the ignition key, and took the chance of pulling out at once behind a careering tram into the homeward-bound, savage flood of competing traffic. In the rear-vision mirror I caught a glimpse of the two women's faces pale in the gloom when the shop-window lights flickered on them as we went forward.

Irma's head was resting against the back of the seat, and her delicate eyelids were closed as though in the extreme of an absolute exhaustion. She looked frightened. With an air of lively concern, Miss Werther was caressing her dark hair, from which her hat, like McMahon's, had fallen or been flung.

Beyond Richmond the branch road turns north-west. We had driven aslant the sunset glow above the blue blackness

168

of the mountains where the light flowed up into the cloudless sky with a pure radiance almost white at the level of the aerial horizon, and faded through pale gold to the imperceptibly deepening blue of the zenith. After eight miles we began the slow series of climbs towards Hill Farm, leaving a last village to sink with the land behind us as the road swept in arbitrary curves and zigzags between taller and taller trees.

Hill Farm is on a curious, roughly defined plateau which drops suddenly on the eastward side. The road became a firm bush track, and the towering trees that seemed to but actually did not meet overhead so darkened the way that I had to switch on the headlights. In their penetrating downward glare the most recent wheelmarks of old Jack's light cart could clearly be seen, and I knew by this, and by the sweet, nippy smell of the thin mountain air, that rain had fallen here more recently than it had in town. As I drove up the familiar way I thought again how wise and leisurely the original maker of Hill Farm had been, to cut his track so that the place was approached from the rear in a gradual ascent and a final level stretch northwards along the mountain side, rather than to attempt to breast the swelling bosom of the plateau's eastern limit with deep cuttings into that dead clay subsoil which becomes like a cold reddish glue during the winter rains.

After Miss Werther had helped Irma into her coat, nobody spoke at all during that unpleasantly fast progress which only the foothills beyond Richmond slowed down. I was glad to be able to concentrate on handling the car, a business at which I am no expert but which does not

169

interfere, as speech does at such times, with thinking. Once we had left the outskirts of the city, the grime and slickness of the factory district south of the University, and the hugely depressing sprawl of residential wildernesses beyond, my mood changed. It always does, here. When the unsullied plain is visible at last on either hand, and the mountains in the distance slowly cease to be a flat navy-blue dado at the foot of the wall of sky and begin to show themselves in all their depth and complicated splendour, a surge of joy and content gathers force in my breast like the urge to sing on a fine morning; and I think, always, that I should leave the city and live a country life, farming the plateau with old Jack to guide me, keeping myself for ever away from the deadly contact with the people of the city, from the greedy fears and the frightened greeds which seem to be the two aspects of their whole being.

I think this, many times each year, whatever the season, whatever my city preoccupations; but—like most other escaping travellers in the same scene, who must think similar thoughts—I shall never do it. Because I am not a nervous man I shall never have the impulse, pure and strong, to break with habits of living and working, and above all with the more subtle and implacable habits of memory.

We passed occasionally by tree-trunks and open spaces that I recognized, signs of the home-comings of years. Remotely below on the right the blur and sparkle of the lights of civilization's fringes could be seen sometimes in passing vertical panels opening and closing between the crowded trunks of huge turpentines and aspiring red and white gums; and over the plain thus briefly revealed hung the pale, forgiving haze of the last blue daylight. The thought came into my mind that, as it was Friday, as likely as not Jack had shut Donna in her wire cage, milked early, and gone off on his grey horse to the nearest pub, at North Richmond, south-east of us and miles away. If so, he would not be back until midnight, asleep on his homing animal as comfortably as an Oriental prince in a howdah. As the trees thinned and the boundary fence halted us, I looked for his light, and as I was closing the sliprails behind the car I saw it, bobbing through the orchard between the cottage and the shed where, years before, he had built a big brick fireplace and set himself up, solitary but not lonely, silent but always ready with an answer and a sharp jest (especially about marriage and the horribleness of women), and casually skilful at everything he had need to do.

He saw my lights at the same time, and raised in salute the storm-lantern he was carrying through the dusk. Underfoot the earth was still clearly visible, and above the mutter of the engine I heard the sudden minatory barking of Donna, and the graver bull-roaring of Jack's dog Ike. It was a moment of such comfort that I did not get into the car at once, but for a full minute stood waiting until Donna's approaching clamour became, abruptly, a series of exclamations of wonder, incredulity and delight as she allowed herself to recognize who had come.

'We are here,' I said into the darkness of the rear seat; and again for a moment the thought of those two women, distracted, over-civilized and alien, in these still and empty solitudes made me frown. No imagination could force them to fit, here; but I realized this now without undue dismay, for my sense of my own ease, like that of a man closing his front door after him as he comes home, gave me strength and confidence in what I had undertaken.

The small bitch flashed like living copper across the steady beam of the headlights, and welcomed me with small whines and groans of pleasure until I felt god-like for that moment. When I let her in upon the seat beside me, however, she went rigid and the hair of her thick winter coat rose stiffly between her shoulders.

'Speak,' I said. 'It is my spaniel—her name is Donna.'

Both the women said her name, but she was not reassured. In her two years of life she had never seen a female human being, nor smelled one. She growled unhappily on a high protesting note, and as we moved forward towards the barn, where I kept the car beside Jack's cart among odd bits of farming machinery, she put one paw, with an air of mingled question and authority, upon my left knee and let me see the whites of her eyes. Not only was she quite unused to strangers, but she was pathetically jealous of my attention whenever I was about, though Jack assured me she grieved little once I was gone.

He was waiting with the lantern. He smelled pleasantly of rum, his evening refreshment after the day's work. I took the usual half-bottle of it out of the glove-box and watched him slide it into his hip pocket without a word, before I explained about our visitors. He listened in silence, sucking at his cold pipe, and nodded when I added that there were peculiar circumstances and that the younger woman was unofficially under my protection for the present.

'I remember,' he murmured gravely into my ear,

'I found one woman quite peculiar circumstances. I reckon two would be very peculiar.'

They would have to stay on for a while, I said, and he must not let them worry him, for it would not be for long. Then I helped the two of them out of the car on to the warm earth floor of the barn, where the air carried the sweet ancient odours of the cow and her milk and her feed from the byre next door. Jack held the lantern high so that he could see who was here. For the coldest part of the winter the cow lived under the same roof with him for a time each night, but for most of the year she came in only to be milked at night and in the morning. A wooden partition wall divided their quarters, and through a square opening cut in it he could commune with her when he felt like it. He was partial to cows.

The two women stood close together while I introduced Jack, who looked sharply at them, pulled some inches of pipe-stem out of his toothless mouth, and to my surprise shook the hand of each in turn. My mind was set finally at rest when of his own accord he led the way to the kitchen door of the cottage with the lantern held so that they could see their steps, and, once inside, began to light the lamps.

It is a comfortable cottage, made and lined with hardwood that has darkened with the passing of half a century or more to the colour of cedar where it is protected from the weather. Two rooms, used as bedrooms, open out of the living-room, which has the biggest floor-space in the house, with casement windows looking north and east across a wide veranda.

In winter, the north side is warmed by the northerly sun; in summer the eastern side, the front, is cool from midday onwards. Whoever built it must have found good timber cheap to obtain, for the floors are of that loveliest of building hardwoods, Western Australian jarrah, polished to a deep rosy brown and as indestructible as teak. It had been Jack's habit, since first he saw the interior of the cottage several years ago, to polish these floors once a week with a paste of his own making—a concoction of bees' wax and turpentine to which he added the dissolved crystallized gum of one of the mountain eucalypts—and this he did whether the cottage was in use or empty. Thus it invariably had a welcoming air of masculine fastidiousness, with the clean old furniture that matched nowhere except in its look of comfortable ease, the gentle brilliance of the bookshelves which the floor hazily reflected as it did the windows and the pale winter curtains we put up every April, and the fireplace of scrubbed brick, where in the colder months I always found a clean fire set ready for my match.

It was these details of care, which I could not myself have seen to, that made me prize Jack's tenancy of part of my land—as much of it as he could manage alone—and consider well any act of mine that might send him wandering again; for he had an independence entirely his own, which was either the cause or the result of his sincere indifference as to where he lived or what became of him. He was by far the most solitary human being I have ever known, but he was not what is called, with weak slickness, 'anti-social'. It was simply that, like the miller of Dee, but without his minor-keyed jollity, he cared for nobody.

So I had a disproportionate pleasure in the sight of him laying and lighting a fire in the kitchen range which, if

Jean had not died, I had meant to replace with a kerosene stove. For men's use, the range was far more pleasant, and I was glad I had never done what I once intended. Jack, I saw, was playing the host's assistant, and if the grimace of a smile he wore in any company was, as I suspected, a little wider and thinner than usual, it was still untroubled. I left the women in the larger bedroom in front, where we carried in Irma's luggage and Miss Werther's travelling bag, and changed into more comfortable clothes in the other room, which was my own. Already beyond my open window the south was dark and starry above the high wall of the spur, and the sweet and nourishing air had the edged cold that follows rain in the mountains and threatens a wind from the west. Passing into the golden lamplight of the big room, where as I bent to light the fire I could hear the subdued voices of the two women through their closed door, I brought my wandering and lazy thoughts back to consider my immediate duty.

They would need warming drinks and hot food. The night was far colder than night in the city. I remembered the coffee among my parcels, the fish and the *batons* of white bread, with satisfaction. There were always eggs and cream and several sorts of tinned food in the tiny pantry which shared with the neat bathroom one end of the long kitchen itself. I had partitioned this off at Jean's wise suggestion, when I was having the cottage and its outhouses repaired and extra tanks installed to ensure a sufficient household water supply in case of the unpredictable winter or summer droughts. There was little now that the human heart could wish for, here, I thought, as I came to a decision to turn the kitchen and the food supplies over to the women, so that as soon as possible they might feel that first faint authority which makes for comfort in a strange place.

Miss Werther joined me where I knelt in front of the fire watching it draw up sweetly while I felt over Donna's skin for ticks. This human habit caused her much bliss and self-abandonment.

'I have been telling Irma you would not mind if she went to bed,' Miss Wether said, 'but it is useless. She says it would be bad manners, also she wishes company.'

She too had changed from her city clothes into a tweed skirt and a brilliant woollen jumper with a high neck, and she looked both younger and more agreeable, for her sallow skin and jetty eyes had not gone perfectly with the black coat and frock she had worn earlier. There was another improvement—no diamond flashed back the streaming firelight from anywhere about her person. She was rubbing her plump fingers together slowly, as though to restore normal feeling to them; when I raised my eyes to hers I caught her smiling down widely at me, showing her large white teeth.

'You miss my jewels,' she said, nodding. 'They are locked up where I usually keep them. In Europe, Mr. Fitzherbert, the refugees carry their savings with them, so, for safety. Today I too am a refugee, a little. Who knows what can happen?'

She was laughing as she spoke. I stood up and moved in a chair for her. Irma's voice called from the bedroom with startling gaiety, 'I am not going to bed, if that is what you are saying.'

Donna sprang up from under my hands, and barked sharply once. Miss Werther called back, 'It's all right, darling.' I quietened the bitch again, thinking that those two women, far from being ill at ease in unfamiliar surroundings, were now in a vast good humour.

'We are both excited,' Miss Werther explained in her lilting voice, sinking comfortably into the chair and stretching out to the fire her feet on which she now wore strong golfing shoes with rubber soles, so that her fat insteps no longer bulged. 'We are excited,' she repeated, drawling the word nonchalantly, 'because this is such a very nice place, and you are a very nice person, and you have a very nice little dog.' She glanced sideways at me with a sly and friendly humour, folding her hands in her lap peacefully.

'That is what I hoped,' I said, 'though it may be a bit early to judge. Except about Donna. She really is very nice. Would you both like a drink? I have whisky and sherry in that sideboard.'

'Thank you, I drink very seldom,' she said, 'but it would be good for—' and she jerked her head sideways and back to indicate the bedroom door. Automatically I looked that way, and as I looked Irma came out, turning to close the door behind her very carefully, as though it were fragile. Once again, as when I had first seen her, she was wearing pyjamas and over them what I believed to be the same thick green house-coat, cut Chinese fashion and fastened high at the neck with that golden medallion or button as big as a florin. Her hair hung fine and loose to her shoulders, and she stood for a moment very still and erect against the dark wood of the door, looking round the room with a kind of severity before she came towards us and with a smile sank down on the floor beside Miss Werther's chair.

At the same time Jack looked in from the kitchen and said to me with a leisurely wink, 'If you folk want a cup o' tea, kettle's boilin'.'

Nothing could have been more matter-of-fact; and nothing could more surely have made me aware of how peace, the great maternal, mysterious and timeless peace of the mountain night, had settled over us, over the cottage and the land, like a blessing spoken from the altar of a supreme divinity.

At Hill Farm one sleeps well. The enormous silence of the mountains at night is oppressive at first to some ears, half-sealed against the imperfect night of the city, where always there is an unbroken undertone of sound from darkness to dawn. In the mountains, night sounds are only of bird or animal, sudden, subtle and brief, emphasizing without even ruffling the silence itself, which flows down from the peaks and up from the valleys like the light of the summer noons, embracing and engulfing consciousness.

All round and over the cottage the silence held fast, but some unfamiliar stirring movement within the walls woke me after midnight. At that hour a man wakes as a rule with difficulty from the depths of first sleep, but tonight I came full awake at once, and from habit looked at my watch in the same movement.

Somewhere, the sound of stealthy, mysterious movement continued; stopped; resumed. Lying in the dark open-eyed, I decided after a minute's bewilderment what it was. Someone was at the fireplace in the big room, pushing the burned logs together over their bed of coals. I lifted back the bedclothes and swung my feet to the floor, feeling for slippers. The cold had become hard and sharp, giving the sensation when I moved of ice passed lightly over the skin of my ankles.

No light showed under the door, but when I opened it I saw that the tall old standard lamp whose wick I had left turned low was still alight by the hearth, and that a dark scarf had been placed round the yellow shade. In the faint downcast radiance below this screen I beheld Irma's bent back and bared heels as she knelt on the hearth rug. Her face, intent and quite lonely, was lit rosily by the glow of the embers she was softly coaxing into flame under the half-burned wood.

In the last few hours she had become so accustomed to my presence that I had been able to watch her unguardedly, and thus in my turn I had come to be more at ease where she was. My position as host and as it were custodian in my own place was a strong one. By my very passivity, which was only at first an effort, I let her know this, and let her know I knew it too. While they with cheerful talk and frequent questions to Jack or me, where we sat silent by the inside fire, had made a meal ready, it had occurred to me—for I admit that by now I was thinking of her constantly—that she had likely never been able to depend completely upon the presence and behaviour of a man. With men she could not relax herself inwardly; there was always a game, often dangerous and never wholly pleasant, to be played; from moment to moment she must, so to speak, count her cards.

Here, in the safe solitude of Hill Farm, her safe friend by her side and two safe men thinking not hers but (as she supposed) their own age-old fireside thoughts, she found herself without an opponent, and—to persist in the metaphor—without use for whatever cards she might pick up. All that had been to do was done: there was no conceivable outcome to this situation, yet she was more secure from fear or the need to act for herself than she had ever been since early childhood.

What her own thoughts might have been I could not know. Abruptly, the years of flight and pursuit, real or half-imagined according to the circumstances, had ended, in a way she could not have foreseen, in a place that until tonight did not exist for her; and at the beginning, when she came out from the bedroom and looked about her with that air of severe investigation, rather like an animal in strange surroundings, she must have been bewildered by it all. As one sometimes does, she may have had the feeling that her mind and her consciousness were not functioning properly for her.

Then, little by little, mind and consciousness revived. When we three sat down to supper at the kitchen table of scrubbed pinewood—where Jack would by no means join us, preferring his own fire and his own food—she was like another person altogether. Even her face had changed, and for the first time I saw it naturally animated, with a moist shine in her eyes and lips and a glow of warm blood in her cheeks and sometimes her throat, as though the warmth and a little wine and the stronger draught of this strange freedom of the spirit had renewed the very tissue of her blood itself.

With her dark hair drawn back now to the nape of her neck and enclosed chignon-wise in a net, as she always wore it for kitchen tasks, she had a brave, naked look of candour, in spite of the queer, sly, Slavic slant of her eyes and brows and cheekbones. She looked at once slightly cunning and more than slightly vulnerable; and for the first time I saw how small and flat her ears were, with that clean, unweathered, delicate look of women's ears, naked as shells newly warmed and dried on a beach in the sun, and with round lobes as red in that light as if they had been rubbed with geranium petals. The lamp on the table between us showed her clearly to me, while I hid comfortably in my own peace of mind and watched the change arise and finally claim her.

How completely it had claimed her, this released and little-known self, I was quickly to learn. She now was quietly and steadily blowing upon the responsive embers, and small rags of flame were flapping noiselessly up and down from the heated logs. She could not have heard my door opening, for she did not turn her head or falter in her task, and the look of loneliness remained in her face. But of this I am not sure, for she neither moved nor faltered either when I crossed the room silently and seated myself on the rug at her side, drawing up my knees under the thick dressing-gown I had hurriedly put on in the dark; for the cold was gnawing at my ankles like icy water. She remained kneeling and bowed forward, supported on her elbows and hands like someone doing homage to Prometheus; her loosed hair hid part of her face that was at once pale and ruddy in the increasing firelight, and her pursed lips were dry with the heat, so that now and then she licked them and pressed them together before inhaling and blowing out another earnest breath. Not for years had I seen anything so moving and lovely, in my world of gas-fires and electric radiators, and vain, self-conscious women. My heart went out to her as it sometimes did to Alan when I watched him absorbed in one of the tremendous occupations of childhood.

At last she sat back on her heels, flushed and pale, and turned upon me the curious deep gaze of her eyes now again—as I had seen them the previous afternoon—not cool opaque blue but hot violet; and with a sort of scared, childish triumph she smiled.

'You could not sleep?' I murmured casually, though my pulse had quickened as I watched her with something more than compassion.

'No,' she said in a soft, unpenetrating whisper, 'it is too quiet . . . Never have I known such quiet as you have here.'

'The mountain silence,' I said; but she shook her head quickly, watching my lips with listening eyes.

'It is not silence. I can hear it—something—I do not know what. I can hear the mountains themselves.'

I thought of D. H. Lawrence in the Darling Ranges in Western Australia, listening to the overpowering self-assertion of lost Lemuria in the seething stillness of the moonlit valleys. Here, on the fringe of the eastern coast, the mountains have a different psyche, a different voice, more vigorous perhaps, less ancient and toneless and indestructible; but it is there, the same mysterious, compelling sense of *being*, quiescent and all-powerful like a tiger watching, which travellers say is to be discerned nowhere else on the earth's surface. It has the quality of a threat withheld and a hunger so profound that the mind at first turns from it in alarm, and sleep, as Irma had found, seems impossible; as though only by remaining awake can one avoid suffering some gigantic and obscure conquest of the soul.

'It will pass,' I said. 'Do you want anything—a drink, or food?'

'Thank you.' She shook her head, turning back to the vigorous spectacle of the revived fire burning upwards for ever yet never able to depart in flight. By leaning sideways I could reach a pipe and tobacco on the top of the low flanking bookshelves on my left. I felt a need to move, to make the small, protective movements with my hands that the business of filling a pipe and lighting it calls for. While I did this I watched her, and she watched the flames in steadfast, dreamy immobility. So some minutes passed, and the night bent over the cottage. I too felt as though I were about to fall into some timeless and beneficent trance as I smoked and looked my fill at my companion in this solitude.

At length she moved, careful to make no carrying sound, and sat down with her slippered feet stretched out towards the warmth. My hand lay on my knees, and she hesitantly put her own hand under my arm and covered my fingers with hers; and this time there was no force or urgency in her touch, which seemed to be without thought.

'I have been thinking,' she murmured. 'You are so kind that I do not know what to do.'

Once again, outside all reason, my heart which had been stilled began to beat more hastily. I felt a great urge to silence her, to put my hand over her murmuring lips and ensure silence; for it suddenly seemed to me that only silence would save us both. But I could not move and I could not speak. Some word of warning stuck in my throat like a solid thing which would not be properly swallowed. I could only remain carefully unmoving, hoping to appear unmoved, and stare into the flames, while that small part of my mind which was not wholly absorbed by its violent awareness of her wondered what time it could be, what time had passed.

'Why are you so—rigid? We are alone. There is no one.'

Her whispering voice seemed to come from another part of the room, because she had turned her head away like a person hiding laughter or grief or some feeling not in keeping with her lightly-breathed words. I still found nothing to say, still felt my own inward cry of warning stifled in my throat. It was a moment of extreme peril, and I knew I must at all costs survive it; yet I was paralysed, powerless to draw away from her in body or mind, for she had become mistress not only of my fleshly desire but of my compassion, and, though I could master the one from long habit, I could not quell and drive down the other which, freed, must—I thought—take all with it.

What was at stake here—and for all my agitation I saw it clearly, clearly—was not my simple faith-keeping with the memory of my dead wife. I found no virtue in that now save a way towards peace of mind sometimes. What was at stake was that life of the mind to which I still aspired, and in which I believed my eventual spiritual salvation lay. The girl at my side with her averted face and her arm linked with mine held out to me not only the trivial temptations of the flesh, from the yielding to which any priest can absolve an indulgent man, but also, and far more terribly, the temptation to abandon a strengthening way of thought which alone made possible the worldly life I lived.

I was afraid now, in my turn. It is clear to me now, long afterwards, that my faith in my own carefully-nurtured inner strength had not until this moment been tried with any force. At the time all that was clear was that abruptly, unforeseen as an abyss at the feet of a night wanderer, a choice of my own devising was being put to me. It was a choice between possessing her, as instinct and bodily wisdom so tenderly urged me, and possessing myself, now and for ever; for even then, in the turmoil of my mind, I knew that such a moment could never again in my life come upon me with this fierce, unpardonable surprise.

In the same instant as I knew this, my choice was made.

I thought out all this afterwards, certainly, in the long and leaden years of war and separation. At the time I was aware only of the profound confusion of mind and spirit when, of all the three aspects of being, only flesh saw clear the way and leaped up strong to pursue it. The rekindled fire at our feet was a springing reflection of the fire burning up again, after a long time, in the secret places of my body and my imagination, burning so well and eagerly that I felt no shame, only an agony of regret, pang after pang of futile longing for what was within my grasp; tearless and bitter as the juice of desert aloes whose bitterness is that of an earthen desolation.

It needed no words to let me know what was in her mind, but she did speak, with her face still averted from me.

'I do not know what to say to thank you for this kindness and as you know, there is nothing I can do in return, nothing. Only one thing, and for a woman it is too easy to be enough.'

'It is also too easy to accept, believe me. I would not impair the value of your generosity so readily.'

'You want me—you?'

'Yes.'

'Then take what you want. It is so little—if you knew . . .'

'I do know, but it is not so little to me.'

'It is yours.'

She moved very slightly towards me, and I saw her face at last, and realized, confusedly, that she had been hiding tears. Without hesitation now I took her in my arms, in the silence that followed our quick whispered exchange. She came to me irresistibly, and I supported her so that she was half-sitting, half-lying across my knees, her head and shoulders in the bend of my left arm. For a moment she remained arched and rigid; then as her form sagged against me she reached up with her free hand to pull my head down near her lips, and began a whispered babble of words.

What she said I would not recall if I could. Even at the time, even when she spoke in English, I did not understand one half of it. It was like the endless nightmare spate of words uttered in delirium, and seemed to have little to do with me myself; I remember thinking oddly, as a man will on occasion think of anything to save himself, that her breath bearing such words as I recognized should rightly have scorched me, instead of striking so gently warm and sweet upon my cheek, and that her still form should have been contorted to give a final force to her soft, frantic speech. With my ear near her mouth I found, when I opened my eyes again, that I was looking at the shadowy hollow of her bosom where the silken pyjama jacket had fallen open as she lay back in my arms; and if I closed my eyes it was not so that I might not see but that I might see for ever, and for ever breathe the delicate, warm perfume of her hidden breasts; for it is by such mortal things, and not by nobility or badness of character, that a woman in the end becomes unforgettable.

Minute after minute, for I know not how long, she whispered her urgent confessions of desires and despairs, now and then pulling me closer with her arms across my shoulders for emphasis. It did not matter that I understood so little, and that little unwillingly. It was enough that she was making a full, incoherent confession of all that life had done to her, all she had done to life. She was a soul in torment, I thought; and I held her in my arms as though that were the most natural thing in the world, as though we had always been together so. Of all her hurried whispering, I retained (of course from vanity, and as a kind of solace to my aching flesh, to the immense regret that had come with my inevitable choice) only one phrase, which she repeated two or three times at intervals: 'Only you have'—I think the word was 'abstained'; that at least was its meaning. 'Only you have abstained,' she said, not knowing of course that my abstinence, if so it could be called, was in fact a positive choice in favour of what I believed to be my own salvation; not knowing consciously, it seemed, that every part and fibre of my body at that moment craved her with a need that, had I spoken, would have cried aloud. In fact, had she not lain so still in my arms, whispering on with such apparent necessity to speak, I do not think whatever resolution I still clung to would have withstood her. But when, for the third or fourth time, she said, 'Only you . . .' I turned my face so that my lips came against her rapid mouth. I did not want to hear any more, and I kissed her so that she fell silent and began to tremble like someone in a fever. With my free hand I caressed her face and hair until the trembling ebbed, became spasmodic like the sobbing of an exhausted child, and finally ceased. Her fragile eyelids lay so still upon her eyes that she seemed to sleep; and only by a deeper breath now and then, by a sigh, by the slight movement of her fingers behind my shoulder, did she show that sleep had not in fact come upon her.

So for a long while she lay in my arms. The fire sank down and I could not move to feed it. All sense of time's passing had gone from my mind, and my body had put aside its craving unawares. Like a boy with his first love in his incredulous embrace, I wished that the timeless moment were timeless in very truth, and that our two selves at one, with nothing given, nothing received, might rest in this waking dream.

'Your lady friends is gone, I took them to the buss stop in the cart yes-day, they might of bin headin west or back Sydney way, didnt say. The young one nearly through a fit when she found you was gone without sayin but the other she just larghed she reckoned you was no fool whatever you done. The night you left the skreetch owl come down the mountin, that scared em a wile til I told em what it was, said it was a sine of rain not a murder or a gohst!!! If you can get Horderns to send new shoes for the cultivater, arent any in Richmond yet and I got to get on with the top field.'

188

FOUR
THE RATIFICATION

Ten days after my visit to Hill Farm, on the twenty-third of August, the warning I had received that Friday afternoon was justified when it was announced that Russia had signed her non-aggression pact with Nazi Germany.

Even in the midst of the uproar and the lamentations, fully aware that this was a death-knell, the exploding of a detonator which would quickly set off the main charge, we pursued our affairs within and outside the office with deliberate conscience and sanity, in what looked to have become an insane world.

The full enormity of what was to come in the end was, to many of us, grimly adumbrated in the behaviour of the German Chancellor to Sir Neville Henderson during those last unreal days of peace. We had glimpses of a man either whipping his very soul to a frenzy of baseless personal resentment, a bull before the charge, or in the grip of a power which he had conjured up only to find, too late, that he was at its command, not it at his. I believed, then as now, when there has been time to look back, years in which to think again almost soberly, that it was the latter; yet in the later part of the war, just before the invasion of Normandy in strength, a dream came to me which I have never forgotten. In this, between the usual ragged beginning and the apparently rational and quite irrelevant change into other dreaming, I found myself talking (in English) with Hitler on the stage of an immense and empty auditorium, a quiet conversation of which, when I awoke, I could recall only one remark, made by the Chancellor in conclusion. He said as he turned away, 'I am an Austrian. My mission is to destroy the people of Germany, and I am doing it.'

It was a good dream, and for some days afterwards I experienced a recurring inner excitement, a sense of almost exultation, whenever I thought of it. Had it come in September of nineteen thirty-nine, it might have made those first days of declared war less like the unpeopled nightmares of sleep which they evoked. As it was, sleeping and waking were nightmarish indeed. We felt we were so far away; we felt the helplessness none of the threatened nations could have felt, for we were, as it seemed in the beginning, helpless without being threatened.

The quick, fantastic changes in everyday life could be accepted with an effort of will; the disappearance of office colleagues and private friends, or their mysterious trans-figuration into people not only in uniform but in the grip of a flushed and bustling excitement, trying to pretend they had not changed, was comprehensible and, at odd moments, enviable to those of us who dressed and lived and worked as we had always done. At that time, because of Alan, because of my age, and because my office intimated firmly that such action would be opposed, I made no effort to approach any of the services; in truth, after the first moments of instinctive consideration while Mr. Menzies's voice still sounded in my ears, I scarcely thought of such a thing again until nineteen forty-two, when the Japanese seemed likely to invade this continent from the north. Scott had me in to explain to me the attitude of the management, which was, roughly, one of repressive exhortation to the whole staff: a combination of 'Do your bit if you think you must,' and 'The *Gazette* must come out as usual.' There were not so many young men on the staff in those days, and it was possible without lack of a show of patriotism to stress the importance of publication at all costs, while at the same time drawing up a list of official correspondents which should silence criticism when added to the list of those who had already joined up.

Scott, in his booming voice and with a face of jovial anger as usual, spoke very kindly to me, explaining that not only had I not been considered for a correspondent's assignment but also as time went on my present useful-ness on the spot was bound to increase largely: 'for crimes abroad breed crimes at home, my boy, as you will find for yourself.' And so, of course, it did turn out, in ways none of us foresaw then.

For Alan's sake, above all other considerations, I was heartily glad when Scott told me that my name had been forwarded to Army and manpower authorities as that of

191

a staff member indispensable to publication of the paper. After that night at Hill Farm, I was aware of changes taking place within me, and Jack's letter, in the middle of the week following my secret departure before sunrise the following morning after some hours of sleepless thought, seemed to speed these changes forward. Like a man who has survived a severe physical ordeal, with all its excitement and fear, I felt for some days a lassitude of body and spirit, and a slowly decreasing bitterness of regret, a growing conviction that by the very sorrow and shame of the choice I had made the choice itself was in a sense endorsed as right. Of Irma I could not think clearly at all. She seemed to be lodged as it were within me. She was too near. I was seldom unaware of her in waking hours—never, it seemed, for a moment—but I could not think of her objectively yet, and did not dream of her at all.

The dreams came later. For the present, I found myself impelled to go over and over my impressions of that last hour we had spent together. I thought she was young and wise enough not to be offended, as an older woman would likely have been offended, by my seeming rejection of her modestly-proffered 'return'; but she was painfully bewildered, like an honest man to whom it is pointed out that the coin of the realm which he has tendered as legal payment does not ring true. Even in my desperation, I tried to explain, with slow words which sounded unconvincing enough, I know, when they were spoken, that I was not made for the enjoyment of evanescent loves of the flesh, and that while I believed I loved her now I must force myself to realize that I hardly knew her, or she me, and that a bodily union with neither background nor future, and with only desire in common between the two indulgeants, was to my mind an act of ignorant self-gratification in human beings, just as surely as it was one of the utmost naturalness in all other animals. Men and women were different, I said; and generously she did not laugh. I showed her how I had desired her, with what hungry fires, and she seemed to believe me, though without comprehension yet; I told her how I had become a sudden field of battle between two ambitions, of which the one that in that moment had seemed the stronger had withdrawn, not vanquished but out-argued and disarmed. I told her, as clearly as I could, all that was in my heart and in my mind: the dead but not forgotten love I had had for Jean, the living love and compassion for my son, and the strange feelings, of pity and passion, she herself had aroused violently in me, and which I had never before felt for any woman, nor—I had thought—would ever feel again.

And she—she let me talk, lying back in my arms with closed eyes while above her I whispered to the dying glow of the fire which from time to time settled itself more comfortably with an answering whisper and shift of coals. She let me talk, always of myself, my life, my body, my spirit—seldom of her, never of what she might feel and think, never of her hungers, her fortune, her destiny; and there in my arms her loneliness must have increased with every word of mine, inconceivably burdensome.

It was this thought, not the nature of my final choice, of which I was later ashamed; for she said nothing, pleaded nothing, made no move again to woo my consciousness away from myself towards herself. She lay there still and listening, and I have often wondered whether, for all her tiredness of body and mind after that long strange day's excitements, for all her feeling of the ultimate futility of every well-meant gesture and every larger human effort, she perhaps found it in her heart to laugh at what could only seem my elaborate self-justification for the subtlest and grossest discourtesy a man can offer a woman who has proffered him herself.

If she did laugh, and with whatever scorn or bitterness, she gave no sign of it. In the end, after we had sat together huddled over the fire as it died, and after I had assured myself that she was warm enough—and god! how delicately warm, how resiliently alive and weighted she was—I persuaded her to return to her bed, and so went back to my own.

It was then, lying sleepless in the dark which pressed its icy kiss on cheek and brow, that I began to feel that sense of unease and shame at the thought that my talk could only have increased by many degrees her awareness of her own loneliness. The more I thought of it, the more grievous did it seem, until I felt I could weep for what I had done; yet—and there was no consolation in the thought—I thought I could not have done otherwise. It was incumbent upon me, by the vow I had made to be to Alan more than a father only, to save my own soul: that was what I was faced with, all my waking hours; and a casual taking and giving in love, under the stress of loneliness and fear and desire, could not but seem a step back, not a forward step towards the strength needed for any act of true salvation. I had a treaty with my

194

own soul, to save it. For years I had suffered my own loneliness unassuaged; I had not known the consoling arms and the generous body of love; I had mastered spontaneous little desires, and quelled imagination with the sturdy weapon of deliberate thought. Every physical appetite I had considered and gone about to command, even the incomparable lust for sleep. I did not see how I could, even if I would, cast aside this discipline in one breathless and unthinking moment, not for all the young and melting womanly beauty in the world.

But the shame persisted. I had been wanting in something, and had tried to conceal the lack with words; and the more I thought of it, there in the darkness, in the poised, watching silence of the timeless mountains, the more convinced was I that she had not been deceived, that what I had lacked, somewhere, somehow, was charity. Yet I knew now that I loved her, not only with the heart.

Thus while the long hours before dawn moved slowly on, and the earth turned eastward with ponderous, unthinkable speed, I decided to go away, for I did not see how the two of us could be together in the company of others, this coming day, so soon after the half-achieved communion of the night.

I determined upon going, leaving the two women to be at peace together, leaving Irma to compose her mind while at a distance I tried to do the same. This seemed wisest. Then, after a week had gone by, and time had passed its healing touch over us, I would return, to find what I might; and the thing which—as I knew in my heart—had by no means been concluded there in the warmth of the dying fire might come to proper issue.

There, however, I was wrong.

Jack's note when it came on the following Thursday confounded me. For days, in fact ever since before my arrival back at my flat that Saturday morning, I had been imagining the reunion of the coming week-end, wondering how I would ever pass the time that must be passed. I would arrive once more in the dusk, this time to find the cottage not empty with a cold and polished expectancy but brimming with light and life and the clear, lilting tones of the two faintly foreign voices. Even in the darkness of my departure, as I looked back to where it stood between the fruit trees and the starry pallor of the eastern sky, I must have been imagining how it would be, because during the unhurried drive down to the city, towards the faint coming of dawn far out above the Pacific that sank unseen with my descent to the plain, I was aware of a compensating element of pleasure underlying the weary discomfort and self-criticism of my thought; and this stayed with me, and grew as clearer thinking made room for it, all through the next few days, until Thursday.

For a moment I was as confounded by Jack's note as a child is by the calm removal of a treasured plaything. I was at once indignant and inconsolable. It was in that moment that I finally, wordlessly admitted, by what I felt without thinking, how much the image of Irma, her voice, her silences, the lightness and neatness of all her movements, the feel and weight of her abandoned person in my arms, and her self within this sensible show—and even the immortal soul within the mortal self—had come to mean to me. Imagination had been secretly feeding love more quickly than the reality could have done. The result, as I deciphered old Jack's calm, untutored pencilling, was devastating.

Now, being poorer and richer in heart, and also wiser, I can perhaps look back with the feeling of a smile at my reactions then, and at what I felt, a week later, when I saw that *Bulletin* poster on the street corner. For all my aspirations towards what seemed to me the aloofness essential to living and working well, I was young still, and my youth gave itself away—the beating heart, the indignation as at a betrayal, and the deeper, more helpless feeling of deprivation and despair. Irma must have had her own reasons for such a sudden retreat. (Later I found out what these were, and they were simple: with my unexpected, unexplained departure, she felt once again unsafe. I had behaved unpredictably after all—twice in a matter of hours, by two improbable withdrawals from her—and all her uneasiness returned. She felt she must disappear yet more completely, and as two days passed, then three, without word from me or about me, her speculations again became fearful. The thought that returned to obsess her, until it assumed unreasonable proportions, was that in my work I was mysteriously connected with the police. On the third day, after Jack's return from another fruitless visit to my mail-box nailed to its tree at the junction of track and road, she decided to move; and with her, decision was always action, as I might have known. By noon on the fourth day, she was gone, dragging Miss Werther with her as far as Blacktown on the way back to the city, where they parted, and the Jewess last saw her waiting, severe and unapproachable and somehow pathetically childlike, for a train that would take her beyond the mountains, which now, since her visit to Hill Farm, began to look to her like a bastion enclosing security. She seemed to think that by crossing them she would out-distance fear, and be safe.)

At the time I did not know her well enough, or know enough about her history, to have followed her reasoning for myself. The main obstacle to my understanding of what seemed her obscure motives was also simple: it would have taken much to make me believe that it was now I of whom she was now uncertain and miserably suspicious to the point of fear. In my mental arrogance I would not readily have believed that after she had been rescued, so to speak, by me and comforted by me, held in my arms and caressed and kissed by me, she could doubt my integrity or my feelings for her. What I would not have taken into account, the very thing that must have weighed most in her measuring of the situation, was the fact that—with whatever goodwill to us both mattered not—I had rejected an offer made for the first time in her life with utter unselfishness, and by a fierce stroke of irony for the first time declined. She was above all a woman, intensely conscious of the fact too, and however well her mind had been trained in the vicious schools of political cunning she had attended, this awareness of her essential self must have fretted instinct when reason might have thrust it aside. In effect, I was not to be wholly trusted; but at the same time no amount of argument would have convinced me that that was her chief reason for vanishing westward while I pleased myself, in the midst of a world poised above chaos, with dreams of our less troubled reunion in fewer days than—had I but known it—there were to be years between our parting on the genial hearth and our next meeting.

I was driven further towards desperation by McMahon. Since his tipsy collision with me in the side entrance that afternoon, he too had been from time to time obsessed with the thought of Irma, for reasons very different from my own. It seems he had seen her once in the back bar of the Newcastle Hotel in George Street, not far from the Quay, when he was hobnobbing with one of his numerous sources of political scandal in what then was the only saloon bar in the city which would serve women; and this man, a self-styled Communist I gathered, had had much to say about Irma into McMahon's neat, uninquisitive-looking ear. Some of it was the truth, much of it hearsay and guess-work, and not a little of it simple malicious invention; for it was apparently true enough that the girl was jealously or nervously disliked now by many Australian members of the Party which she had flatly and unequivocally abandoned. Moreover, with her exotic appearance—and in the dark and shabby back bar of the Newcastle, crowded with those second-rate artists and writers and musicians and artists' models who seemed to enjoy the glamour of being mistaken for politically intelligent thinkers, she must have looked exotic and exciting indeed—she should have been more approachable than she was; for such was her aloofness that it was even rumoured (among those who could have thought of few more slurring accusations) that she was a virgin, who had won more by unhonoured promises than her Party sisters had by enthusiastic performances.

Possibly she had seen that they were talking about her, for before he could think out some means of approaching her in person she had disappeared. Now he was sometimes quite sure, sometimes uncertain, that he had seen her in my company. Even had he known that she had vanished, shepherded by little fat Miss Werther, into the back seat of the waiting car there, it would have meant little to him then, for he did not know that the car was mine, and I took care he never should learn this. According to his state of mind, he now taxed me with having secret acquaintance with her, now settled irresistibly in my visitors' chair for a discussion of her rumoured history.

I was nonplussed. Any too-emphatic denial, any indignation at his friendly, careless gossiping, would have made him really suspicious. That is the sort of man he was. That is why he had made such a name for himself: he missed nothing—nothing but an objective view of his own shortcomings. He was, even to me, potentially dangerous. I soon understood why it was that his political contacts talked so freely to him: they felt an urgent need to divert his attention from themselves . . .

He did me one service, however. He did talk of Irma, and so enabled me to think once more of her as apart from me, rather than a part of me. She began to stand as it were one step away, at once more vivid and more unattainable than she had ever seemed. I found the contemplation of her, thus, more painful and less soothing than one would have expected. Heard of from the neat lips of the mildly-intoxicated, friendly McMahon, who was in fact ignorant of any real connection between us, she became intolerably real, being imagined, and, being absent, wellnigh intolerably desirable. More than once I had to plead an engagement, and leave him, the room, the office itself. I was unwillingly and ridiculously in love with a girl of nineteen.

This state of mind, rather like the exultation of despair, persisted up to and beyond the ill-omened twenty-ninth of that month, August—up to and beyond the declaration of a state of war between Australia and Germany which followed Mr. Chamberlain's announcement to the empire; it survived the voice of the Australian Prime Minister that evening of the third of September, and my own few minutes of still almost incredulous horror as I realized that Alan must now grow up in a world at war. Without interrupting work or the times of waking and sleeping, it existed along with these, so entirely that I could be said to have been living two lives. Only Barbara, and Hubble, whom I did not count as important now that Irma had disappeared even from my own ken—only they knew that something was changed in me; but only Barbara guessed what it was.

Although we spoke intimately, we did not make intimacy a personal matter; and so I was surprised when, on the afternoon of the first day of September, the official first day of Spring, after a not unusual silence during which each of us had been occupied with private thoughts, she spoke abruptly about myself.

'Lloyd, I know it's not my business, but I've been wondering—are you in love?'

Her tone was light and apologetic, as though she felt she must ask the question and be done with it, lest, unasked, it stand between us. I too had known that my preoccupation with thoughts of Irma had set up from time to time a barrier as it were of glass; but I was surprised at the direct question—surprised but not disconcerted, because after listening to McMahon on several occasions I now had a desire, the more suspect to me the more it grew in urgency, to speak of her myself, to cleanse my memory of some of the things that neat, dangerous, friendly little man had said.

Warily—and it shows my state of mind when I say I was already capable of being cautious even with Barbara—I pretended not to understand.

'I mean with that girl,' Barbara said.

'You mean with Miss Martin, the model?'

'I mean with Miss Martin the woman. Oh come on, Lloyd—forget I spoke.'

Her affectionate mockery was disarming. I had known her for more than eight years; with Irma I had not passed eight hours. How could I dissimulate further? Nevertheless, as the affair was not yet by any means clear in my mind, I avoided an answer as straight as her amiable question deserved.

'Barbara, I don't know what it is to fall in love. Miss Martin has made me feel pity and indignation on her behalf. She has thrown herself on my mercy—if you allow the exaggeration. What sort of a man would I be not to be moved by all this, and affected by having done all I could to help a fellow-creature who was afraid?'

'Who *was* afraid?' she said. 'Then she isn't any more?'

'Heaven knows,' I said. 'I do not even know where she is, now.'

'You mean she ran away even from you? Oh surely, Lloyd . . .'

202

'No,' I said. 'I mean I ran away from her, if you like to put it like that.'

Barbara said 'Oh' and paused, and then said it again in a different way. I saw she was half-smiling.

'What do you mean by that?

'I mean,' she said, 'that you've answered my question, and also I'm sorry I asked it. As I said, it is no business of mine. Forgive me, Lloyd.'

'Nothing to forgive,' I said. I looked at her directly, and was moved to see how good she was. The conversation drifted.

'One sometimes asks a question thoughtlessly, and realizes too late it was a piece of juvenile impertinence.'

'Not between you and me, Barbara.'

'Well, thoughtlessness between you and me would be a pity, in any circumstances.'

'I don't think you did ask a thoughtless question. I think you wanted to know, and I can even answer it in a way. The girl seems to have become a temporary obsession, that's all. I cannot get free of the thought of what sort of a world it must be that can create such a set of circumstances and place someone like that in the middle of them—like a moth in a spider's web.'

How well it sounded then, and how ignobly near the truth it was, I thought afterwards.

'What do you think of the girl herself? Is she—you know—as innocent as the moth?'

'No,' I said, driven to frankness. 'To me that is the tragedy of the thing. She is a warning example of the double meaning of Henley's claim to be the master of his fate. As for being the captain of one's soul, that is so much nonsense. It always puts me in mind of a Manly ferry. No. This young woman, Irma, has herself to blame for her present state. That is not either tragic or abnormal, I know, in human life. What is, is this—that she had long since cut herself off completely, as she thought, from the sort of life she had been forced to life. She wasn't forced in the beginning, but who is going to condemn a child of fourteen, barely fourteen, a precocious child at that, familiar with most of the major cities of Europe ever since she could remember first being dragged about the continent by her mad musician of a father—who is going to condemn someone like that, a mere child, for making a wrong choice from the generous fullness of her heart, and not realizing it for three or four years? Yet the fact remains that she did choose to become a Communist at that age, and now she is paying for it. The life she thought she had done with is catching up with her, even in Australia. She regards this country as her last refuge, and suddenly finds that for her it is no safer than anywhere else in the world. To you and me that might seem unbelievable, even at a time like this, but not to her. And not to me now, after I have heard what she had to say. You will be interested to know that my belief in whatever she told me was prompted in the first place by her warning, ten days before it happened, that there would be this Russo-German pact. I believed her then sufficiently to pass the information on to Scott and the police for what it was worth.'

'I see,' Barbara said. 'I wondered at the time why I got a special memo asking me to send anything to do with Russia to the editor before getting it set.'

204

'So you see,' I said, 'how one would be ready to believe other things, in retrospect anyhow, such as her insistence that she was in personal danger from some European Communists pretending to be refugees who arrived by the same ship. At first, I admit, it sounded suspiciously like a motion-picture melodrama or an Oppenheim thriller—what are you laughing at?'

'I was just thinking of the picture your words gave me—the poor child telling you all this, and you clutching your beard and looking more and more aloof. Do go on.'

'But I don't clutch my beard,' I said, taking hold of it; and so we both laughed, and I realized it was my first easy laugh for many dreary days.

'Well, that was what made me suggest my place in the mountains. We managed to get away—she and a Jewish friend of hers named Linda—good lord!'

'What is it?'

'Miss Werther. I had forgotten her. I should have rung her up. I imagined she must have gone too—what a fool!'

'Just a moment,' Barbara said. 'You haven't told me the rest of story. How did you get away. Do you want to use this phone?'

'It can wait now,' I said. 'Only one of the copy-boys could have guessed that we left this building together. It was rather a fantastic business, but she wanted it that way. She had been trailed, she thought, since she left her lodgings that day, but had put her watcher off, she believed. Our only moment of danger was when Tim McMahon came in just as we were about to leave. He was rather tipsy. He thought he recognized her—he did recognize her, I mean, but he was not sure whether I knew her or not. He's been trying to find out ever since.'

'McMahon,' she said. 'You know, of course, that he's in very deep with the local Communists?'

'But Barbara—he's a Catholic.'

'Doesn't matter. Con happened to tell me a few things about Tim McMahon once, when he was in a bit of a rage over one of his bad Canberra articles. What I say is quite true. He's not a Party member—no, he's something worse. A sort of under-cover man.'

I was trying to remember the various monologues McMahon had treated me to lately, and to review them in the light of what Barbara had told me. He might have been doing his best to find out not what I knew about Irma but whether I knew where she was. After all, the man was not always drunk, and often, I felt sure, not as drunk as it suited him to pretend to be. I had learned to recognize him sober by a seemingly natural mannerism of his, of removing his spectacles and slowly polishing the thin convex lenses round and round, revealing in full by this action a face that looked curiously blind and anxious, the helpless face of a man incapable of duplicity. I imagined I had noticed him doing this more often of late; and he had assuredly returned to that one subject by direct or oblique ways which in another man would have been boring. McMahon, even when he was being a nuisance and an unwelcome interruption, was never boring. He himself saw to that. One could not help listening to him. I realized it was possible that he had mentioned seeing Irma apparently with me to someone to whom there might have been more in it than there was to McMahon himself—at first. It would need but a word, to a good Party sympathizer ('See if Fitzherbert knows where she's got to, Tim.'), to put him on his mettle and on Irma's trail where it appeared to vanish as it joined mine.

'He came in, rather unsteady, and bumped into me, and his hat fell off. There may have been more to all this than I realized, after what you've just told me. He muttered something about "the little lady Communist" as though they knew one another—by name and sight, at least. What I'm wondering now is why she didn't say anything to me about him later? As we drove off I noticed in the mirror that she seemed to have had a bad shock, but I thought it was just the strain of getting away quickly. I must try to find out more about him.'

'I may be able to tell you enough,' she said, and I realized suddenly how seldom and how impersonally she spoke of other members of the staff, even to me. It was this that made one feel so safe with her, this that with her fine habit of tolerance towards others helped to make her a woman of such quality.

'I was thinking of Irma's point of view,' I said. 'Miss Werther may be able to tell me, if she is in Sydney after all. I do not want to get anyone involved with McMahon through my own ignorance, you understand. These things can be so messy . . .'

'Tell me the rest of your adventure,' she said.

'We got to Hill Farm, and had a very pleasant evening. They seemed to settle down well, and old Jack quite took to them, I was glad to see. Evidently there are women and women, after all, even for that famous misogynist. We went to bed fairly early. At half past one she woke me by making up the fire in the big room—it was a cold night. She had not been able to sleep. We talked for a while in whispers, sitting by the fire.'

It all came back vividly, painfully, as I spoke about it at last: her face in the firelight, her fingers on my hand, the weight and warmth of her across my knees, the swelling heat of her lips against my own, and the eventual silence.

'She seemed to think I expected some return for helping her. I had not even thought about being kind. She apparently thought of it all as deliberate kindness, and she—she could think of only one way to repay me that was within her power. I understood well enough what she meant. I said it was too much to accept . . . You don't think me shameless to talk like this? I am trying to explain what happened later.'

'Go on,' she said with a sigh, looking down at her hands on the table intently.

'You know, I suppose, that all new human contacts are somehow embarrassing to me, as well as being very interesting. One tries not to let either the interest or the embarrassment show. As for casual love affairs, I can understand their attraction without ever feeling it—without ever seeing myself give way to it, I mean. That night, everything that might have been propitious for another man was wrong for me, the way I am apparently made. She had come to me for help, and I gave the best I could think of. She was in my own house, and also, in a way, quite at my mercy. That evening she had been exquisitely lovely because she was happy. And above all, she made the offer—it was no suggestion, it was a pathetically generous offer—she made it herself. For anyone else, to take her at her word would have been not only easy and delightful, it would have seemed the only decent—yes, *decent*—thing to do. For me it was not like that. There were other considerations, very deep ones. Say if you like I am made unnaturally, but understand that for me to have taken her at her word—and I assure you I really react no differently from the way other men do at such times—to have taken her at her word then, of all moments, would have been exactly the opposite of decent. I expect you, as a woman, to see that it would have been calamitous, another chapter very like previous ones, I gather, added to her unhappy story. Added, as usual, by her own helpless contriving. I feel sometimes that that girl craves for one thing only—complete extinction . . . For my part, it would have been a self-betrayal. You will not laugh at this, I know. My personal ideals may be ridiculous in a world like ours, but to my best ability I am loyal to them.'

'My dear boy,' she said softly, looking up wide-eyed, 'I will certainly not laugh. Do go on—we are friends.'

'It is because you are the truest friend I have that I talk like this. Someone must know—I must tell someone.'

'Tell me, then.'

'I am loyal to those ideals, and nothing can be, or seem to be, so selfishly, bitterly cruel to other people as this kind of loyalty. It appears to benefit only the person practising it. It appears to. But I tell you, Barbara, it is most difficult to sustain, in the welter of human contacts and relationships, because of the way a man is made. Self-indulgence gets more friends than self-denial, and always has. This loyalty needs constant protection against many of the common human characteristics of the man himself, and demands many sacrifices. The sacrifices are not chosen by the loyalist, they are merely unforeseen and not understood by the victim, whose very misunderstanding as often as not makes the sacrifice a voluntary one—and, as I say, an unforeseen one. One thing always happens then. The loyalist is held to blame.'

'Yes,' she said slowly, 'I admit for a moment I did feel a bit shocked. I knew what she must have felt. Now I see what you mean.'

'Well,' I said, 'that is what happened. I could see no other possible choice.'

'That was what you meant about running away?'

'That was it, in a way. I suppose I did start my departure from that moment. I left before daylight. Since then, all I know is what old Jack had to tell me,' and I took out and handed to her the note I had carried about with me ever since, reading and re-reading it with less and less surprise, more and more misery. That perfect picture (did he but know it) of the two women hearing for the first time the appalling cry of the screech-owl that lived higher up the mountain above the plateau was what moved me more than most of what he had to say; that, and the mention of how the younger one 'nearly through a fit' when she found I had gone secretly away. Yet quite evidently there was nothing else I could have done about it.

'That is all I know,' I said. 'She has gone completely this time, as far as I am concerned. The trail is lost unless Miss Werther knows—if she did not go with her. I don't suppose she did. It would be impossible to guess where Irma would stop, if she stops at all. As for me, I would not say I had fallen in love with her. I just cannot forget her.'

'You see why she left the cottage, I suppose?'

I shook my head unhappily: no.

'Why, because of you, silly,' she said. 'Your behaviour was unfamiliar. Nothing more—not insulting, as you seem to think, just unfamiliar. To anyone like Miss Martin the unfamiliar would be highly suspect. She probably found she couldn't believe in you fully—you know the expression, too good to be true—and what a woman can't believe in she doesn't trust for a moment. So she went. Poor child—but what else could she do? You must see, Lloyd, she wasn't in your position. She didn't have a choice, she had no ideals left to fortify her, the only sacrifice she could make was the one you repudiated, however kindly. I only say this because I want you to feel you see her side of it as well as your own.'

'I have been trying to do that for over a week, and now you have done it for me. It makes it no easier for me, personally, to know that I can do nothing for her now. The whole thing is complex. I ask myself whether to hold on to one's personal ideals is not just an extreme form of vanity, an insane egotism, and yet, you see, if I did not remain loyal to mine I cannot see what good I would be to anyone else in the world—and of course by that I mean Alan. When I reach that point in this interminable argument, the moral question arises whether such an attitude to a son is not unnatural in a father, whether it is not perhaps sowing seeds of future trouble when the boy is grown and aware of me and able to think a bit for himself. To this I answer myself, in the persons both of interrogator and of witness, that a

211

part of my self-discipline, even now, is to learn to make no demands upon him whatever. To do without love. I do not want love, I want him to be free of me from the beginning. In fact, Barbara, I had to choose that night between the boy and the woman, and I chose the boy. Habit. I would always choose him, so long as I could be of use to him. That is why—now I see it plain enough—the choice was inevitable.'

'You don't suppose that by choosing the boy you reasserted to yourself your right to a claim on him?'

She surprised me.

'It could be so,' I said. 'If it actually was so, then the best thing I could do for both our sakes would be to go out and shoot myself.'

'Don't be extreme, Lloyd,' she said mildly. 'I imagine you are doing what you think is right and good the whole time. Wasn't it the counsel of Polonius to his son, "To thine own self be true"? Isn't that the advice you're trying to follow?'

'I don't know, Barbara, I don't know. One question's answer seems merely to ask yet another question, until I feel I am getting nowhere. It could easily be that I set far too much store by what I dare to suppose is my future importance to Alan. Yet supposing I were—not there, so to speak—and he wanted me, and later I learned of it, later when it was too late. You see, I am obsessed with the feeling that I must always be there, the whole of me. So often my father was not there when I did need him, without knowing it. Alan is spiritually unarmed. Most naturally optimistic boy-children are like that—taking knock after knock and unable to help coming up smiling. I cannot bear to think of

212

that as his future—I would be so deeply to blame, if I did the easy thing and went after my own interests regardless of him. He will remain unarmed until he gets his first real wound—and god have pity on whoever gives it to him.'

Barbara said nothing for a while, but sat looking at the pale fingertips of one immaculate hand. At last she looked up with a slight smile to say, 'I can't help wishing you could take this business of fatherhood a bit less seriously, a bit more easily. I can't help thinking a certain amount of harmless irresponsibility on your part might be for the ultimate good of you both. Take that as the passing thought of a mere woman, if you like, but do take it, and bring it out one day for consideration.'

'You are giving me Eve's counsel, lady,' I said mildly, 'and you know what came of that.'

'Yes,' she said, and her shrewd eyes flashed suddenly, 'Adam's awakening to true wisdom through what is called sin or suffering by some, and self-realization by others. Adam's separation of himself from his god, so that he learned to worship something other than himself. That's what came of Eve's counsel, and much thanks she's had for it—nothing but the execrations of every Adam ever since, poor thing.'

'Don't let us talk about it,' I said. 'Tell me about yourself instead of about Eve. We must be topical. How are things at home?'

'All right,' she said, recovering herself with her usual disconcerting ease. 'I don't care for all this nonsense about the maternal show of bravery and a stiff upper lip. Brian is ready to go, and we're going to do without his visits for as long as we have to. My main trouble is with old Molly. All the Irish is coming out in that woman—the crying Irish, with occasional unconvincing bursts of the fighting Irish. You'd think he was her own only son, instead of mine and one of three, by the way she goes on. I sometimes wish Con hadn't been so fond of her for the shameless fun he used to get out of playing up to her. I could do with someone a little—firmer—in fibre just now. Ever since Con died she's set herself against my way of bringing up the boys. It's still going on. Patrick and Terence still lean her way a bit in their weaker moments. I wish they could have gone to that school of Alan's.'

'The only thing I have doubts about, as far as Alan is concerned, is that Townsend's system may give him the idea that there is a virtue in not conforming mainly to the social pattern. I may be wrong. I foresee him going through a period when he has more imagination and intelligence than he can cope with at his age. When he is twelve he will go on to Shore, I hope, and live with boys only. I cannot say I care much for the idea of boys and girls living in close proximity for the first years of adolescence.'

'I wish I had a daughter,' she said. 'I don't want to become one of those mothers people mean when they say, "She simply lives for her boys." That awful gaiety, Lloyd!'

'I know what you mean. They are, in fact, sexually abnormal, and it seems to me about time our society recognized the fact, instead of praising it under the name of devotion. Not many people know the real meaning of the word. It is misused to hide a number of gross crimes of conduct.'

'How stern you look when you talk like that,' she said. 'Like a sea-captain ashore—still stern and dependable even as a pedestrian.'

'Especially the pedestrian part,' I said. She waved that aside. 'What I want to know is, what are you going to do about yourself?' she said.

'Work.' I got up to go. 'Tell me one thing. Why have there been none of the usual interruptions today?'

Her easy smile lightened her answer: 'I had a feeling it might be the last talk of this sort we'd have for a time, so I told them in the other room I simply wouldn't be in if you came. I bet that made them smile knowingly—or are they used to us by now? Tell me, Lloyd, just what do the people here think of you and me? I'm really shamefully out of touch with the rest of the office, most of the time.'

'I never bother to wonder what people think here,' I said. 'Ours is not the only innocent friendship in the place, though I doubt whether any of the others is as good and as lacking in self-interest.'

She laughed. 'You do keep yourself untouchable, don't you. I hope you always can. I hope you're always spared the self-betrayals the world offers us so often.'

A minute or two later I left her. The next time we met, during the following week, her son had been sent to an advanced training unit. We were officially at war with Germany, and the final over-running of Europe had begun. Her feeling about our last talk had not been wrong.

For the men and women of my profession, or trade as my father had insisted upon calling it ('for come, my boy, admit

215

you will be trading in the human passions, from intelligent curiosity down?'), the six years of active warfare could be described as years of prosperous discomfort.

There was almost an over-supply of news made ready to hand. 'The war angle' applied to everything, from women's fashions to stock-sales at Homebush and crime in Darlinghurst. The idea of violence and death, incomprehensible still, became commonplace and meaningless, its mysterious fascination now only a legend. We knew they were impressive years. What we did not realize, because of their often brilliantly-lighted darkness, was that they were to impress and alter beyond remembrance the whole mind and manner of the civilian community.

The men and to a less degree the women in uniform were impressed and altered under our very eyes, even before they had gone abroad. We expected this. They became men and women of another race, unconscious initiates into the mystery of how to be a sheep proudly, hardly less strange though of course more nearly related to us than were the plump, heavy-drinking, over-courteous young Americans with their—to us—astonishing, naively uncouth adolescence who came to the country later, on the heels of General MacArthur.

The war, the idea of it, claimed them at once. As they dressed differently, so they thought—when they did think—differently; and the others, the men and women of the civilian front, showed them a startling degree of humility that was to continue for the duration. Once more, as in my own childhood, the voice of the fighting man was heard up and down the land, like a drunkard's in a church hall during a welfare-society meeting. It was heard and listened to, suffered with every appearance of enthusiasm, and obeyed with a readiness that must have been gratifying to those minds that could be called normal only in such abnormal times. The old values, the old words, the thoughts of the philosophers and the poets, were for a long time forgotten, or, remembered, remembered mostly with impatient scorn. This was war, the killing season. Man's life and soul, it seemed, could be divided into those of the man of the time of peace, and of him of the time of war, two men without a bond between them. The bombs fell, the guns dinned, the blood ran brightly, and the future of the race was not worth imagining.

Through it all, the news flowed in along overburdened channels of wire and air, coming from all over the continent and all over the world. There were no silly seasons now, those times in the newspaper year when it seems impossible to fill the paper, when news-editors become irritable, and the youngest cadet suspects an underlying futility in his joyfully-chosen profession . . . or trade. On the contrary, most of us were over-worked, and some received more money than was good for them. Money had begun to change hands with its inevitable wartime carelessness, because no costs were being counted anywhere, except in the hearts of a few men and women; and the whole country's sudden preoccupation with secondary production, factory work, not only denuded the land, the whole source and security of Australia's existence, of men and the girls they should have married, but also set free a flood of currency which, like the workers, swirled into and round about the capital

217

cities so that from very early in the years of war the face of city existence was suddenly and ominously changed.

The Americans, when at last they came in interesting enough numbers, were never absorbed, as they were to some extent later in Europe, where fragments of their roots still clung, for here the native-born community, barely eight million strong, would have been too small even in peace time; and now, with hundreds of thousands of younger men and women—approaching one-eighth of the population in the end—in uniform and often engaged overseas, the friendly, boastful youngsters from across the Pacific, eager as adolescents in their sexual curiosity, their uncomprehending enthusiasms and their schoolboy passion for food and drink, were conspicuous to the very end. Wherever they went, in Australia as in other parts of the world, they never quite achieved popularity with the people, despite their efforts, despite what they and we were told; but the years of advance publicity spread by talking-pictures and imported gramophone records and wireless programmes made them in one way or another invariably spectacular; and the impression they in turn made upon the life of the bigger cities has endured—sometimes tragically. We were to discover the secret of the American way of life—that it offered the greatest ease for the least effort; or, as one of their officers told me with a wink as rich and heavy as a slice of fruit-cake, 'pleasure without payin', son—pleasure without payin'.'

But they paid—they paid for everything, willingly and twice over, and nearly overthrew our own domestic economy by the effect their full pockets and liberal ways had upon prices.

I had quite a lot to do with them, both on and off duty; and, though I found it was possible to accustom oneself to the curious hollow unreality of what they claimed, with sharp, parrot-like cries, to be that American way of life, I could never overcome a depressing shyness of those who lived it and took it with them wherever they went—and they went everywhere. Nor could I ever believe, in spite of what I had read and heard about that country, that the young men, and the men not so young in the higher posts, who invaded our already chaotic life to its further gross confusion were characteristic of the powerful nation they were said to represent.

However, they were news. Their presence affected the papers themselves, and their staffs. We chose to trace to it the most startling development in latter-day Australian newspaper history, when *The Sydney Morning Herald*, the property of generations of Fairfaxes, older than the *Gazette*, abandoned its old-style, conservative 'open-up' lay-out (based on that of *The Times* of London, of which it had long been a devoted if not always impressive under-study) for the modern American front-page presentation of the morning news. As well as recurrent and inevitable special articles about the young American soldier abroad (including a couple of my own in which I was allowed to hint at the effect these foreigners were having on Australian crime methods and statistics), we printed for their benefit and that of their numerous Australian friends (and even more numerous parasites) more and more news from the United States, of a sort we had not bothered to use before. It meant a recasting of our American offices. At the same time, America wanted more news—of the acceptable, 'we're-over-there' sort—from our own end, and their papers mostly had their own representatives, as well as those of the big press agencies, in Australia, so that even the newspapers felt within their walls the full impact of the invasion.

It is said that out of it all, out of the increased tragedies and mis-marriages and other youthful crimes (including the soft debauchery of a surprising number of adolescent girls in the cities) good came, in the firmer drawing-together of the two young nations; until today they are like suburban neighbours of different ways of life but with a street, a fence and some opposed windows in common—friendly enough to borrow each other's gardening tools and repair outfits, so to speak, but still no more than deliberately amiable strangers, with nothing more in common than a common regard, on the part of each, for what may be gained at least cost to face and fortune from the other.

The war years saw the commencement of this super-ficially enthusiastic playing at good neighbours, while to us the Australian way of life, in climates ranging from the tropical to the temperate—but no lower, except in the snow playgrounds and pastures of the eastern Alps—still seemed preferable, in spite of the heightened clamour in our midst. It was a way of living more like that of the pure British convict stock from which a large part of the population had descended, and its snobbery continued to be concerned with origins and traditions belonging to the British islands from which our ancestors had departed, no matter how ungracefully, as pioneers of a new nation. When, towards the conclusion of armed action, British fighting men from the three desperately-tested services passed through on their way north and east, they were greeted not with caution but with the joy and fury that so often characterize a reunion of blood brothers. It was then that the tragedy of the American way of life suddenly showed clear; we saw that they were a sovereign people without a sovereign, with no fixed object for their love or their hate save only one another, not even a cultural heritage, like that of France, to bind them together gladly at the foot of Democracy's empty throne. By contrast, to our people the British on their way through were as irresistible as a breath of fresh air in a bedroom through the opened window of morning.

Through all this, my own work increased considerably, and I had no assistance in it, for by nineteen forty-two we were seriously short of staff, when the Japanese approached from the north and the most unlikely men suddenly appeared on the streets in uniform. That was no bad thing, for it helped me to keep the piling horrors of warfare as made by my own generation at a certain distance from the point where recognition of them would have threatened sane behaviour. Sane I knew I must keep me, for Alan's sake if for no other reason; for in a convulsed world he was growing nearer to adolescence, nearer to that moment where, as I foresaw it, our ways must separate to run apart for a time on near-parallel lines separated by a whole generation; that moment when—also perhaps for a time only—our half-wordless intimacy of the blood must end, and we must begin to speak new languages, I his, he mine.

During his four years at S. Johns school, about which the brief controversies now rose less often and more quickly subsided, he had developed into his true self in a way that was delightful and astonishing. He was not to be called precocious; Townsend and his wife did not encourage such false growth; but he bloomed fully and freely into a kind of boyhood which filled me with a hot pride I was ashamed to reveal. The perfect, normal health of his flexible young body was repeated in the health and quality of his mind. He never lost what he found at that modest, eccentric school-home—a sort of brightness as it were of the spirit cupped in the cupped hands of secret reserve and quiet generosity. Above all, he had neither malice nor deceit in his heart. I never knew him to lie, or to countenance with amused composure lies in others of his age. The one thing in his character which gave me most unease was his habit of single-minded optimism. It appeared, indeed, when he first learned to walk; and the impulsive fears for his safety which I then suffered I underwent, for always-differing reasons, a hundred, a thousand times subsequently. Then and always, he saw the end and smilingly took for granted the rightness and inevitability of the means—not always wisely, not always successfully. Failure in an enterprise stunned him into temporary incredulity and slow, unchildlike, old-man's tears; success turned him silent and brilliant, or dreamy-eyed at the tremendous thoughts of further conquests of the world of matter and energy. He had from infancy a habit of sitting silent on the edge of his bed in the dark of early evening. Once, when I thoughtlessly asked him what he was doing, he told me without self-consciousness or what would have been a pardonable irritation, 'Just thinking.' It seemed to be a conscious, planned act of thought, after

222

the manner of the religious who withdraws from habits and surroundings at certain times of the day consciously to commune with divinity.

When he was twelve years old, after four years of living rather aloof both from me and from the whole wartime society of those days, he left S. Johns for Shore, as the great Church of England grammar school is called, as a boarder. I chose that school, rather to my mother's distress, when Alan was still a child, for the fact that its final products were boys who had not suffered the rather stifling religious indoctrination of the no less notable Catholic schools, and whose manner and faintly awkward social grace had always appealed to me. My father, after turning the matter over in his mind without comment, told me he thought the choice a wise one, especially when he understood that, as at S. Johns, those whose parents expected it could go to Mass in the ordinary way without being stigmatized or even singled out because of it.

For his own part, my father had never tolerated the idea of putting me to a boarding-school, and I have suffered the lack of that experience all my life. I wanted Alan to be not my own son so much as his own man, above all things, and as soon as might be. When he left S. Johns, in the fullness of summer a fortnight before Christmas, when the whole land was hot and glowing with colour and sun, my mother 'gave' us Miss Molesley—Alan still called her Moley—and I invited her to be my housekeeper permanently, and found her a good room with a view in one of the quieter streets near the Cross and a few minutes' walk from my flat. The war, and the death of her only brother, had aged her noticeably, but she was still an agreeable woman, an intelligent and economic cook in a country where women are no longer always either or both; and Alan was as dear to her prim old virgin's heart as though he were indeed what she called him—'little brother'. As one addicted to the teachings of theosophy, she used the expression easily, but with an especially tender inflection for the boy scarcely one-quarter her age. (Me she had called 'Judge'—to my mother's secret and half-amused indignation—ever since my father died.)

Moley looked after us both, during the holidays, when Alan slept in the big bedroom next to mine at night and by day was freely busy with his own concerns and his successive hobbies. She would wait until I returned, no matter what the hour, and then walk fearlessly and unescorted back to her room through a district that was coming to be known as dangerous. When assignments kept me away at night, as happened occasionally, she used the day-bed in the living-room with its tall windows overlooking the great curve of the harbour north and east to the Heads. It was on these nights that she taught Alan card games. She was a great addict to the cards, and to dramatic and soft-spoken tea-cup reading now and then, when we were *en famine*. In spite or because of the great difference in their ages, and also because of the fever and passionate unrest of the world that throbbed and threatened in the near distance, they drew very close to one another again after the years of separation; and I was content to see it, for Alan was at a time of life when it is good for a boy to have as companion and mentor, if he has not his own mother, a loving, trusting and unsuspicious woman of much older years, when he is not among his own kind. The point of departure between us two, the point of no return, had come, and gone, even sooner than I expected it, and gradually I found myself in the last year of the war faced with a return to my earlier ways of solitude and underlying loneliness.

It was not that Alan withdrew himself. He seemed if anything more friendly and confiding, and sometimes I caught him looking at me with thoughtful surprise, as though for the first time he were seeing in my familiar form the problematical and unknown. No—there was no withdrawal from the innocent and merry intimacy in which we had for some years dwelt like conspirators against time and the world; rather it was as if, with the inexhaustible energy of his youth, he raced ahead, looking back to see at what speed I followed, or if indeed I followed at all.

I was particularly aware of this at the end of his first public-school year, when he came home for the summer wild with plans for sharing the holidays with one or two of the new friends he had made.

At the beginning of the last week of term, early in December, he called me by telephone at the office in the early afternoon. The air-conditioning plant had broken down again during a brief spell of abnormal heat, and the big room was full of still air that seemed to have been breathed several times. I had been at work on a difficult story since mid-morning, writing, telephoning, going out to an interview, writing again and once or twice checking the story, as it progressed, with the police. In order to make the most of what remained of that day's quiet inside the office, before the majority of the editorial staff came in at two o'clock, I did not go out to lunch but remained doggedly at my table. I was hungry, thirsty and half-stifled by the soft heat, smelling of petrol fumes and hot tar, that had drifted in from the glittering black streets to the very core of the building, when my telephone rang once again. It was Alan.

'Hullo, Daddy, isn't it hot? Daddy, are you—do you want to come to the school break-up?'

'When is it, Alan?'

'Tomorrow week—um—Thursday.'

I could imagine him, looking vaguely about while he waited for my answer. His voice did not deceive me with its calm affection; the change from 'are you coming' to the less encouraging 'do you want to come' had told me what was in his mind—what had been in my own mind, safely settled, for weeks and months in fact. I remembered my own over-sensitive boyhood days; I remembered what I had once said to Barbara; I remembered and agreed that boys do not necessarily enjoy being seen with fathers who look thin and pale and wear beards. I had my answer ready, but it needed to be given gracefully. The time for small studied pretences between us, devised to ease each other's minds, had come.

'Just a minute, while I take a look at my diary.' I put down the receiver and took up the little book to riffle through some few pages near the mouthpiece, muttering softly to myself. Then I spoke again. 'No—I'm sorry, Alan, but it can't be managed this year. Do you want Grandmother to deputize for me?'

His voice had not shown any trace of concern in the first place, not even when he firmly told me the exact day; but now, irrepressibly, it lifted with a faint, bouyant relief

226

'I wish you would say shillings, Alan, not bob. I shall post you a few bob today.'

'There—you said it yourself! Thank you, Daddy . . . Well, goodbye.'

'Goodbye, Alan, until next week.'

'Goodbye.'

At S. Johns, during his last year there, he had learned to talk without shyness over the telephone to me. As a result, I could enjoy speaking to him at his new school with a pleasure I could not analyse or describe. Always I left the ringing-up to him, though sometimes, on a free evening alone in the flat, I had had to put aside firmly the temptation to ring him up myself. I knew the very time at which to catch him, between evening tea and the hour of preparation boys of his age put in, before racing off at the shrilling of the electric bells to dormitory prayers and the luxurious horseplay and relaxation of undressing for bed. If there were any idleness in his days, it would be at this time. I never did use the telephone, except once, later, on the evening my mother died; but that was quite another matter.

We had, in truth, reached a phase in our relationship in which, for me, such constant caution and self-restraint were necessary that the exercise of them in his presence made me secretly shy of him. By telephone, talking was easier. I did not have to look and be looked at; I did not have to refrain from telling him to say 'shillings' rather than 'bob' and to try, for the sake of his appearance, to give up biting his nails when he was reading. Alone at my end of the telephone, I could allow to show in my face, no doubt, the pleasure I invariably felt at the thought of his youth and youthful beauty of body and mind.

In those years, the interminable years of a war whose fantastic echoes will never cease to sound somewhere in history's corridors, I had no deep personal preoccupation other than with this boy; no wife, no sweetheart or mistress, no love given to myself above all others. When one does not receive, it happens often that one is more able and eager to give; and so I gave him my love. There was no need to stifle or discipline my emotions. They could be hidden. The things I felt, the feelings his memory or his presence aroused in me were always good feelings which would not have harmed him had they been shown; but the disparity of our ages and my own rather undemonstrative bearing made it unlikely that he ever knew more than that I loved him as it is good for a son to be loved, and proper in a father to love an only son. 'Passing the love of women' had once seemed to me a grossly exaggerated phrase characteristic of the worst in biblical prose, but sometimes in these days, with healthy mental and spiritual values going the way of most material values, wherever the mind turned, wherever the ear attended, I thought that phrase might have a meaning I had hitherto not tried to find.

By then it seemed easy for almost any other affection to exceed the love of women. War does that to a community: it allows the expression to be mistaken for the emotion, the gesture for the feeling that once profoundly prompted it. As I kept my habitual watch over the society which in turn kept me, by its insatiable curiosity and hunger for excitement, alert and profitably employed, I could not help thinking again and again how much the young American soldiery had helped forward the moral devaluation, and how unintentionally, above all in the matter of sexual conduct. They were frankly lustful young men, and in spite of a mass-produced veneer of song and dance and exaggerated courtesy towards women—particularly older women—their lust had not even the grace of an animal's. They had apparently been trained from childhood by their monied masters, the industrialists of the sciences and the popular arts, to be obsessed by the life of the body, exaggerating its needs, valuing its outward and inward well-being with a relentless consciousness and to a degree that seemed to me insane. No appetite, they seemed to say, should be denied for a moment longer than could be helped by any means or stratagem; and of every appetite a man should be proud. The word moderation seemed to have come to mean, in their connotation, a state of vitiated abnormality which should quickly be corrected with the aid of drugs, vitamins, serums and stimulants of every kind. As for restraint, that was not a word they used at all.

It may have been the war which emphasized these common characteristics. Certainly, as the world's highest-paid soldiers, they spent their money with an abandon which came naturally to them, and which was soon expected, especially by the young Australian women, who, now that their brothers and lovers were gone away to fight elsewhere, seemed to crowd the streets of the cities in surprising numbers. Many of these had become women physically since the war's outbreak. Robbed of even the knowledge of the more diffident, naive eroticism of the young men of their own nation and generation, they fell readily into the smooth hands and habits of mind of the foreigners who had come to rescue their country from the Japanese.

Our office policy was to avoid or smother all criticism of our glorious ally across the Pacific. The police, however, were more outspoken, and occasionally even Hubble, that mild man, surprised me by the passion and articulateness of his diatribes: for what I have described as 'unAustralian' crimes had increased both in variety and in numbers. What dollars could not buy could be taken by other means. Their over-large pay and allowances, and the way they spent, came nearer than anything to demoralizing the whole civil life of the cities into which they swarmed, on their way north to death and glory, in the train of the battle-hardened Australian divisions from the Middle East theatres. The *Sydney Bulletin* summed it all up succinctly, as usual, with a drawing of an American soldier helping an Australian wench out of a taxi-cab at Kings Cross: in the two lines of caption, the girl sneeringly asks the cabby, 'What'll you do when the Yanks are gone?' to which he replies tersely, 'What'll *you* do, sister?'

Meanwhile, we had another glorious ally in the Soviets, whose entry into the field came before America's by some months; and at the beginning of nineteen forty-two, with both Russia and America the declared enemies of Germany and her satellites, it was possible—and somehow terrifying—to conceive of eventual victory. A pattern of black and white, spread with apparent carelessness around the globe's surfaces of land and water and in the air above them, began to be discernible; black indicated our enemies and their distribution, and it seemed, on the whole, that the pure white masses—the Western allies, and Russia in the east with China at heel casting a shadow over Japan—were

232

rather better placed, in terms of time and movement. We said to ourselves that, in any case, the aggressor is always at an eventual disadvantage, psychologically and in other ways. It was possible to conceive of ultimate victory; but nobody thought of peace, which was just as well.

After their brief disappearance, the men and women of the Communist Party returned to their former places full of health and strength and with strong and healthy finances, and a natural air of having at last been vindicated. If I had ever hoped to see Irma again, this reinstatement of many who wished her ill seemed to give reason for letting any such hope go from my mind.

By ringing Miss Werther, I had traced her as far as Blacktown station, and there she vanished.

'I wondered if you would ring,' the amiable Jewess said in her lilting voice. 'We have something to talk about. Forgive me if I don't keep you just now on the telephone. Could you come to my office in Castlereagh street, in the shop? Yes? When can you come? I want to thank you for your kindness—to both of us.'

I arranged to visit her the same afternoon, the afternoon I had had that memorable conversation with Barbara; and at a few minutes after half past five she let me into the shop herself. Her eyes and lips wore the remembered gay smile as she crossed with light steps a square of deep, expensive-looking carpet to open the glass door. When I had entered she closed it, letting down the white Venetian blind inside so that we were screened completely from the street. I prepared myself to be thanked again for my 'kindness', and recalled Irma's averted face, her arm linked with

233

mine, her hand on my fingers, the firelight on the delicate skin of her ankles, and her remote voice . . . offering a return for kindness.

It was all so recent then that my heart began to beat heavily in my breast, and for one brief wild moment I wondered whether the little fat Jewess leading me through the front display room to a smaller, less formal room behind it, and across this to the screened doorway of a roomy office, were about to produce to me Irma in person from behind one of the olive-green velvet curtains, as easily and gaily as she would have produced one of her own expensive hoard of furs. But she only moved a deep armchair slightly away from the shaded lamp on the office table, and with a graceful movement of one fat, ringless hand invited me to be seated. She herself took a plain bentwood chair opposite me, full in the light.

'Now,' she said nervously, 'Mr. Fitzherbert, I think it is best I tell you Irma told me what you talked about that night at your cottage. It was all very sad. She does not understand men like you. I don't think she understands any of the really good things in human nature, if I may say so. All her life it has been violence, fear, greed, ambition and one voice shouting down another. Whatever she said to you that night she said for the best. You must not judge her. She didn't know any better, you see. She started life too young. There are some values she never learned to respect.'

She was looking at me intently, her polished black eyes shining tearless and nervous in the light. I had a vivid memory of Irma, all woman, body and mind, knowing so much and yet so little—like a girl in the dawn of physical

234

maturity, like a flower that shows what seems to be the grown seed even before it blooms.

'She talked only of you, the next two days, Mr. Fitzherbert. She has had one love affair in Europe, and it ended in a terrible way, a man who was killed by the Gestapo in Holland. She was too young for all that, you know. It terrified her, because it was the first time she had loved anyone, since her father died. She thought it was mostly her fault he was killed, and so it was in a way, but only partly. She ran away to England, then to here, because Nazis and Communists were both after her now. And you know all the rest, I think. Ah—I am so sorry—would you like a glass of sherry? Yes, please do.'

While she took from the table cupboard a small tray already set with Belgian wine glasses and an exquisite sherry decanter that did not match them except in beauty, I wondered what was the purpose of her preamble; and when she had poured the pale wine, and set the two glasses within our reach, she continued.

'She can never have been a really good Party member, Mr. Fitzherbert. She was young, everybody was becoming afraid of the Nazis, it was something to do to help, and of course all very exciting. They made a sort of pet of her in Berlin, and gave her small missions, and even made her dress like a boy. Poor Irma, she was only a child. She loved it. She believed everything they taught her, everything, especially the things about love having no private place in a society where everything, all ownership, even the human body, was to be in common. That was how she learned first of love—she was only fourteen. What a wonderful society it would be, would it not?'

The abrupt and contemptuous irony of her voice surprised me. It reminded me that I had never really understood how so many Jews could embrace the common-ownership doctrine of the Communist ideology.

'When she fell in love at last with this Maartens, a much older man, she was afraid for the first time of her own Party, and did not know what to do. Well, that was solved for her. The Party in Berlin, for safety's sake—you know she had been pretending to be a genuine Nazi Party member too, by order—the Party let the Nazis know she was Maarten's mistress and that Maartens, as a Communist district leader, was trying to spy on them through her. If she had not heard about this just in time and got away, they would have got her too.'

The picture her words evoked made me feel sick. The idea of the body of a woman one has held in one's arms, however innocently, being 'got' by a cleverly-driven car in a dim midnight street is extraordinarily horrible, especially to anyone who has seen the still-living victims of fatal accidents trying to drag themselves out of the reach of an incomprehensible violence that has already done its work on them. Miss Werther drank some wine, watching me rather nervously still.

'I tell you all this, Mr. Fitzherbert, so you will know what I am going to say next is reasonable . . . Irma wanted you to know she loves you.'

My movement was involuntary, and she affected not to see it as anything but a movement to take the wine glass from the table and raise it to my lips.

'She thought when I saw you again—for she was sure

you would get in touch with me—I could tell you this if I thought it was wise. You see, Mr. Fitzherbert, she tried to tell you that night but it went wrong somehow. The memory of that other love affair, when she was young and ignorant, frightened her when she saw how she was feeling about you. She couldn't help thinking there would be more trouble. Also, you are so—what the French call *gentil*, you know? She was half-afraid of you at the same time because you are different from the other men she has known. It was the first time she thought of her past as perhaps disgraceful to you—that there had been other men. Because she was a good Party member, devoted to the pure beauty of dialectical materialism . . . How terrible her situation becomes, you see, when she realizes what her confused feelings about you really are. And then, in the morning, you are gone, and everything falls to pieces.'

She let her closed hand fall suddenly open in her lap, in a most eloquent gesture of helpless disintegration.

'Like that . . . She does not know what she has done. She knows now she loves you, but all she can think of, every time she tries to get it clear, is that you are somehow in league with the police, and that you know very much about her—all she herself has told you. As you do not want her she sees you cannot love her, so she begins to think you may feel you should let the police know about her, so they can find her if they need to. This makes no difference to what she feels about you, Mr. Fitzherbert. It even makes it worse, so to speak, but now she is afraid again as well.'

'But good heavens,' I said as calmly as I could, 'she must know me better than that. I gave her my word.'

'Do not forget her training, Mr. Fitzherbert. To the Communists, one's word is only something for someone else to take. Giving it means nothing. Also you are mistaken. She did not know you. I do not know you. You are not that sort of man.'

I did not know what she meant; but as I took breath to explain she interrupted quickly.

'Please—do not be offended. I tell you only the truth. You are an Australian, and you look like perhaps a European—French, or Spanish, or even English. You do not behave either like an Australian or a European. We talk about you, and all we know is that without doubt you are younger than you seem.'

I muttered something about being more honourable than they had seemed to think, too. For the first time, she laughed, in the way I had liked when we were together before, in the quiet security of the cottage.

'Without doubt, if possible,' she said. 'It was not a question of honour—women, Mr. Fitzherbert, leave honour to the men, you will find. It's a word they don't use among themselves, women. It was, frankly, a question of what to do next. I offered to come to town and see you. She believed if you said anything it would be the truth, and I said I would ask you what you were going to do, and what you thought best for her to do.'

'I was coming back the next week-end,' I said more roughly than was fair; for I was so confused and unhappy that it made me angry. 'I went away to give her time to settle down without me about the place, since my presence seemed to remind her of her foolish idea that she owed me

238

something for doing what any decent man would have done in my place. Also I had a good deal to think about.'

'She offended you then, Irma?'

'No . . . You must understand I am not merely what I probably seem to you two people—just a man in a newspaper office with a useful house in the mountains, empty and safe. No, I have a background very different from Irma's—particularly different in that fear never had much of a place in it for long. I have two lives to care for, my son's and my own, each dependent largely upon the other. Do you see what I mean? Very few things that she would think exciting have ever happened to me. I am even a Roman Catholic by birth and upbringing, though not a very good one now, I suppose, in the priests' view. Most of my friends are older than I am, and I myself am twelve years older than she is. As for my feelings, I am no casual lover—I haven't enough experience in the art of subterfuge, for one thing. But now I know my feeling for her is the same as hers for me, if what you say is right. Where is she?'

In spite of my resolve, in spite of everything, I heard myself asking the question harshly, in a voice unlike my own. It startled me, as it surely startled her. Her nervous look returned; she made a small placatory gesture with her two hands, and shook her head and swallowed audibly before she answered.

'Mr. Fitzherbert, I do not know. I do not know. When the train came to Blacktown she said, "Help me get my things out, quick," but when I went to get out with her she said, "No, Linda, no. Go back to Sydney. You are all right," and she gave me a push, so hard that I fell back on the seat,

239

and slammed the door. When I got up the train had started. I looked out—there she was, not even looking for me, like a lost child always looking the wrong way. That is the last I saw of her—looking the wrong way.'

In the lamplight I saw two tears brim over her dark-lashed lower lids from her polished black eyes, and slowly thread their way down her cheeks while she felt for a handkerchief. Her fat chin trembled a little; she looked very pitiful suddenly, no longer the rich little Jewess secure in her prosperous business, but a refugee from all that is incomprehensible and tragic in life.

'Forgive me—I am very fond of her. It makes me sad to think what will become of her, poor Irma.'

'She told you nothing of what she meant to do?'

'Nothing.'

'Do you know if she had ever travelled that line before?'

'She told me she had never been out of Sydney before. She said how strange the country looked to her—very hard, she thought it was.'

'I suppose we can safely suppose she is still alive?'

Miss Werther gasped, and put her plump hands to her throat. 'I tried to take it from her. She said, "Don't be silly, Linda. I am not going to use it—yet".'

'I do not know what you are talking about, Miss Werther.'

At that, she seemed to break down completely, wringing her outstretched hands together and shaking her beautifully coiffured head from side to side with her eyes closed.

'The poison. She had it with her always. The little glass bit of sealed tube. They called it the death capsule,

240

in Europe. You bite it, and you are gone. I tried to take it, but she saw me. "Don't be silly, Linda" was what she said. Ah, Mr. Fitzherbert—you must understand—all that talk of suicide is very easy for the young.'

'All what talk of suicide?'

'You never heard it?' She recovered herself sufficiently to scrub at her eyes with her handkerchief and then look at me more confidently, though her mouth still trembled.

'Ah well . . . you knew her so short a time, I keep forgetting. All her talk about you, after you went, made me feel you had known one another ever since she came here. Forgive me. You see, when she was very blue, depressed, she would talk of ending it all. Like many of those people, she still carries the poison—cyanide—with her. It is very quick. She has it with her always, like other people have a little mascot . . . But no! she is too young, and suicide is not for her, not in this country. Surely? It is so easy to talk.'

Aloud, I reminded myself that I would surely have heard. 'She would be traced to Sydney.'

'That's it! You are with the police. No, no—she has just gone off alone again, she used to say it was the only real safety, to be absolutely alone. But of course that is not always so easy . . . I know she will write to me. I know she is still alive and well, somewhere. It is such a big country, isn't it?'

On that inconclusive thought we parted, and I took my confused feeling of regret and concern and an underlying, uncertain joy elsewhere; and though I nursed the thought of Irma's regard for me I could get little pleasure from it in the end.

In truth, now that she had spoken of love, I was not even sure if it were love I wanted from her. Once more I remembered that I had made my choice, with a conviction that seemed to have little connection with my dazzled senses at the time, and nothing at all to do with them in retrospect. The choice, made, was irrevocable and absolute, a living part of my history now. But love, I thought, can die; in a hundred different ways and even from simple starvation it can die and crumble like a dead old leaf.

Nevertheless, now that all was over between us—all the little, it might seem, that had ever been—I did nurse and hug to myself the knowledge that she had said she loved me. Sometimes, when I recalled my own behaviour, it was an embarrassing knowledge, prompting a self-contempt which bruised and bewildered, for I still did not see how I could have acted otherwise; yet for once she was innocent, and I, of all people who had reason to play the Samaritan, had stepped aside from her as though she were a harlot offering to trade.

Sometimes, though, as the weeks and months passed, and the war's apparent false start left us as it were in mid-air, frustrated, still at stretch, I thought that knowledge wonderful in the extreme. The only escape from the unreality of the actual, in Europe and here at home, was by way of dreams—the dream of work, the dream of fulfilled wishes; and I dreamed like any boy. She was my girl. We had known each other but a few hours in all, we were strangers still to each other's history and each other's self that had shaped it, yet in a short hour of being tested we had indicated to each other a whole new world of possible experience.

The image of her was becoming clearer as she receded

in space and time—clearer, yet more complex. Thinking of her age, even in a day when girls become mature, *rangées*, so much earlier than their mothers did, I was repeatedly arrested by the view I had had of her independence of action as well as of mind. She made her own decisions, and without hesitation moved on them. Even allowing for the practice she must have had, in a world where she knew she could count on no sure support from anyone at all in the event of a serious mistake, this complete self-sufficiency was disturbing in one so young, not merely because it was an incalculable quantity but because, as I mused on it, it gave her in imagination an air of extraordinary loneliness. Without consultation, she could leave her job and her lodging; she could come to me and confess things which, to her mind, were too dangerous for any unknown, irresponsible person to hear; she could summon her friend without warning to go into hiding with her; she could leave both the temporary refuge and the friend in a matter of hours, and disappear god knew where, on a train of whose departure she must have known in advance, at a station which, as far as we could tell, she had never heard of before . . .

The whole series of actions argued a deal of cool, determined forethought and preparation, without a word to anyone. I began to think, indeed, that none of my own part in it had been quite by chance; I began to suspect, without much argument, that she had summed me up, from her own point of view, with flashing quickness on that morning aboard the *Empire Queen*, and to realize that she probably knew more about me than, had she told me, I would have believed she possibly could know.

243

Her one miscalculation had been concerned with my response to her whole-hearted offering of her love, not—as I now saw—merely as a return for kind services but because it had unexpectedly become the inevitable ending to all that had gone before it. Flight demands eventual surrender—to something, no matter what. She, poor child, gave herself up to love. I was to be her captor and turn a key on her in her prison of peace. It was her one miscalculation, and a bad one, for which only her youth could be blamed. No wonder that, as Jack had said, she 'nearly through a fit' when she found I had gone wordlessly away, leaving her not even another chance. I supposed, with a wretched sinking of the heart, that she had gone willingly back to her bed that night because already she was setting much store by the bright morning soon to come.

Such thoughts bring no ease. They are like the tongue's worrying at an aching tooth: they incessantly identify the source of pain and do nothing to lessen it. I kept coming back, for a comfort that was each time colder, to the fact that I had been faced with a tremendous decision and had made a right choice. It did no good: it was true, but for many weeks and months the virtue seeped out of it like water from a cracked jar, leaving only a dry emptiness and the formal, useless shape of the jar itself.

In those weeks and months it was easy to turn the mind to private concerns. Part of my mind held scorn for the way I succumbed to that false easiness. Another part, the vast uncharted emotional regions where many a stronger and wiser traveller has lost himself for ever from integrity, welcomed my wanderings with lure upon lure as I followed

244

the witch-fire of imagination and desire. I see now that the self-controlled repressions of the preceding years, ever since Jean's death, had built up a structure of support which was not as strong as I had tried to make it. It was based upon a negative base: what I had used for foundations were more often denials, not—as I had thought—assertions. It was like the young Queen Victoria's strenuous 'I *will* be good' which had the irresistible ring of 'I will *not* be naughty'; and it was just as vain.

All this distracting activity in my mind made me understand later how tremendous the decision had been; and understanding sealed as it were the cracked jar, and poured back into it not virtue but acceptance and resignation, which I am told smell hardly less agreeable to god. I say acceptance, because it is necessary to reason to accept an accomplished fact; but instead of resignation one might say relief, because I was realizing at last that if I had chosen Irma instead of my concept of myself (which included and largely was Alan) I should have abandoned that alternative for her as wholly as I had abandoned her for it. There could have been no compromise, not only because it is against my training and my nature to compromise but also because, with her, compromise would have been impossible. There would, of course, have been the appearance of it; but Alan and my aspirations to the impersonal, Olympian viewpoint would have been set aside in my mind together, the one to grow untended and, by my standards, without love, the other to be in all honesty forgotten.

I began to suspect, at last, my own limitations. I was still too unmatured to dare to devote myself to more than one heart-felt cause. Singlemindedness, like self-sufficiency, imposes its own penalties. It too is an ultimate loneliness.

So, it appeared, we were both destined by our decisions to be lonely. This thought, arrived at in due course, sent me back to the cottage like a homing dog to a deserted mastery. Three weeks after I had driven from it into the south-east, aslant the winter daybreak, I was back there with a fast-beating heart and a belief, a mad hope somewhere unacknowledged within me, that she might have returned, secretly impelled like me to come back to the point of departure, with that dreadful human hope that, just this once, one may be given a second chance.

I went in a fought-down frenzy of haste, like any schoolboy to an uncertain assignation. Once more I drove at an illegal speed, outside the busier thoroughfares, and once more an irrelevant gaiety welled up in me, like the urge to sing on a fine morning, as I cleared the last straggle of suburbs and wheeled the car fast into the opening plain, where fewer and fewer houses were to be seen, and where the mountains marched towards me like a wave that changed as it came from dark blue to green, from flat to a cleft and tossing complexity of austere pride.

Today, however, morning was at my back and I travelled towards a pale and hazy sky. By the time Richmond was left behind and the river crossed, the mists were coming down upon the highest crests, with imperceptible speed; and as I turned off north-west on the unsurfaced country road of red gravel and hardened clay I saw the nearer ranges in a sudden magic of definition, their over-clear green turning black again by contrast with the white and heavy vapours that rolled down into the innumerable valleys and ravines and narrow gullies before a descending curtain from beneath which they seemed to have escaped like forerunners. Their whiteness and apparent lack of all movement as I climbed steadily nearer turned the revealed depths of the immense eastern mountain forest into the likeness of a stereoscopic photograph, and along the lowest edge of the curtain individual trees stood out, stark charcoal drawings that were slowly swallowed up from below until only the solid-looking, craggy tops of them could be seen, like islands about to sink back into a white ocean.

The cottage, I knew, would be mist-bound already, and I concentrated my thoughts on the road itself, and on seeing my mail-box on its tree to guide me to the turn-off. A fog formed on the windscreen before I realized I had plunged into the thin lowest fringes of the mist; in another minute, with the windscreen-wiper jerking and clicking inexorably across the glass, I could see only twenty yards ahead of the car between the looming and vanishing trunks. My headlights now seemed to exaggerate the unnatural silence of the misty mountains closing behind me, and what had been bright day when I left the city was now a pallid greyness, a vision of the silence itself, on every side, beneath huge trees whose leaves were already dripping as they turned the ocean of vapour into water upon their chilly surfaces.

Donna met me at the gate. As I put up the rails behind the car, thinking of why I had come, I knew with absolute certainty that I had come for nothing after all; yet still that hope which was only a wishful dream made me hasten to cover the last few hundred yards. One look at the cottage when it became properly visible in the mist might have sufficed. Its withdrawn, motionless look was now that which houses take on when mist or rain comes down heavily upon them, shutting in and intensifying the life they contain. No sound, no light came from it, but more than this it had no soul.

Having let myself fall into the clutches of excitement and anticipation so wholly, I could not stop now. When the car was put away, and no one appeared in answer to the sharp, lonely rapping of the horn in the darkness of the barn, I made for the cottage as though committed to a definite and pressing purpose, though I had none; and as I passed beneath and between them, the leafless fruit trees opening late in the mountain air their budded flowers along each polished twig dripped moisture like tears on my bare head and my beard; and Donna danced along at my side with joy and impatience, tenderly mouthing my hand each time it swung back as I walked.

The kitchen was clean and empty, and smelled faintly of wood-smoke and ashes and the split wood Jack always kept there in a deep recess by the stove. It was a sad, cold smell. Nothing was out of place—dishcloth, soap-saver, brush, all were on their hooks on the window-frame over the sink, dry, unused this many a day. The silence of the mountain mist was inside the house; nothing lived there except the bitch and myself, both listening, both knowing there was nothing.

In the big room, the pale curtains kept out the paler daylight. I flicked them aside with the backward wrist-movement of years of habit that sent the wooden rings to the ends of the rods with a small dead rattling sound. Immediately the profound and empty silence of the mist, so different from that of the mountains themselves at night, resumed its full occupancy of the place; and suddenly in the careless garden of shrubs in front a thrush began to sing with accurate and penetrating sweetness. I listened until it stopped and flew away, unseen the whole time, through the blank world of the mist. I did not know what to do next.

There was a clean fire laid as usual in the ruddy depths of the brick fireplace. The polished floor between the rugs reflected vaguely every surface that caught the humble light from the windows, and the windows themselves, rectangles of barely discernible grey. All trace of use was gone from the room. I stared at the sheepskin rug before the hearth in disbelief.

In the front bedroom, the two beds had been stripped and made up again with clean linen, as the visible creases in each pillowcase, each turned-over sheet, mercilessly showed. I did not even know which one she had lain in, wide awake in the dark in a strange place; neither of them, in its military neatness, seemed ever to have felt the weight of that strong, warm body whose strength and warmth I instantly felt again across my knees and in the crook of my left arm. Jack, as always, had cleared the whole place of every sign of living, moving human beings, and women at that, no doubt as soon after they were gone as he could find time to do it. I imagined him at work, his rope-soled espadrilles hushed on the floors whose polish they scarcely clouded, his pipe-stem gripped firmly in toothless jaws behind the stretched lips that made him appear to be smiling to himself the whole time. I remembered how he had told me he had once been to sea for a year or two, in his various ways of escape from his now rather legendary wife; I supposed it was there he had learned this habit of ascetic tidiness which, in that cottage, could make the rooms beautiful without flowers. Whatever he did he did in the same way, tidily and thoroughly and without seeming to think about his actions. His fenced fields, with the furrow running dead north and south across the gentle slope of the plateau, were each complete and four-square, with the rabbit-netting in perfect condition even at the gates. The kitchen garden, sheltered from the south beyond the barn and the partitioned shed he and his cows shared, each in her season, was a model of clean economy and fruitful industry; yet I could not remember ever having seen him actually at work in it. 'The truck-garden' he called it almost scornfully; yet once, months after I had been talking idly to him about the use of herbs in cookery, and their reputation for being important to health in our almost Mediterranean climate, when I had forgotten the whole conversation, he took me to that small patch of enclosed ground and indicated a warm corner with the wet stem of his pipe: 'There's your 'erbs. Writ to Yates—all they 'ad.'

He was thorough without even a show of effort, enthusiasm or boredom. It must have been nothing to him to sweep and dust and wash and polish away all traces of a couple of women he had never seen before and would never see again. Staring at the natural grey colour of the sheepskin rug, beaten so free that it appeared never to have felt the weight of human bodies, I could imagine him doing it, and thought how good a thing it would be if one could clear and clean out the mind in the same way.

In my own room at last, I changed into working clothes before going to the kitchen to light the fire in the mercilessly-polished stove. Stoves, I thought foolishly, are polished so that they shall radiate as little heat as may be, and no doubt the same effect is achieved with what is commonly called a polished mind: the more polished it is, the less warmth it gives out. How polished was my own mind? Or perhaps it did not matter—perhaps there had never been a fire there anyhow; until now?

Before the kindling wood began to crackle as it took the flame, I heard the muffled thudding blows of an axe higher up the mountain, dulled and unechoing in the white mist. The scene that came into my mind showed me Jack in soiled sandshoes and trousers, the belt tight below the swell of his ribs under the white sports-singlet he wore when he went wood-getting. With his pipe held strongly, he would be addressing himself—there was no other word that so accurately described his attitude—to a dead tree while his grey horse and his black dog Ike waited at a proper distance, too familiar with it all even to look his way. His axemanship was characteristically clean and quick. It reminded me of yet another allusion to his past he had as it were let fall some time, between mouthfuls of food perhaps, or slow puffs at his pipe. He had done a bit of timber-getting, he said, but—using his favourite and most deceptive expression with a sharp, un-smiling glance at me across the intervening space—it was 'too much like hard work'. He had the shoulders and hips and nimble feet of a good timber-man; and I had seen him looking with shrewd consideration at my few acres of forest above the cleared upper end of the plateau where it melted into the steeper slope of the soaring mountain. He told me it was wood for the taking, easy to get and easy to get out. In the end we decided to let it stand a few years more. Now it could wait for I knew not how long, until the war was over.

I was thinking about Jack, listening to his axe thudding, so that I should not too clearly remember Irma in this kitchen, her face in the tender lamplight rosy and golden with the colour in her cheeks and lips and the revealed lobes of her ears, and the shining candour of her slanted, sly-set eyes looking frankly at me across the yellow table as she laughed with us. How happy she had been, and I too, with Miss Werther between us at the end nearer the stove trilling away in her lilting voice, apologizing to me every now and then for a sudden spontaneous remark in German, at which Irma had frowned and shaken slightly her dark, smooth head with a glance at me inviting the other to remember: 'He does not understand you.'

Well, I thought now, as I rinsed and filled the heavy iron kettle, it is there, but it is over, finished, and I have made my choice and shall stand by my decision. Yet when I had set the kettle on to heat, I could not resist looking again through the whole place, Donna at my heels. She followed me about with a look of patient contentment on her bright brown-eyed face, between the golden fall of her ears that gave her the appearance, in some moods, of an intelligent blonde film actress. I even looked round the small

252

bathroom next to the larder; but everywhere was a clean impersonality, with not a trace even of myself or of Jack, not even a dark, unidentified hair, a fingerprint, the ghost of a breath on the mirror's icy surface that mockingly showed me myself only, and in reverse at that, so that it was not even I whom I saw staring self-consciously back at me.

When the fire was firmly in, I took another axe and set off along the north headland by the bank of the little hurrying creek towards where Jack must be chopping. Before I had gone far, the thudding blows ceased to sound through the obliterating mist, and after a pause of seconds I heard it—the groaning brief crescendo of noise as the felled tree tore its dead branches free from the arms of its living company, and flung itself slowly and for the first time and finally down upon the earth that had nourished it for half a century, and upon which, standing upright and defiant and beautiful, it had lived and at last begun to die, high above the scanty scattered life sprung from its own seed.

When we came to the place, old Jack was sitting on the clean stump, smoking imperturbably and looking with mild amusement and distaste at the prostrate silver trunk and the branches that had not smashed in the fall raised now in frozen, rigid gestures of self-defence. It was a large tree. When he saw me he nodded amiably, his lips stretching wider and his sea-blue, lizard-like eyes narrowing in a real smile.

'Thought I heard the car. Just come in time. Must of knowed sumpin,' he said moistly round his pipe-stem. I paced the trunk and looked over the branches, trying to see the thing as two or three months' supply of good firewood.

253

There was all of that. Above us the mist drifted in the green tops whose canopy showed no wound; for the tree had been too long dead, and the seasons had healed over the gap it might once have left, dying.

Later, we got to work with the saw, and in this exercise, when I had remembered how to perform it with least effort, I slowly found a peace of body and mind I had not known for a long time. Perhaps this was the secret of old Jack's imperturbability, this dissolving of the mind's tangles of desire and foreboding in unceasing bodily labour, at no matter what, without haste and without end. The snarling hiss of the cross-cut blade, sharp and well-set, rubbed out thoughts and names, and even memory let fade the remorseless pictures that have no words. We lunged rhythmically at each other eight feet apart, down on one knee, listening to the greasy passage of the blade deeper and deeper into the solid trunk, and soon it was necessary to kneel down lower and rest on the free hand, until we could cut no nearer the ground. Even the two horses working together could pull only short-length loads of the heavy hardwood in that dense forest, and we made several more cuts before leaving the saw for the axes. I remembered with surprise the fire and the kettle; everything but the work had gone from my mind. Wiping of the chilly sweat, I went down with him to make tea. The dogs followed, after their fashion, ranging to hunt in the misty undergrowth but returning sometimes to see that all was well with us. On our left the little creek tinkled coldly unseen in the twisting depths of its rocky bed.

By the end of the day we had finished with that tree and got a lot of it down and stacked in the lean-to wood-shed on the north side of the barn, away from the weather. I felt wonderfully weary and cleansed in body and mind. Jack had not shed a drop of sweat nor shown anything but a lazy amusement as at some peculiar characteristic of his own of which no one else knew. While I ran off a bath and soaked my pleasantly-aching muscles, he put on his patched coat and fed his hens and milked his scornful-eyed cow. Donna sat on the bathroom stool with folded paws, drenched with mist and shuddering herself warm, and now and then, between brief dozes, looking down sceptically at my white skin under the colourless hot rainwater in the tub. She was no longer beautiful like a film star, and I told her so, while she wagged her feathered stub of tail frantically in acknowledgment of unexpected compliments. It was an hour of warmth, of profound and unthinking physical and mental peace; for this, and not for a woman or a ghost, I had come.

While Jack and I drank a glass of whisky by the kitchen stove, I remembered I had not brought his flask of rum. It was the first time I had forgotten it; and though I knew he did not depend on me for his modest supply of it, I was put out. He looked surprised.

'Must have sumpin on your mind,' he said. 'Maybe it's this war they tell me's officially opened.'

'Maybe it is,' I said; and I told him I should not be staying that night as I was on duty next morning. He may have remembered that that in itself had seldom been enough to prevent me staying, but I did not think even he, for all his shrewd and smiling silence, could have guessed that the quarter-hour following my arrival, the unused beds, the cloudy smoothness of the sheepskin hearth-rug, the lifeless and immaculate kitchen where once we had so gaily sat down to our meal in the lamp-light, and the whole clean emptiness of the cottage, without a trace of unaccustomed movement anywhere in it, had made me feel for the first time like a stranger there; and I could not stay just yet, after my coming and my animal-like searching about and about had been fruitless.

Yet he took me by surprise when he said, 'You young fellers is all the same. Dress a bit o' meat up with a few weird doodahs and give it a foreign name, and you'll eat it every time, if it burns your guts out . . . Anyway, you'll be takin' a risk goin' down in this,' and he waved his glass at the window. To hide my consternation and to avoid answering the first part of his remarks at all, I went to look outside. Dusk had come invisibly. Beyond the dark reflecting panes there was only a hinted whiteness catching the light of the lamp behind me.

'I have driven up and down in worse,' I reminded him, and he answered after a while, somewhat obscurely, 'Yes—but not when there's a war on.' In the window I could see the side of his face and his shock of flat grey hair in the lamp-light. He had not bothered to turn and look at me to see how I had taken what he first said. It was the first time I had ever heard him volunteer a comment in any way personal upon me and my affairs. No doubt he rested secure in his knowledge that with a smile and eyes and a voice as non-committal as his he could have said almost anything to almost anyone without causing more than a rapid, startled self-inspection. In any case, I liked his wry, probing wisdom, and his air of being mildly and constantly amused, even when he was alone. There could never be trouble of a personal sort between us; he was, in addition, twice my age and harder than I had ever been.

But at that moment I felt incapable of referring to Irma with anyone at all, in however indirect a way of speaking. Telling him to help himself to more whisky, I went out through the cold, moist air that was not yet darkness made tangible, as it would later be, and backed the car from its place among the farm tools and light machinery in the barn. When I returned through the dripping orchard to the kitchen, regretting its quiet warmth and light as though I had already left it behind me in the lowering night, he was still standing by the stove, his face, so ruddy and bright in contrast with the flat thatch of his grey hair, turned sideways still from the lamp as he looked at his thoughts in the corner of the room.

Unconcerned to dissuade me any further from driving alone down the difficult track in that mist and darkness, he spoke coolly of Irma.

'What become of the little foreign lady?'

'Nobody knows,' I said. 'She changed trains at Blacktown and disappeared west.'

'I heard you go, that mornin',' he said. 'You ain't no fool.'

'You can hear me go again now,' I said. 'Sorry about the rum.'

'Think nothin' of it,' he said courteously. 'I always got a drop left.' He added, rather surprisingly, 'Like the widder's cruse.'

We briefly shook hands, and he said, 'Well—take care o' yourself. See you some time.'

It was several weeks before I did go again, however; partly because I was still disinclined to spend a night at the cottage, and partly because several changes were taking place in the office, and some of us were working overtime a good deal, covering a sudden brief staff-shortage, and unobtrusively keeping an eye on the settling-in of some newcomers. More men than might have been expected in a staff where the age-average was not low had been drawn into the slowly accelerating current of war running now through all human affairs. Individual changes near the top affected us all: when the news-editor's assistant took on a liaison job with the navy, a complicated series of upward and sideways moves followed, for the *Gazette* of those days still held wholly to the policy of internal promotion from a careful if not always happy reserve of strength—a two-edged policy, some thought, which reaped both the sweet fruit of ambition and the sour fruit of discontent. The argument in its favour, a negative one, was that the discontent was not as bad as it would have been had we done as other offices did, and brought in new blood at the top rather than at the bottom, thus avoiding the disaffection so often caused by putting a newcomer in a high post and so arresting that subtle upward movement, slow though it may be, which keeps any office staff alive. Because of this policy, even today the *Gazette* seems to find outside replacements on the upper levels unnec-essary; and only the *Herald* has lost good men less frequently. (The argument that both papers are resultantly dull misses the point, which is that the majority of newspaper-readers are dull too.)

Scott, in his booming voice of angry good-humour, put the administration's attitude clearly.

'If we can't replace one of our own men with one of our own men, then we are short-staffed, and if we're short-staffed we can't go on producing a newspaper.' And he added once to me: 'If a man's left hand doesn't know what his right hand's doing in this office, he'd better start teaching it at once.' On another occasion, apparently concerned with this same matter of domestic policy, he shouted back into his room from the open doorway, to someone evidently still there within, 'Any man here who thinks he's indispensable had better seek other employment, by god!' in a voice to be heard all over the building.

But with the development of world-scale war, for the second and perhaps not the last time in the lives of so many of us, things became different, even in the most conservative establishments. Promotions were sudden, and replacements at the ladder's foot more frequent. As the war, with its calamitous false start that ended with Dunkirk, gathered more directed energy as opposed plans were made and put in motion, and the battles were joined, men were lost who had to be replaced abroad from the Sydney head-office staff, however indirectly. The newcomers at our end, many of them very young, many of them, as time went on, having been formerly in one or other of the services, needed careful handling and unobtrusive supervision as they adjusted themselves to the strange and exacting life.

The sudden Japanese threat in nineteen forty-two

caused a long period of panic recruitment complemented by a panic wave of enlistment which together swept civilians of all ages and occupations, men and women both, into the ranks of the fighting services and the administrations behind them. During all those six years of war I and my colleagues were hard-worked and more highly-paid. Private relaxation became almost a public affair. We gathered together among ourselves more closely; pleasures were less decorous among the decorous, more uncontrolled among the carefree and the distressed; and as goods and necessities lapsed from plenty to scarcity—particularly those goods that helped to heighten the relief of worldly pleasures and for which there was thus an ever more urgent demand—what began to be called the black market came openly into being, and insidiously took its place in our lives and thoughts, prompting few protests because it was based—as it still is—on fear: the fear of being thought mean, or poorer than the next fellow, and the fear of not having what the next fellow had for his greater worldly comfort. Its persistence to this day makes it clear that it was never a wartime vice, to pass inevitably away after the ending of warfare, so much as it was from the beginning a characteristic if not of the whole nation then at least of the three eastern major states facing America across the troubled Pacific. Fear, the driving force behind most human endeavour in the democratic society of today, was keenly heightened, intensified, in those bloody and uncertain, shameful and despairing years; and mankind has so progressed, and improved its state so far, that the only soporific to comfort fear is money—more and more money, acquired no matter how.

I was fortunate in having a very modest private income assured to me by my father ('to himself at least, my boy, a man must cut some sort of a decent figure') whose active value varied with the times while its face-value remained unchanged; and I lived in such a way that even with the increased costs of Alan's schooling I was able to save money and invest it for him in my turn. The knowledge that money is available, rather than the possession of it, is of considerable importance to a growing boy, and I was glad to think he would not have to suffer the small, distorting heart-breaks of any degree of poverty.

In my own mind, as in the minds of most thinking people in those days, the subsequently much-publicized and even more neglected 'four freedoms' had already been clearly defined as a proper objective for the whole activity of living. Secretly almost from myself, I had added one more—a freedom from love, as human beings mostly know and show it: as a misty shape of overpowering emotional claims, amorphous and terrible, upon the consciousness of the loved one, from the simple beginning—'You must love me, for I love you'—to the last dreadful expedient, when the beloved seems about to escape finally from the talons of love, of spectacularly-acknowledged renunciation, in itself the boldest, most desperate and selfish claim of all.

I did not want to be loved, I thought, even by my son. By making provision for his freedom from at least the sharper material wants, and so perhaps from many worldly fears, I hoped to have enabled him, as he grew older towards manhood, to meet me when he chose and on his own terms, as two friends with disparate worldly interests may meet upon the common ground of humanity and warm mutual examination in speech and silence. I myself had always felt the lack of someone to whom I could talk and stammer out the record of my growth without making of confession a hostage to my freedom (it was what I meant when I spoke to Barbara of my own dear father as so often being 'not there'), and it seemed possible that if I were supremely careful of my mind and heart, that they should not too much show in me, Alan might not suffer that lack, which is a fruitless, wry suffering not good for the soul.

This intention was always alive in me, even when I was with him. It survived many dark disturbances of mind when I was alone, and made tolerable even the black depths into which a man may find himself being drawn, now and then, when nervous exhaustion for a time spurs on self-criticism towards the shades of nightmare insanity, and the whole past of his life seems to stand in question, and to be damned as worthless. Even at such times, hearing the plash and suck of the blacked-out, starlit water of the harbour against the stone wall of the swimming-pool below my bedroom window, thinking that there, if anywhere, lay the gentle peace of oblivion and the merciful end of thought, I could think of Alan and not, in imagination, drown; I could sometimes recall Scott's seemingly contemptuous epigrammatical obituary on a newspaper colleague who had committed suicide by drowning: 'Water is no solution,' and see the truth of it beneath the surface twist of wit, and know that death in that way would be for me not only the unholy thing my Mother Church so rightly held it to be, and not only a cowardly act of courage, but also comparable to that gesture of love's ostentatious renunciation which I detested, and which would have placed upon the boy's eager young shoulders a burden that must, like time itself, grow heavier as he grew older and more nearly understood what I had done, and why.

Looking back, I see and know that my sorriest lack in those years was of a wife. It is not that I wanted consciously a wife who loved me; my own private fifth freedom would make that plain. I had once been loved, with a young and joyous devotion as profoundly moving and impelling towards god as the music of Bach, or the smell of spring roses in the cold air of a starlit dusk, or a child's face in the absolute innocence of sleep.

I had been given that love, and in moments of gloom I would fearfully imagine that the gift had exhausted the giver to death like sleep after a splendid toil. It was not this that I wanted ever again. I could not have borne it. What did I want, without knowing it, was a companion in the sleepless nights, a voice to answer mine if I cried aloud the many hidden cries of ordinary daily speech, and the untroubling presence always of a being not my own, a body and mind and soul all feminine to complete my masculine identity; in my care yet not of me; not for me, yet not withheld in ignorance that I too was a complementary being.

Twice in the weeks following my useless visit to Hill Farm, where Jack lived on in amused solitude far from the talk and stresses of war, I had to speak to other people of Irma.

I do not include there McMahon's occasional monologues, for since the declaration of hostilities he had seemed to lose his former prying interest, and besides, he had much

263

to do in keeping track of his excited State politicians, and in finding, in unpublishable detail, who was feathering his nest most warmly. Some of his stories were scarcely credible, shocking even to me in their revelations of small pettiness and insatiable self-interest; and I let him see this deliberately, for the more astounded and disgusted I became the more satisfaction he found in retailing his useless information; and the less likely he was to remember Irma.

Her name was first mentioned, after weeks in which it had sounded only in my own mind, by Miss Werther. That kindly and amiable person rang me at my home, where I could talk and listen without interruption. Even in the brief exchange of our greetings the lilt of her voice suggested that she had interesting news. As I sat back at my table in the firelit lounge room which was also my home office I could imagine vividly her black, polished eyes shining brighter with pleasure.

'It is about Irma I am ringing,' she said, 'of course. Why else should I trouble you in these terrible times? Mr. Fitzherbert, I have had a letter. She is in Perth—very far away, is it not? Yes, but there she is, teaching French and German in a school for girls. And she lives at the school. I am so happy, Mr. Fitzherbert, you can imagine how happy this makes me. Are you pleased?'

'Yes.'

'Her name is different. She is now Miss Irma Francis, a French orphan. How clever she always is, you know. I myself could never have gone on so long. It is the gift of youth. She sends you her warmest greetings.'

'Thank you—if you write please give her mine—my warmest greetings.'

264

'She hoped you might write to her. I will give you her address. Have you a pencil and some paper there?'

My hand was trembling as I changed the receiver to my left ear; and it surprised me. I had not heard her name for so long.

The address, I found with a tremor of excitement, was that of a 'select' private academy for young ladies—a girls' school—not far from Fremantle and overlooking Melville Water, one of the spacious salty lakes made by the Swan on its approach to the sea. I knew it at once, for the house, large and gracious and old in wide grounds, had belonged to an uncle of my mother's. I had even lived there for a time as a child, during the other war, when wartime duties parted my father from us for long periods, and that kindly old man had asked my mother to cross the continent and run his diminished household for him; for he was a widower. Of all this I knew little at the time, for I remember only a childhood sense of ceaseless pleasure and well-being while the old world fell finally to pieces over our heads. My most welcome memory is of the sweet smell of pine needles in hot sunshine, and the smell brings back childhood now more vividly than any other reminder. In the gardens there were always flowers in bloom, always birds singing in the pines and the giant fig trees, doves by day and magpies day and night when the moon was near and past its fullness. On the smooth croquet lawn the painted hoops were as white as the white *click* of yellow mallets against coloured wooden balls, and in the near distance, beyond the privacy of the bookleaf cypress hedge, so lemon-scented in the sun after rain, Melville Water stretched blue and glittering between and above the peppermint trees' dull green to the thicker blue of an horizon of low hills . . .

It all came in a thrilling flash as Miss Werther gave me the address. I had not thought of it for years, and now it was the more intimately pleasing, in a way I could not describe, because I had been there before Irma was born, and because she was there now where, in the midst of hellish war, I had been so innocent and so happy.

In a country always poor in school-teachers, it was little wonder that she had had no difficulty in finding that employment, with her easy command of languages and her modest demeanour; and later I realized that because of the discipline she herself had had to learn, and because she also had that small, complete air of authority on occasion—an authority rather of intellect than of will—she must have made a very good teacher indeed.

All I did at the moment was to throw the amiable Miss Werther into a passion of delight by telling her of my knowledge of the school when it was my home. This gave her immense satisfaction, and I felt grateful to believe how much and how unselfishly she cared for the fortunes of that young woman who had come to my country for no material gain but as to a refuge for the harassed spirit.

We ended our conversation with an agreement to meet for coffee soon so that she could show me the actual letter. I had not said I would write, and though I was often impelled to do so I never did, for what could I have said that would have made sober sense in a sedate girls' school thousands of miles away on the other side of the continent? Nevertheless, at last and for the first time since I had known her I was able to imagine her moving in her smooth, youthful way against a real and (however altered) familiar background of walls and trees and dark-panelled halls, with the blue of Melville Water shining beyond the bookleaf cypress.

The second mention of her name was made by a man who was a stranger. We never found out who he was, though his ill-intentioned purpose in approaching me was fairly evident.

I had never seen him before, and I never did see him again. It is possible that McMahon knew who he was, but that too I let remain uncertain.

He was announced by a boy as 'Mr. Martin'. The name itself was so often in my mind at that time that for a moment it meant nothing, spoken aloud, and I must have shown instinctive suspicion, for the boy repeated it, adding doubtfully, 'That's what he said, Mr. Fitz.' It was, in fact, the boy's tone of doubt, of allowing that it might not really be 'Martin', which brought me to my senses and the immediate present. The name is common enough among the groups of less usual christian-surnames, but I knew only one Martin, and that was not a man.

'All right—show him in, please.'

When the boy brought him, I was already and by instinct on guard. The visitor's hint of a stiff bow, from the waist, as his name was pronounced, made me more suspicious still. I seemed to have no doubt at all that the visit was to do with Irma; and in the same instant, in a flash of exact memory, I could hear Barbara's voice telling me of McMahon's private connection with the Communist Party.

'Sit down, Mr. Martin,' I said without rising.

'Can we go some place where it is private?' he said, rolling his dark eyes slightly at the crowded room.

'You can speak here as privately as you can in Pitt Street.'

It was so exactly a repetition of the opening words between Irma and me on her visit to the office, all those months ago, that I could have laughed. This time I had no intention of using the wireless room, for something about him had already turned suspicion into dislike in me. It was always so—anyone in any way connected with Irma I accepted or rejected in a matter of moments, at the first meeting. While I tried to rationalize my feeling of dislike, I looked with care at the cause of it.

He was, quite evidently, a foreigner, very dark of eyes and hair, very pale of skin, the hair worn long and sleekly combed from a straight forehead horizontally lined and somehow too small for the rest of his face. His lips were red and wide, but petulant, not humorous, as he waited in vain for me to get up and go somewhere 'where it was private'. His large eyes were the eyes of a liar or of a professional stage dancer; someone to whom words themselves meant nothing; and I observed already that he had difficulty in keeping his white, black-haired hands from gestures as he said softly, with a look meant to be full of mystery and promise, 'It is a very personal matter.'

I nodded to the chair by which he stood.

'Don't be afraid, Mr. Martin. If you know anything about newspaper offices, you must know that in the general room it's impossible to listen to other people's private conversations.'

He seated himself, drawing down the corners of his mouth and raising his shoulders in a shrug of exaggerated resignation, as if he regretted, after all, having come. On his knee he rested a satchel of imitation crocodile skin which would have placed him fairly accurately even if he had not said a word in his rather thick foreign voice. As usual, I waited for him to speak, while I made a note in my mind of his clothes, from the wide shoes of foreign make over dark purple socks to the padded shoulders ('self-raising shoulders', my father would have called them) of his costly brown suit. He was one of those Europeans who seem to have been born to shrug, roll their guilelessly watchful eyes, and to do things with their mouths and hands in a fashion so hypnotic that, without remembering a word they ever say, one has a lasting recollection of them always doing those things, like images on a motion-picture screen not wired for sound. He might have been French, Hungarian, German Jew, or—except for his accent—a native of southern Italy, Cyprus or Malta; I never found out whence he came, but that was his sort of manners and dress and colouring.

'I hope you may be able to help me,' he said with a meaning flash of his eyes that meant nothing to me. 'I am in search of someone very dear to me. A lady.'

He popped the word out impressively, with a following upward jerk of his mobile eyebrows; then, getting into the swing of it, held towards me one manicured hand, palm-upwards, in graceful supplication. 'No, no—please, please do not laugh.'

I was not laughing, and I told him so; I had suddenly seen what was coming, and was waiting for it.

'The lady is my sister. Irma. Irma Martin . . . little Irma.'

There were genuine wet tears in his eyes, and he was watching me so closely for a moment that he could not bear it himself, and had to rest those lustrous dark eyes by looking away from mine for a full second before resuming his intense stare, which I returned so irresistibly that I was able to see, as though magnified several times, the burning brown of the irides, minutely ridged and grooved like creased velvet under water, surrounding the mysterious receptive holes of the pupils, sooty black with a pin-point of light at the bottom of them. They made me think, irrelevantly, of some novel display in the window of a chemist's shop, made of cloth and coloured glass in a setting of enamelled cardboard.

He must have leaned forward in order not to miss any slightest reaction of mine to that name; for I saw him slowly sit back on the wooden chair and avert his bold, hooded gaze to the satchel, which he began to open fussily on his knees. I still said nothing, for I now disliked him so heartily that I knew my face must have remained perfectly blank under his brutal inspection. I also knew without doubt that for all his soft and emotional manner he was probably dangerous.

'You do not know her? Come—I think you do,' he said coaxingly yet threateningly—as I thought—while he looked up from the satchel with a coming-and-going smile that had little to do with his eyes or his hushed voice. Then, with a positively melodramatic glance round the room behind him and on either side, he slowly withdrew from the metal lips of the leather bag a silver photograph-frame containing a portrait which he hid with his spread hand; but in doing this he accidentally allowed the satchel to slip to the floor, and, in leaning to snatch it up, afforded me a brief glimpse of the face of the sitter. It was, as I had known it would be, Irma's face, grave as a ghost's. Moreover, I knew enough about police photography to recognize even in that brief glance that it was a photostatic copy of an original photograph—not quite the sort of thing a loving brother would carry, frame or no frame, as a momento of his missing sister.

He had in one awkward movement recovered his satchel and turned the portrait face-down, not realizing he was too late. A more skilled scoundrel—for I was now convinced of his scoundrelism—would have withdrawn it face-downwards in the first place, if he had wished to conceal it from me.

'Look,' he said, unruffled by his little scramble, 'I will show you her picture and you will remember her. No one could forget. Not even you, my friend, who must see so many faces . . . See.'

He held the thing out suddenly at me, as though, like his announcement of her name, the revelation must confound me into showing all I knew in my face. I had time to observe that a rubber stamp in the top right-hand corner of the original had been imperfectly erased.

'Yes,' I said slowly, very slowly and as it were thoughtfully, a man making an obvious effort to remember. 'Yes . . . I seem to know that face. Irma Martin, you say?' I shook my head with a smile. It is horribly easy, it is a pleasure, to lie to a man about whom one feels as I now felt about this creature before me, with his hypnotic gestures and his evil watchfulness.

'I do not know that name, Mr. Martin.'

'Never mind.' He permitted himself to seem very excited. 'You know her! My sister I begin to think is maybe dead, how do I know? She is here, my Irma! Tell me, please tell me where is she?'

'I have no idea.'

'Ah.' He sank back, snapping the smile from his lips. 'But you have seen her.'

'Perhaps—a long time ago,' I said. 'She arrived in some ship with hundreds of other refugees.'

'Yes, yes,' he said, 'the *Empire Queen* . . .'

'How do you know that?' I said abruptly. A man who is himself perfectly clear about the facts of the case can seldom help giving himself away if you omit one you believe he thinks important. 'You thought she might be dead. You say she vanished. Yet you know what boat she travelled in. What else do you know?'

'Nothing, nothing at all,' he said, pleading with his face and hands. 'That is why I come to you, to beg you . . .'

'Why not the police?' I said. 'It is their job, not mine, to trace missing people. You should go to the Missing Persons Bureau.'

'Not the police,' he said warningly. 'Irma would be frightened—very frightened. Always in Holland she is frightened—the dam' Gestapo, you know.'

'The dam' Gestapo' must have sounded singularly weak even to him, for he made haste to cover it with an explanation he doubtless thought would convince my Australian simplicity: 'We are—you know—Jewish, Irma and me.' He rolled his eyes a little, and sighed.

272

Just for one moment I felt a bloody impulse to clench my fist and smash it into his insolently grimacing face. The words 'Irma and me' brought home to me as nothing less than witnessed violence could have brought home the fact that her former danger had never been imagined at all. I looked at the person calling himself Martin, and saw him clearly for what he was—a pimp, a back-alley killer who would use a knife or poison—women's weapons—not for gain but because he was a coward and a hireling without hope of escape from his employers; a dangerously humble creature who would indulge to the full such appetites as were permitted to him; perverted in body, mind and soul ever since some fateful mistake of over-confidence had put him in the power of those who could find a use for him on such occasions as this . . . A feeling of sickness came into my throat.

'If the police frighten her, she must have something to hide,' I said coldly. 'In that case, is it not unwise to come to me, on the faint chance that I might know where she is? The police are friends of mine.'

For all his prompt grimacing, he could not conceal the momentary look of hatred and contempt in his dark, full eyes; but again he had his answer ready.

'No, no,' he said, 'there is nothing. It is just she is frightened of even the name: *police*. For so long we have been . . . *on the run*, as you say in English.'

I perceived that he did know enough about Irma, or at least about people of her kind in similar circumstances, to give me cause to be careful.

'What makes you think she should still be on the run in Australia?'

It stopped him only for a few seconds.

'If the police are your friends, you must know, Mr. Fitzherbert, there have been Nazi agents even in your own wonderful country.'

'That may be so, but they have not drawn attention to themselves by Jew-baiting. Is your sister a Communist?'

'No, no,' he said again hastily. 'Not now. Once, you understand, we were all—sympathizers—but we have been betrayed.' Once more the eyes upturned towards the ceiling, the little resigned sigh. He was in a quandary, for he could not be at all sure how much, if anything, I knew of Irma's past. The photostat copy of her portrait, which he had put away with many cautious glances about him, was probably an N.K.V.D. one if what she had told me were the truth; and I had no further reason to doubt her on the facts. The camera had not missed those faint traces of a circular rubber stamp's imprint in the corner, suggesting that the original was a file copy.

'I do not quite understand all this,' I said, purposely to provoke him. 'You say your sister is not a Communist, which means she has nothing to fear from anti-Communist elements which may be in this country from abroad. You say first you had lost all trace of her and were beginning to think she was dead, yet you later tell me the name of the ship she arrived on. If you knew what ship brought her, you had only to go to the police and tell them. Sooner or later they would have found her. She need not even have known they were trying to trace her, if you had asked them to keep it dark. Our police may have different methods from those of the police you have had to do with in other countries'—I watched him blink at that—'but they are not fools, nor are they gangsters. In spite of all this—and I assume you had the wits to think it out for yourself long ago—in spite of all this, you come to me, to tell me in a rather peculiar tone that you think I know your sister, even when I say I do not. Why?'

He was discountenanced, and showed it. Even the talk of Irma as his sister had been unreal from the start, a crude attempt to cover the fact that he had come—no doubt by direction—straight to me, which he would only have been told to do if there had been strong evidence somewhere that I knew more about her than I admitted to knowing, or at least that I had seen her more recently than on the distant August morning of her arrival. As far as I knew, only McMahon had seen us within speaking distance of each other, apart from Barbara, whom I trusted, and the wireless monitor . . . and of course the copy-boy—and Miss Werther—and Jack . . .

It was absurd. The only person in a position and at the same time with conceivable reason to betray to these unknown hunters the possible fact of any association between us since her arrival was McMahon, whom Barbara had described as an under-cover man. I would only need to mention him, with his notorious habit of drunkenness, to hear all knowledge of his very existence denied. Such a denial would make any explanation even more impossible to this sly, lying, dangerous sneak who was now obviously trying to think of a credible answer to my question.

'Why come to me?' I said again. He had lost his manner of caution and appeal, and began to look sullen, though not in the least frightened as I had hoped.

'You were seen with her . . . recently,' he said at last, bringing out the words unwillingly and with difficulty, like

275

a man suddenly uncertain of the idiom of the language he is using.

'Impossible,' I said more coldly than ever; and then, to my own surprise, I began to laugh silently. The whole situation was absurd. He had mishandled his part from the beginning, and thanks to his careless lies I had him, as they say, on toast; and I was glad, I enjoyed watching his sullen discomfort, which was for himself alone, for his collapsing vanity, more than for the futility of his mission. He dared not tell me who had seen Irma with me, even if he himself knew. Mention of the always-intoxicated McMahon would not only have made him look ridiculous, but would have threatened or actually destroyed the future usefulness of that friendly under-cover gentleman.

'Look here, Mr.—Martin or whatever your real name may be,' I said at length, 'you have come to the wrong man. In fact, I suggest you have come to the wrong country. Wherever your sort go, they expect to inspire fear, or to arouse a fear already dormant. In Australia we have never had to live in that sort of individual fear as yet. I doubt if we ever shall. You come to me with the obvious purpose of finding out the present whereabouts of someone you say is your sister. That alone shows how little you know of things here. No reputable newspaper man—no one but a drunken sneak,' I said, for I was becoming angry again at the thought of McMahon, 'would give your sort of person the information you seek, even if he had it to give, which I have not. On the contrary, he would, if he could, get into touch with the young woman at once and warn her of your presence and your inquiries. It seems to me you do not mean this young woman any good. Do you know what I shall do next? I shall telephone to the police—they are, as you know, my friends—and I shall give them a very careful description of you, and advise them to look into your papers and your history. Make no mistake, Mr. Martin—they will find you and find out all about you, and decide whether or not you, as an alien, are a desirable person to have at large in this country which you seem to think is populated only by fools, knaves and traitors like yourself.'

I was so angry, for the first time in years, that I was enjoying it without shame. The pompous words, however quietly spoken in that busy room, sped from my lips as glibly as any rehearsed speech, and with furious conviction. As for him, he actually shrank against the hard back of the visitors' chair, his face paling to a faintly greenish tinge and the rubbery smile coming and going on his face with the effect of a nervous tic. He even held out one hand as though begging me to desist.

'Recall,' I said, 'that we are at war with Nazi Germany, and so, technically, with her allies. If by any chance you come from either the one or the other party, beware. A nation at war, Mr. Martin, does not waste time arguing with spies and foreign pimps in its midst, not even a nation as easy-going, as slow to suspect strangers, as this one. As you give me the impression of being a liar employed by other liars who do not care to reveal themselves in person, you are probably everything else that is bad and contemptible. I suggest you go—not only out of this office, but out of the country . . . if you can get out of it fast enough with a whole skin. If I could find it in myself to do so, I should

277

take every possible step to make you suspected by the people who hire you, and you know what that would mean. Read the papers, Mr. Martin. See how often one after another of you foreigners is beaten up or found mysteriously dead in some back room somewhere, or drowned in the harbour or fatally injured by an unidentified vehicle that failed to stop after the—accident. Read the papers, Mr. Martin. They do not tell one half of what happens in the shadows of this city or the other big cities of this continent. Think carefully of what I say, and take my advice and go—if you can—or join the Australian army where you have a chance of being lost even to your fellow-thugs, if the Army authorities do not decide to hand you over to the police at once. And now I must ring the police Aliens Squad.'

It was of course a shameless performance, but I have never been sorry for it. He was a sort of man one would actually regret having treated decently. While I spoke, rapidly and in a low voice with my released anger roaring in my ears like a far surf, he seemed to become smaller and more puppet-like, and by the time I had finished and was reaching for the house telephone, he was on his feet looking thoroughly frightened. I am quite unused to causing people to show fear or even to feel it; for all my deliberate reasoning to the contrary, I was still sore and sick at the thought, prompted by the innocent Miss Werther, that it was fear of me that had made Irma resume her blind flight which had brought her into my life in the first place. I realized with disgust that perhaps in her distracted mind there was little to choose between this wretched incompetent creature and myself now, even though she had said she loved me. It is not hard to love that which will destroy the lover, and earthly love and fear are in essence equally strong, equally self-destructive.

I lifted the receiver and said clearly, 'Get me police headquarters please, Inspector Grimes of the Aliens branch,' without letting him see I was holding down the trestle-bar. When I turned from the instrument I was rewarded with my last sight of him, walking with his padded shoulders slightly hunched, like a man who fairly expects a knife-blade in the back, through the doorway of the general room, and so out of my life.

I was glad to realize that my anger had vanished with him. I am not given to violence. From childhood I had been trained to believe, and later to understand, that violence achieves nothing against its object, while at the same time it inflicts a self-defeat upon him who gives way to the urge to do it. I had come to have a contempt for warmongers and a horror of war-making as a deplorable but ineradicable human characteristic, as inalienable in the human race as the compulsion to love. All the time now I was confronted with the evidence of this characteristic, day by day for six years, eight years, ten years—it seems for ever. My son grew up to know little of any world but a world at war, wholly or locally, from the time when he first understood what the word meant. Our glorious Russian ally—as one or two men like Winston Churchill always anticipated—grew to become a nursery terror of nightmare proportions in the United States of America, and in time the acknowledged potential enemy of the whole western world. Even in my own country the echoes of a frenzied violence sounded, as they sounded more loudly in other dwindling places of true freedom on the earth's surface.

Without foreseeing all these things at the time, I sat there at my table and told myself I should be ashamed of the recent impulse to which I had nearly given way; and yet I was not ashamed.

It may have been that I felt a blow had been struck for Irma against fate in the person of a dapper and venomous representative of her persecutors. I may even have felt convinced that her safety was now more secured than it had been, flee though she might to the outer limits of oblivion. Whatever it was, I was pleased with myself as the anger left my blood, and happier in thinking of her than I had been for a long time.

Just before she lost consciousness for the last time, not very long after she had been confessed and received the benefit of extreme unction which is one of the kindliest ministrations of my Church, my mother's fingers stirred in my hand and I saw she was looking at my face. It was a strange, traumatic look such as one might turn upon something as recognizable, evocative and lifeless as a mask of clay. Her eyes were aware of the surface of my face and nothing more; they moved from my hair to my lips, rested on my own eyes without entering them, strayed from side to side measuring the width of brow and cheekbones, and in fact went over my face several times as though not her eyes but her hands were searching it in the dark, as she sometimes used to do when she sat on the edge of my childhood bed, before saying goodnight, after she had put out the nursery light. In those days I would laugh softly at the moth-like touch in the warm secure darkness. Now, when she was about to die, I found it infinitely moving and pitiful, and to hide from her indifferent eyes my sudden grief at this foreseen yet unimaginable parting I raised the hand I held and passed it over my face in the way she had been wont to do.

'So like Alan . . .'

That was the last thing she said, and I hardly heard the words; for she spoke with the dragging voice of a dreamer or a drunken person, and I remembered she had been given an opiate to make death's coming less of a surprise to her fading consciousness.

This happened early in nineteen forty-five, and to this day I could not swear to whether she meant I was like my father or like my son, named Alan after him. The years of war had played havoc with her mind and body, for though she tried to conceal it I knew she had never recovered from the incredulous sorrow of my father's death, and had little energy left from this concealment with which to resist the succession of days and years of peculiarly personal horror the war flung at her. More than once in moments of thoughtful privacy with me she had seemed to confuse me with my father, and had said things, incomprehensible to me, in an idiom he evidently would have understood.

There was little I could do for her, beyond ensuring that her failing bodily resources were properly cared for by a trained nurse poorly disguised as a genteel companion and housekeeper—for nothing would persuade her to separate Miss Molesley from Alan or Alan from me; and in any case she needed the skill and impersonal handling of a qualified nurse. All her life she had been regular in her observance of Church ritual, confessing herself modestly once a week

281

and attending two Masses, as well as occasional special services on certain saints' days, and vespers irregularly but often during the summer evenings, Like many intelligent women, she found a profound pleasure and self-fulfilment in the temporal and spiritual aspects of the Mass, and I took to attending her when I could, though our only regular engagement to worship publicly together was still the habit, which was rather an impulse than a habit, of joining in the lovely midnight ceremony of Christmas Eve.

She never mentioned my increased assiduity in going with her to church, and I wondered whether her occasional moments of confusing me with my father might not have been encouraged by having me with her far more often when she went to her devotions; for at such times during their marriage he had been with her always. Never during their long life together did he allow her to see the growth in himself of the scepticism which, he told me, was beginning to embitter his last years, and for which, as for my mother's slow bodily weakening, I could do nothing.

He felt himself to be spiritually sick, yet he was not sure . . . His moments of doubt, which he attributed once in my hearing to having been over-zealous in his youth, became more frequent though never quite intolerable as he grew old (he was forty when I was born); and, while they made him impatient, of himself and of the value he came to set upon reason at the expense of faith, they never spoiled his enviable sense of humour. 'I believe, my boy, I shall be glad to die and clear up this matter once and for all,' he said to me. It was the sort of thing which, in his tender consideration for her, he never said to my mother; and so, though she never knew it, in the end he had begun to grow apart from her.

'Women have the divine gift of faith in a degree which we shall never understand. If we perceive it in them, we should recognize and honour it, and attempt no more, lest we find that like earthly beauty it is the outcome of perfect bodily functioning.'

I found that in one of the *Unselected Letters*, a series of unfinished notes and fragments of thought which he began half-heartedly to put into publishable shape just before he died. Indeed, this scepticism of his had seeped more deeply than I realized into his whole life; that is to say, I never realized how obscurely distressed he himself was while he lived through those last few years of enforced retirement from the Bench and the judicial work which he had loved with a love he described as 'both unseemly, my boy, and infinitely chaste'. All the important developments of his life happened belatedly. He had taken silk late, and married late, as marriages are made in Australia; my mother was thirty-five when she bore me, and he himself had only recently been appointed to the magistracy. When he was fifty-five he was appointed to the Supreme Court, from which he retired nine years later. Only his death, at seventy-two, was perhaps a little premature for the rest of us.

Unlike some of his colleagues and contemporaries, he held that the courts of law were no places for the parade of judicial wit, however sedate and austere; he maintained that a judge who was deliberately witty might be thought to betray boredom rather than an alertly following mind, and as a result he sometimes entertained us at dinner with remarks which, he said, he could have made while the court was sitting—if he had thought of them. These he noted down tidily in scattered notebooks under a proposed title, *Best Left Unsaid*. He never had a book published in his lifetime; and when, some months after his death, I carefully went through all these random writings of his I found that the only connecting thread was that widening lode of scepticism, which never became cynical because in him thought was balanced and profound as well as sharp and sensitively probing, but which nevertheless reflected the secret distress of his spirit. For this reason I made no attempt to carry out his part-serious, part-ironic plans for publication, and put the papers away until after my mother's death, when, having culled them again, I stored the gleanings at Hill Farm, and with a little harmless grieving (for he was a good and gentle man) burned what remained.

It seemed to me that my mother, at the end, must have meant that I was 'so like Alan' the husband. The Fitzherberts, judging by old likenesses and copies of earlier portraits, had been pre-potent for generations. Not only the white skin and dark hair persist: the cranial and facial structure has changed little and imperceptibly if at all. Apart from this, I could not have been said to be very like my father. I never had his sense of humour, certainly never his easy wit with which he was always so careful never to hurt any human being except, in fun, himself. I was an only child, but he was not. As a younger son in a family of somewhat eccentric intellectuals, with a father and an elder brother and a sister who were for the most part talking over his head or making sly game of his serious church-going, he nursed his wit in the first place as a sort of defence of both himself and his mother, whose unfeigned piety he had inherited too young, and whom her brilliant barrister husband treated, I believe, to a good deal of verbal bullying mixed with sardonic courtesy in place of affection; and it was only later that his native good temper took conscious pleasure in being witty for what to most people was wit's sake. In fact, he considered good wit a gracious aspect of good living, and symptomatic of a proper sense of leisure.

I inherited the aspirations but not the quality of his mind, which belonged to a more leisurely age than mine, and the inevitable, unconscious loneliness of a solitary childhood made me, too early, prone to a gravity that by no means became my years. He was the only one of the three children who had married; nor had I cousins of my own generation on my mother's side, for she too was an only child. This small, restricted trio of relationships in my childhood made me quite incapable of forming easy attachments for the rest of my life. Human associations, as I knew them, were so tender and precious that it was impossible to believe they were not also very rare; until I married, most of the few friendships I did form for young men and women of my own age I myself overbalanced and let fall, by weighting them too readily, too soon, with too much value, too openly. I was that most embarrassing of creatures, a serious-minded young man.

In Alan, as he grew older and bloomed in the glowing warmth of adolescence, I saw more of my father than of myself. Of this I was continually glad; by it I was on occasions elated, for he promised to have his grandfather's wit and temperament, without the underlying bitterness that blossomed, pathetic and barren, in the old man as we last knew him. In the year of my mother's death and the war's official ending in most parts of the world, he was fifteen, white-skinned where the sun had not lightly browned him, dark-haired and with the wide-set eyes which have been the Fitzherbert's most persistent characteristic in a skull that seems never to have changed from its earliest depicted shape: so wide from temple to temple that the top of the head looks flattened, above a face that narrows from high cheek-bones to a long chin which deceptively makes the base of the lower jaw look narrow too. 'The family jaws' and 'the family forehead' must have been mentioned as often and as matter-of-factly in the hearing of my forefathers as they were in mine. It was almost certainly the reason why, for generation after generation, except for a time in the foppish days of the eighteenth century, the males of the line wore beards. A beard saves such a face from appearing to be a sly caricature of good looks, with every feature exaggerated. It gives a mildly piratical air that does not lack dignity and is not unduly noticeable.

Alan had the family forehead and eyes, but a better line of jaw and mouth more full and mobile, less repressed-looking, than his forebears'. His eyes in their wide-apart deep sockets under perfectly-marked eyebrows had an increasing penetration as he began to find and keep the inexpressible secrets proper to his age, the secrets no man has ever learned before; but above all, the arched brows gave them a delightful look of merry humour never overshadowed by the broad thoughtful pallor of the forehead above them, from which his dark hair was brushed aside in a thick curve. To me he looked what he was—a scholar and an athlete in the making, one who thought his own incommunicable thoughts and dreamed his own dreams untroubled by early introspection or any sort of doubt or fear. He was never lonely. He filled me with delight, the mere thought of him filled me with a delight that paid in advance for anything I might do for his sake.

At the same time, he made me wary of love. As he came nearer to me once again, and, paradoxically, became also more individual and apart from me and all others, the practice of that warm indifference at which I had always aimed stood me in good stead. By the end of the summer holiday which he turned fifteen, he showed signs of being willing to treat me as a friend, with a sort of respectful familiarity which I tried—and tried in vain—not to find flattering. A negative, tacit insistence on his association with friends of his own age and interests, which my continual absences at all hours of the summer days and nights made easy and unemphatic, merely added to this quite filial familiarity an unexpected but charming, amused yet tender show of sympathy for 'the breadwinner'. He did not chatter, but he had sudden impulses to talk without ceasing for half an hour on end, about anything that had apparently been occupying his thoughts; and sometimes before, sometimes after these bursts of gay, irrelevant speech he would sit looking at me thoughtfully in silence, as though asking himself 'Should I tell?' or 'Should I have told?', or follow me about the flat idly without a word, uncertain in his own mind of something said or unsaid.

When he awoke, in those early mornings, he awoke wholly, apparently with forward-looking not retrospective thoughts, into a vitality of mind and body he must have found hard to check in that comparatively restricted space—what he wanted was a place of rivers and fields and mountains, as I knew from observing him during the occasional weeks and week-ends we spent at Hill Farm in the winter and spring months. In the flat that first summer of official peace I would hear him, through the lifting veils of my own sleep, busy in the kitchen at the coming of first light soon after four o'clock those December mornings. Later he brought cups of tea to my bedside where I slept in the corner of shadow between the eastward and the northward windows—a pleasure I had seldom known, outside country hotels on rare occasions of duty, for fifteen years. With his cup in his hands he surveyed through half-closed eyes the blinding brilliance of sunrise upon the harbour beyond the wide-open French windows and the stone balustrade outside, while doves bargained monotonously with each other in the garden of the building next door, and the gulls screamed their arrogant slate-pencil exasperation near and far above the sparkling water that reflected a blind stipple of flights up on the white ceiling.

It was a waking pleasure to watch him, angular and smooth in his swimming trunks there in the blaze of hot eastern light. Morning after morning, in the changeable summer days of that December and January, I found myself coming by varied ways of thought to the same point of unanswerable query: what would women see in him, a few—a very few—years from now? I saw him leaning in the frame of the open windows, his thick dark hair wet and brushed neatly aside, his deep, candid young eyes moving their regard, which changed so subtly as it moved, from me to the spectacle of sonorous and vivid day roughly cupped in the huge twisted hands of the harbour outside, and back from the day to me; I saw the duality of adolescence—the speaking, smiling boy, ageless and vivid as the morning light that swept across him into the room, and within the boy who seemed so conscious of me and the outside world the other, the brooding self, unconscious of its house of flesh, of the world, and of time.

There can of course be no certainty of what women will find, or fail to find, in some sorts of young man. Social manners change with the generations; circumstances of upbringing differ from father to son, and of the probable relationship of a man to women not much can be foresaid. Good looks, of which Alan would surely have more than either my father or I had had, seem to count for little, if there is not informing them a strongly masculine spirit, erect and positive in the presence of a woman. The existence of this spirit may not always be discernible in the middle years of adolescence, even in a country where bodies and minds mature early, at sub-tropical speed; but I imagined I could detect it sometimes in the boy: in his new, unostentatious modesty with Miss Molesley concerning such matters as his linen and the privacy of the bathroom, for all that he passed most of the year in the boldly-outspoken world of boarding-school boys—or because of that, it might be; in his masculine sensitiveness at this age to words and tones of voice, his frequent choice of solitude, and his carefully unemotional friendliness and affection towards me.

It was necessary to forget my own rather circumscribed and unnatural boyhood in order to approach an understanding of the boy's present being and probable development in the society he would live in; and I found it hard to force myself to forget. It was necessary also to realize that the very fact of having been reared by strange hands among the bull calves of the coming herd would likely give him a normal physical, animal appeal to women, which I had certainly never had, during and following the sequestered, segregated years of my own first youth. This profound difference of our social selves each from the other put beyond likelihood all chance of friction between us. We thought and spoke one language most of the time, but beneath the surface of word and gesture and appearance there separated us a distance not only of time but, more mysteriously, of kind.

He was perhaps more nervously masculine than I had ever been. I knew I had never had much direct physical appeal to women—not enough of the bull there, and too much of the sacred hart; if they had been attracted, it was by the ordinary observances of cleanliness, good clothes, the manners my father had taught me, and my own pleasure in hearing them talk. My friendships, such as there had been, were rather of the intellectual sort, with speech and thoughts for currency. That was why the years-old attraction I had felt in myself for Irma and in her for me had taken me, against my will and judgment, by storm.

I wondered what would happen between that girl and me, were we to meet again now, after the long silence and the memories of six years, a silence and memories without calm. I wondered if my heart would beat again, as it did sometimes beat in her company, like a boy's who again and again, half-disbelieving, sees his girl at his side; and whether she herself had changed with the violent, fretful changing of the times. I knew I myself had aged as a man does age when he watches a son grow towards manhood, and feels his sympathy and understanding of the coming man deepened by the keen remembrance of his own boyhood, his own dreaming youth with its decreed innocence and ignorances, its moments of instinctive foreknowledge, its gradual awareness of truth and error, right and wrong, as conscience is born like a kernel in the seed of the ripening fruit. These experiences a man relives, if he should take upon himself the task of true parenthood; and they, by a sort of paradox, both age him inwardly and make him younger; the rod of the husband becomes the more pliable bow of the father, and there is an enlarging of thought from its absolute discipline to a compassionate curve of reason.

Irma, the girl, would now be a woman of twenty-five. With an unholy pang of physical jealousy which I had felt more than once, and cursed, during these last years, I wondered what men had had to do with her, what flowers and scars must distinguish from the sapling I had known the maturing young tree she would now have become. All I did know of her was occasional word heard from Miss Werther. The amiable little Jewess had prospered during the war years, thanks to a native foresight in buying such stocks of furs as would have made any ordinary dealer lose sleep—and buying them before the war began. From time to time she rang me at my flat, and her lilting voice with its seemingly indestructible tones of kindly good humour brightened the moment always with the same words: 'Mr. Fitzherbert, there is another letter . . .' She would briefly outline the contents, and always there came the final almost reproachful ending—'She sends you her warmest greetings and hopes some day you may have time to write.'

Well, in six years I had evidently had no time; and in six years her greetings could still remain her warmest. I had never written, for what could I have said? I saw her letters later, over cups of coffee or at some luncheon table, as each one arrived, half a dozen in a year perhaps, letters as fluent and neat as the handwriting in which they were set down. Of our eventual reunion and its outcome I could foresee nothing, or I might not have gazed with such dreaming content and self-commendation at the boy leaning his shoulders back in the white frame of the open French windows, with bright morning hot and eager as a promise behind him.

'Sir,' he said with a sort of tender impudence, 'you are very broody this morning.'

'If you had a boat,' I said, 'you could get round the harbour and see it at its best, from water-level. You could also visit some of the islands.'

'Too much like hard work.' He had picked up that expression from old Jack, for whom he had a respectful admiration that pleased me and amused Jack. He had few social and even fewer of the intellectual affectations of his age; sometimes I heard him telling Moley how he wanted his clothes pressed and his handkerchiefs folded, but he never minded copying Jack's haphazard ways of speech, which he apparently accepted uncritically as part of the man. It was Jack who had taught him things I never knew myself: how to milk and handle a cow, and how to ride; to think of a dog as your equal in vital importance to itself, and your superior in natural dignity; how to sharpen tools and use them with a loose wrist; many useful things that trained body and mind to work together. Their association, which continued day-long and into the dusk whenever we were at Hill Farm, contented me deeply; in practical matters Jack was the ideal mentor for Alan, making fun of his mistakes as I would never have done, and sharing with him long periods of industrious silence in the paddocks or the barn or high up among the great trees that hid the mountainside. He learned to lay an axe to a tree as I had never learned, swinging the four-and-a-half pound head in such an exact imitation of Jack's own classic style that because it was correct and easy, and he was very young, it became a habit. He could skilfully set rabbit traps in runs his own eyes assured him were used often, and conceal his revulsion under Jack's cool miss-nothing gaze when he had to kill the hysterically screeching creatures next morning; but after the first experience of this necessary extermination of the pest he could never eat a rabbit dish again. It was no matter: he was learning, and to Jack's delighted question: 'What's this? Mean to tell me when you're a doctor y'ain't ever goin' to kiss a woman again after you cut the first one up?' he could reply with a lofty air that made the old man choke with amusement, 'Women are quite a different kind of animal, you see—don't you always tell me so?' It was the first time I had ever seen Jack laugh. In return, he spent half a day teaching the boy how to sharpen a knife and work leather. From Jack and Miss Molesley he even learned to cook. During all these fascinating exercises his classroom studies were set aside so completely in his mind that any chance scholastic allusions that might escape me as the three of us sat by the fire for a short hour before bedtime were met with a momentary blind incomprehension in his drowsy eyes.

Thus he had grown, in the tutelage of many masters of whom old Jack, his ancient sly sagacity untroubled by the remote chaos of a world he had done with, was not the least worthy; he had learned by the time he was fifteen to use his head and his hands together. To me his life, what I knew of it, seemed full and wholly good.

'What then?' I said, preparing to get up and change, and join him in the pool below where the water of the rising tide looked agreeably bitter and clear and cool against the cemented stone.

'I was going to Ken West's for the day—when you've gone to the office—to play tennis, if I may, please.'

'Very good.' I put my feet to the floor. He came to take away the empty cup from the top of a pile of books on the night-table, and to my surprise he ruffled my hair with his hand as he passed me. It was one of those rare gestures involving contact between us at which he was far more adept than I would have been had I ever risked volunteering them, a thing I had long ago ceased to do; for boys of that precarious age seem able to tolerate only the rough touch of other boys without embarrassment; and in Alan's case there was also an inherited unreasonable wariness against actual physical contact with those of his own blood. I had felt the same with my own father, and to a less degree even with my mother; the old man once told me, when we were discussing the more inexplicable aspects of heredity, that one way his father had of reprimanding him had been by grasping him by the back of his neck with his naked hand. 'After that, even to shake hands with him in later life was always a conscious effort, don't you know?' he said, adding thoughtfully, 'Yet there was never a cleaner or a more honest man, according to his own standards, which were high enough in all conscience.'

Alan's casual brief touch, daring yet innocent of familiarity, was like that of a friendly animal that has no cause yet to fear your weight of years or your human intellect. I did not look at him or speak, but smiled for him to see, thinking how it was very much a gesture not of his age but of the times and his generation—such a gesture as I, for example, would never have thought of making towards my own father, though I realized (by far too late, alas) that it would doubtless have pleased him, after his own brief surprise, as it had pleased me now.

While I closed the Venetian blinds to darken the room against the heat of early morning, and changed into swimming trunks, I listened to him in the kitchen whistling above the sound of running water; and at the opening of a door I heard him stop in the middle of a bar to say with sudden glorious gaiety, 'Hullo Moley my dearest old darling. Why don't you slip into a two-piece swim-suit and come for a paddle with the pater and me?'

Her reply had the comfortable, timeless security of a habit whose origins were forgotten by all but Miss Molesley herself; and even she could not exactly tell me how she had come by the one remark above all others that had confounded Alan since earliest childhood with its air of mad profundity.

'There's them as do, and there's them as don't, and I be one of them as do don't.'

His summer laughter followed me into the cool sanctuary of the bathroom like a breeze.

Like most people who tend to be over-serious in their whole daily life, I have always been easily taken by surprise by circumstances which to another, livelier mind would not be surprising at all.

I was surprised in this way that it should have been Barbara who at last gave me first-hand information about Irma. Nothing could have been more natural, one might say inevitable, than that it should be she, of all people in the office, who saw the girl again before any of us—she who spent so much of her working time thinking and writing about new clothes for other women, and looking at the show of them. It was quite usual for her to go by air to Melbourne for the private showings of spring and autumn fashions, taking her own photographer with her and managing to make of it a short two-day or three-day holiday in the city she liked so much better than she liked Sydney.

At the end of April, when I was already allowing myself to look forward to Alan's first-term holiday, Barbara flew up from Melbourne one Thursday forenoon, and telephoned me from her home across the harbour, where she had gone direct from the airport to recover from the effects of air travel, which invariably made her feel sick for some hours after landing.

'Try to get over for dinner,' she said weakly over the telephone. 'We're having a new dish, and you can have it whenever you say, if you're busy. I want to show you something and tell you about Melbourne before I get all tangled up in the office again.'

At five o'clock I took a cab from the office, and was with her twenty minutes later, where she lay pale but alert under a rug on the cane lounge in the sunroom of her high Seaforth home. That room looked south and east fairly down beyond Middle Harbour to the vertical gateway of the Heads veiled today in an evening ocean haze; and the plains of blue water, darkening in the last full daylight, were stippled with the last of the failing north-east wind, the dying wind of summer.

'Lloyd,' she said, when her elderly Irishwoman had talked herself backwards from the still room that seemed made only of glass and polished wood and air, 'I feel as though I'd been away a terribly long time, this time. Give me your hands—no, both of them, my dear boy—I feel very old at the moment, Lloyd, and I need your youthful support.'

She pressed my fingers against her forehead, first one hand and then the other, with her own warm fingers.

'Nothing ever does any good,' she said wanly, against the inner side of my wrist. 'I've tried sedatives and glucose and goodness knows what else, and the only thing that ever helped me was a flask of whisky during the flight itself—and then I felt worse afterwards than usual. I think we should have a drink now. Brian will be here to dinner. The latest is, he doesn't want to leave the R.A.A.F. now, having come through with a whole skin, the lunatic. In that cabinet there by the door—whisky and a siphon. I wish Con could see

297

him now with all those ribbons and things. I do feel so proud of him, even if I don't understand much about it. Con was a great one for colour in uniforms. He said it was the Scotch in him, and when I asked him what Scotch he simply laughed and said, "Imported." Do you suppose he meant whisky or immigration?'

After fifteen years she still spoke of it as though it were yesterday's conversation. I reflected, as I mixed two drinks, that I could not any longer feel that way when I remembered Jean. Men are more faithful to an idea, women to a remembered reality. Alan had at length replaced her as fully as possible in my life, and if there were still an emptiness, like unacknowledged physical hunger for food, to be felt in me at times I was too used to that now to be troubled any more by it—ever again, I thought with satisfaction.

No sooner had this satisfaction declared itself so complacently than I was called upon, with divine irony, to pay for it, when Barbara, having swallowed some of her drink thirstily, sighed and spoke again.

'Do you ever hear from Miss Martin, Lloyd?'

'No, only from her friend whom she writes to sometimes.'

'If it's not an impertinent question, how do you feel about her now?'

'I hardly know if I feel anything, Barbara.'

'I had to ask, because you never do show much—you don't let on, as Molly says. One has to guess . . . Besides, I saw her and spoke to her in Melbourne, and I've brought back an off-the-record photograph she allowed us to take to show you. I hope you don't mind. It was my own idea.'

'How was she?' I watched the day going peacefully away over the ruffled fields of dark water; it seemed at that moment the only peace left, in the world or in my senses. When I looked back at her, Barbara was smiling, and there was a faint return of colour to her face.

'Very well. Really beautiful now. She has taken part of Melbourne by storm, all in a matter of weeks—the rich part. There is nothing of your refugee about her now, I assure you. All the same, I felt when I spoke to her, or rather when I listened to her, that she was still in search of a refuge. You know—that not-quite-happy feeling some beautiful girls seem to have?'

'I know. We all have it, probably, but only the beautiful ones show it, because we look at them so much more carefully. We try to find what it is that we have not, and in the end we find what we ourselves have that they have not.'

She shook her head a little impatiently but with a look of laughter.

'That drink has made me quite intelligent again, and it's no good you being clever just to avoid the issue. The subject was Miss Martin—she's known as Irma Francis professionally, by the way—and I still say she's not as happy as she ought to be, considering her success.'

'And I,' I said firmly, 'still say that is true of anyone you like to name. Frankly, I think you're trying to draw me, Barbara, and I don't quite know why.'

'Frankly,' she said, 'I am, and I should have known you better, I should have known it was impossible as well as unfair.'

She took from the cane garden-table beside her a

manilla folder which I had noticed was bulging with photographs, and put it on the rug over her knees.

'I wasn't really trying to draw you out, you know,' she said. 'Or was I? Dear me—the worst thing about a woman of my age is, she seldom knows what really goes on in her. The honest truth is—and this is the honest truth, Lloyd— I am so fond of you after all these years that I think I'm just slightly jealous of this girl. You don't mind?'

'I would be flattered if I could believe it.'

'Not at all—it's she who must be flattered, since it's true . . . Oh dear—just for once, Lloyd, relax and give me a kiss. I'm still rather up in the air after that damned 'plane trip.'

She pulled me by the shoulders, and needed little effort, to get me near enough so that we could kiss one another warmly; and I had to think hard to realize that it was the first time we had ever done that, in a world where kissing is so easy as to have no longer the value even of a betrayal. She smelled very warm and sweet, very feminine, as though she had stepped out of a warm bath not many minutes before. I was aware of her long after she drew back and unconsciously rubbed her lips with the back of her hand.

'One gets to like it, I believe,' I said. 'The French have a proverb about it—they say that kissing a man without a moustache is like eating an egg without salt.'

'A man made that up, I'm sure. For a beard too, add pepper. Lloyd! Don't look so shocked.'

'I was not feeling shocked. I was thinking nothing so nice has happened to me for a long time.'

'Well, here is something nicer still. I don't so much

mind giving it to you now.' She slid out the photograph that lay uppermost on the pile in the folder. 'Look at this. That is your reward for being sweet to me, and don't say I'm not generous.'

The likeness was a seated full-length with a matt surface that gave it a positively tactile quality. Irma looked sideways at the camera and so at me, and Louise, Barbara's photographer, had caught her in such a lively way that the direct, sidelong look along the high cheekbones made her seem about to turn her head fully and smile, no matter how long one continued to gaze at the face so perfectly portrayed.

Bones do not change. She was perhaps a little thinner, or perhaps only the studio lighting made it seem so; and there was delicate emphasis, not alteration, of the hinted shadows in temple and eye and cheek. I had never had such an opportunity to examine her face in detail at my ease, and my heart was overcome with a surge and thrust of infinite longing, infinite melancholy (encouraged no doubt by Barbara's kiss still warm and full on my mouth), as I observed the fine generosity of her almost-smiling lips on which the light shone moistly, and the slanting set of her eyes that were not quite sorrowful like the eyes of an Oriental, and not quite sly, but rather could be said to resemble the eyes of a fearless wild animal. They too seemed about to smile.

This upward line of her face had been emphasized since last I saw her, I thought, perhaps for the occasion, perhaps by the firm touch of time. Her hair was long now, drawn smoothly back from brow and temple to show her ears, and

301

coiled and rolled into a large dully-gleaming knot lying on the nape of her neck with the appearance of solid metallic weight that subtly enhanced by contrast the modelling of her throat and ears and the whole enigmatic yet mobile face. Her skin in the unglazed surface of the print seemed to glow from within, warmed and informed by her life.

Barbara, leaning back on the head-rest of her lounge, was looking at me as earnestly as I had looked at the portrait.

'She let Louise take that as a favour,' she said amusedly. 'It isn't for printing, of course. She still won't be photographed if she can help it. It's probably only a pose or a habit now.'

'I never saw her in evening dress, of course,' I said.

She laughed so delightedly that she took me completely aback.

'Lloyd, you ass, that is a nightgown, and a very marvellous thing too—what we call a creation. Look again.'

I felt myself blushing like a boy. It was so, of course; my eyes had been intent only on the turning, me-recognizing face, and I saw now how the gown revealed in a half-concealment the white fullness and candour of her bosom, the arch of the unseen protecting ribs narrowing to the line of waist, spreading again to the weighted hips and thighs from which the stuff of the skirt fell in a shimmering rhomboid, like water in the sun, to the rug on which her slippered left foot rested before her. She leaned back on her left hand; in her right, slightly raised, was an elaborate hand-mirror into which she gave the impression of having glanced one moment earlier, and from which, as she let it sink to her knees, she was about to turn her face fully. The whole pose was formal, a stock pose of the shops, but I had never seen it caught before with such an effect of arrested or incipient movement.

'Louise has excelled herself,' I murmured.

'Well,' Barbara said, 'I think so, but she's a perfect subject, as you can see. Continental-trained—we don't see many of them here yet, and none of our girls can quite catch that air of actually owning the gowns and things she wears. It's not a matter of looks—Miss Martin is not a perfect beauty, like some of the Melbourne and Sydney girls. That's why her face is so interesting. She has irregular features, as you'd find if you measured them as an artist does, but she also has life and character. That's what counts. She must love the work—or else she is so well-trained that she can't help it. Whatever it is, she's made a name for herself in Melbourne in a very short time by selling everything she's shown, so far as I could gather. She must be earning good money. There's competition for her in the trade, I know that.'

It was like listening to the story of a stranger.

'As far as looks go,' I said, 'she does not seemed to have changed much. She looks older, of course, and yet in some peculiar way she looks younger. It may be professional habit, but I see no sign of the not-quite-happy look you talked about. She looks, in fact, almost mischievous here.'

'She had reason to look mischievous. But let me tell you from the start. After the show I introduced myself while we were all having cocktails—it was like most of those affairs, half-business, half an informal party, with buyers and the Press and various friends and relations. The models changed and came back to meet us, and Irma—everyone calls her Irma now—she was almost mobbed when she came in with some of the others—women as well as men, and myself among them. She took it very well. Just once I noticed her face change, when some man took her familiarly by the arm, and she rapped out in a low voice, "You would do well in America, sir." You couldn't tell whether she was angry or frightened—she tilted her head back and opened her eyes very wide—I could only think of a nervous horse. But most of the time she was smiling and talking with the rest of them . . . I'm trying to give you a picture of the goings-on.'

'You are succeeding.'

'She has peculiar eyes, Lloyd—you may have noticed them. A most unusual sort of blue, but quite suitable to that type of face with its slanting lines. The way she has her hair done in that photograph made her far the most remarkable-looking female in the room. I watched her, I suppose, more than was good manners—I was thinking all the time of what you'd told me about her and you—and really I think you acted very wisely. Now don't misunderstand me, Lloyd. I am speaking my mind. I have a feeling she might not have been good for you. There's something about her that is not—not *you*, if you know what I mean?'

'Yes.'

'Well, all right, you needn't agree with me. Anyhow, I must have stared too obviously, for I suddenly found she was giving me a nice cool steady stare herself. I felt quite embarrassed. I felt my age and a bit more—like an inquisitive old woman. Women can look at one another in that way. The only thing to do was to introduce myself and explain what I supposed she thought were my bad manners. And in any case, I was curious because of you, as I say. I mentioned you straight away—said I was sure you would like to know I had seen her, after all this time. Of course it was clumsy. She looked away and said, "Oh—do you think so?" and she was blushing. Again I didn't know whether she was angry. I felt perhaps I'd made a much worse mistake this time. When you think of it, it would sound condescending in those particular circumstances. I didn't mean it that way. I was just trying to be friendly, Lloyd.'

She spoke almost pleadingly. 'Naturally,' I said, taking my share of the lie.

'The only thing I knew about her was that she had been frightened and lonely—a long time ago. When I spoke to her I could see she was neither, any more. On the contrary, she apparently has a large acquaintance down there, a lot of foreigners among them, mostly women. Her poise has nothing to do with her job, either. Models are a vain crowd for the most part, and nothing is more easily thrown off balance, if you know how, than a vain woman. But in Irma's case there's no vanity at all. She was much more composed than anyone else there. I made the best of my blunder and left her. Five minutes later, there she was standing beside me as though she'd risen out of the carpet. Is all this of any interest to you?'

'Yes, the way you tell it.'

'If you weren't such a gentleman you'd point out— and it'd be quite necessary—that it all came from my own feminine inquisitiveness, which in turn came from my sort of possessive feeling about you. You see, I've worked it out for myself. Damn it, why do you think I've been lying here feeling so particularly wretched all the afternoon, not caring what became of me? At least you must admit I'm trying to be completely frank with you.'

At the moment I did not follow her wholly. Only in memory, afterwards, did what she was saying take on any special meaning. Looking now at her, now at Irma's portrait of a girl forever about to turn and speak, I heard her with my ears only, while in my mind the scene relived itself, vital beneath its seeming insignificance.

Irma suddenly appeared at her side, not as though she had approached but as though she had materialized. It was an unconscious trick, inexplicable, proving that ordinarily the eye sees only a fraction of the masses and movements within its range. I never got used to seeing her in one part of a room at one moment, and finding her at my side, or disappeared, the next instant as it seemed, Barbara, to whom she was quite a stranger, was startled.

Irma smiled her upward smile that could make her face as radiant as a child's with pleasure, and surprised my dear Barbara still more by saying with an air of gay conspiracy, 'Now I think we may talk more privately. Too many people listen. Please call me only Irma. If you remember me by any other name, please do not use it here.' While she was speaking, she led her to a seat in the corner, and sat with her back to the noise and the faces.

For quarter of an hour, strangely uninterrupted, they talked about the models from overseas which had just been shown, and Barbara found that unlike most mannequins she could speak with intelligent and critical authority about the clothes she and the others wore.

'I didn't realize yet that she was quite a brilliant designer herself, and that two of the most interesting new suits we had seen were her own ideas. Everyone who saw them was busy saying, "Typically Parisian, my dear—unmistakable" and trying to place the unfamiliar name, some invention of her own. I said it myself, and of course we were all quite right— they were typically French, because she had meant them to be. One doesn't necessarily have to be German to play Beethoven.'

While they talked Barbara studied her, and became more fascinated by her; and the more fascinated the more uneasy she felt, without yet realizing, she said ruefully, why this should be. It was like having before her every piece of a jigsaw puzzle but being helplessly incapable of imagining the finished picture. It needed only one movement, and the whole thing would assemble itself. It was Irma who made the move, by saying abruptly, 'Tell me, Mrs. Conroy—how long do you know Mr. Fitzherbert? I know him so little, whatever you may think.'

Barbara, embarrassed again by that 'whatever you may think', said we had worked together on the same staff for nearly fifteen years. Irma regarded her steadily for a moment, and then, smiling and shaking her head, said with her sudden air of ancient, gentle authority, 'It is quite strange. You both belong to the same world, you are both lonely people, and yet you are still just—friends. After fifteen years. Why did you want to see me, then—me, particularly?' And at that the simple puzzle fell together with overwhelming inevitability.

Like most newspaper people of ability and worth, Barbara had trained herself never to rely on instinct before reason, even forcing herself to set aside some of her native

307

womanhood to do so. Irma, on the other hand, arrived at and accepted causes in lightning flashes of instinct alone, and had acted on her conclusions often long before reason caught up with and endorsed them. This she had had to do many times in her earlier years, when as likely as not her freedom, or even her life, depended upon her being quick and certain of what she meant to do. This, unintentionally and as it might be by innuendo, she had now done again. Barbara, confused as a girl but outwardly composed in a manner suited to her years—she was forty-nine—turned the completed puzzle around to face Irma, and reversed their positions by saying with a calmness she did not feel, 'I am so fond of him after all these years that I wanted to see for myself the woman he could fall in love with.'

To this Irma merely nodded, as who should say perfunctorily, 'I understand', and a moment later excused herself and disappeared among the increasingly noisy crowd of men and women in the room.

'Do you know, Lloyd, I spent half the night thinking over what had happened,' Barbara said. 'I felt rather a fool. You must understand that all this talk about how I feel about you means nothing more than what it says.'

'We probably feel the same about one another, my dear,' I said.

'Oh, no doubt—no doubt.'

I may have missed the irony in her tone. I was full of a sudden tenderness and confidence towards her, which was perhaps isolated in my mind by having drunk a second glass of whisky while we talked.

'I can only say I can't imagine how I would have come through these last fifteen years without you, Barbara. That is the honest truth. I have depended on you more than I ever knew, more than I have on any other woman I ever knew. You never have to feel a fool on my account. You know I find it hard to show affection in the usual ways that come easily to most people, but that is only because I have been purposely training myself, because of Alan. The affection has always been there—the love, if I may use that word. Not many men and women have had the pleasure we have had, of being able to speak the truth simply and unhesitatingly to each other always.'

I had taken her hands while I spoke. When she withdrew them from mine it was to raise herself from her reclining pose with a faint sigh. In the near distance the front door was opened and closed vigorously.

'Brian,' she said to herself; and to me, 'I know. But you have to remember that even friendships like ours are different for a woman—I suppose because a woman is always liable to be wanting a little something more, without knowing exactly what it is . . . If I did feel a fool that night, lying awake listening to Louise asleep in the other bed, it was mostly because I'd had to go all the way to Melbourne in a wretched aeroplane to find out from Irma—of all people!—the simple harmless, *harmless* truth in my own heart. That's what seemed so foolish. Anyhow, I was determined to see her again, to make the whole thing clear. I can't stand tangles and misunderstandings. Life is complicated enough even when it's as simple as mine is. So I went early to next day's show, and saw her by herself. We persuaded her to pose for Louise, and once she had agreed she quite sold herself to the idea, and started worrying about what to wear. I don't mind telling you I was very much amused by her choice, until she asked me did I think it would offend you, as it was to be a memento for you? I said the garment was too lovely to offend even a saint. She looked perturbed and asked if you were that sort of a person. Certainly not, I said—I hope I did right? Anyhow, I asked her, merely from curiosity, why she chose it, apart from the look of it. She laughed a little, and said, "It is just a garment without period—it means nothing at all. Tell me, why do women wear such things?" and I reminded her that many women-look a good deal more attractive in them than out of them. She accepted that quite seriously. Louise wormed her way into the *Sun-Pic* office and made this print. She was rather sad about scrapping the plate—I have an idea she made more than one print, just between ourselves, for her own files. Irma looked at the print a long time, and said, "Please give it to him with my warmest greetings"—just like that. And that's all . . . Do get me another drink. I've been talking too much. Oh dear, I feel so much better.'

Brian joined us. He had changed into a tweed coat over his uniform shirt and trousers; when Barbara told him to get his tunic so that I could see all the ribbons on it, he only laughed.

During dinner, Barbara and he chaffed one another gently in a very mother-and-son way that was not even meant to conceal a deep mutual affection and interest. As always, I was made to feel myself one of the family by being involved in their badinage every now and then; and it was

310

easy to laugh when Brian said in his light, quick voice of a young air-force officer to whom authority is habitual, 'Mother, I have a suggestion. You and Lloyd should get married one of these days,'

He went on, 'You may laugh, but what could be more natural? I think it's a jolly good idea. You both do the same work, you have the same interests—rather heavyweight ones, I always think—and Fitz needs a woman to look after him now that he's getting on. You can tell by the worried look.'

'How old do you think I am?' I said.

He considered, looking at me shrewdly.

'I did know, years ago, but I've forgotten. About forty-five, I should guess, sir.'

'You compliment me, I suppose,' I said. 'Thirty-seven. The "sir" only makes it a worse mistake.'

We laughed at his embarrassment, without meeting each other's gaze; but the whole time I was wondering what Barbara had 'made clear' to Irma, and I knew I would never ask her, from an obscure conviction that she would tell me the truth and complicate our easy relationship in some way I could not quite define to myself.

Into my mind had come that expression of Jack's, in his clumsy writing and his deft speech: '*You ain't no fool.*' This afternoon Barbara had unconsciously endorsed this when she said, '*You were wise to go away from her . . . There is something about her that is not you.*'

The only two people in the world who knew they could say whatever they thought right to me without presumption had independently applauded what I still thought was an act at least of temporizing, if not of self-mistrust or even cowardice. Realization of this had come to me while I was washing before dinner, with Barbara's conversational, patchy, puzzling picture of Irma obsessing my thoughts like an undecipherable message, and Louise's formidable portrait of her shut in my brief-case in the hall. Smoothing hair and beard and moustaches, all showing silvery hairs now, in the glass over the hand-basin, I stared as impersonally as a stranger at my own eyes reflected there, and with exasperation saw nothing—the reflected face meant not a thing, it was like some unconvincing mask bolted immovably into place over all that had ever gone on within me, all that was fretting within me now.

What was it, and was it in me or in Irma, that had made those trustworthy and wise people who had only an intelligent humanity in common to put into almost identical words a common thought? '*You were wise to go away . . .*' '*You ain't no fool.*' Were they praising what they assumed, in their own respective integrities, was my modest knowledge of some weakness, vulnerability, worldly inexperience in myself? Or had they some impression of Irma very different from all those of my own?

I felt a moment of crying fury against . . . I knew not what. Was it against this wooden, intently-staring face in the mirror? Or the suspicion that the human character is ultimately not only unknowable but basely and worthlessly so? Or merely against the futility of all intentions to live and accept life in others without confounding feeling by outfacing it with judgments, without confusing and debasing judgment by making it drunk with feeling, when the two were of worlds apart?

The short roar of fury fell silent in my ears. I recalled for no reason, with a disgust as sharp as when he said it, a remark of McMahon's in the week following Irma's disappearance, when he pestered me with seemingly idle monologues about her: 'Any woman with eyes like hers gets a reputation for being as sexy as hell, old boy.' At the time I had not noticed it more than various other of his unembarrassed personal remarks, but I had heard it well enough, for it came back to me now, rude, trivial, the sort of remark so easy for a man like McMahon to make about a woman like Irma, but at the same time overpowering. It might explain why both Jack and Barbara felt the same doubt about her, in relationship to myself; or more likely the same doubt about me . . . as though I had barely escaped some humiliating misfortune at her hands.

While they talked with unhurried, affectionate banter among the candles burning, I was told, in my honour, I was so engrossed with thoughts of her that I believe at one time I actually decided, while Molly was garrulously handing round the dessert, to go to Melbourne and see her, come of it what might. At least there would be a clarity; the action would precipitate whatever sediment was clouding our minds and our lives. By now my frank obsession, sprung from years of neatly-repressed impulses and desires, included a doubt of Irma, herself. The reality did exist; how did I know that I had not been for years cherishing an elaborate and detailed fiction? This possibility, and all it implied of cruel lack of self-realization in me, of cruel self-deceit and deceit of others, so alarmed me that I almost choked on the spoonful of iced pear I put into my mouth as I thought of it. Brian's brisk slaps on the back at least let me groan aloud to ease the moment of its horror.

'I'll run you over, if you really have to go,' he said kindly—he was not going to 'sir' me any more, for he had to go himself to some meeting in the city; and in the car as we went he talked more intimately to me than he ever had talked of his ambitions and the worth of his war-time experience as a navigator. Ordinarily such confidences would have warmed and pleased me, but now I was cold, cold, with even the slight optimism of the whisky I had drunk faded to a dullness of mind, and some sort of frightened, lonely ache like an obscure physical sensation at my heart.

That night, and every night for the next two weeks, I slept badly, turning from dream to dream, tormented by uncertainties and doubts as never before in my life when they turned, as they soon did, from Irma to me as their object. There was an increasing desire in me, confusing thought, to leave the *Gazette,* Sydney, the State, the country itself: in fact, to cut and run from some incomprehensible situation poised implacably on the eve of development, dragging Alan with me to avoid calamity. It was a pity I did not give way to this one unreasonable desire of my life. Only the knowledge, in periods of normal mental control, that running away inevitably brings one face to face with the thing fled, the faster the sooner, and in a condition of exhaustion to boot, prevented me from taking some action which with part of my mind I knew I should quickly have regretted.

At the end of that fortnight, Alan came home from school for the May holiday; and Irma arrived unannounced and unexpected from Melbourne to spend a short week-end with her old friend Miss Werther.

When Miss Werther telephoned me that Saturday morning with her bubbling news, all confusion was swept from my mind so suddenly, so completely, that I felt weak and had to sit down. The feelings of threatened calamity that had shadowed me day and night since the evening of Barbara's dinner went away like a cloud on a change of wind. In its place shone as it were a light of warm pleasure, emanating from a positive source of determination. Everything now seemed supremely simple. Alan was here. Irma was here. All that I most loved was now at hand, within call.

The relief of mind was momentous. I heard with joy the monotonous squealing cries of the pearl-grey gulls beyond the breakwater. In the kitchen Miss Molesley and Alan were washing the breakfast dishes in a cheerful communion of which the short clatter of plates and cutlery made a part. Through the closed leaves of the French windows I watched the knife-headed, knife-winged gulls, dagger-beaked, black-capped, red-eyed, ceaselessly hunt the grey water under the smooth grey of the sky, looking down and from side to side as they flew in a way that gave their quick, unhurried flight the perfection of absolute self-assurance maintained in complete unconsciousness of effort.

Miss Werther's amiable lilting voice, excited and hasty on this occasion, still sounded in my head.

'You must come to dinner, won't you, please? Come early this afternoon. You will have so very much to talk about. Ah—what a happy surprise this is for me, Mr. Fitzherbert.'

It did not seem to me, at the moment, that I would have so very much to talk about. I felt it would be enough to see Irma again and be in her presence. As for conversation, to be easy in such a reunion at least some community of experience is needful, some mutual knowledge and shared continuity of thought; and between Irma and me, separating us solidly still like a wall which will transmit the futile rappings of attempted communication, but nothing more, there were over six years, mostly of war and strain and desperate self-preservation amid the inexhaustible, crashing debris of a whole world's slow destruction.

I looked into my mind, to see whether the manner of our ancient and unreal parting after one hour—the first hour and the last—of joined embraces of body and mind would add its weight to the great bulk of this separation; and I found that it would not. It mattered no longer, except as a beginning (not an end), and beginnings, however awkward, take on with time's passing a charm of the half-forgotten, the wishfully-distorted, and all memory of them is hazed and coloured by years of less and less anxious thought. It seemed to me, indeed, that we might start very well from that point of departure. If this meeting should prove, in spite of all my intentions, to be barren, then we would have a conclusion, six years old, ready-made, its purpose nearly completed now, in which momentarily to resume our roles, and withdraw.

If there were no barrenness, if imagined promise were to be realized, as I had determined it should be, then the point of departure became a point at which openly to resume what had never been abandoned—the nourishing of our mutual interest and attraction. There was now the difference made by her old, oblique confession of her love, and by my own admission, to myself at least, of mine. As for any future, I did not think of it. I merely felt that now, since we were about to meet again, free from the alarms and distractions that had once made us stiffly cautious of one another, there could be no more reserves of thought or speech, no more real separation.

Alan had his day planned, and Miss Molesley could enjoy one of her few worldly self-indulgences—that of preparing and eating dinner alone with him. Long ago my mother had explained to me that Moley's joys were of the spirit, which made her an admirable companion for my mother; she never sought, yet never rejected, enjoyments of an earthly sort, but was mostly careless of them. I could not quite reconcile this with her firm addiction to card-playing. It may have been that to her the ages-old mysteries of the numbers in combinations in which she allowed no element of chance somehow proved in innocent visual forms the existence of the divine logic in which she happily believed.

Her care for Alan had for a long time made my own life easier to order. I felt once more the cat-like comfort and security of having a home which someone was running for me. She did for Alan most of the things a good mother would have done, without exciting or embarrassing him with any of a mother's formidable shows of outlived but persistent gross affection. Deprived of Jean, that charming being now no more than a wraith in my memory, he could have had no better tender—he had only known and accustomed himself to a father considered by a lot of people to be 'a little strange', 'a cold fish', or 'a reserved type'—you could take your pick. As I recalled to mind these descriptions of me that had come to my knowledge over the years, I could smile with not very happy satisfaction at the success of the mask I had contrived and worn—even though the sight of it in Barbara's mirror so recently had filled me with exasperated fury at I knew not exactly what. The thought was in my mind, as I sat watching the gulls reel and recover for ever against a sky the colour of themselves, that this mask would soon be lifted, if only for a brief space.

Miss Werther lived comfortably at Edgecliff, within easy walking distance; it would take little more than half an hour to get there. I chose my way by Darlinghurst Road and the Cross. The day was still grey and windless, pressing down over the city with a belated warmth that presaged rain; but not even the weather, and the huge Saturday-afternoon reaction of faint, half-drunken melancholy that rose like a vapour from the vacant metropolis sprawling to north and east and south to meet the descending sky, could affect the Cross's air of violent, intimate life. The clamour of taxi-cab horns rises above the swimming tide of voices that speak, one would say, all languages known to man, above the sound of the passage of feet that have trodden the streets of every country of the world. Not only Sydney, but Australia itself seems shut out from this place where the rest of the world is at home; yet figures show that Australians predominate. The thing is, they do not perambulate as naturally as do the Europeans and Asiatics here; they must, like me, be going somewhere, if it be only to the nearest bar or café, while the others are happy merely

318

to be walking, to see and be seen, up and down the same few hundred yards of pavement, by brilliant fruit and vegetable stalls, flower shops clogged with colour too solid to have meaning here, dress-shop windows as passionately austere as the caged homosexual faces peeping round their enclosing, excluding curtains; libraries, antiques-dealers, cheap open-fronted cafés; and the shops, not closed today in spite of the Sabbath, selling kosher and imported foods.

It resembles a jovial nightmare, with undertones of rough passions and vitiated lusts and purchasable laughter. It never wholly sleeps; and just as at night there is a lurking illusion of unburied day, so by day there pervades it something of the less fettered freedoms of the night, and time becomes a different, wayward thing in which the hours can pass like minutes, the minutes like days.

Above all, it bestows the desirable gift of anonymity. All there are forever strangers whose caught fragments of speech, dropped on the air like scraps of innumerable torn-up letters, have no relevance and no more meaning than that of the detached words themselves. Here it is possible to hide, indefinitely and in a fashion not over-restricted, from all authority, but not from one's own kind. It is possible here to die by violence in a locality where a scream may be a laugh or a laugh a scream, and where the muffled cries beyond the partitions may be of love or of death, and go unheard, or, heard, unconstrued. The strange air belongs, as though conditioned through the years by alien throats that have breathed it in and alien lungs and tongues expelling it in the airy transience of speech, and as though localized by the intensely personal quality of life here.

In one short block down Bayswater Road, all this has vanished, and even the receding sound of it is obscured by the noise of east-bound trams and the scurry of passing traffic heading eastwards for the immense stretch of richer and superficially more sedate residential suburbs marching in from the Pacific coast, set down but not crowded between the coarse and violent worlds of the city and the beaches. The traffic passes through the Cross without touching or being touched by it; and it is this feeling of a graver, potentially dangerous stream of wholly law-abiding life going by without pausing to intrude that gives the Cross itself, and the area of which it is the vigorous heart, much of their air of nonchalant, secure isolation and intimate privacy. It was this that had attracted Irma, as it attracted every other educated alien arriving for the first time at the port or the aerodrome of Sydney; it was here she had lived her obscure year of uncertainties and stifled impulses; from here fled, and almost here in the end returned.

Edgecliff is beyond the curiously desolate brightness which, like all waterside public reserves (mad name!), Rush-cutters Bay Park has when the weather is fine; a brightness that on grey days becomes dulled and unreal, like the throng of racing and pleasure yachts spiking with their bare masts the high northern horizon from where they lie moored in the bay itself. No one cuts rushes there now. The swampy inlet of the harbour, where the convicts of a century and a half earlier bent to embrace the reeds under an alien and undreamed-of sun, has long since been reclaimed for sports and embraces of a happier kind. It lies sunk without character between two dwindling hillsides of roofs and windows, one sloping down from the east, the other from the west. Its north boundary is the harbour whose waters it scarcely clears, and the main artery taking the life-stream of traffic to and from the city arrests it on the south.

This day I saw consciously none of these things. Indeed, I was climbing the hill to Edgecliff from the bottom of Bayswater Road before the sense of increased effort woke me clearly to my whereabouts: as so often happened when my time was free, I had passed through the very centre of the Cross without realizing it, lulled in profound thought by the familiarity of the way.

I was, in fact, deliberately making myself wary of anticlimax, the empty reality that follows vivid and interrupted dreaming. Only the memory of my morning's feeling of determination remained. What I had determined upon I still could not have said, other than that it was something the opposite of flight—not pursuit but a stand. My days of acting wholeheartedly the following, enamoured swain were past; they had been gone long before I met Irma the first and the second time. Rather this determination, it seemed as I walked, was in effect a change of my whole mind, from an attitude of rejection to one of readiness to accept whatever might come to pass between that strange young woman and me. As I realized this, the memory of the morning's feelings reverted to an awareness made stronger yet, calmer yet, and yet more relieved; and in spite of the steepening hill into Edgecliff I lengthened and quickened my step.

Miss Werther's flat is approached by a ramp leading down below street-level. Between the wicket gate and the entrance door which is for her private use stretches a narrow suggestion of a formal garden, as wide as the frontage and six or eight feet deep, symbolized into two standard rose trees without flowers, in two rectangles of smooth buffalo-grass lawn flanked on all sides and divided in the middle by strips of pale concrete roughened to make a secure footing in rainy weather. Her door, on the right of the ground-floor facade, had the word *ONE* neatly done in brass, screwed on its single panel in separate brass letters, and below it a small brass plate inscribed modestly in black, like a doctor's, *Linda Werther—Agent*.

All these details I took in as I approached, that day, and I have never forgotten them: I could reach out my hand now, formally gloved, and touch with one leather finger-tip the snub black bell-button in its brass setting that showed minute traces of cloudy polishing-fluid round the sunken screw-heads. When this door was opened, it opened on a new life for me.

Irma had opened the door, wide.

Without a word, she stood back to let me pass, and closed it again, shutting us into a long, lighted hallway which appeared to run the full depth of the building, opening into a sunroom made, it seemed, all of glass from ceiling to floor. Through the glass, between pillar-like flutings of opened curtains, one saw at once a high-walled garden further screened by tall young maple trees whose remaining leaves, tenacious in the mildness of the early winter, were as bright as any of the scattered groups of dahlias that had lingered into May in the coastal warmth,

322

and hotter in colour than the chrysanthemums blazing coldly yellow and white in the dead light against the warm tones of the brick wall.

All this I thought I had seen in that first instinctive glance investigating strange surroundings, but it is more probable that I saw it so clearly only later; for at the moment all I seemed to be aware of was Irma, silently there with me, her face very pale and her smooth hair very dark in the airy hallway, taking my coat and hat and gloves like a servant, but unlike a servant not looking at our hands, not for a moment looking away from my own look bent upon her; until she turned abruptly, and put the things down on a semicircular wall-table under an ancient, misty mirror, behind her. In the mirror's depth her eyes still met mine, with a slightly mad look.

I had not thought of anything to say for this moment, and I left it to her to speak first. I had not even imagined the moment itself in advance, for I had never been here before; it would have been as impossible as imagining the moment and the circumstances of one's own death. When she turned quickly back to face me, I heard the faint catch of her breath between her parted lips, but she too remained silent, calm and erect and pale—only the transforming mirror had made her look mad—and so we stood facing one another without embarrassment, perhaps feeling only an unusually intense and frank curiosity, perhaps not even that, for I know not how many seconds.

At last, and unsure whether we had paused or not, or whether I had but imagined this to prolong the sensation of my own surprising delight, I held out my hand and said her name. Her blank expression gave place to a look of sober amusement and pleasure as she put her firm warm fingers round the back of my hand and her palm against mine in a grasp at once frank and secretly intimate.

'Yes,' she said, laughing a little, 'yes—it is me—Irma. You needn't look so *surprised*, my dear friend. Here I am.'

With her head thrown back and the faint colour discernible again under the fine skin of her slanting cheek-bones, she had an air of offering herself to my scrutiny with enthusiasm. Our hands still clung firmly together in a clasp it seemed neither of us was willing, as I was certainly unable, to end. I could not have freed my hand from hers, for I was holding her whole self in mine. I drew her towards me, and she came readily, and all that I had supposed to have been between us—years of war, years of separation under the shadow of a clumsy and ill-reasoned parting—all this might never have been, as her body touched mine from breast to knee, and her face loomed slowly enormous and disintegrating and vanishing as her eyelids closed over her blind eyes a moment before I too shut out all sight in absolute, perfect awareness of her immaculate and naked being held once more in the strength of my left arm.

FIVE
THE INFRINGEMENT

Possession is not wisdom, which comes completely, it seems, only after complete renunciation. I do not properly possess wisdom myself because I have never been able to renounce my aspirations to it as ultimately the one worthy prize in this life. As in the profound mysteries of the simple act of love's physical consummation, there is a moment when the experience so urgently sought, and the striving after it, are magically fused in one flash of unearthly identity; only to be flung apart in that same moment by the piercing thunderclap of achievement.

Not to possess is to know, and be wise; to possess is to embrace the whole, and, by doing so, to cease to be embraced by it. I take it that is what my Lord meant to imply, when, as it is reported, he said that unless men become as little children—full of the absolute wisdom of the defeated new-born—they shall not know the only heavenly kingdom, that of the mind governed by the spirit.

By her death I possessed Irma wholly for the first time, and in that false possession was deprived of her wholly. I foresaw and accepted this, for with it went my final renunciation of something I could not help but hold more dear, if only because it was something virginal, uninfringed, unique—a young man's mind. What had been infringed was, after all, a trivial thing: no more than the treaty she and I had made together four years earlier.

It was possibly made earlier still—ten years earlier, when first one and then the other drew apart from the tentative first embraces of a mutual possession which must surely, then, have ended more quickly in mutual destruction. I choose to believe, and must subconsciously long have felt, that there was an agreement made between us, unknown to either, when we first stood face to face in the airless cabin of the refugee ship *Empire Queen*, and that to her though not to me some inkling of it may have been mysteriously apparent when she as she thought lightly claimed me with a meaningless kiss as her 'first Australian friend'.

Except in moments of unselfconscious passion, neither of us ever took kissing easily, and as we were both, in different ways, as much the creatures, the willing servants of habit as are even the most eccentric men and women, it was too late to change, should it have seemed necessary. In the airy silence of Miss Werther's hall there was no movement, that day, of simple passion such as sets two people clinging helplessly mouth to mouth as though to draw the very life from each other's parched and famished lips.

Nothing so simple as that at all, though for one agonizing moment, six years before, there had been, as there was to be again. This reunion, inevitable and unpredictable in even its largest movements, merely flung us together as sea-borne bodies are flung ashore by some wave at last larger, more strenuous than the offering and withdrawing waves that have supported them before it.

We seemed each to lie in the arms of the other, but I found I was taking the weight of us both, standing there before the old and misty mirror which, when at length I opened my eyes, showed me her head and shoulders supported by my left arm and my right arm firmly about her waist. Over her raised shoulder, the complete self-abandonment of her pose, with her back to than ancient glass and her eyes closed secretly in her pale, averted face resting upon the dark stuff of my coat, I saw my own wrong-sided image of head and shoulders; and the mask was lifted. It so surprised me momentarily that I looked away and back again, hardly recognizing in the shadowy, contented countenance reflected there my own. It had to me an almost indecently frank look of surprised happiness. I felt like acknowledging it with an ironical salute.

Irma must have sensed immediately the slight shift and focusing of consciousness in me. She had at times an almost animal awareness, both more and less than physical, of what the other person's mind intended, and a way of anticipating it that was at once exasperating and delightful. (It gave her a consummate skill in the delicate art of all love-making.) When I looked down at her face upon my breast I saw now that she had begun to smile, still without opening her eyes, as much as to say with deep satisfaction, 'I could have told you it would be like this.' Like all true expressions of profound emotion, hers at that instant managed to convey two opposites—a sense of triumph, a sense of defeat.

With one accord, in a transitory new world where instinct ruled reason absolutely, we drew apart in space—if not in time—and I was able to study her with a more objective view at last. The six years since I had seen her had made her almost mature in appearance, as though her beauty, strange and informal, were settling finally into the mould it would show forth at the time of her death. As Barbara said, she was no perfect beauty; the lines of her face contained some subtle contradiction, and what one took for beauty was as much an inward-burning warmth as any outward show, for all the exciting Slavic modelling of brow and cheekbone under the delicate humidity of the skin. There were new lines at the outer corners of her slightly upward-drawn eyes, and a new firmness and repose about her mouth which modified its shape of secret voluptuousness to a cool maturity I found much to my liking. When, standing away from me, she had ceased to smile, it wore still that expression of faint, unconscious melancholy which I had glimpsed in the cabin of the *Empire Queen*; but this expression too had softened as though little by little her memory of the past were fading, to give place to confidence and hope.

The veiled, calm scrutiny she gave my own face apparently satisfied some last question in her mind, for with that impulsive movement I so well remembered she laid her hand upon my arm, almost as though she needed to prevent me from going away again; and she said with a new intimacy in her faintly accented voice, 'Come—let us go into the light,' and as she said it I remembered her 'Can we go where it is private, please?' that had really started all this, that mid-August afternoon in my office in the city. My mind was already busy, collecting our beginnings. I saw again the direct look, rather of command than of appeal, in her blue-grey eyes, with which I had so readily complied once before, and I surrendered myself now with satisfaction to this modest and assured authority in one so much younger than myself.

We were alone in the apartment. Miss Werther, with a frank delight I could well imagine, had already been engaged to play bridge all that afternoon, Irma told me with a faint, humorous grimace; she would return in time to give us a late dinner—did I mind late dinner? There would, of course, be things to eat and drink before that. I did not mind; in the circumstances in which I found myself, seated beside her on a sort of divan of Manila cane, a huge affair which might have been meant to live on but which sprawled easily without crowding the spaces of the lightly-furnished sun-room, I cared nothing for what happened to time or domestic details. I was wholly taken up with looking at Irma, as she was by being looked at by me, in a mild sort of ecstasy, as though she were something I had created myself. Probably I wore something of the same expression of absorbed speculation I had seen on Alan's face at times when he would sit, for thirty minutes on end, regarding some completed piece of his own handiwork, in the days when under Jack's tuition he first had learned how to use his hands and other small tools delicately, to make models

329

of ships and aircraft that must have seemed to his freed imagination atremble with perfect life—as Irma seemed to me now.

It was apparently not easy for her to tell me much about her life in the years of war. Each successive set-back, or near-disaster, for either side, had come at her like an unexpected blow in the half-dark. To women, I had noticed, war remains to the end a series of mystifying and reasonless happenings unconnected by any thread of purpose. They are unable to find relief from the intolerable expectation of the next thunderclap of battle joined, as a man can, by considering the whole future as a near-impersonal problem capable of being solved, or at least guessed at. She was herself a child of Europe; she knew the capital cities, the villages, the life of the peoples of that continent far better than I knew those of my own much younger one. Every movement of the warfare on land became increasingly imaginable to her in its setting as the storm of conflict moved up from North Africa through Italy by land, westwards with a gathering force of brutal, revengeful frenzy from the punched-in elasticity of the Russian borders, and coolly, relentlessly north, east and south from the misty bomber-bases of the British islands. Secure from violence now in the land of her refuge, she could not think of it as ever having been truly endangered by the slow southward flood-water movement of the Japanese; the shameful fall of Singapore and the shocking loss of the whole of one of Australia's few infantry divisions she had accepted as inevitable, in view of what was known privately of the futile and apparently corrupt self-complacency of the local administration there; and she

330

could not turn her thoughts from the chaos into which her native countries were being thrust by the desperate hands of 'the three enemies', as she called the Western allies, Germany, and Russia; 'for Russia, you understand,' she said with that memorable air of gentle patience, 'is already the enemy of all that is left of the world.' She had wanted only to draw her growing sense of temporary security about her, like a fabulous cloak that had the power to make her invisible; and as it came to seem less temporary, as she was more and more casually accepted, even welcomed, by the kind-hearted (though to her mind politically and economically backward) people of the enormous western State that contains one-third of the continent, so she drew it the more closely about her, avoiding altogether the mere chance of contacts with the refugees from Europe who had by now become the country's major import, and beginning to lose her sense of foreignness in the enjoyment of the modest, lawful exercise of her own personal authority, as a teacher and a confidante of those young girls.

She knew Miss Werther had read me her letters; she had always hoped I myself might have written, and always understood how I, like her, finding so much unsaid between us must feel I could say nothing. Linda in her replies never failed to mention my interest in her welfare.

I asked her at length about poor Mr. Sampson, a name in her letters I had reason to remember, and she laughed and looked sidelong at me, her half-closed eyes shining.

'He was very young, you understand, only a boy.' Again she laughed gaily with that sidelong glance of youthful mischief that made her look like a sly schoolgirl.

I remembered very well the unease I had felt about poor Mr. Sampson, and the relief that followed it when we learned that she had left Perth for Adelaide. There had been little mention of new friends in her letters; I gathered that she sometimes went out with men and women she had met—people who were never more than names, seldom recurring in the letters. But once she explained, with suitable punctuation, that one man had proposed marriage to her, '—*but imagine my surprise, for he is only a boy, 27, and he does not know me though he thinks so, poor Mr. Sampson!*'

This letter, which I could not put out of my mind for weeks, had been followed at the end of that year—nineteen forty-three—by her announcement that she was going to a new post in Adelaide; her only regret seemed to have been that she would be leaving behind her the fabulous ocean beaches of blue-green surf and blazing white sand on the Western Australian coast. Nothing more of poor Mr. Sampson; and when once more she moved on it had been to Melbourne, 'to take up my real profession again'—much to the excitement of Miss Werther, who from time to time made plans to fly down there for a week-end, but never did go, in the end, chiefly I think because she felt Irma was now so near, only four hundred miles away, that it was needless to worry about her any more than if she had been back in Sydney.

'Well?' I said, smiling at myself and my remembered unease and jealousy of a long time past.

'I only put him in for you.'

'The devil you did!' I said involuntarily. Her half-bashful

332

confession made me realize more than much direct description could have done that by then she was already a different person from the girl I had last seen prostrate with misery and exhaustion at Hill Farm. I could not look often enough at her, sitting beside me demurely cross-legged on the soft divan, looking rather Oriental and mysterious altogether in that attitude, in her usual suit of pyjamas covered by a house-coat of corduroy velvet, smokey-blue to match her eyes, and, as before, fastened high at the throat with a medallion of large and bizarre design.

'You made me jealous. Do you like making people jealous?'

'I don't know—sometimes, a little bit.'

She was looking at me seriously again, with a grave, speculative expression, as though all this had shed some small new light on me for her. After a while I began to realize that she was in fact not seeing me at all.

'Mr. Sampson,' she said severely, 'was very honourable, but he could not help touching one now and then. At night. I had many pleasant afternoons with him—the beaches, the country, the mountains—for he had a car. But when it began to get dark he began to shut up his talking and start touching. So.' She negligently reached out one hand and touched my face, my neck, my hands hanging loosely clasped between my knees, and my knees themselves. 'It was the—the same old thing, but all rather honourable, you understand. So is a spider honourable to spin its web, and I felt as though a spider web was being spinned all over me, from here—' she gestured lightly 'to here, here to here. One of these nights, I thought, poor Mr. Sampson is going to complete his web, and I am going to be well and truly in the middle of it.'

She tightened her lips, and looked at me for a sign of comprehension. I was busy trying to sympathize with the very comprehensible activities of poor Mr. Sampson, and hating the thought of him.

'So—goodbye poor Mr. Sampson. When he finally understood to leave me alone, and said goodbye, I cried, my friend. What do you think of that?'

'What can I think? You wanted him back at once.'

'No no . . . I cried because I liked being touched kindly—but not by poor Mr. Sampson.'

The silence that fell between us was effortless and serene. Beyond her averted face I could see through the glass walls the autumnal privacy and colour of the garden within its high enclosure of warm-looking brick. A curse of sparrows descended upon the smooth expanse of grass between the tree-lined brightness of the borders, like a settling of grimy leaves blown in from some far city street, and at once fell to scavenging and quarrelling with brutal appetite. In the fading grey light the flowers held their colour close, without radiance, like flowers in a water-colour painted with conscious boldness by an indifferent artist.

At my side, Irma had fallen into some reverie of her own, very remote from me and the immediate present. I could not keep my eyes from her for long at a time. With her feet tucked neatly under her, her head bowed above the taut, convergent arches of her thighs, she sat quite still in that extraordinary immobility of an eastern sage; but it was not a held pose, it was like the perfect stillness of some animals, certain birds, that have no sense of time passing, and to whom the world is in motion only when they are themselves static. It is an immobility that gives a fleeting impression of a profound wisdom secretly held; but I learned later that it was her own way of thinking most freely, by letting her whole body relax its weight. In sleep, too, she lay in the same way, in a perfect stillness that seemed not breathing, and that frightened me for one bad moment, the first time I observed it.

When she raised her head and looked swiftly at me and the room full of clear grey daylight all about her, I knew at once, with a small tremor of disappointment, that it was not of me she had been thinking, as I had been of her. In a voice of comical dismay she exclaimed 'Oh!' twice, and quick as a cat was standing beside me, ankle-deep on the rich rug under my feet.

'Forgive me—I get them now.' Her unEnglish accent was momentarily more marked, as though she had been thinking in some other tongue; she noticed it too, and mocked herself, nodding vigorously: 'Yah, Ay git zem,' and went away laughing, to return a few minutes later wheeling a service-tray on which there were bottles and glasses and several kinds of unfamiliar small savoury foods.

'There. Linda is perfect,' she said largely, with emphatic satisfaction, as she seated herself and pulled the service-tray to her knee. 'All this she did while I was lazy after luncheon. Come—eat. It is all good, I assure you. Nothing but the best for darling Linda's friends, always. And there is to be no dinner for—oh, hours.'

I drank some whisky of a brand I thought had long since disappeared from any market, legal or illegal, and tasted with a gravity that amused her immensely the various little highly-flavoured delicacies ('to eat when one is in love,' she remarked enigmatically) on the plates, while she drank one glass, and then another, of an unbranded wine that looked like claret, for which she had not so much developed as recovered a taste during her sojourn in South Australia, its home, and which she told me was an authentic *vin du pays* of the purest quality. A claret, yet not a claret—did I understand? Yes, I understood. Then what a pity I should be drinking whisky, which in this country was surely only a drink for the night. Did I drink whisky often? No? Then what? Nothing?

'You Australians,' she said dispassionately.

The afternoon waned in the walled garden outside like a chord of music struck and held, fading. I was in such a state of content by now that I could have wept with compassion for the rest of the world. Men who have been drinking heavily for days reach, I believe, a similar state of mind at some unforeseen moment. I had reached it and as suddenly passed beyond it simply through the breaking within me of a drought that had, I saw, dragged relentlessly on for years. I shut my eyes the better to savour the fullness and depth of this strange melting sensation, which reminded me not irrelevantly of what I had supposed the earth to be feeling once, at Hill Farm, when rain had at last broken a drought of almost eighteen months' duration; when cracks a finger's breadth had opened in the baked and apparently lifeless ground, and young trees whose tap roots were not plunged deeply enough where they grew apart from the protection of the mountain forest died where they stood, under a merciless succession of brassy suns and wizened stars . . .

After all, nothing had happened dramatically between us after that first irresistible coming-together in the airy silence of Miss Werther's hallway. It was as though we had lived long side by side in this room with its walls of clear glass and its opened curtains like fluted columns of thick blue stone supporting on the tiled floor the high white ceiling. We had descended two steps to get there, and it was this that made the ceiling seem unusually high: the floor was lower than that of the rest of the apartment, and the sun-room itself with its tiles and more recently added glass had probably once been an open veranda or *loggia* on the same level as the enclosed garden outside.

Nothing had happened, but at some time, before the coming of approaching night, before the return of the fat and amiable Miss Werther who had so ingenuously flung us together here in peaceful solitude where the outside world could not penetrate, something, no matter what, had to happen, or I should never be able to leave this place, to return to my own life, my son, my home, my own particular privacy and order, womanless and imperfect now in my memory.

I looked again at Irma, and found her regard once more bent questioningly upon me.

'What did you want to know?'

'Why you came.'

'Ah—you know that. Did not your friend tell you about me? Did she not give you the picture?'

'To both questions—yes.'

337

Characteristically, she did not ask, 'What did she say?' but went on in a matter-of-fact tone, 'Well, what else could I do but follow her here, my friend? Do you know what? When she went away I suddenly thought to myself, "Now she has seen me and knows all, that Mrs. Conroy will certainly make off with him at last—after all those years!" That is what I thought, and it troubled me. Did she?'

'Good lord,' I said, laughing with a sort of exasperation, 'no! To begin with, she is a woman of nearly fifty—'

'To begin with, to begin with,' she said, and she positively giggled like a delighted child. 'Listen to him, the man, giving his reasons on his fingers, one-two-three. No, my darling, my beloved, say only, to begin and end with, she is a woman.'

Her voice broke from hysterical laughter to tears as bright as happiness. She moved over to lean against me, her arms about my shoulders, her face against mine, laughing and sobbing softly at the same time.

'So am I a woman,' she said in a stifled voice, while her recent words of reckless sudden endearment rang in my ears, *my darling, my beloved, my darling*, again and again like bells falling downstairs, uttered with conviction and relief; and again I held her in my arms across my knees where in the abandon of the moment she had thrown herself. There was so much that was innocently animal about her, warm and fond; and because at such times the mind, humbly abashed perhaps at what it beholds, has a clever habit of substituting less disturbing and more familiar images for present actuality, I had a passing mental picture of Donna at Hill Farm greeting me with reckless yet fully-controlled

338

enthusiasm, hurling herself upon and all over me when I sat in my chair by the fire in the big room, nuzzling and licking and tenderly nipping at my hands and face in the passionate re-establishment of all her old claims to my person and my attention. It would hardly have surprised me if the young woman in my arms, the weight and warmth and resilience of whose body were just as vital and as little to be tamed as Donna's at that moment, had licked and nuzzled me in the same way. She was like another person; yet even while I heard her and felt her in my hands she was gone again—not far, but apart.

I am glad to think now, though then I did not know, that it was always to be like that. She had scarcely any habitual attitudes or poses. This was in part the secret of her mystification of me; for I had been raised and trained myself further to observe a recognizable external pattern of conduct, just as one continues throughout life to pronounce the words of one's whole vocabulary according to usage; whereas, with her, conduct was similar to her use of language, perhaps conditioned in the same way as her English was, coloured and sometimes made wayward by the idioms of the other tongues she knew so naturally. Unlike any animal I can think of except a cat, she remained unpredictable to the end. There was no training her beyond what she already was, even if one had wished to do so; and what she was was a woman in complete control of her faculties who, like most women, always knew what she was doing with herself.

If, as it may seem, she wronged what she had made of me, and with me of us both, it was no more than seeming.

She never wilfully did injury to a single soul—never, never. That is why, having lost her utterly in possessing her wholly, I cannot forget her.

Nor—though the memory has nothing of the other's stifled but persistent anguish—can I forget how Alan took the news of her death, that early morning.

He came home with Hubble and me in a sustained mood of unabashed good humour, which seemed even to be increased and justified by the policeman's half-jesting lecture to him, where he sat jammed between us in the front seat, about the obligations of his father's son—of all people—to keep the peace. I did not hear all of what Hubble said. While I looked unseeing through the glass at Darlinghurst Road opening to our steady advance, until we had passed through the false and faded noon of light and shadow at the Cross, they kept up a friendly conversation on my right, with Alan calling Hubble 'Sir' now and then, and once, with a grave face, 'Inspector', and Hubble equally gravely correcting him in a way that might well have silenced most young men of nineteen or so. Hubble, I realized numbly, was thoughtfully keeping his attention from me; and as we drew near our home, the home now reduced by half by the hopeless emptiness of the flat next door, I marked his mood with dull misgiving, and was half-inclined to let him sleep it away, thinking he would be perhaps sufficiently calmed or even dulled by sleep then to be spared the suffering of too much immediate shock.

However, the thing was decided for me by Alan himself, for when we reached the landing and turned towards our own door he hesitated at the other as we came abreast of it, and bent his handsome young head to listen. Knowing how soon and how completely I was probably going to lose him, I looked at him as it were for the last time then, and the twisting and gnawing of two griefs in me were given pause for that moment by a welling-up of indescribable pride robbed of vanity by the same underlying, humble compassion I had felt for him since first I saw him, red and black-haired and crumpled, shortly after Jean had passed on her life to him. As I looked, I thought—with the utter futility of all such thoughts—'If only Jean had lived, none of this would have happened.'

He was tall, and never so pale as I had always been, for his youth was a different youth from mine, much of it spent out of doors in the sports he enjoyed with the deprecatory nonchalance proper to his present conscious attitude of an intellectual young man of good family. In spite of having lately indulged in what could only be called a back-street brawl, he had managed to put his clothes in their usual somewhat fastidious order, and smooth away his black hair neatly from the bland expanse of his brow. At the moment his eyebrows, dark and straight and rather thick, of the sort held to denote an intense, single-minded power of concentration, were drawn together in a frown of listening. Standing near him, in that long moment which marked an end and a beginning of our relationship, I caught the faintly bitter, aseptic smell of laboratory chemicals that had not washed out of his skin and his hair (Irma's habit of pretended disgust had been to cry, with stiffly repelling hands, 'Go away, go away, my dear doctor, how you stink!'

341

It was strangely heartrending to remember this, and at the same time to think of her lying both in his eager young arms and in the cold and final embrace of metal-bound, insulated darkness.)

'Not a peep out of her,' he said, after a few seconds; and he stared at the flat nickelled setting of the keyhole as though it were keeping from him some trivial mystery he felt he had a right to know. At even this late hour she was usually awake, waiting for my coming. He drew his hand from his overcoat pocket, one knuckle raised to knock.

'Oh—don't waken her,' I said. 'Don't try. Don't try.'

I should not have spoken. He let his hand slowly fall to his side and looked at me over his shoulder curiously.

'She'll love to hear of this *fracas*,' he said; but his smile was suddenly doubtful and almost frightened.

'Let us go in,' I said. 'It can wait.'

I opened our own door hastily, and he followed me in and paused in the small entrance lobby to hang up his coat, while I withdrew the key and slipped home the latch, shutting the door finally upon our life up to that moment. Going as usual straight to the kitchen, he left me standing there heavy and useless and not sure of what to do next. I wanted nothing so much as to get to bed and drug myself to sleep.

'Come and sit down for a moment, Alan,' I said from my table, when he came out of the kitchen with a glass of milk and a few sweet biscuits in his hands. 'I have some bad news for you which you may as well hear now.'

In the light I saw that there was a bruise already darkening on his cheekbone beneath his left eye. The milk and biscuits, the childish supper of every night he had ever spent in the flat with me, moved me almost to tears by its very incongruousness with what I knew of him, with what he had unwittingly done to me. On my knees my hands began to sweat and tremble. I did not see how I was going to get through this thing decently; I felt sick, horribly sick now.

The look of faintly guilty alarm that had come instantly into his face when I finished speaking gave place to an expression of equally sudden concern. With a gentle precision he put on the table the glass he had been holding, and laid the brown biscuits in a small pile beside it.

'You don't look quite yourself,' he said. 'Let me pour you some brandy.'

'Whisky,' I murmured, but he went on as if he had not heard.

'The thing about bad news,' he said—too lightly, poor boy, for he was unpractised in deliberate deceit—'is that until it's told it always seems worse than it is. Drink this slowly, the doctor says.'

Again I saw the faint, worried smile come and go on his firm young mouth, while his eyes were steady in their helpless anticipation of trouble, brilliantly blue in their clear whites under the dipping shadows of their brows. I drank the nauseating mixture of brandy and water and thought how I, who knew what was to be told, was desperately perturbed while he, ignorant for one last moment of what I was going to say, and obviously expecting to hear me speak of something which for the rest of my life I must forget I ever knew, was as essentially calm as I was trying to appear to be.

'It's about Irma,' I said, when speech could not be put off any longer. With a start, he stood up from where he had been sitting on the table's edge, and in silence took the empty tumbler from me and turned away. I too stood up, making the movements slowly like an old man. His face when he looked at me again was paler than mine had ever been, surely.

'I have to tell you, Alan,' I said, 'that she is gone from here . . . gone . . .'

'Dead,' he said, making the word ring softly in the silence of the lighted room where so often we three had all been merry together. Quite surely, she was in some way with us then, making a small face at the sound of the meaningless word on the young lips that had kissed her own; but she was freed of all union with either of us now. I seemed to hear as I had so often heard her dispassionate unEnglish voice saying lightly, 'You Australians,' and I looked about the familiar place like a stranger, but saw no trace, nothing that had been hers except the two of us, father and son in an irresistible communion across the glass top of the table.

'She was found drowned,' I said, and under his breath he cried 'Oh no—drowned! She could swim like a fish.' The half-emptied glass of milk in his hand worried him; he set that too on the table.

'Sit down, my child,' I said, addressing him as remotely as a confessor so that he could taste and recognize the taste of grief in decent loneliness; and we both seated ourselves like very gentlemen, without meeting each other's look and so admitting death's fatal intrusion between us.

'Where was this? What happened?' he said, and I said, 'I can't tell you, Alan. I cannot say. No one will ever know.'

It sounded as I meant it to sound, a simple statement of ignorance. I feared nothing, for I had nothing now to betray: it was done.

While he sat opposite, staring at the tumbler as I stared at him, with a sort of disbelief, I told him how it was that I had by accident been there to identify the unknown woman in the city morgue earlier that night, with Hubble and the police surgeon. I told him of our entry to her flat and of what we had found there—the note, the empty glass tube from which the remaining tablets lay at that moment in the locked drawer under my hand, unknown to anyone, for use should I fail myself one day. There was nothing more I could tell him that he needed to know. The picture, itself fragmentary, gave an impression of completeness, of an irrevocable end.

Three times during the short recital he spoke when I paused, without moving his frowning gaze from the clouded tumbler before him.

'I can't seem to believe it,' he said the first time, his white face strained and tearless. 'She was the happiest person I ever knew.'

Later he said impulsively, still without looking up, 'It must have been ghastly for you, Father,' and it was then that I understood a simple thing: the shock though not the keenness of his grief had been dulled as it struck at him by his enormous—and irrelevant—relief in finding, as he must suppose, that after all I was ignorant of the relationship that had bound the two of them together in secret.

In the end, when I had finished all there was to say now, and was wondering how life was supposed to go on

345

from this point of finality, he slipped lower in his chair and turned his head to look directly at me. In his candid eyes of a young and honest man was a look of such pain and confusion that I could not meet his gaze. When he spoke, his voice was low, but it tore at my mind like a cry in the profound silence.

'I never believed anyone I knew could die—like that. I always thought god—looked after good people.'

I opened a drawer and took out a box of mild sedative powders.

'Take two of these and go to bed now. You look worn out. As you go to sleep, try to tell yourself we, the living, have a duty—to go on living as well as we may. You in particular have a duty to humanity which you are learning how to perform now. Think of all the lives you will save. Think of all you have yet to do.'

'Sleep,' he said, as though it were the only word he had heard. 'Just now I wish I could never wake up again, ever.'

'Listen,' I said, giving him two of the powders, 'there is one lesson very hard to learn—that we can never really know what is in another person's innermost mind, Alan.'

'Not even you and I can,' he said with finality, and I saw that nothing I could possibly say could touch and comfort him yet. At the door he turned, as if to give me his usual affectionate good-night; but instead, leaning against the frame for a moment with his fingers ruffling up his thick hair over his frowning forehead, he said in a strained, angry voice, striking at me as any wounded animal in the frenzy of its pain will strike at the gentlest hand, 'I think you ought to know she was the first person I ever really loved—the first person I ever knew who really loved me. That's what makes it so—'

The open doorway was empty. Whatever his last word might have been I never knew, for only his own mind could have heard it. Hearing his step receding, fighting a terrible impulse to go after him and ask what he had meant, I stood holding on to the table, looking at the untasted biscuits, the unfinished milk—a child's supper abandoned—and over and over in my mind repeated themselves the trivial words of absurd protest, not against him but against the fate I had devised so ably for my own enactment: *What about me? What about me? What about me?*

Irma and I were married six months after her first visit to Sydney since her departure more than six years before. The ceremony was a civil one, very simple and final and somehow suited to our long-delayed union. Two ageing men taking their ease in the November warmth of early summer in Hyde Park, opposite the office of the city registrar, seemed to be waiting there especially to act as witnesses to this and other small worldly events to which their years made them indifferent. They showed neither surprise at my proposal nor recognition of one another's existence; one of them, looking up at me with a bleak glance, permitted himself to remark that 'he hoped I wouldn't regret it like he did', and the other said, 'Sure, sonny.' Afterwards, tucking away their *pourboires* hastily, they returned across the swarming square to the park, apparently to different parts of it too, without a backward glance either at each other or at us upon whose worldly union their laborious signatures had been set like those of a couple of worn-out demi-gods.

That moment, as we descended the steps of the yellow sandstone building alone and unremarked, was a concluding moment of a whole part of the life of each of us. It had about it an inevitability that robbed it of surprise.

After the far more elaborate church ceremonial of my first wedding, I had felt myself a different person, not altogether easy at the thought of the (to me) immense responsibility I had now sworn to assume, for the bodily and spiritual well-being of the nineteen-years-old girl walking with such modest joy beside me with her hand in its white glove resting formally upon my arm. Today, there was nothing but a sense of relief that all formality, down to the first and only witnessing of the strange signature *Irma Fitzherbert* was ended; a sense of relief and satisfaction at the conclusion of an episode which, by intruding briefly upon our two separate lives, had brought them officially closer together. Unofficially, not even the eventual night of this day could (I thought) make us more intimate in the end than we had already become; and although I was quite wrong in this, by the time I remembered the thought it no longer had the least significance.

All had been arranged secretly; all was to be settled and made secure before Alan came home from the end of his final year at Shore, where this same day he was sitting for the last paper in his matriculation examinations. Our reasons for this secrecy were several and simple—most of them. Irma's naturalization papers, which were issued on the strength of the false papers with which she had entered the country, would not have stood up to any extended investigation. She also meant to continue working at the fashionable *Chez Madame* salon, where she had been welcomed back with surprise and complacency, at what seemed to me an excessive salary, and where the single state was still strictly *de rigeur*. For my own part, with a fastidiousness by no means unreasonable to either of us, I had refused even to contemplate the thought of Alan living in the same household as his father and his father's young bride. There was also, I think, a very slight uncertainty in my mind as to how he would accept even the thought of me having married a second time. One does not expect reason to overawe the instincts of the very young, especially the muddled instincts connected with such a person as a dead and of course forever virginal mother.

In effect, when the flat next to my own fell vacant a month after her first visit and I took it without hesitation and without even consulting her, she was delighted. Fortune was favouring us from the start, she said, crossing her fingers contentedly. Like me, she had grown used to living alone, and there still remained in her the ghost of her former conviction, which she had explained to Miss Werther, that only in solitude could one find real security. Subterfuge, too, had been a part of her most exciting years, and she did not find it hard, I think, to see in the arrangement of separate, adjacent establishments much that was innocently exhilarating. From the beginning, she was inclined to treat the whole affair as a grown-up game to be played straight-faced, harmful to no one because no one would know of it but ourselves, and providing us with a secret such as the intimacies of the body never quite had for her.

She began to move into the flat on successive week-end visits, until the time when her Melbourne commitments ended after the spring fashion-shows; for she had taken up no further engagements down there since her earlier visit to *Chez Madame*. She was living almost as she chose, at no one's beck and call, and revelling in it while it lasted. She made herself a familiar figure to Alec, the caretaker, and his daughter Emmy, who explained that she was 'very high-class' and would be an ornament to any building. 'I hope you mean as a tenant, Emmy, not a statue on the roof?' 'Oh go on, Mr. Fitz, I mean on the inside.' Finally she met Alan.

Alan at that time was nearly seventeen, well-grown, beautiful with health. Though he had never distinguished himself in any sports he played tennis and Rugby football with an agreeable intelligence and dash, like so many boys of his age, without setting much store by these achievements; and all his life his two great athletic pleasures had been swimming and—thanks to old Jack—riding. All these activities went well with his (to me, incomprehensible and rather frivolous) love of dancing, and enabled him easily to 'cut a figure', as my father would have said. Indeed, that shrewd old man would have been in his own fashion delighted with the boy as I was, secretly, in mine. Unlike me at this or any other age, Alan was instinctively at home in any company, and had already made without forethought or conscious intention a secure social life for himself among his own kind. His school holidays now were days and nights of pure pleasure, of music, dancing, innocent love-making, gaiety, wit and frequent late rising in the mornings. All this seemed good, to me; he was shaping just as I had hoped and

350

planned for him to shape—away from me above the surface, so to speak, while his roots and mine touched beneath it in more and more casual, inevitable and ripening communion, openly remarked by neither of us and probably scarcely realized by him. I could think of us as two trees of the forest, of which the older, the parent, first shelters and at length makes room for the younger.

To my surprise and gratification, Irma did not make what had come to be the inevitable comment of those who saw us together for the first time; a comment which, because it was irritating and invariable, we now treated as a private joke: 'absurdly alike'. Fatuous and inane phrase, it probably concealed some obscure resentment in the minds of those who gave tongue to it.

Going down together, we overtook her on the stair, and Alan met her simply as the new tenant of the flat next to our own ('and it is sincerely to be hoped that she doesn't have too many rowdy parties,' he said later with a grin). She went down and out into the light and air before us, and waited there, trim and demure in her tailored suit whose skirt the wind from the harbour was pressing sideways against her knee. Alan murmured in my ear with unsuspected knowledgability, 'Melbourne, London or the Continent—definitely not Sydney, would you say?' 'I am not up in such matters,' I said aloud, and we joined her in the cool winter sunlight of the August morning.

It seemed to me a propitious meeting. They took to one another easily, for the boy had a youthfully gallant way, saved from being familiar by a suggestion of embarrassment, with women—even with Miss Molesley most of the time: his presence always caused her to sing modestly to herself as she went quietly about the flat—rather, Irma told me, like the manner of young French or Italian men, 'but without their way of pretending at once to share a naughty secret with one'. This easy friendliness in him often had the effect of making me feel more aloof and reserved than I really was, and that in turn amused him, and afterwards he would tease me with amiably mocking imitations of myself meeting a girl in his company; but I never minded this, for once in an expansive moment he told me that, 'beard and moustaches, stick and gloves and all, you are far the most presentable parent I know, my dear sir'.

Even Irma, I think, did not realize my happiness that morning. I was walking in bright sunshine and a following wind with the only two people in the world I knew how to love, the only two people who cared to love me. I felt I was twice as rich as anyone we passed. There was a temptation to turn to them in the warm fullness of my feelings and say, 'Love one another, for I love you both.' It would have been a sort of whole-hearted gift, wholly to be understood in value by myself alone. Three years later I remembered that temptation during a night spent in an hotel bedroom, but then it was a temptation no longer, for the gift was by then not in my benefit to bestow.

Irma walked between us. Not until she was seated in a taxi which Alan had with characteristic good fortune seen unengaged and hailed for her did she look at me fully; but the quality of that brief, mysterious glance, its flash of absolute recognition and a sort of hot impatience, made me stand there still when she was gone, as though she were

352

looking at me yet. Alan's voice freed me from the long moment of captivity.

'You see, sir, I was right—definitely not Sydney, nor Melbourne, nor London either.'

'I have heard Highland Scottish accents very like that,' I said, 'and for that matter there are Highland women with just such fey expressions of the eyes.'

'Don't prevaricate, boss. For an ace crime reporter, you miss one thing. You never saw a Highland lassie who would dress that way, even if she could.'

'How is it you are so well up in these esoteric matters?'

His laughter filled his eyes and mouth and turned the faces of passing women towards us as we entered Darling-hurst Road.

'It was you yourself, and Jack, who were always telling me how important it is to be observant in all things,' he said. 'And then, of course—one gets around, you know.'

'I know,' I said with affected severity. 'But I don't want you to get around so regularly that you find you are literally travelling a circle.'

He pressed my arm unexpectedly, giving me the full warmth of his attention as unselfconsciously as a child in that strolling, hurrying crowd. Irma, whose one swift look was still dazzling my own mind, had passed completely from his.

'I like it when you impart a moral precept in public,' he said cheerfully. 'You look like a Conradian conspirator. I don't mean to be rude. It becomes you, Father.'

'I should never have dreamed of speaking to your grandfather like that, now I come to think of it.'

'Now you do come to think of it, how can you be sure he wouldn't have enjoyed it—'

I guessed he had been about to say '—as much as you do?' and he would have been justified. His cheerful boyish swiftness, even if it was—as one of his older masters had told me—a little above his years, always pleased me; but for the moment I was saddened, with the rich melancholy only possible to one who is at present wholly happy, almost too happy. What he had lightly suggested of my father was only too likely, and I was realizing it too late. It was the old man's very worldliness that had always held me a little apart from him; that, and his stupendous memory for legal citations, made me slightly in awe of him even in his gentlest moments, which I suppose were frequent enough. He had somehow kept me from the world, perhaps for the very reason that he himself had such an observant, inquisitive, insatiable passion for it until his last years, when with an equal passion of contempt he threw it aside. He reminded me of a drunkard who will in some moment of sobriety make his children swear never to take a drink. It was not that he had ever tried to encourage me to forswear the world. He would have considered that an impertinent error in a parent. What he did try to show me, not unsuccessfully, was the world's faithlessness to men of good faith; and so convinced was he of this faithlessness of mankind to the individual man that in the end, as I have said, it seemed to destroy his own faith in the faithfulness of god to mankind.

If this were his tragedy, I had no doubt contributed helplessly to it by my own small apparent lack of faith in him. It was not so, but it might well so have seemed to the old man. I had never teased him as we walked the street on a sunny morning. My love had been too grave, too unaccented by the lighter syllables of human intercourse. There, as I went along the public way beside my own son, I prayed it might not be too grave still, for him in his turn.

'You are very broody, sir,' he said, scattering the shadows of these thoughts in his own rightful fashion—for if I wanted his company I should seek it on his terms, not mine. That word had left childhood with him and become useful now as a way of telling me I was being unduly silent and serious. It always did me good. For the rest of that walk, down William Street and across Hyde Park, we discussed the coming year at the University. Never doubting the certainty of being able to matriculate in November, he was already more concerned with textbooks than with the New Year publication of examination results; and we made our way to the shop of Angus & Robertson where, as booksellers to the University, they might be expected to indicate the basic requirements of a first-year medical student. His supreme self-confidence so near the time of the matriculation examinations would have amused his grandfather . . . Perhaps because of my happiness, I had the old man much in mind these days. Even as we passed into Hyde Park, crossing College Street from Boomerang Street under the stony benignant gaze of the exalted clerics above the gates of S. Mary's, I recalled how he had always raised his hat to the unseen high altar in the great dark-grey cathedral behind us ('as an example to the less faithful, my boy, and a warning to the over-devout'); the faint mockery I detected in his eye as he did so was only a mockery of himself as one

355

who sometimes, even then, doubted the infallibility of the divine majesty symbolized within.

When Irma and I met later in the Botanic Gardens for a luncheon *al fresco* in the shelter of a grassed bank flooded with sunshine, almost her first words were of Alan and me as child and parent. The encounter had meant a good deal to her—more by far than I realized at the time.

'But you are not alike,' she said. 'It is not that you seem too young to have a son so old—so—what do I say?—*rangé*, assured. The temperaments are different, and maybe it is this that makes silly people find you too much alike. They are confounded by the physical. There, you resemble each other. *Here*, and *here*,' touching her head and then her bosom, 'no . . . What a gay boy!'

I knew I was not 'gay' as she meant it then; I did not know she was used to enjoy such gaiety as one enjoys an *hors d'œuvre*, as a promise of the meal to come.

'*You* are my meal,' she said, explaining this, with tremendous approval, some time later; and by then we had been married long enough for me to hear such remarks without even a mental demur; for her enthusiasms for life had, since our union, become so warm and her consciousness so relaxed and all-embracing that together they swept me away on the full tide of being, and I understood at last, in my very bones, what was intended by the abused expression 'a new man'. I was truly a new man, in that I was for the time no longer my own man. Irma claimed my body with the genial appetite of certain female spiders; but my soul she left alone in increasing content.

Because of that animal power of spontaneously reacting anticipation, she was naturally graceful in the ways of love, which she could lift from gravity to the butterfly realms of delight, from silence to laughter and so by a sudden progress to blind ecstasy, peace and oblivion. She seemed blessed with that chastity of mind which makes of the commonplace a thing of suddenly-revealed beauty, and to every gesture of intimacy gives innocence and a sort of inspiration. In advance, just as a wise surgeon may use premedication before beginning his delicate, god-like task of transfiguring an imperfect human body, so she, with the wisdom of instinct, lulled to sleep the last sick doubts and self-questionings of my mind; and when it awoke it was transfigured. I can say of her no better thing than that she gave freely what I could receive, and took what I could freely give. Because I had known, in all my thirty-eight years, of no such profound experience, with all it brought of self-discovery and a rather belated flowering of native manhood, I found it inevitable—but neither dangerous nor strange—that with me she became as it were a divine obsession. To this I gave myself so wholly that it went beyond or beneath consciousness. She was an essential part of me: she was of my essence.

So secure and destined was this love that the worldly details housing it seemed to settle and arrange themselves without any pressure of ours. Each of us worked at the work we knew, in worlds so disparate that our hours together could never be surely foreseen, even on week-end days, because of the uncertainty of calls upon my own time. Alan, in the room next to my own, slept the deep sleep of the enthusiastic student whose days were full of learning and laughter, serious sport and light-hearted play. He never

357

woke at my return home, near or after midnight, and I fell into the habit of going directly to Irma's door, which opened to my key to reveal to me beyond the farther end of the entrance lobby her reclining figure stretched on the blue floor-rug, with an electric radiator at her feet in the winter nights, and, winter or summer, her head pillowed near the concealed speaker of her big, powerful wireless receiving set which, night after night, brought her the foreign-language broadcasts of the B.B.C. and the native tongues of half Europe and Asia. Only when I was kneeling at her side could I hear the subdued voice, meaningless and agreeable, going on and on in the midnight silence of the curtained room.

With a bodily assurance that sometimes awed me, sometimes moved me to an inexplicable compassion, according to my mood and how I had been thinking of her, she pulled me down firmly against her without much changing her own relaxed position, and ran her fingers through and through my hair and across my forehead until I could remain still not a moment longer under the light, dragging touch. She never mentioned the broadcasts; I never even knew, unless by overhearing some chance closing announcement, where they originated. For the most part she turned off the receiver when I was at her side, rarely motioning me to silence while she listened a little longer. I never did understand what satisfaction she had from this perpetual listening, night after night, stretched on the blue rug in the dimly-lighted room, listening absorbed to the faint mosquito voices babbling near her ear of a world which had hunted her at last into the refuge of my arms.

Sometimes, it is true, she commented aloud later, as if to herself, on some antipodean happening which seemed to me obscure and aimless at the time, yet which, to her, apparently swelled with a dark significance and portent. In such instances what she foretold with a lightly prophetic air of having seen it all before often came to pass, in some way or another. She could not withdraw herself completely from the world of her childhood and her wild youth; her knowledge of European politics and temperaments and emerging personalities was ingrained. I wondered how much of her waking time she gave to thinking of the Australian present, how much to the European future, which obsessed her somewhat as she herself obsessed me. The more secure she felt with me, as she came to see she was really and essentially a part of my own life, the more fearlessly she let herself examine how that world went on in its desperate forward struggle, without her; but now her comments and speculations were without heat any more; she had extricated herself from the cauldron during the very years it had been boiling at its most furious rate. After the boil-over, the bubblings and slow fermentations and exhalations that followed one another or coincided on its repellent surface she could observe now without emotion, without bitterness, without distaste. She had left no one of her own there; her observations were aloof, cool, and sometimes even amused. She reminded me of one playing a game of chance with no stakes offering to stir the faintest passions.

Alan and she became fast friends during that first easy year of our marriage. Gradually, as we all settled into the positions determined by this new life of each one of us, we gathered more freely together, and I began to envisage the day, a few years hence, when our marriage itself could be openly admitted. Miss Molesley she set out with secret deliberation to charm, in a fashion that showed me yet another aspect of her character. She treated her with an almost Oriental respect as a sort of Number One Wife (though Moley did not know of that gracious sinocism, and would certainly not have suffered its application to her own modest duty to me and Alan), as an elder and therefore a wiser woman to be, if not consulted, at least listened to without interruption or demur. I did not learn for some time that she and Irma had fallen into the way of taking a cup of coffee together in my flat on some of the mornings I was not at home, until I noticed a remarkable difference in the coffee Moley herself began to serve us when there was occasion. That wholly admirable creature, to whom I owed so much of Alan's material well-being, then confessed that it was 'your friend Miss Martin' who had one day offered to show her various European ways of blending and brewing the ground beans. With a straight face she quoted Irma—who had in turn been quoting a hard-faced, temperamental little old Dalmatian *maître de cuisine* of her acquaintance—as having insisted that 'the coffee she boil, the coffee she spoil'. Coming from the colourless, old-maidenly lips of the good Moley, it sent Alan (who had heard it and mocked it before) hastening abruptly from the room with his table napkin muffling a choking fit.

By winning over Moley, Irma also won, by unspoken consent of the other two, a right which she carefully never over-used to come into our home when we were all three at leisure. Unlike mine, all her evenings were free. I took to spending more of the daylight hours in the office, less of the nights, as far as was possible, and this modification of my times of absence seemed to suit us all. When he had no night lectures or private engagements—and he seemed to engage himself less often now that he had Irma to talk to and take about a little—Alan came home for dinner; when Moley and Irma joined us for that meal we sat down four very happily; and occasionally—but not too often—Irma had us to her own table, where, when Alan was absent, I dined privately with her, though I was supposed to be in town. It was a small and harmless subterfuge to which we came to look forward very much.

Belatedly, as such things go in Europe, she had taken to exercising her natural skill as a cook, now that she had space and the means to do this. As a married woman—married however secretly—she would feel ashamed, she said, not to be able to handle every household detail herself; and she explained that in Europe the first requisite of a good wife was a good table, which remained the standard by which a man's friends and family judged the wisdom of his choice. *Du reste*—with that inimitable sidelong look—'it does not matter if she beat hell out of her old man'; and as for the other good things of marriage, the pleasures of the bed and of parenthood, all faded (a wise, long nodding of her head, as though I had contested this), but the pleasures of a good table, never.

Though her savage little old Dalmatian friend—he was, in fact, Austrian, but in Australia that was no better than 'German', and long before the war he claimed Dalmatian citizenship—told her with scorn that the only good cook was a man cook, and would demonstrate his contention in her own kitchen by bringing ingredients from which he prepared notable strange dishes in a passion of curses, song, and lamentation that caused Alec to go uneasily up and down stairs several unnecessary times; and though she herself believed this inherently and from experience all over Europe, yet she gave us from time to time a meal that caused Alan to look at her with surprise as well as his habitual frank admiration for a beautiful woman, while Moley's normally sedate, observant silence at table became noticeably more ruminative. All this filled my heart—as it was meant to do—with pleasure and a pride I dared not express until, in the depths of the night long afterwards, she became again my own dear, her head pillowed upon my breast and her hand in mine as warm and firm as a child's.

For a long time, few of her former acquaintances came near her. She was a habit they had lost, just as they tried to lose their other unAustralian habits, and after hearing her talk of them in her matter-of-fact way I admit I was glad it was so, though when they returned to her, later, I neither could nor wished to make any sign of protest. Part of our happiness came about through our expressed desire never to assume any 'rights' involving the will or the tastes and opinions of the other; and because we were no longer children this was a desire that could be satisfied without reservation, too. She knew how much of my thought was devoted to Alan, and in her calm way acknowledged that there my duty lay; for her earliest training had nourished in her, wisely or not, the conviction that in these matters a woman gives way to the rights of the male, and no amount of shrewd indoctrination of the theories of sexual equality in the social system had caused that conviction basically to weaken.

Yet she had a profound sense of possession, and looking back even so soon on the last, hopeless situation that developed I am urged to believe that it was this, more powerful than reason and conscious will, that moved her. Beneath the lighthearted jesting assertion to me, in the blissful aftermath of love's self-abandon, that I was her 'meal' there must have been a stark and evident truth which we were both too blinded by the splendid show of love, in our different ways, to see. Because of Alan, she had once gone hungry.

She had never dealt in half-measures, never really known compromise. It was not likely that she ever forgave Alan, in the deepest honesty of her unconscious being, for having once had a stronger claim upon me, body and soul, that she had had. I never knew how much she still needed her freedom, that freedom of spirit which she had hunted in flight, like a jack-o'-lantern in a dark swamp, all her life, and which to the end she never hunted down. How near it she came I shall never know, for I do not know where her impulse to possess and engulf me would have rested satisfied. It may have needed my own death, rather than hers. These things I think of with a bitter humility and in no spirit of judgment; for how can one dare to judge, how can one be other than humble before that which has taught one not only the meaning of happiness but the belief that happiness does have a meaning, after all?

I should say, as an epitaph in honour of her own goodness, that she alone regenerated and confirmed in me my earliest faith in god. A woman can do that for a man. In the light of this truth, how can her least noble worldly actions appear as anything but shadows that attest the light's source?

Most sorrows can be concealed from most people, but joy has a quicksilver way of showing itself. It weakens the effort needed to conceal it by prompting a slightly unbalanced self-confidence, like too much alcohol in a healthy man.

The two women who knew I had joyfully resigned myself to my obsession by Irma were of very different temperaments, and already had their own opinions about it. Miss Werther, irrepressible now and convinced it was—as in a sense it was indeed—largely her own doing, was filled with an embarrassing satisfaction at the sight of us together—embarrassing, anyhow, to me, though not to Irma ('You do not understand, my friend—she is a witch, who wishes us well. In the villages at home, I would have given to her our bridal linen.').

Barbara's reactions were not so simple nor so ingenuously shown. For some reason she had seemed to avoid our former easy intimacy, since that evening when I last dined at her house across the harbour. If I had told anyone about my marriage, I should have told her, as the only other living being, after Irma, whom I considered to have any sort of claim on my full confidence. For obvious reasons and some not so obvious instinct, I kept silent with a regretful effort; but I could not keep from her my changed state of mind, for she was a woman, with a woman's awesomely discerning eye for such things. She was also a friend, and as such she could mention the matter naturally.

'I was at *Chez Madame* a week or so ago,' she said, one afternoon in March. The day was humid and stifling, and for some minutes the only sound in the shaded room audible above the rumble of traffic below the windows was the click and whirr of the swinging electric fan.

'It was the first time I had seen Irma since she left Melbourne, though of course I knew she was here again. I looked at her, and I've been looking at you, and if I may say so you remind me of a couple of children in love!'

Among other things, I was learning from Irma never to feel, and certainly never to show, surprise at that sort of frankness in a woman which, in a man, would seem both brutal and insolent. It was not Barbara's sort of remark, either; if I had changed, so had she. She seemed to have withdrawn a part of herself from the perpetual gift of self she still offered in the name of friendship. There was about her an elusive air of self-criticism, regret—I do not know; and at the same time she as it were pressed my confidence nervously to the last drop, meeting me with a newer eagerness as though I were the possessor of some secret she longed to learn.

Inevitably, with the one-eyed vision of a man deeply in love for the first time since his youth, I sometimes compared her, against my will and most unfairly, with Irma; and her goodness and quality were for a moment cancelled out, preposterously, by the evidence that she was a generation older. By contrast with Irma's, her quiet poise was the outward sign of a weariness of body and mind, not the powerful, trained control of vital energy and profound passions. Such moments to me were of sheer misery and bewilderment. Fortunately they were but moments, transient. I could not long have borne the spectacle of my dearest and most faithful friend's image distorted in the glass of my own unaccustomed emotions. I should have had to beg her forgiveness for merely thinking of her so, without my heart.

'What do you expect me to say?' I murmured. 'I can think of only two things. One is that you are still what you have always been to me—indispensable.'

'And the other,' she said lightly, 'is what?'

'The other is that this—this other matter has not sprung from nothing. For seven years I never forgot her nor made any approach to her of my own accord. For six years not a word, written or spoken, passed between us, and what little was ever said to me about her was as often as not disagreeable. McMahon—'

'Oh, forget McMahon, for heaven's sake. He's gone, anyhow.'

'McMahon,' I said stubbornly, 'painted a vicious, lurid picture of her history and her character just when I was concerned that she should be spared further misery in the only country left to her for a refuge. Many things have been put forward in her disfavour. You yourself thought I was wise to have parted from her when I did. You were probably right, but the point I am making is that I had every reason not to remember her, not to waste time remembering her. Yet I did. And at the same time I kept faith with myself, with Alan. I think anyone knowing him as he is now would admit that that job was done with love and thought, even allowing for the good material, I worked at it conscientiously, for seven years.'

'Like Naboth's vineyard,' she said with all her old tenderness.

'If you like . . . Anyhow, the thing I want you to remember is that I have not acted like an unpredictable youth—I was never that, more's the pity—and I have had time, eternity, for thought.'

Leaning forward to put her hand over mine where it lay, rather surprisingly, clenched into a fist on the table, she said kindly, 'Poor Lloyd. I've never thought of anything or wished for anything but your own happiness, where you and I were concerned. If you've found it at last, I'm glad— and good luck, and god bless you, Lloyd.'

We were at one again, content with each other's occasional company as before; yet it was not to her I turned when Irma tried to end her own life.

The question one instantly, arrogantly asks of such an act as attempted self-destruction is always *Why?* I was, after all, too good a Catholic and too much an egotist to have thought of asking, say, *Why not?* That, I think, is the question my father would have preferred to ask. Always, of suicide, that death of most mysterious and faith-shaking form, one craves for denials of reason, not logical explanations. Murder we accept, but the other we deny . . .

It was towards the end of the second year of our marriage, and in my simplicity I thought my own happiness was become as nearly absolute as would ever be possible in a world over which was spreading a slow chaos of inhumanity more terrifying than that of any warfare. The carnal growls of the victors eyeing each other over the mauled corpse of Europe were mingled with and echoed by the occasional drunken bacchanal screams, across the timeless Pacific, of the self-styled cultural, spiritual, political and economic leaders of what they called, with witless irony, 'the free post-war world' of the forgotten four freedoms. In the midst of this self-obsessed destruction of mankind by man, from which the true spirit of man must shrink and turn away its helpless face, the innocent love and faithkeeping of two insignificant people seemed a thing of beauty, a banner of salvation in a world of eloquent and smiling madness.

I believed Irma thought as I did, but I knew she was sometimes saddened, sometimes maddened by those interminable foreign broadcasts to which she still listened. Yet by no sign apparent to me was it intimated that her mind had diverged at some unknown point of the way to disappear into a blind cleft in the rocks, a trackless wandering where, unheard by me in my confident progress hand-in-hand with what was now only an illusion, she could cry aloud some anguish of the spirit too simple for simple words, too profound to be imparted in the strangled whispers of transient passion, too incomprehensible for hope to console it.

The October morning was brilliant and windswept in a newly-rinsed world of clear distances and familiar details made vivid again by the swift and glassy air. After nearly a week's absence on a hideously entangled case of rape and murder ending in a two-day man-hunt by the police through the forests of the north coast inland, a case whose every successive detail, at which even now memory shies aside, had sickened me as it was brought to light by the cool and insatiable methods of police investigation and reconstruction, I had returned late at night to the city the previous day, and after a conference with the booming, angrily genial Scott made haste to get home where I could put aside the very clothes I had been wearing, and so perhaps divest myself of some of the mad, clinging horror.

My own flat was dark and empty, but Irma was waiting for me, lying as usual on the thick blue rug by the wireless receiver, in a suit of white silk pyjamas covered by the inevitable house-coat, this time of a dark red velvet I had not seen before. She was magnificently, strikingly beautiful as she rose to her feet in that one strange fluid movement that seemed so effortless, and stood looking at me with the half-startled, half-mischievous look I had never quite got used to. Then she came quickly towards me.

'No—don't touch me,' I said. 'I have just finished with something particularly foul. When I have had a bath and change, I shall come in again. Will you wait?'

'Of course.' She watched me go with a surprised, studious attention. When I returned, half an hour later, supper was set ready for me, and a small fire chattered softly in the grate, teased by the west wind rushing across the moonlit roofs of the city. While I ate and drank, and she sat on the floor sipping her evening drink of hot, sweet coffee laced with brandy, I did an unusual thing: I told her a good deal, though not all, of the case the police were about to conclude. I was tired, yet I felt a sick and sleepless need to talk. When I had done, she leaned her head against my knee, looking up.

'There is no limit,' she said sombrely, 'to the terrible things men and women will do to each other for love.'

By my view of her tilted head, her backward, slanting eyes looking up at me with unfathomable appeal, I was reminded as irrelevantly as ever of Donna at Hill Farm, and this in turn made me think, with a sensation of physical thirst, of the thin, pure air there, the smell of wood smoke, the deep brick fireplace, the grey sheepskin rug on the hearth; cleanliness, silence, peace, Donna gazing up . . .

'You ain't no fool.'

I had no reason just then to hear the dry, unemphatic words. I must have been half asleep with my hand resting heavily on the dark smooth shape of her head reclined against my knee.

'Let us think,' I said, 'how we can get away to the cottage tomorrow without telling too many lies. Will you come?'

She put her head far back, and smiled faintly while I examined the novel appearance of her face upside-down. I had never thought of looking at it from such an angle before; it showed up the light, broad bone-structure with foreshortened exaggeration.

'I shall go to Linda's,' she said. 'You shall go to Hill Farm. With you will go a mysterious dark lady named only Mademoiselle X.' (She pronounced it *'Eeecks'* with complacency.) 'In effect, myself.'

Subterfuge in any form still delighted her. She even took a mad pleasure in walking behind me in the street with no sign of recognition, surreptitiously digging me in the back in a crowd and, when I turned, apologizing charmingly as to a stranger. I never knew what she would be at next when that mood of incomprehensible gaiety overcame her. I once overheard a Viennese medical friend of hers tell her quite seriously that she was a slightly manic-depressive type, but I could never believe this, for her self-control was too good: she acted rather as she planned to act than as though forced by an inner compulsion superior to her conscious will. Next day, however, I was to remember that Viennese doctor's pompous words.

Our rare week-ends at the cottage, contrived with difficulty, always delighted her in prospect, as they did Miss Werther, who was invariably a useful party to our going. Each time, Irma amused herself by thinking up some new fable to cover the fact of our leaving town together. It made her as light-hearted as a child.

'What about Alan, though?' I said. 'Has he engagements?'

'Ah yes,' she murmured. 'One must not forget Alan.' Then she laughed softly. 'You shall do the lying to Alan, my friend. It is your penance for having such a charmingly credulous son.'

'Charmingly credulous' was not how I would have described that young man, now approaching his eighteenth birthday. It was probably one of her occasional mistakes of language, so rare these days as to be at once noticeable. If so, it was nothing for comment, and I only remembered it a long time later.

In the wild brilliance of morning, waking in my own chaste bed, I felt cleansed and absolved, able to forget yesterday's heavy thoughts of death and violence and the gross madnesses that can arise like evil spirits from the smashed seal of intolerable sexual repression. At nine o'clock, when I knocked at her door, Irma was up but not dressed. Of Alan there had been no sign. Moley said he was gone when she arrived, and added that the teapot was still hot and that he had had breakfast. There would be no occasion for evading both lies and the whole truth, face to face with him, and felt relieved of my 'penance' when I had written him a note to tell him I was off to the mountains for the week-end, and would see him soon, on Sunday evening.

'No need to do penance, after all,' I said to Irma while she poured coffee. 'Alan has disappeared.'

'You are joking?' she said sharply, putting down the pot with a startled look. I thought, she is up too early after a late night listening to a story I should have had enough sense not to tell her. 'Yes,' I said, 'I only meant he has gone out early, before eight o'clock.'

'He goes all day today in a boat, a yacht,' she said dreamily. 'How lucky for him, such a wind. How I hate it, blowing, blowing.'

She spoke without particular feeling. I watched her graceful movements about the table for a while, and left her when she had smoked a cigarette and put out the butt in the dregs of her cup. We were to meet in an hour's time; as I went out the door I saw her go towards the telephone as though to ring Miss Werther, only to halt and turn to look after me just as the door was closing. Afterwards I tried to think of anything unusual in her behaviour, but there was nothing—only that hesitation by the telephone. She was not used to hesitate over anything, great or small, on which she had decided.

372

We were to meet in the city before the week-end rush of Saturday noon, and get out of town with a clear road. I walked to the garage to get out the car, and drove it to a corner parking area, the site of a demolished office building now hedged in on two sides under the sky by the naked walls and blind-looking inward windows of more lasting buildings. At the office, warm and stuffy after the racing wind in the streets outside, and full of the sour, fusty smell of paper and printing ink and ancient city dust, there was nothing that really needed doing, no one about but the cleaners at their lonely tasks among the echoes. For an hour I sat smoking, thinking over the past six days more coolly now, and filing notes and copies of a few documents I had collected. Hubble, when I rang for him, was not in town.

The time passed slowly. For some reason I felt a vague, uneasy depression rising in my breast—perhaps a nervous reaction, I thought, from those last days of suppressed horror, with which the dead, drained atmosphere of the office contrasted without bringing relief or ease. Written down in full, the inexorable reconstruction of a combination of incest, rape and murder would have seemed like the nightmare imaginings of a Freud gone mad. Since my marriage I had become rather less resigned to observing the extreme aberrations of human behaviour. They sometimes haunted my dreams at night. Scott would have said I was becoming soft . . .

The feeling of depression gathered into an ache of uneasy fear. I felt as a man may feel who has left something of vital importance unattended to until too late. As though it might have had something to do with her—there was nothing I did now that seemed not to have something, in some way, to do with her—I telephoned Irma's number at the flats, but she did not answer. That was natural: she was almost due at the street corner in Parramatta Road where she had decided to wait for me; but in a sudden access of nervousness I at once rang Miss Werther's flat. When the amiable Jewess told me Irma had not rung her up, panic seized me by the throat as though it had been waiting in the back of my mind for just that moment, just those words.

Only a partial and inaccurately-collated memory of my next movements comes back to me now. I must have acted with great swiftness and precision, for in retrospect I seem to have transposed myself without pause from my office table to the door of Irma's flat, to be in the same moment putting down my telephone receiver and turning my key in the lock of her door; whatever happened between those two sets of actions was evidently of only secondary importance to my immediate, absolute knowledge that something was dangerously wrong. I do recall thinking that whoever drove the taxi that pulled in as though expected at the front entrance of the office as I ran out must have been divinely sent, divinely trained, for with more skill and knowledge than any police driver I ever knew he managed to avoid all main streets and crossings between Macquarie Street and Darlinghurst Road, and had me at my address in a very few minutes, according to my watch.

The door opened, and I closed it before I called out. My voice sounded dully through the silence of the familiar rooms. A sixth sense told me that the place was not empty, that somewhere there was life in it, and for the only time in all my experience of assorted horrors I knew the sensation of the hair slowly stirring and trying to rise on my scalp. Then I moved.

There was after all no mystery and no horror about it. Irma lay across the wide bed with her knees on the floor, her face turned sideways and her arms outstretched in a pathetic attitude of striving, as though to climb upon that low elevation had been a little beyond her. Her averted face wore a faint, frowning look as if she were disappointed or confused.

I looked round the room in a moment of mad helplessness. There was a folded paper on the dressing-table, held flat by a small half-empty glass tube I had seen once before, marked *Poison* in red type easily legible from where I stood inside the door. The whole scene, like so many in which she had figured, was extremely formal and correct in detail—so much so that I choked down a wild upthrust of laughter as I felt frantically for my pocket-book.

Between the calling of her name and the finding of the telephone number I wanted, not a full minute could have elapsed. I was dialling the number in the next room before I realized I was not still looking at her; even where I stood I could still hear her heavy, grievous breathing sag and lift, sag and lift, somehow far less real, less credible to the sense than the windswept screams of interminable disaster of the scattered gulls above the harbour outside.

'Fitzherbert,' I said to the cautious, suave voice that followed the lifting of a remote receiver. 'This is private and urgent. Please come straight to my address—you know it. You will need apomorphine and a pump . . . Yes, taken orally. I will wait for you on the landing. Please hurry.'

Providence so far was in my favour. The suavely cautious voice was that of the one man I could trust implicitly in this business: he lived a minute's distance away, in Macleay Street; he had been at home. Only my habit of keeping a list of certain 'silent' telephone numbers known to a few of us outside their subscribers' personal circles had saved me now—that, and the prior fact that by accident I knew more about this Doctor S— than was good for him; more, perhaps, than was good for me, since he knew I knew it. It was the sort of knowledge of which the police, who shared it, would have been glad to have proof. I never intended to admit to anyone that I could easily have supplied such proof (as S— also knew); the enforcement of the law was not a thing I was qualified for, in any case; I certainly had not foreseen a time when my information would possibly be the indirect means of saving a life.

I had to believe it would be that. It was necessary not to think otherwise, to think in order not to give way to the panic fear which danced somewhere in the back of my mind as I felt the unfamiliar dead weight of the body of my love trying to slide from my arms, when I used all the strength of which desperation is capable to raise her up against the pile of pillows and cushions I had flung against the headboard of the bed. What made it worse was that her eyes were half-open, and seemed to look over my shoulder with that sidelong glance, at once mischievous and shy, of a knowing school-girl, taunting me horribly with her clever escape. Through her bright loose lips the heavy breaths came and went, exhaustedly.

The kettle on the kitchen stove was still quite hot. It

gave me a moment's hope that not much time had passed before I found her—everything depended on that. A rinsed coffee cup stood inverted on its saucer on the metal draining-board of the sink, tidy like the whole flat; even this last thing she must do tidily, oh god, I thought, lighting the gas under the kettle and almost running back to the bedroom to snatch the folded paper and the little glass tube and stand over her for a few seconds like an executioner, before I went out again to the door, and out upon the landing. There I took one long look at the words written so neatly on the white paper.

Lloyd darling, I have no world of my own and can't can't live in yours any more. I look at the water of the beautiful harbour and it calls me . . .

It ended 'Goodbye Fitzi darling—IRMA' after a line or two more which I did not quite understand, though there was not much sound of hysteria in the words set down so tidily. My mind shook at the use of her most intimate pen-name for me—'Fitzi'—even while in one glance it memorized the rest. I put it quickly into my note-case and slipped that back into my pocket as I heard the entrance doors open and close with a springing thud in the distance below, and the rapid bounding steps of S— on the carpeted stair.

In the few seconds while he was running up, I wondered what the sea had to do with us now. It seemed a fantastic possibility, or merely a possibility in a world of insane fantasy, that she had meant to get down and into the harbour by the service staircase we all used in the summer to reach by the quickest way the seawall and the swimming pool; and that the drug had worked more quickly than she realized it would, before she could even fling herself on the low bed to snore away life alone. If it had been her idea to go down by the wall that made a walk to the old unused boathouse, with its water-stair never used since the flats replaced a private mansion fifty years before, it would have been in accord with her tidy ways, it would have emptied the flat and the world of her very neatly. But I never knew she listened to any call of the sea outside our windows. I realized with shame and terror that there must be many things about her I never knew, after all.

'In here, Doctor,' I said to the suave, wooden-faced S—, who had not lost a breath for all his haste. I recognized that peculiar controlled tension of a doctor in a hurry. When we stood at the bedside in the sweet-smelling room, where I suddenly felt like an intruder, a stranger, I showed him the half-emptied phial of tablets, and told him I believed she had taken them in coffee. He dumped his bag on the bed beside her, and brought out a hypodermic needle which he sterilized with methylated spirit, asking me at the same time for a silver spoon, hot water and matches. I brought these as he emptied the barrel of the syringe on the carpet with a splutter and hiss of air as the plunger went home. Then he shook a tablet into his cupped palm and took the spoon.

'Pour a little boiling water—scald the bowl,' he said. 'Have a match ready.' With his eyes on Irma he whipped a bottle of saline solution from his coat pocket, took the spoon, dropped the tablet into it and covered it with the saline. 'Light a match and hold it under the spoon.'

The tablet dissolved almost at once as the match boiled the solution. Carefully he let it cool and began to draw in and press out the hot fluid into the syringe, warming it, filling it at last with all that the spoon contained. Then, holding the fine needle downwards pointing to the floor, he felt with his left hand at Irma's flaccid left arm inside the elbow.

'Take her hand and turn it palm-upwards and pull it out to you,' he said. He felt for the vein with his eyes closed. I had seen the injection given, but not without a sphygmomanometer. As if divining my thought, he opened his eyes, keeping a finger in place above her straightened elbow. 'I'm taking a chance, without the wind-bag,' he said with a cold look upwards at me; and delicately, between two finger-tips stretching the satiny skin taut sideways, he pushed in the needle without bothering to swab a patch. I felt her hand like warm lead in my own, and watched the plunger steadily go down the marked glass barrel of the syringe until it fitted into the inside of the head. Lightly his hand withdrew the needle from the vein, while his other hand felt for the swelling that would tell him he had missed or completely penetrated the vein walls. I could see no change in the surface contour of that rounded upper arm which was like humid satin against the lips. The risk had succeeded.

'You will have to help me, Fitzherbert,' S— said without a glance, bending over her and raising one eyelid casually with a fingertip. 'You don't know when she took it, of course? No one ever does in these cases. Get more water and a bucket—cover the carpet with something if you don't want a mess. And hurry. We've got to be quick here.'

When I came back, he had stripped to his shirt-sleeves and was rapidly rolling them up.

The following hour was grotesque but too impersonal to be in the least moving. I found myself admiring the controlled ruthlessness with which he used his great strength, while I was feeling the drag of exhaustion at my shoulders and the backs of my legs. At last, when he had wiped the dew of sweat from his face for the last time, and for the last time examined the pupils of the sightless doll-eyes, he said, 'She'll do, I think. It was lucky you found her. Half an hour later . . . You'd better have a nurse. I can't manage a hospital bed even if you wanted to risk it, which I take it you don't. Your friends the police wouldn't help you here because it's just the thing they've been waiting for to pin on me. I don't think you want to tell them. But I can get you a nurse for twenty-four hours for observation.'

'If possible, I don't want anyone,' I said. 'Can I be trusted to do whatever is necessary?'

For the first time since he had come bounding up the stairs, he looked at me steadily.

'I take it you can be trusted just as fully as I can—in everything,' he said evenly. 'Did it occur to you just now that if this young woman should have died—accidentally—not even I would have been willing to sign a certificate? In fact, not I of all people. Even with the farewell note she left, you would have been in an unusual position for a man like you, Fitzherbert.'

I had thought of it, and of the inevitable discovery of my legal relationship to Irma.

'A note?' I said. 'I don't see it.'

380

'Don't be a fool,' he said dispassionately, getting into his waistcoat and coat. 'Every pretty woman who tries to kill herself with a slow-acting poison leaves a note. You don't *see* it because it's in your pocket, probably . . . Very well, young man. Stay with her yourself. Be better—I don't trust even my own nurses all the time. Watch her pulse and respiration.' He tore a leaf from a notebook and began to write on it with a gold fountain pen. 'Send someone straight away to a chemist with this, or they'll be closed. When she starts to come out of it, for god's sake don't excite her in any way. Give her a dose of this. If either pulse or respiration starts misbehaving, ring me at once. I'll be at home all day. But I think she should be all right now.'

I said with some hesitation, 'I would like you to let me give you a cheque.' He had played my game with absolute fairness, according to my own ideas, and I felt suddenly weak and at a disadvantage. Now he was staring at me out of his bold, expressionless eyes of an oldish man still hard and cold as iron, and for a moment I understood why he had gone for so long unpunished for his misdeeds, from the harbouring of injured felons to crimes of a far more serious nature.

When he spoke his voice was as soft as a snake in dead leaves.

'You wouldn't think of soiling those aristocratic fingers by handling my money, now, would you, Fitzherbert?' he almost whispered. 'Well, strange as it may seem, I feel exactly the same way about yours. When you are as old as I am, you too may just possibly find you have grown sick of the odour of sanctity . . . Well, there's nothing more I can do here.'

He packed his bag, and washed and dried his hands in Irma's bedroom, and was gone; and I realized as the door closed upon him that it was his strength and indifference together which had enabled me to come through the last hour without a thought of myself. I took from my note-case that neatly-written note, and read it again, but could not bring myself to destroy it, although I felt this should be done, if only out of compassion for the inert sleeping creature under the blankets on the wide bed. As for the phial with its little stack of white tablets, I forgot about it until, undressing late that night, I found it still lying neatly in my outside coat pocket, and automatically locked it away in the drawer with the useless revolver and the now-meaningless letters.

All I wanted to do was to get away and hide myself until I felt I had regained a proper degree of self-control; for as I looked at her lying there, with her dark hair spread like a fury over the pillows and her swollen lips in her face of hollowed wax, I began to tremble, and it was all I could do to hold back my tears.

After ringing Miss Werther on the lounge-room telephone to ask her if she could come, I sought out Moley, who had just come in from her Saturday morning shopping, and, for once not caring what she might come to think, sent her out in haste to the nearest chemist with S——'s prescription.

Then I went back to Irma's flat, to sit beside her and listen to her easy breathing and to the baffled screams of the gulls etched upon the sound of the west wind pawing the window-frames; to sit beside her, and to wait—I did not quite know for what.

The waiting begun in physical exhaustion and mental bewilderment that Saturday afternoon never really came to an end. Other things screened it, but it remained, like a listener behind a curtain.

When she had recovered, with the rapidity of natural good health nursed by Miss Werther's unexpectedly matter-of-fact presence, from the amount of drug her blood had retained, we were obliged to look at one another for a time like strangers. Even in the mountains, where by arrangement with our respective employers we were able to go for the remainder of the week following, there was a change in our association. I realized that there comes a moment when the heart finds it has done with ecstasy, when the wonder of the mind is dimmed by the sadness of suddenly-recognized incomprehension; when 'I love' becomes 'I will keep faith' and 'I know' is modified and ennobled to 'I believe'.

For some days she was shy of me, as though too soon I had surprised a secret in her. She would have me near her but would not willingly look at me. I thought at first it was shame, either for a thing imperfectly done by her who would always choose perfection, or for the faulty impulse itself, that had made the attempt fail; but these things seemed not to weigh upon her at all, and as for the intended self-annihilation, she appeared—as did every other would-be suicide I ever knew—to think no more about it than if it had been something someone else had dreamed. In the end, when my compassion for her seeking death had stilled to a simple, grateful relief at the sight of her alive and no less beautiful, I began to realize that whatever thing she had found suddenly intolerable, that bright morning, was

383

withdrawn, not banished; that she did not know whether at some unknown future moment it might become intolerable again.

If so, I should be just as helpless as I had been this time; for I knew enough about attempted suicide to know that nothing—least of all the expressed determination to make the attempt—could be surely regarded as symptomatic of the state of mind in which the attempt itself becomes as inevitable as a thing already done. I had not known, and I never should know, when that state of mind might abruptly develop and command her.

Until we left for Hill Farm, ostensibly taking Miss Werther to look after Irma, that kindly little Jewess's presence in her flat relieved my own part in the whole affair of the likelihood of appearing suspect either to Moley or to Alan. She, good soul, sincerely embodied what the politicians describe as 'grave concern'; he, on his side, was aware only that his delightful friend and neighbour had been taken ill in some mysterious way.

'Woman trouble,' he said to me that evening. 'We are learning something about these things this term. I wish I had been here, I might have been of some use. What were the symptoms?'

'Would you not have been embarrassed, Alan?' I said. 'I believe medical men do not really like having their friends for patients, whatever the layman thinks.'

He tossed his head in a way that had lately become a habit with him, and laughed at me across the warmth of firelight between us.

'No woman could embarrass me,' he said cheerfully.

384

'I like them too much, they interest me too much for embarrassment to come into it. Not having grown up with a mother may have had something to do with it. You know what I mean, Father. I know nothing much about them, and yet sometimes I feel I know everything about them. Yes, you can smile. I'm too young, I know. They don't *frighten* me, that's what I mean. Perhaps starting life at S. Johns had something to do with it. The beautiful ones are usually too vain to be frightening, and the plain ones too frightened to be anything but—pathetic.'

I set my teeth on my pipe-stem.

'One thinks a lot about these things,' he went on confidentially. 'They may not always be our better halves, but biologically speaking they're our other halves. All the same, from what I can see they're the bane of a doctor's life—even most of the women connected with the profession, hospital staffs and women doctors and so on. Not that doctors could ever do without them. But I'm beginning to realize the practice is rather a—a priestly thing. There's a good deal more than just skill and learning and memorizing in it. Just as there is in law. The interpretation is what matters. All the greatest doctors since Aesculapius have been more than just learned men, haven't they? A sort of communion comes into it. A sort of communion with the spirit of life itself. Or am I talking nonsense to my clever old Pop?'

'I don't think so,' I said; and I thought of the force and power of Doctor S— that morning, wondering what some of his Macquarie Street patients would have said could they have seen him sweating there in his shirtsleeves, his hard, expressionless face bent like an iron mask to the labour. Something more than skill and learning had been at work there. It was like watching the actual performing of a miracle. His last remarks, about his money and mine, came back to me, and I felt unaccountably humble at the memory.

'Or Jesus himself,' Alan was saying with more assurance. 'The modern Apollo—half-divine, the greatest healer in recorded history. A doctor must have faith, like a priest—that's what it is. So no wonder they tend to find women a nuisance.'

'I hardly follow you over that last jump,' I said. 'Do you mean you think women don't have faith?'

He turned to me fully with a rather disarming look. 'Not the impersonal selfless faith I was talking about.'

Donna was once more heavy with young—Ike's doing again, Jack told me.

'They trick me,' he said. 'They git off into the bush, and come 'ome opposite ends o' the clearin'. A man can't keep up with 'em—not at my age.'

'Next season,' I said, 'we'll take her to a stud somewhere, if I can find the pedigree. You can sell the pups. She might as well earn her keep, with a family history like that.'

He grinned more widely round his pipe-stem, with a flicker of his eyes.

'What about ole Ike? You goin' to deprive him of his greens? They's good as man and wife—better,' he added hastily. 'She don't argue.'

Irma stepped back from the little golden swollen creature when she flung herself panting upon us, with a movement of disgust she had not been quick enough to conceal. That alone showed she was not as perfectly in command of herself as she was used to be.

'Ignore her,' I said. 'She sees no difference in herself, you know, except perhaps that she feels all dog again. Complete.'

'Does one need—that, to feel complete?' she said with sudden amusement in her old sidelong free look. 'Would you like me to look like that?'

'It was a speculation, not a proposition,' I said, and her laughter set Donna to barking and capering and biting at my idle hand with gentle teeth.

The cold west wind lasted until that night, when during the dark hours, waking from time to time to listen to Irma's peaceful breathing, I heard too the more frequent hollow stillnesses between weaker and weaker gusts. By sunrise it had dropped completely. The sky was exhausted of it, void and clear as a dome of pale blue china.

'Summer comin',' Jack told me. 'I reckon she'll be a wet 'un again.' But he could not say what made him think so. He only pointed to the ants. 'See 'em movin' higher and puttin' away all the tucker they can git. They ain't often wrong.' But really he could feel each coming season in his blood, like an animal or an insect.

Irma spent that day in a long chair among the trees of the orchard where she could watch us and hear our voices while we worked a bean crop with the hoes. In the dapple of light and shadow under the thick leaves of peach and apricot, apple and plum, her face glowed like transparent gold. Sudden gold lights shone in her dark hair drawn down from her smooth crown in two plaits that rested on her serene young bosom. I noticed always the change in her, and longed to question her about herself alone in the flat that Saturday morning; but she seemed to have forgotten the affair, and was idly gay and tender and at peace with herself. My eyes of a troubled lover discerned, however rightly, an ebb and flow of the faintest melancholy, as though for a while she had stepped out of a natural role to observe her own playing of it. I could make nothing of this. I wanted to put to her the one question that haunted me: *Why?*; but if knew she would not, perhaps could not have answered me intelligibly. So there was this veil of invisible gossamer between us. At night, in the darkness, it seemed to drop aside, leaving her wholly at one with me again when her head lay on my breast and her hand held mine firmly with the warm, authoritative grasp of a sleeping child's.

It is hard even now to believe what I certainly never suspected then: that in those few days of halcyon weather there had begun a sort of Indian summer of our life together. Two people about to part who do not desire a parting draw closer to one another than at a meeting, which loses more immediate import the more it promises of a future. Neither of us, I believe, consciously foresaw any future other than a secure and happy one, and I for my part had not realized that it was possible for her to go from me utterly where I could not follow; but she, in some deep place in her mind, must already have known that this, to me a possibility as unlikely and as certain as her very death, some day, was for her inevitable and not very remote. She clung to me like the departing traveller whose imagination outruns time. Not seeing it, I thought only that she was more dear, more tenderly passionate and passionately tender than I had believed even she could become in the security of her final refuge within the cave of my mind, the walls of my arms.

Jack looked at her as he had looked at the ants, with mild, unhurried calculation. He seemed even pleased at our frank alliance, which—to shock him—I was tempted to tell him was quite legal; but his gaze, turned casually upon Irma where she lay under the shining, laden trees in air that swooned with the smell of ripening fruit, or sat between us happily at the yellow pine table in the kitchen (where she had somehow persuaded him to join us for meals), gave away nothing of what he was thinking. Never again did he tell me, 'You ain't no fool', but evidently his quiet observation of her had reassured him about something— like his observation of the ants, informing him of some probability, good or bad mattered not—and now and then when they happened to be alone together I would hear his quiet drawling Australian voice, interrupted by her quick, unEnglish interjections of sharp surprise—the unforgettable, startled way she said 'Yes?' that goes on and on in my mind—and her sudden laughter thrilling the still and limitless air.

I am sure she, like the traveller, did not desire any parting; in fact, sometimes it seems certain that what happened did happen because unknown to herself she sought some yet closer, impossible union with me. She had, however, grown old too young. Unlike Donna, she had passed beyond hope of that sense of completeness which for a woman is in the end the only pure worldly happiness, however come by. By the time I might have persuaded her that a child of ours was the one seal heaven itself would ever set upon our earthly destinies, it had become too late for me to talk of such a thing; or so I felt. I had taken too long to convince myself of it, in the first place: it was unnaturally difficult for me, for too long, to imagine her carrying and bearing and suckling a child, for my one intimate experience of a woman doing so had ended in a personal tragedy for the child and me which, having been too young at the time to comprehend it, I felt might happen again. Also, no doubt, her quality of being perpetually virgin, new, unknown even by myself, made me reluctant to move forward our marriage from where it stood arrested, as it were in the midst of its consummation, by the worldly secrecy surrounding it.

No human relationship, of course, can remain long suspended in timelessness. Like a bird in flight, it depends on movement, its own or the supporting air's, or it must fall and disintegrate. Only man in relation to the god of his faith can dispense with the awareness of time passing, or of his own passage through time. At noon on our third day at the cottage the 'bus passing inaudibly in the valley beyond the southern spur walling the plateau left in my mail box a telegram recalling me to my office in the impersonal, authoritative way to which all newspaper men have to accustom themselves. We had to leave that afternoon.

Irma was not as disappointed as I had feared, or hoped, she might be. It was almost as though she had expected this abrupt ending of our sojourn; her casual shrug of the shoulders, when she handed me back the telegraph slip covered with an awkward, legible handwriting of some country telephone attendant, seemed to acknowledge the inevitability of such endings. There was neither surprise nor regret in her face, and I recalled how much of her life had been spent in going somewhere else. There was always, in one form or another, a poor Mr. Sampson waiting for nightfall to begin spinning his tenuous web from which one must break free; or there was a telegram, or a word of warning passed from mouth to ear, mouth to ear until it arrived to set one in motion once more. Even then I did not see how futile it was to suppose she would ever enjoy an absolute peace, an absolute security, for long. She was the bird in flight, which must move or be moved, or fall into nothingness.

We reached the city at sunset, when the thickest traffic had emptied from the warm streets, into which the tall dark walls of the deserted shops and offices distilled a duality of lights and deepening shadows all faintly blurred and misty in the early summer evening. I left the car in a side-street while I went up to see Franklin, the chief of staff; but I was too late—he had gone home. On my table, conspicuously placed, was a memorandum from Scott, asking me to go to Melbourne by air that night, if possible, or first thing next morning, to do some special articles to tie up with a particularly sensational underworld feud down there which had been threatening to break out openly for some months and had done so the night before. At Hill Farm we did not interest ourselves in news of the outside world, and I was unaware of any details. Nothing could more firmly have ended that brief escape from earthly reality into a deeper reality of the mind than this assignment to study and report

391

on some of the simpler, more uncivilized passions of that outwardly most civilized of Australian cities.

Irma looked at me in the driver's mirror with a faint grimace of resignation by which I knew she was again shrugging her shoulders as she had done over the telegram. We travelled up the coloured width of William Street to the evening brilliance of the Cross without speaking. It was the dragging, inconclusive end of an episode which had begun with a yet more dragging inconclusiveness barely one week before. In the mood of depression I was already fighting off, the thought of home was far more appealing now than the memory of Hill Farm behind us. I felt again the existence of that thin barrier between us, that veil of gossamer whose origin I could not divine. I was heading for privacy and security myself now, taking her with me like a man afraid to enter them alone for fear of finding even there the barrenness that had so inexplicably descended upon the world.

Amid this confusion of thoughts and undisciplined emotions of fear and love, the image of Alan rose clearly like a standing tower in a ruined plain. I could, I thought, leave Irma in his care, and take at least a little comfort from knowing that something of myself, of my body and mind and spirit, mysteriously divorced from me yet inalienably of me, would remain to keep me in her mind while I was gone.

In Darlinghurst Road I drew in to the kerb so that she could go to one of her shops and buy fresh food. One keeps little in the cupboard in that place where the food-shops stand open day and night brilliant with invitation. To Irma this was so natural that to have remarked on it would in itself have been remarkable but with Miss Molesley it was different, a fascinating, suspicious and faintly disreputable hospitality of the streets, which at a wink might vanish like some fairy-tale invention. She still did her marketing on Friday and Saturday mornings, as she had been taught to do, with an air of facing an agreeable but tricky adventure. Irma shopped every day of the week, like most habituées of the district, and took a lively pleasure in it, sometimes engaging in brisk conversations with fellow-Europeans on this or the other side of the counter, in various languages, and coming out into the street with a look of tolerant surprise to right and left, as though she had just returned from another country.

This evening she wasted no time, but even so she was cheered when she returned to the car. It was the hour when faces are changed in the glare of the neon signs to green and blue and red and yellow masks, momentarily unrecognizable in their flat planes of light and darkness. The warm air was languid and muddled with the smells of food and flowers and petrol fumes overlying the pervasive smell of lively humanity. We drove off unnoticed among the crowding cars and taxicabs, and so came to our own street falling away beneath occasional dim lights, spaciously roofed with starless deep blue, and to our own empty entrance, unseen, unexpected by a soul. When I had switched off the headlamps, and the wall that closed the street had vanished against the darker northern sky, she put her hand upon mine on the wheel.

'It was very lovely,' she said. 'Let us say goodbye here if you go tonight. It will not be for long, no?'

'Three of four days,' I said. 'I shall probably be back on Tuesday.'

We said goodbye, I with the familiar ache of every parting from her, she with I know not what feelings; for I believe she did not yet understand her own heart, nor foresee where it was leading us.

We said goodbye, and after I had turned the car I too ascended the well-known silence of the stair, and at my own door stepped as always now from one side of my life to the other, like a man crossing a room to an opposite window that opens upon a different world, while the room itself, his external habitation, remains unchanged, accustomed to his movements, arranged to make them free.

Alan was reading by the empty fireplace. He looked up from the page, where his finger marked the point at which my voice had interrupted him, with an abstracted look in which for a fraction of time there was no recognition at all. Ever since childhood he read with an exclusive absorption hard to reconcile with the otherwise lively awareness of his senses.

'Hullo,' he said, 'you're early,' and then he jumped up so quickly that the heavy volume thudded on the floor a yard away. 'You're back,' he said with immense surprise, and bent down to pick it up kindly as if it had been a cat. With his face still away from me, he asked, 'Is everything all right?'

'The office wants me to go to Melbourne,' I said. 'Is Moley here? I have to be at the airport in two hours.'

'I'll tell her,' he said, and put down the book and went quickly away. Looking closer, I saw he had been reading a work of Krafft-Ebing, who like Sigmund Freud is still only a name to me; and as I went to change and pack a suitcase I was thinking somewhat dispiritedly that like me he lived in more than one world, and—as thought took its own determined course—that, while this multiplicity of the mind's existence and ambition continued, to talk of peace between nations, or even between the people of one nation, or of one city, or one household sheltering two generations or more, was a self-contradiction; for if the whole were the sum of its parts, and those were in disunion, however imperceptibly, then the whole (no matter how tightly wrapped in words) would remain disunited, and the statesmen and pseudo-philosophers talk in vain.

I thought, 'I must be getting a cold,' and looked out the warm undergarments Moley had long since given up expecting me to wear. Melbourne's climate is even more erratically unpredictable than Sydney's, for all that it boasts a lower average annual rainfall. On my table ready for cutting were the last few days' papers which I had not seen, including this day's; I put the lot in my briefcase to read in the aeroplane on the trip down. They would give me enough to think about until I was in touch with our Melbourne office and the local vice-squad and C.I.B. chiefs. I knew what I was expected to do, and had my own ideas on how to go about it; and it must be said for the *Gazette* that, if it did take no cognisance whatever of a man's free time, between annual holidays, it also left him alone to do in his own way most of the jobs assigned to him.

Alan stood in the doorway when I looked up.

'You are muttering, Father,' he said rather diffidently. 'Anything I can do? It's like their cheek—giving you time off and then sending you to Melbourne in the middle of it. How is Irma now? Is she coming to dinner?'

'Bless me, I never thought of that,' I said. 'Go and ask her, will you?' but I knew she would not come, after that strangely melancholy parting in the darkened car. Yet when he came in to say, 'She says she's just going to bed,' I was disappointed. In the end, he and I dined alone; Moley had excused herself to go to some meeting from which she could not get back until after I was gone. With a sudden upsurge of gaiety and self-derision, Alan waited not ineptly upon us both, and we spent an hour alone together, for the first time for more than a fortnight. Peace of mind returned to me in that peaceful hour of the boy's optimistic companionship.

'If you had time to drive me to the aerodrome,' I said, 'you could leave the car at the garage on your way home. We can leave early, and you need not be late back. Irma would probably be glad of your company. I think she found Hill Farm more dull than she realized.'

My own words surprised me: they were true. She did think Hill Farm was dull—not too dull to be borne, but dull nevertheless. She had never lived away from cities, all her life. I only slowly awoke to the inevitable implication in what I had said—that it had been dull in spite of my own company. After that Saturday morning, the whole of life must seem like a heavy anticlimax for a time, I supposed. She had imagined herself dead. Perhaps I should have given more thought to her helpless shrinking from the approach of Donna so full of life, her richly-bulging flanks concealing her usual shapely form; perhaps that pregnancy was more staringly significant than I had realized when I told her to ignore it.

'Yes,' I said, 'go and see her, anyhow. You always know how to make her merry.'

That too was true; but it did not explain the long, considering look he gave me when I said it. I opened my lips to tell him the whole story of the previous week-end, but closed them again because I did not care to speak to him of it without thought of every word. At last, 'We seem quite to have taken her into the family,' he said thoughtfully. We rose together from the table, which he began to clear while I went to the bathroom for my toilet kit. It occurred to me as I looked hurriedly at my dark, hollow reflection that I seemed to do a lot of peering into mirrors these days—I who had not had even the excuse of doing it while shaving, for most of my life. It suggested—the face I peered at without recognition suggested—that some sort of self-doubt had arisen or returned to trouble me, coming upon me in the midst of my happiness. I looked back along the line of days, but for all their unevenness no one stood out warningly to say, *It began here*, and a common thread of purposeful delight led through them up to the very moment where I was. With a sudden firmness I resolved to do what I had resolved to do several times in the past two years: to ask for some sort of long-service leave, on the grounds that I felt I was beginning to grow stale after more than seventeen years of studying and writing about crime. It sounded simple. I would make it so.

The resolve made my mind easier. When Alan left me at the airport with some time to wait, I was content to be alone in the middle of the excited crowds of travellers and their friends, coming and going, with the prospect before

397

me of many hours of absolute solitude in a city where I was not known to more than a couple of dozen people by sight. Irma, in the care of Miss Werther (whom I had advised of our return, independently of Irma herself) and sometimes of Alan too—particularly of Alan, I thought with a warm tenderness for them both—would be as comfortable, I tried to think, as she was in my own care.

It was a comfortable thought in itself, at the beginning of a journey.

Had I but realized it, my departure for Melbourne at such a time, with so much unsaid between Irma and me, was a fatal mistake. I might have saved the whole fabric of existence had I not gone. However, I have admitted to being a creature of habit, and it has been one of my habits to comply rather than to argue with the decisions of my editor and our employers, even when I might have been sure of a sympathetic hearing. Since childhood, my feeling, or rather my conviction, has been that I was never the sort of person of whom the unreasonable is demanded, either by men or by circumstances. So I must also admit that whatever has been my good or ill fortune has for the most part been the direct outcome of my own will in action.

When I returned, a day later than had been planned, from the southern capital the dice must already have been thrown, the fall against me. Whatever followed followed inevitably, but only one person—Irma—was in a position to see this, and I think she did not see it. It took me another six months to learn, very suddenly what had happened to me, to all of us; but after that there was no waiting: certainty and a course of action became clear in my mind in a night. To what end that course led has already been shown.

For a moment, it seemed that everything I had ever done, every ambition I had ever had, for the happiness of the only two people I loved was turned from an honest intention to a ridiculous and insanely selfish attempt to shape their destinies to accord with mine. This cannot be done; but I had committed myself too far, and whatever I had done I could not undo; I could not go back, and to go forward was impossible for three of us together. The only one who mattered now was Alan, who had barely begun his life of usefulness as an alleviator of earthly pain, a healer of fleshly ills. Of the other two, the one he needed least was the one who must give him up—must give him up without seeming to do so . . . without knowing of a renunciation . . .

After my return, there promised to be no more inter-ruptions to the irregular routine of life as we were living it, together and apart, in these two adjacent flats above the moody ocean of the harbour. Alan was studying hard, perhaps too hard, for his third-year examinations, which seemed to him a sharp turning-point in the whole long way towards graduation and qualification as a medical practi-tioner. Things had gone well with me financially, thanks to a broker who was a personal friend, and not through any shrewdness of my own. I could afford to think of offering Alan post-graduate work abroad after he had done enough hospital-walking here; my own wants were small, and Irma, for whose clothes and housing I paid, had insisted from the start on paying her own household running expenses, maintaining severely and unshakeably that her freedom of movement and her privacy were more than those of a married woman, and must be bought by the one enjoying them, to keep their savour. She would have kept herself wholly, but this, like some other ideas of hers, was difficult for me to comprehend and impossible to endorse. 'Very good,' she said at last, with a mocking sigh. 'I'll save the money for my lonely old age.' After that, she would not let me speak of it again.

My ignorance of her secret self must have depressed her. Once, in an hour of great weariness at the height of the summer, when the wet heat foretold by old Jack's ants lowered like a steaming threat from zenith to horizon, I suggested that we could, with properly circumspect preparation, at last make known the fact if not the date of our marriage. I would not have confessed it, but I was tired and irritated at times by what seemed to me an increasingly unnecessary deceit of all who made up our world. I wanted to claim her openly as my wife and companion. It seemed to me that Alan, who had lately been unusually aloof with both of us, would be pleased.

She would not have it. Her finality surprised me. Why? She could give no reason save that she was happy to live as we did. I gave way to the oppressive heat and my exhaustion, and murmured something like 'What about me?'

'My friend,' she said almost sharply, 'you are happier than you know. The change you suggest would soon make you realize it.' She paused, and her look of animation left her face, which became composed and thoughtful as she said, 'Anyhow, a marriage such as ours was not meant to suffer the anticlimax of the breakfast-table. It would blunt the edges. And then—there is Alan.'

Very well, I said after some consideration, he could move now to quarters of his own, near enough to take whatever meals he chose with us, but still apart, in his own place. It would please him to feel that his comings and goings were known only to himself; he was too old now to have to think himself accountable to anything but his own conscience.

She looked at me and laughed softly, shaking her head with that air of ancient sagacity that had never changed over the years since first I saw it aboard the *Empire Queen*.

'My darling, you will never part with him.'

It was the nearest we ever came to a quarrelsome disagreement.

Ironically enough, it was I myself who began to feel insecure that summer, and to feel the need of some sort of a refuge of my own. The more evidently satisfied she became with our way of life, the more my sense of the unreality of it all increased. She had never been so gay, or seemed so lovely; she throve on the intolerable heat, of which even Alan, who was in a subdued and almost irritable state sometimes, complained. I put down the change in him to excessive work as well as the hard summer. After the new year, when without much enthusiasm he went off for a holiday on the south coast with three young men and four girls of his own year, I sent Miss Molesley away for three weeks, the probable time of his absence, with enough money to go wherever she liked within a day or two's journeying, on her first proper holiday since the war's end.

I had the flat to myself, and as much of Irma's company as my hours of work allowed. For once the wall dividing our two flats seemed as it were to melt, though something less tangible remained between us, tantalizing and bewildering me when I was away from her. We had never spent so much time together—we could waken side by side in the hot light of the early January mornings without the need, now, to part at once and meet again. This was secrecy of another kind, against an alien world for whom we did not care; and if Alec in his cool den below-stairs suspected what we thought was well and gracefully hidden we did not care, and he never made a sign. (It would have been too much for Emmy, who had become Irma's devotee at a distance, to learn of such goings-on, anyhow, and his job depended on her presence there.) Once he had conquered his inclination to suspect Irma in all things as 'one of them reffogees, Mr. Fitz', he had let his good nature bustle him into a defensive liking for her which she found enchanting. She could no more do wrong than I could, he seemed to say with his shrill, deprecating laugh.

I know well enough now that it was Alan's absence that set us more profoundly at peace with one another. After the examinations, and over the Christmas and New Year holidays, he had seemed to be with us the whole time, unable to settle his mind to any one thing, like a man afraid that a plan he has launched irrevocably will fail. For the first time in his life he suffered those onsets of a black and furious depression which for generations seem to have been a family characteristic of ours and are common enough in many people of vastly different mentalities. He could not understand these experiences, and for reasons quite other than those I supposed he sought Irma's company evening after evening, whether I was at home or not. Because of the summer lassitude at the end of each day, I was often enough content to sit or lie still and read, or work on a collection of articles on juvenile delinquency and its origins in the home, which I wanted to put into shape for a book. It was pleasant to know that those two, secure in each other's care, were what Alan called 'doing the beaches' in the car, or sitting absorbed in some theatre together, or, most often, visiting or being visited by the friends Irma seemed to have made again during the last few months in surprising numbers.

While he was gone, disporting himself outside time on some southern, cooler beach with his own friends, she paused as if to take breath and refresh her energies, and let herself sink contentedly under the spell of the heat she loved. Incredulously, perceived that those hot months were like a prolonged spring to her; between November and April she took on a sort of tropical bloom and a passionate and coolly untiring energy. Her skin was in texture and almost in colour like that of a ripening apricot. The sun never hurt her, for she exposed herself to it the year round; and I remember with what a pang of delight and wonder, like a boy's, I had seen her on the screening stone balcony outside her bedroom windows stretched supine, nude and indescribably chaste, the ivory and rose and black and delicate gold of her weighted body scanned like music by the blissful light, and in the bar of shadow at the foot of the wall her face, as quiet as though, open-eyed, she slept. By summer's end she was radiant with the warmth she had bathed in every morning, so that to touch her was like touching the skin of someone newly dried after a bath; but yet there was none of the summer's soporific heaviness in her vivid body, and it was almost as though she had taken into herself for a secret, delicious gain the energy I had lost to the sun as the sweating weeks went by.

She had this energy, and hoarded it for her own purposes. It was a thing as much of the mind as of the tissues of mortal flesh, and I do not remember one moment's sadness in her as she made this pause like some solitary explorer who, having completed one journey into an unknown interior, pauses to let experience overtake imagination before launching himself body and soul upon his next mysterious quest.

Among her visitors, who all seemed to me recently-acquired friends, the most familiar to me was the Russian refugee violinist Kalmikoff. He was a type, a heavy, indignant man with a face somewhat like that of Josef Stalin, but without the Georgian's eyes of humorous peasant cunning and intelligence; his curved Hebraic nose overhung with a sort of angry melancholy a thick dyed moustache, and the same conflict of melancholy with angry scorn could be seen in his fleshy eyelids that seemed too heavy even for the large eyes whose dullness occasionally flashed fire when he spoke from the heart—which was seldom.

He appeared to be obsessed with Irma, not as a woman but as one who had behaved like a fool and who might yet be saved from the consequences and rewards of her folly; for, having somehow escaped after the war from the realms of the Russian proletarian dictatorship—as they cosily called it—he became a weighty and overbearing apologist of Communism in the country he had chosen as a refuge from what he regarded as Communism's relentless pursuit

404

of himself. He had all the unreliable fanaticism of the late convert, all the intolerance the apostate harbours towards another's apostasy. Irma seemed to him a free person. He could not bear it.

He was a type, and there are hundreds, thousands like him in the country now, bravely and securely giving battle against the native optimism, the tolerance, the slowness to suspect, to hate and to condemn which are the damnable characteristics of their forbearing hosts, whose money they take while deploring the system under which it is made. Kalmikoff himself was, like so many foreign Jews, a man with a considerable air of culture overlying that capacity for fear which has made so many of his race successful in material ways. While Irma obsessed him as the biblical shepherd is said to have been obsessed by the strayed lamb, he amused her in a perverse way. 'Keep to your fiddle, Kalmikoff,' I heard her say more than once, choosing the moment mercilessly; at which he would seize his encased violin—it never left his side—and raise it aloft to dash it on the floor. It never crashed down. He was too much a musician, and in any case he never could face a real and simple issue. She laughed at him, and he shouted dully at her, and now and then they fell into a second or two's agreement about the egotistical American dream known as the Marshall Aid Plan—though for very different reasons. Kalmikoff, with that turgid and elaborate humour only possible to the humourless, repeatedly referred to it as the Marshall Truman Western Bloc-Aid Plan (a pause while he trundled his heavy eyes round the room to collect laughter), but I knew that Irma saw it as a threat to what little we had

405

all left of Europe's native spiritual integrity and cultural dynamism; nevertheless, because it was much in the news in those dead, vivid days, she appeared to agree on reasons as she did agree on the opinion, that it was a bad thing.

Sitting apart by the wide-open windows, I was able to watch her excited mobility during the interminable, inexhaustible and tireless arguments she and the ponderous violinist had far into the summer nights; and I envied her and her friends their amazing ability to distil from the squashed pulp of a whole harvest of words the intoxicating, volatile stimulation they gulped down with such unquenchable thirsty relish. Of one thing only I was certain: not one among them meant to do anything about the existing evils and urgent changes they took to pieces with exclamations of fury or approval. In this habit of using up their whole supply of reforming energy in passionate talk of reform, they had one thing in common, at least, with the people of the nation that has given them refuge from all but themselves and their indispensable, irritating fellow-refugees. In a sort of waking dream, myself a refugee from the unbearable futility of the too-oft-spoken word, I could see how easily they might become a nation within a nation (not only because so many of them were Jewish), as explosive within the land that was nourishing them as would be so many dangerous and ineffective messiahs born in a merely mortal world.

Exciting and interminable though their foregatherings were, they seemed to have no real effect on Irma. She would stretch like a cat when the last visitor, sibilantly vocal to the end, had torn himself away from the doorway, the stairhead and the street entrance—all points that had somehow developed a powerful magnetic attraction for these foreign hands and elbows and feet; and then, calm and warm with a kindlier warmth than that of the humid summer midnight, she would sit down beside me on the floor with her head against my knee and tell me how little 'all that' seemed to matter to her now. When I asked her once what they would think did they know of our marriage, she laughed until she was all but helpless; and when she could speak at last, with tears running from her upward-drawn eyes, she said, 'My dearest friend, they would then not *think* I was mad—they would *know* I was.'

'Would it make them stay away?' I said casually; for in truth I began to grudge them the hours that might have been mine. She gave me the familiar, mischievously sidelong look I did not see so often now, and laughed again, but differently, with an underlying sadness that puzzled me to remember.

'Nothing,' she said soberly, 'nothing in the world would make them do that . . . You see, I am one of them.'

Though at the time I denied it, her calm assertion stayed in my mind as self-criticism by the loved one can do. For me there had always been in her a core of absolute steadfastness very different from the inherently volatile natures of the strange people who had taken to gathering about her. As I had never lied to her, but given her an absolute and soul-searching frankness which—I suspect now—must have bored her extremely when she thought of it, if she did so more than seldom, so I took her for the embodiment of truthfulness, to such a degree that even when it would have eased my mind to believe that she lightly lied, or mockingly exaggerated, I yet could not entirely believe, since that did not accord with my image of her.

And in this I was misled: that always, always it was my own image of her in which she appeared to me, until long after Alan's return and our glad resumption of the more regular life that now more than ever seemed to be shaped by the slow turning of the academic year. Not until the end did I find it possible to admit—and then only with my mind, not with my unschooled heart—that she might be other than what I, with absolute faith, imagined her to be. To the end, and beyond, I loved her in a way I think sanity will not pardon, nor my god condemn.

The only accusation of betrayal I make here is directed against myself. A man finds it hard to forgive his own guilt of self-deceit, and if others are involved, they become only the more worthy of compassion, the more bitter and unfor-givable and forlorn the guilt seems.

On the night of the eighth of May in that year, when it became abruptly evident that my life both as a father and as a husband must have ended some time since, without my having known it—when, to put it brutally, I found myself in the peculiar position of a father cuckolded by his own son—my first impulse was towards incredulous laughter at the impossible. If I did not give way to it, neither did I give way to the passion of anger which slowly took its place, and which burned down to ashes in its turn like a fire with only a handful of hollow sticks to feed on, and no one to tend it.

It was four years almost to the day since Irma had so unexpectedly arrived from Melbourne to spend a short week-end with her faithful friend Miss Werther. In terms of the range of human emotions, that is a long time; in terms of thought and memory not so long. As I walked homewards, looking at the bright autumnal stars revealed by the withdrawing clouds from which a little rain had been falling before midnight, I remembered with unusual clearness my thoughts and feelings that late afternoon, up to the moment when I saw my own leather-gloved finger extended to press the bell-button at the door of *Linda Werther—Agent* in Edgecliff Road; up to the moment when, having closed the door upon us in the airy hall with its framed view of bright garden beyond, and having taken my things to put them on the wall-table under the dim mirror, Irma withdrew her eyes from mine in the reflection, and turned, and was in my arms.

Perhaps the picture was unusually clear because I was tired from too much work, too much concern over the subtle, irresistible change that seemed to have come into our passionate and calm relationship in the two apartments overhanging the restless waters of the great harbour. Change there was without doubt, yet I could not put my finger upon it as I had upon Miss Werther's door-bell, nor would the definition of it have again opened a door between us. I could not see it except, so to speak, out of the corner of my eye; when I looked boldly and fearfully for it, it was not there. For us, I thought, all was the same. We still laughed and were silent together, in mutual love and possession (I thought); the summer pause, when love had seemed only a stillness like too much peace, had softly returned to a forward movement without direction but also without end, and to seal the wholeness of my life Alan had come back to make us three once more.

In all this could be seen no alteration but a slow ripening; yet my sense of alteration, unable to fix on anything that would focus and contain it, spread like a haze over the sun and robbed my world of its full clarity and colour.

No one expected me tonight. One of those special assignments that sometimes came the way of senior members of the staff had taken me by air to Brisbane that morning, and through a mistake I could not trace I had been supposed to stay north overnight and return the following day. This had turned out to be unnecessary as well as undesirable—these days I was loth to be away from home a minute longer than I must—and through the Brisbane office I had had the good fortune (it was no less than that) to be offered a seat in an R.A.A.F. bomber going as far as Richmond on a return-to-base flight.

From Richmond, where the aircraft was put down 'blind' (as it was later explained to me over a hurried drink in the Mess), a staff-officer going home late took me as far as Kings Cross in an official car. Everything had been comfortable and pleasant, and also exhausting, as I found when I stretched my legs on that final walk along the few quiet streets beyond the Cross to my door. It had also been too sudden and hurried for me to have sent a telegram ahead of me, had that been possible.

What happened next had nothing to do with the day just ended, and if I remember the two experiences together it is with the same sense of disconnection with which one might look at a motion-picture record of oneself, being incredibly both actor and onlooker at the one moment.

Half-way up the last flight of carpeted stair, I could see

410

that both my door and Irma's were open—mine wide open as if left that way by someone in haste or expecting to return at once, and hers no more than a few inches ajar, sufficient for me to know that what light was showing came from the open door of her bedroom on the far side of the dark living-room, from the reading lamp by the bed, which sent out into the larger room a flat, low radiance that reached the opposite wall and was reflected dimly towards the door.

Unconsciously I hurried my mounting step, thinking of illness, and then, aware again of my own wide-open doorway, stopped with a feeling that something was wrong not with anyone there, but with me. In the warm silence at the top of the stairs I heard nothing for a moment but the beat of my heart's blood in my ears; and then, with a thrill of unreasoning fear that changed itself even as it came to fearful recognition, I heard from beyond that scarcely opened doorway a low moaning sound that was suddenly cut off as though by a hand on the slightly parted lips from which it issued.

Then I heard the voices.

'Irma, my darling, my darling, I must stay with you. I can't go now.'

'But yes—you can.' To my immense surprise this ambiguous reply was full of stifled laughter. It was followed by a slight rustle of movement, a murmur of unintelligible words, and then Irma's voice again, low but quite clear and in perfect control.

'So. Be more gentle, my friend. Now.'

'Teach me to be more gentle, then. Teach me.'

For a few moments, while my mind tried to make its escape from these impressions, I had not allowed myself to

411

recognize Alan's voice as the other. Now I did, with a wild urge to laugh to which I did not give way, lest it shock them, my two beloveds. They were in the dark entrance hall, out of the line of that faintly-reflected light which revealed only a vertical section of the pearl-grey wall the colour of the seagulls' wings. There was not even a shadow on it. I was near enough to hear faintly not only their murmured words but the hushed quickness of their breathing, and without volition my feet began to descend the stairs, backwards, feeling for each step like the feet of a man being thrust slowly and irresistibly backwards towards an abyss. Some attraction beyond my power withheld me from turning my face from that vertical line of pallid light, and I was still staring at it when it was eliminated by the abrupt soft closing of the door.

As I turned at the half-landing to continue my descent more safely, I saw that the light in my own flat was still burning with cheerful welcoming brightness. I had a momentary, impatient urge to go up again at once and turn it off; but I did not do so.

If it had been difficult not to stroll away up the dim street laughing loud and long, by the time I found myself sitting fully dressed on the edge of a barren bed in a strange hotel bedroom it was equally touch and go whether I gave way to the disgraceful rage of jealousy that threatened to overwhelm me.

This too would have been laughable to anyone who, unlike myself, had realized that I was jealous not of Alan but of Irma—not of my son but of my wife. Now that the situation was sufficiently clarified to point a need for some

412

sort of action, I think I should already have realized this; but I did not, my upbringing tried to convince me that in these confusions of deceit and betrayal it is always the man who is to blame; and when I say my upbringing I mean of course my mother's, who always thought what was held to be the correct thing. My mother, did she but know it, would have been entirely in favour of the crucifying of the man she spoke of as her saviour. So of course would most people who call themselves Christians, if they had been alive and in Palestine in those exciting times.

Fortunately, in the end cool reason asserted itself successfully against the feather-stuffed arguments of upbringing, but not before I had experienced the bewilderment of a conviction that it was somehow quite wrong to think of thrusting the boy aside with a violent shoulder and reclaiming what was my own from his ignorant grasp. Denied the poisoning satisfaction of solving the immediate problem this way, my mind for more than an hour was denied any satisfaction at all. I was so obsessed with the thought of that woman as a victim, of men and circumstances, that it took me at least that long to understand that she, my beloved, was not in his grasp, but rather that he—my beloved—was in hers. Persuading reason to proceed in this direction was for a long time like the attempt of a drunken man to drive a horse at a wire gate. The gate, like the spurious instincts nurtured by upbringing in the dung of fear, merely had to be set aside: clearly the way led beyond it. In the end I got down, so to speak, and opened the gate.

It is easy to talk like this afterwards, when all is over. It was not easy to think at all, at the time, and I sat rocking myself on the edge of the bed that did not want me, fretting and whimpering like a punished child to whom for the moment punishment is all. Like such a child, too, I searched for comfort and indignation among the strangely weightless arguments of self-righteousness. I thought, have I not spent altogether more than half my life doing, at no little cost, what I faithfully believed was best for those two people, who had with the soft closing of a door ajar become discernible to me as the strangers they must always have been?

And sometimes I thought simply, Oh god, what is to become of me now?

Gradually, however, the horse of reason persuaded the fuddled driver that the way led beyond the invisible steel of the gate, and that he must incommode himself if he wished to go further; but the way itself was not yet clear to be seen.

Any ordinary mind would long since have realized that I was, in matters of the body, over-fastidious. The only person I knew who sensed this and fully approved of it, at least as it affected my relationships with women, was old Jack. I remembered, with a desperate hope of buoying up my self-esteem, how he had said, 'You ain't no fool.' After all, that was a criticism not of Irma but of all women (I told myself in confusion, as the winds of passion blew this way and that); and surely it expressed approval of me, as a sort of corollary?

I began to try to think what Jack would do in my place—only to have to ask myself, what was my place? I was a man whose second wife is seducing his first wife's son. The son does not know the circumstances at all, because of a piece of short-sighted cleverness based on his father's excessive physical self-consciousness; he not only supposes that his step-mother is an unattached young woman but also that he is the instrument of seduction . . . And if I did not like the taste of that undiluted dose of bitter truth, I must nevertheless swallow it.

It made no sense to me, put simply—that was the only trouble. Generations of dead Fitzherbert men and women scowled and shook their ghostly faces at all attempts to be so simple. With steady finger-bones, they pointed to the society of my own day as if to indicate that they could never have clone their part in building it upon such preposterous foundations as simplicity and truth. There was, moreover, no such thing (they seemed to say) as simplicity in human relationships. All relationships were only a matter of holding chaos at arm's length by the exercise of a constant, tremendous effort. One moment's self-deceit, and chaos claimed its own.

I knew well what old Jack would do in my place. He would go away. I could hear him telling me, with a twinkle of amusement at himself, 'I'd git for me life.'

If I did that, it would be a coward flight from inevitable catastrophe—a running away from my son's eventual spoliation and abandonment. I knew Irma—I knew her as no one else living knew her; and now, in the shrieking electric light of that hotel bedroom, full of death and departure and the empty postures of love, I was obliged to admit to myself with shuddering, whimpering humility, with rage, with shame and with truth how fatuously slight was my claim upon her; if, indeed, I had any claim upon her at all. She was right, she could do as she liked. For if I had done

415

anything to make easier her life, I thought, how much more she had done to beautify and expand and make rich and human my own. And in spite of this, she was a stranger. Her love was the bird in flight, like her whole being; she must move on; for her there was no refuge after all, no place in her own heart where she could stay still. Poor Irma, poor child. She would be better dead.

It would have been better if I had let her die, that wild and brilliant morning months before. She knew best. I should have sat by and listened to her snore out her life, and then crept away and in the final test of courage resumed my own. None of this—my mind immediately said 'foulness'—none of this foulness of fermenting passions could have happened then. But I had wanted her, as before god and man I wanted her still. It is always the same, said reason: what you want and obtain ceases to be what it was, becomes its opposite. The most fair becomes the most foul. The more embracing the possession, the more irrecoverable the loss. In self-abhorrent imagination I shared her adulterous bed. I had meant to be pure in thought and deed, and marriage had seemed to me the only purity of bodily love. Why, else, had I not taken her six years before, six months before, when she would have been mine for not even the asking? I could have quelled that liquorish heat in her, those battling limbs, that arched, triumphantly defeated torso again and again, and gone my way and been not even obliged, if such had been in my mind. But no—I must have what they had told me was purity in the eyes of my stern-faced, loving god, and in choosing purity I had now drawn down upon my own flesh the impurity of the damned. I too would be better dead.

Lying back, half-on, half-off the bed, with one arm across my eyes to keep them dark from the light which I was afraid to turn off, I tried to imagine my own death and its effects on those two strangers; but instead, since this was impossible, I sought a vision of Alan lying dead at my feet, dead in his bed, dead in a hospital, in the street, in the restless waters of the harbour. Each time I forced my imagination to look at his face, it was hers I saw, her voice I heard saying with tender irony, 'My darling, you will never part with him.'

I could not think of Alan as dead because clearly that was not yet his fortune. He was too young, too unripened in mind and body, with too much good yet to do; this that had befallen him, how long ago I did not know or dare to think, was a slight thing, and none of his doing. I approved the courage and restraint of his passion, even while the thought of what that had been fed upon, under my very eyes and with all the encouragement my ignorance could have given it, was a sheer choking agony that made me sit upright again to wipe away the sweat that chilled me as it sprang prickling from my skin. Courage there was, and restraint there must have been, for again and again I had obliged him to keep her company, I had thrown them together until the sight of her, the mention of her name, the mere passing of her doorway each day, must have been such painful pleasure and sweet temptation as only a virgin youth could know, and only a strong heart and a noble mind endure as he must have endured it.

And she—how clearly in the end one sees these things—she had inevitably felt towards him at once a vague

417

and indeterminate resentment as the son and the robber of her lover's youth, and that sweet, gratifying attraction any older woman must feel for his virginal innocence, his erect and manly youth. Both these feelings, so interchangeable as to be without separate identity, could be assuaged in the way she had described as 'too easy for a woman'; and in that assuagement, doubly confirming its instinctive rightness, was also her complete and final possession of me.

From this point, and I saw it at once, she must go forward alone.

SIX
THE END

It is a formidable thought, to those who like myself believe in god as the principle of good informing our lives, that there is always to hand the means of taking or despatching the life of another human being.

It is always there—if it be no more than one's own two hands it is there. For the most part there is a saving lack of motive; sometimes, though rarely, of opportunity. Without the motive, the means can have no power nor the opportunity occasion; but with the means always at hand a man might destroy his whole family one by one within an hour, as men have done, without any preparation whatever, though never without that conscious or sub-conscious forethought in which motive, the spring of action, is forged with such dreadful secrecy.

The remarkable thing about this secrecy is that the mind can keep it even from its own knowledge. I have discussed cases of the sort with my friend Hubble. My own contention is that a man committing a homicide has always been capable of committing a homicide, no matter how unlikely the circumstances surrounding the deed itself may be. This, *per se*, as Hubble laboriously and exactly pointed out, argues the absolute assumption of some degree of premeditation, no matter how honestly and credibly both the murderer and the circumstances deny it. In the minds of all of us, pressed down, sealed up, forgotten if it ever was known, is the vision of another's death at our hands, which in same way, at some time, consciously or not, we have seen and recognized; and the face of the dead is the face of love.

More than any other noumenon, the strange, unearthly identity between death and love has obsessed the dreams of men since unrecorded time. Love and sacrifice, love and death, love's own self-annihilation and the annihilation of its object, in the moment of its perfect bodily expression, are part of all consciousness. For men and women, to love is to destroy; to be loved is to invite destruction.

The means are always at hand, if death is to solve a problem from which life offers absolutely no escape. As dawn with fearful slowness revealed the murdered stone face of the building opposite the hotel bedroom window, with first only a curdling of the darkness into barely-seen rectangles and lines of shadow, and finally a dismal greyness of Victorian architectural detail impossible to look upon as the work of man, I found that the last hours of the night had with similar slowness brought me face to face with the one conceivable choice—a choice between Irma and myself, as to which one of us Alan could less unhappily do without.

For it was he, of course, who alone mattered beyond the moment. In the fruitless consummation of our love, Irma and I in ourselves had already ceased to count; our marriage, barren of all but an uncertain worldly security for her and offering her no refuge from her dreadful craving—as I had told Barbara—for absolute extinction, and for me a division of self into two irreconcilable parts, came not as the beginning of love but as the end. Whereas I had Alan, to call upon my duty and my care, she had nothing—certainly not him: for in possessing him she must lose him as I must lose him in denying him her. Thus, even lost to both of us, he alone had significance still; my importance as a guide would lessen quickly now; Irma meant nothing, retained nothing. Not even a last refuge remained for her to seek when she withdrew from my encircling arms, from my heart's cave, and left them empty again.

I undressed to the first sounds of traffic in the street below, loud and sadly echoing in the grey coulisses of the empty city, and huddled myself together between the clean yellow blankets. In the hotel itself, sounds began—the clanking of mops in buckets, rushing of water from taps, and somewhere remotely below the scraping crunch and ring of coke being shovelled into a furnace, and the voices which at that grey hour sound so wide-awake and purposeful. Warmth spread slowly through my cramped and rigid limbs, relaxing them. In the glaring light that had saved me all night from complete darkness I fell at last into a short sleep from which a girl in a black dress and a white apron woke me, with a tray from which she took a cup of tea. Sitting there in the normal light of morning, I drank the cup off slowly, and the tears ran weakly and briefly from my eyes as I thought how often Alan had stood with me at that hour, leaning in the frame of the open French windows while with half-closed eyes he assessed the promise of the day across the eastern harbour. I cried to myself in the weakness of waking again, wishing he were still a boy at school, wishing that the promise those years had seemed to hold had been sustained always on the verge of a wondrous fulfilment, wishing that every action of my life had not so positively curved downwards to this moment of timeless and intolerable loneliness.

Given the motive, means and opportunity will always present themselves. Precision of thought and action and the ability to see the thing whole, from beginning to end, are all else that is needed. Afterwards, forget what you can and let the pitiable memory of what cannot be forgotten be a punishment more divine than any devised by mankind in its futile dream of self-protection. So long as there are men there will be murder.

It is probable that I had always imagined Irma dead, for reasons other than that I loved her. It may even be that I substituted my love for her death from the beginning. When, in speaking of her refugee friends, she had said 'I am one of them', it had been true, and my heart if not my mind acknowledged it. In her own way, in my own microcosmos, she was one of the despoilers of my young and eager and unblooded country, a land as old as earth itself and as young as Alan. She had come into my world shyly, hungrily, seeking a refuge in which to pursue her own obscure and worthless ends; but she had pursued them as one herself pursued, in beauty and with ineffable grace and lonely, unflagging courage.

This quality of courage seemed to be embodied in the cast of her face. The Slavic cheek-bones, the flying grey-blue eyes, the full firmness of mouth and chin gave it a look of ancient bravery like that of a face on a centuries-old coin. I looked at her in the soft lamplight of early night, as with a smile she took from my steady hand the cup whose contents would kill her. In the poised unreality of that moment before she began to drink it (so strong, so sweet, its aroma blending headily with the fumes of the heated brandy) I knew how real had always been my admiration of her, the delicate and controlled and noble animal set apart by some subtly exaggerated womanhood from all other women I had known.

As she raised the cup to her lips she raised her eyes to mine in a long, meditative stare, and in that moment I believed that by virtue of some ageless instinct she knew what she did when, mouthful by mouthful, without a word passing between us, she drained the cup almost to the dregs. With her left hand she held the saucer in her lap. I reminded myself automatically that I would need to wipe it and the cup's handle. Its pure whiteness enhanced the fine secret glow of her skin under the delicate artifice of the nylon pyjamas she was wearing for the first time that evening. For once, because I was too intensely aware of how alive she was to be able to keep silence, I had expostulated earlier with her about this pyjama suit, which by its clinging weight and transparency revealed more of her person than it concealed.

But she had silenced me by saying gently, 'It is for you alone, my friend, I promise you.'

With a sense of its meaningless irrelevance, that yet was somehow relevant to I do not know what moment of our past happiness, I comforted myself with a conviction that at least no one but myself should see her alive in it. If I had said so, she would have agreed, but I did not say it, for I could not tempt her now to a lie; the unreality of the hour, too unreal to bear the stress either of fear or of pity, would have made my own words meaningless too . . .

We were in the bedroom together. She tried, clumsily for the first time in my experience of her, to get the hair-brush against the smooth hair she had not uncoiled. Later I picked it up where it had fallen softly on the floor rug; now I had to get her on to the bed, where I laid her down, alone, terribly alone. She said something which I still think was 'Now are you satisfied?' and the full realization of what I had done came to me then as she seemed to fall asleep.

By my watch it was an hour since the tide had turned; I had heard its coldly amorous slap and kiss on the stones of the breakwater that led like a path straight into the unused boatshed with its old water-stair opening out of its floor and a ribbed ramp going down on either side beyond the stone steps. That was now my destination.

It never occurred to me that I might be heard or seen as I took her down the service stair by which I had returned in the darkness an hour earlier, by which I would again return and leave soon. I was impersonally occupied with an extreme care for her person as we descended; had her hand or her foot struck the wall or the safety railing

I would have felt it with tremendous concern. And nothing untoward happened. No door opened as we passed; no faint impact trembled through her warm indolent body as step by step we went down together into the night lying secret and immense upon the rising tide.

I felt that in the safety of my arms she had, after all, come to no least harm.

Text Classics

textclassics.com.au